The Fallout Kids

A Post-Apocalyptic Survival Thriller

Jordan Weir

Live Big Press

Copyright © 2026 Jordan Weir

All rights reserved. No part of this publication may be reproduced, distributed, or transmitted in any form or by any means without prior written permission of the publisher, except in the case of brief quotations embodied in reviews.

This is a work of fiction. Names, characters, organizations, places, events, and incidents are either the product of the author's imagination or used fictitiously.

ISBN: 979-8-9956392-0-6

First Edition

Published by Live Big Press

Cover design by Jordan Weir

To the people in my life—
those still with us,
those who are not,
and to the new ones reading this…
thank you.

PART ONE
PROJECT: FALLOUT KIDS

CHAPTER ONE

The room was silent.

A red light blinked to life above the camera lens.

Someone cleared their throat.

From the overhead speakers, a voice drifted down. Flat and precise.

"I am recording. You may begin whenever."

The camera adjusted slightly, focusing.

The silence deepened. It pressed against the walls, heavy and watchful beneath the sterile hum of the lights.

Fabric rustled. A chair shifted.

He leaned forward slightly, elbows resting on his knees.

Still, no words.

Only the steady pulse of the red light.

Waiting.

His heart began to pound harder the longer the silence stretched.

A long inhale filled the room, slow and deliberate. It stayed trapped in his lungs for a moment, held until it almost hurt.

A shaky breath escaped.

For a moment, it sounded like someone trying to remember how to speak.

Then—

The blue glow of the numbers above the door burns my eyes. I'm forced to squint, fighting back the tears threatening to spill over. It's the most beautiful shade of blue I've ever seen, richer than the endless sky on a cloudless summer day. Yet, it's also the most terrifying thing. It's the spark that ignites the fear burning in my chest, fueling the tears edging closer, promising to fall.

3 — *My heart pounds, fast and hard, like it's desperate to break free, racing against the seconds slipping away.*

2 — The pressure in my chest is suffocating. I force each breath deep into my lungs, steadying my legs to keep from buckling beneath the weight of the moment.

1 — The thought of what's on the other side of that door paralyzes me. Or... what isn't.

As the final second ticks away, a blaring horn cuts through the thudding heartbeat in my ears, its deafening sound making me flinch.

The airlock door groans open, and I freeze. My body goes rigid, drowning in a silence so profound it feels like the world itself is holding its breath.

I step through the airlock and into the world I've been shut away from for so long.

The heat is overwhelming. Sweat beads across my skin, heavy and immediate, as if the air itself is too much to bear. Sulfur slices at my windpipe like a thousand tiny razors, choking each breath. Smoke hangs low and heavy, clinging to the air. It scratches my eyes raw, as if my lids were made of sandpaper. I wipe at the stinging tears, struggling to face the reality I've feared for so long.

The world has been set ablaze.

Buildings are nothing more than shattered remnants, piles of rubble where once-thriving structures stood. Concrete and steel lie twisted, collapsed into heaps of unrecognizable debris. Cars, now rusted, hollow shells, stand forever frozen where they met their end.

Gone are the fields of green, the trees swaying with the breeze, their leaves vibrant and alive. The sky is a lifeless, suffocating gray. No trace of blue, no birds soaring, nothing to break the oppressive stillness. There is no color left in this world.

Everything is ash. Everyone is ash.

Through the haze of smoke and smoldering ruins, I catch a glimpse of something, faint and distant. As I push forward, the shape becomes clearer, and my heart plummets.

A house on fire.

I move toward it.

With every step, this crushing feeling starts to build.

Finally, like a bolt of lightning through my chest, the realization hits.

I know this house, this is my house.

Panic surges as I race toward it. The flames grow more furious. Their dance more erratic, flickering in and out of focus like they're toying with my mind.

The heat presses down, slowing me, pushing at my resolve. Each step is a battle. The flames lash at me, their crackling louder and louder. They taunt me, daring me to get closer.

But I won't stop. I can't stop.

Finally, I reach the front yard. Flames rage from every window and doorway, devouring everything inside. The house feels alive, consumed with a fury that turns every wall, every beam, every scrap of furniture into fuel for its wrath.

I stop short of the porch, heart hammering in my chest. My hands fly up to shield my face from the heat as my eyes squeeze shut.

And then, amidst the roar of the fire, a voice cuts through the chaos.

"JASE!"

"JASE!"

"HELP ME!"

I squint through my fingers, desperate to see past the flames. Through the smoke and heat, I catch a glimpse of someone standing beyond the wall of fire.

For a split second, the flames part, almost mocking me with a brief window of clarity.

There, in the inferno, is Eli. My brother.

He's standing there alone, screaming my name, begging for help. The terror in his eyes, the raw fear in his voice, sends a chill through my spine, freezing me in place.

But before panic can take hold, I don't think. I just react.

The searing heat no longer matters. A primal urge surges inside me, driving me forward. Without hesitation, I leap for the steps with only one thought driving me—save my brother.

Just as my foot lands, our eyes lock again.

In that instant, time seems to stop at what I see in his eyes.

The fear is gone. His eyes are hollow now, brimming with a profound sadness. His lips quiver, and then, with a pain so raw it breaks my heart, he whispers:

"Why did you leave me?"

The words slice through me like molten steel, cutting deeper than any flame. My breath catches. Guilt surges like a tidal wave, crushing every rational thought. My knees buckle, and I collapse under the weight of it. I search for words, I want to explain, to apologize. But none exist. His eyes demand an answer I'll never have.

There is no answer, no words to make it right.

The weight of regret pushes down on me. My body trembles, struggling to stay upright. His words echoing through my mind.

But then, the heat bites my skin again, burning through the paralysis. Clarity strikes: I can be there for him now. I can save him. We can figure out the rest later, after we both make it out of this burning hellscape.

I shoot to my feet, driven by a desperate need to get to him. I leap for the step, muscles coiled with explosive force, ready to carry me into the fire. My boot slams into the step and then gives way.

The wood splinters as the floorboard beneath me collapses, plunging me into the decaying structure.

And then everything stops.

The flames vanish.

The heat, the smoke, the suffocating air—they all dissolve.

The house crumbles into ash, scattering and blowing away silently on the wind.

For a moment, the world is eerily still.

Then, faint but unmistakable, his words echo once more, carried on the gentle breeze, as I watch the ashes float away:

"Why did you leave me?"

"Why"

"That's when I wake up," he said, his voice tight.

"The sterile white lights overhead burn my eyes, forcing me to squint. My body's drenched in sweat, the pillow and sheets soaked through. My heart's pounding like it's about to tear free from my chest."

He dragged a hand down his face, his fingers trembling.

"And the fire… it still clings to me. I can feel it crawling across my skin, even though there's nothing there. No scorch marks. No burns. Nothing."

He swallowed hard.

"My lungs ache. I can still taste the sulfur in the back of my throat. But the air down here is clean. Crisp. Pure. It's like the world I just left behind never existed."

A hollow laugh slipped out. "I tell myself it wasn't real. Just a nightmare."

For a long moment he said nothing.

Then, quietly—

"But the weight's still there."

He rubbed the back of his neck, staring at the floor.

"The guilt. It won't let go. It just sits there on my shoulders… growing heavier every day."

His voice tightened. "The fear of what happened up there. The fear of what happened to my brother."

Silence stretched.

"And no matter how much I want to escape it…" His jaw clenched. "There's no blade sharp enough to cut it free."

He paused, breathing unevenly. Then he lifted his head and looked directly into the camera.

"This is Alpha-One. Day three hundred and fifty-eight." He hesitated a moment, like the words had become a ritual.

"End recording."

From the overhead speakers, the voice returned—unchanged, emotionless. "Recording ended. Thank you, Alpha-One. Your Echo Loop has been logged."

With a hiss, the hydraulic doors to the Operations Command Center slid open.

Olivia stepped inside, tablet in hand.

"Good morning, Alpha-One!" she greeted, her voice laced with sarcasm, a mischievous grin tugging at the corner of her mouth.

The moment she spoke, the tension in the room shifted. Her presence cut straight through the heaviness of Jase's recording, dissolving some of the darkness clinging to him.

"Good morning, Beta-Three," Jase shot back, rolling his eyes—an intense blue that barely hid the affection behind the challenge.

Olivia, as she was now known to everyone, was one of six subjects selected for the study.

Three men. Three women.

When the project began, their identities had been stripped down to designations: Alpha for the men, Beta for the women, each followed by a number.

At first, it had felt clinical. Appropriate for a scientific study. Now it just felt ridiculous.

The longer they lived inside the Ouroboros, the more the labels sounded like something meant for lab animals.

"Pretty early for your Echo Loop, isn't it? Another sleepless night?" Olivia said, her eyes flicking down to her tablet as her fingers moved across the screen.

"Yeah, I guess it is," Jase replied, his voice quieter than usual. "Just had a few things I needed to get out."

Echo Loops were supposed to be simple. Weekly video logs for the Principal Investigators to monitor their mental state without personal interaction. Just another clinical requirement of the study.

But after everything changed, the recordings had taken on a different purpose. For most of them, they'd become something closer to therapy. A place to dump thoughts no one else wanted to say out loud.

Without looking up, Olivia asked, "Let me guess… you had the dream again?"

Jase exhaled slowly, brushing a hand through his tousled brown hair.

"Yeah… same dream, same result."

Jase shifted his weight, broad shoulders slumping as though the air itself pressed down on him.

At just over six feet, he was built for strength—his frame carried the kind of muscle earned through use, not vanity. He was undeniably good-looking, though it was clear he didn't put much effort into it. Sun-kissed skin, earned from long hours outdoors, gave him a rugged, earthy appeal.

There was a sharpness to his features, a focus that lingered even in quiet moments, as if his mind refused to rest. Despite that edge, something about him always drew attention, an unspoken confidence that didn't need polish or pretense to be noticed.

"So… smoke, fire, ash, full-blown panic attack," Olivia said, her voice a mix of teasing and concern.

Jase pressed his lips into a tight line and nodded, shame flickering in his eyes. This wasn't the first time they'd had this conversation, and it was wearing on him.

"And yet… still no me? I'm starting to get jealous, Jase!" she added, lifting a brow and throwing a playful glance over her shoulder.

A reluctant smile tugged at his lips. He scratched at his chin, trying to hide his embarrassment.

"Guess I just never make it that far."

"Well, maybe you should dream smarter, not harder," Olivia teased, a smirk returning as she refocused on her tablet.

The humor lingered a moment, but Jase's smile soon faltered. His shoulders sagged under the weight of something deeper.

"It's always just him. Always just Eli. Alone." His voice heavy with pain that never seemed to leave him.

Olivia's playful tone softened into something gentler, sincere. "Because you left him behind."

Olivia knew Jase better than anyone else in the facility. From the moment they met, there had been an unspoken understanding between them. Something that felt inevitable, as if their lives would have crossed paths even if the outside world had never fallen apart.

She turned toward him, brushing a few loose strands of blonde hair back from her face. Most of it was tied into a short ponytail, though stubborn pieces always slipped free to frame her jaw.

At five-ten she carried herself with an easy confidence—lean and athletic, the kind that made Jase suspect she'd once been a soccer player. She always laughed that off, insisting she'd trip over the ball before she ever scored.

Now her blue eyes fixed on him—sharp, perceptive, almost unsettling in how easily they seemed to read people. But beneath that intensity lived a warmth she rarely let anyone see.

It showed itself in moments like this.

High cheekbones and pale skin gave her a striking look, but none of that mattered to Jase as much as her smile.

Even down here, buried beneath steel and concrete, that smile felt like sunlight breaking through the clouds. For a heartbeat, it made him forget the weight pressing down on them all.

"Jase, you're overthinking it," Olivia said, her voice steady but gentle.

She moved toward the wall panel of humming servers, and popped it open, revealing a web of wiring and circuits. With a quick tug she freed a cable, plugged it into her tablet, and typed a string of commands.

"We don't know what happened up there. Hell, for all we know, nothing happened at all."

She glanced back at him.

"But whatever it was… we'll deal with it when the time comes. You don't have to carry it every day."

Jase crossed his arms, his jaw tightening. He took a slow breath, but the thoughts gnawing at him refused to loosen their grip.

"I know that, Olivia. But something obviously happened. Something bad, or we wouldn't be stuck down here."

He shook his head slightly. "And it's not just the uncertainty… it's the guilt. Knowing I'm safe while he's out there. Alone."

His voice dropped. "I should be out there protecting him. Not down here, cut off from the world with all of you."

Olivia glanced up from her tablet, her gaze locking onto his. There was no pity in her eyes, only quiet understanding.

"You think I don't feel that every day?" she said softly. "I'd give anything to see my dad again. Anything just to hear his voice one more time."

She paused, the softness in her expression sharpening into something steadier. "But I've learned something down here, Jase."

Her eyes held his.

"We can't change what happened up there. All we can do is stay focused and ready. Because when those doors finally open, we'll find them."

Her voice hardened with resolve. "We'll find Eli."

She paused for a moment.

"But first," she said quietly, "we have to make it that far."

Jase's shoulders sagged, the fight draining out of him as doubt clung like a shadow he couldn't shake.

"I want to believe that, Liv. God, I do." His voice thinned, almost breaking. "But it's not that simple."

He raked a hand through his hair, his jaw tightening.

"Eli… he begged me not to do this. Said it didn't feel right. Said something about the whole thing was off."

He shook his head.

"And I just…" His voice caught. "I brushed him off. Like it didn't matter. Like he didn't matter."

Olivia's fingers paused on the tablet. The words hung between them, rawer than he meant them to be.

Jase looked away, unable to meet her eyes. "I left him behind, and now…" His throat tightened around the thought.

Silence swallowed the rest.

When he finally spoke again, the words came out quiet and broken.

"Now it feels like it was all for nothing."

Just over three hundred and fifty-eight days ago, everything had been different. Back then, they were just regular young adults, the future wide open in front of them.

Jase had just finished his junior year of college, standing on the edge of summer with equal parts relief and excitement, until the letter arrived. It came from a government-funded research program, informing him he'd been selected as a candidate for a highly lucrative study.

The program was called Project: Fallout Kids.

According to the packet, the study would examine the physical and psychological effects of long-term confinement inside a state-of-the-art underground fallout shelter known as The Ouroboros.

The letter claimed Jase's physical health and academic scores made him an ideal candidate.

At first, he scoffed. Three months in an underground bunker with strangers? No thanks.

Then he saw the line that changed everything: Compensation includes college credits, monetary reward, and forgiveness of all student loans.

That was the hook. That was all it took.

The rest of the material was half sales pitch, half history lesson. Jase remembered skimming it, barely paying attention at first.

During the Cold War, it said, fallout shelters were critical lifelines in the face of nuclear fear. In the 1950s, the U.S. built a network of underground facilities, but two stood apart in scope and purpose.

The Raven Rock Mountain Complex, Site R, tucked deep in the Pennsylvania forests. Built in the '50s to house top U.S. government officials if disaster struck. Underground chambers, command centers, a place where leadership could wait out the end of the world.

Then, in the '60s, the Cheyenne Mountain Complex rose in Colorado. A hardened fortress, command-and-control for NORAD. Built to survive a direct nuclear strike. More advanced, more resilient than Site R. Capable of sustaining its inhabitants for years. It was designed for prolonged isolation, for a world that might not come back.

That was then. Technology had come a long way since.

The Ouroboros wasn't just another concrete bunker. It was automated. Self-sustaining. A facility engineered to support human life indefinitely. A monument to human ingenuity, designed to outlast the civilization that built it.

Compared to that, places like Site R and Cheyenne Mountain looked like caves.

The Ouroboros wasn't just a shelter. It was the future.

None of that had impressed Jase at the time.

It was the debt. Always the debt.

The catch was isolation.

Total severance from the outside world. No contact with anyone. Every detail of their physical and mental health tracked daily by the facility's systems and Echo Loops.

Ninety days underground. That was the deal.

It sounded hard, but manageable. Endure three months, walk out debt-free.

He had never imagined the doors wouldn't open.

Olivia's gaze softened, her blue eyes catching his and holding them. There was no pity there—only the kind of understanding that came from carrying her own weight of loss.

"You did what you thought was right, Jase," she said quietly. "We all did. We said yes to this because it was an opportunity—because it made sense at the time. None of us knew what was coming."

She held his gaze, steady, unflinching. "And now? It's not like we can just walk out those doors. We don't have a choice."

Her voice softened, but didn't waver. "Eli will understand. He loves you. That hasn't changed."

Jase swallowed, trying to breathe past the knot in his throat. He searched her eyes for something steady, something to keep him from unraveling.

"I hope you're right," he murmured, doubt fraying every word.

Olivia straightened, a spark of defiance cutting through the softness in her expression.

"Then picture it," she said. "When those doors open and you see him again, what's the first thing you'll say?"

The question hit like a punch.

Jase exhaled hard, his gaze dropping to the floor. His vision burned as the words slipped out. "I imagine it every day."

He looked back up at her. "I'll tell him I'm sorry."

Olivia didn't look away. She let the silence settle between them—not as judgment, but as a quiet promise to hold him up when he couldn't hold himself.

Eli had never been as enthusiastic about the study as the others. He thought it was a terrible idea and he made sure Jase knew it, right up until the day he left for the facility.

Maybe that was part of why it stung so much.

Two years earlier, their dad had died of a sudden heart attack, and the loss had gutted the family. Eli carried it quietly, never talking much, but Jase could feel the shift. They'd always been close, but after their father's death, something between them felt fragile, like it could splinter if pulled too hard.

Every summer, without fail, they had a tradition: a camping and fishing trip, just the three of them. No distractions. Just firelight, casting lines into the lake, and making memories that felt like they would last forever. After their dad was gone, they kept it going. Not for the fish, but for him. To hold onto a piece of what they'd lost.

This time, though, Jase knew the tradition wouldn't survive. By the time the study ended, summer would be over, and he'd be heading back for his final year of college. Graduation was around the corner, and with it, whatever came next.

Eli had never said it outright, but Jase could feel it—that fear that this trip, this bond, would slip away just like their father had. That once Jase stepped underground, the last thread holding them together would be gone.

"It's not your fault," Olivia said softly. "You didn't know it would turn out like this. None of us did."

She paused, her eyes drifting away.

"We all have people up there… people we care about. And we don't even know what happened to them. But until those doors open—until we see for ourselves—we have to hold onto hope."

Her fingers traced the edge of her tablet, restless. Doubt flickered across her face, sharp and unguarded, before she forced it back down. She swallowed hard, then crossed the room and stopped in front of him.

For a moment she simply stood there, close enough that he could see the tremor in her breath.

"If I let myself imagine the worst… believe the worst…" She shook her head faintly. "I won't be able to keep going."

Her hand rested lightly on his arm, grounding herself as much as him.

"I need to believe there's something left. Something worth fighting for."

Her voice hardened. "That my dad—your brother… they're still out there."

A quiet breath escaped her. "That we still have a chance."

Jase's heart sank as he listened, guilt pressing harder against his chest.

He didn't answer right away.

Her words settled into him, heavy and unrelenting. The tremor in her voice, the way she held herself together—it all landed deeper than he expected.

"Liv..." His voice faltered, quieter now. "I'm sorry."

He swallowed hard, forcing the words out. "I didn't mean to weigh you down. You shouldn't have to carry that. Not because of me."

His gaze dropped for a moment before finding hers again. "You're the one who keeps me steady... and I hate that I'm making this harder for you."

He ran a hand through his unruly hair, frustration flickering across his face. "You're right. It doesn't do me any good—and it definitely doesn't do you any good either. I just... didn't sleep. I let the guilt get the better of me."

He glanced at her, his eyes softer now. "You don't deserve that. I'm sorry."

Olivia's expression eased, the tension slipping from her features. Her hand lingered on him a moment longer.

"It's okay," she said. "We all have our days down here."

Her voice was quiet, but steady. "That doesn't mean you're dragging me down." She held his gaze. "It just means we lean on each other when it gets too heavy."

A small breath escaped her. "That's all we've got down here, Jase... each other."

For a heartbeat, she simply held his gaze. His walls were down, and she saw him clearly.

Raw.

Uncertain.

Human.

Something about that vulnerability pulled her in, more than any strength ever could.

Then, as if sensing he'd had enough heaviness for one morning, her lips curved into a grin. The sadness in her eyes flickered out, replaced by the spark he knew so well.

"You know what your problem is?" she asked, her tone shifting to playful.

Jase raised an eyebrow. "What's that?"

"You need some breakfast!" she said with a mischievous grin. "What do you say I finish this up later and we head to the kitchen? Get your grumpy ass something to eat? That should put you in a better mood!" Her smile spread, infectious in its warmth.

Jase couldn't help it, he let out a laugh, the sound escaping before he could stop it. A genuine chuckle that felt like it had been trapped inside him for far too long.

Maybe Olivia was right. Maybe a simple meal was the distraction he needed, just for a moment. Just to break the tension that always hung between them.

"You know me too well, Liv. That's exactly what I need," he said, the smile lingering as his shoulders finally eased. The weight didn't lift, not entirely, but for a moment it didn't press so hard.

Olivia smiled, clearly pleased with herself. "Alright, let's go get you fed."

She turned to the ceiling. "Ouro, remind me to finish server maintenance later today, please."

A soft, female voice answered, smooth and without hesitation. "Copy that, Beta-Three. I will remind you this evening to complete rack server 2-3C maintenance in the OCC."

Ouro. The AI that ran every system in the Ouroboros.

She was everywhere—doors, lights, water, air—so tightly woven into the walls it was impossible to tell where the machine ended and their lives began.

Always listening. Always watching.

Never seen.

Olivia—despite her easy smile and the fact that she looked nothing like the stereotypical tech wiz—was the one who kept the vast system from faltering. She spoke with Ouro more than anyone.

And sometimes, in the quiet of the shelter, it almost felt like talking to a seventh roommate—one who never slept, never blinked, and never truly left them alone.

Olivia crossed the room, unplugged her tablet with a swift motion, and snapped the panel shut. The servers hummed steadily behind her.

As she returned, Jase caught her hand and tugged gently, guiding her toward the door.

Just before they stepped out of the OCC, he stopped and turned to her. He held her gaze, his own eyes steady with a resolve he didn't truly feel.

"When those doors finally open," he said, "we're going to find them, Liv. All of them."

Her breath caught for just a moment before a wide smile spread across her face. Warmth radiated from her like sunlight breaking through the underground gloom. She leaned into him, resting her head against his shoulder, letting the moment linger.

Jase managed a small smile.

It was convincing enough.

Then he guided her out into the hallway. The door sealed shut behind them with a soft hydraulic hiss.

Inside the OCC, the monitor Jase had been sitting at flickered to life.

The hum of the servers deepened.

Across the screen, a single word pulsed: *Analyzing*.

CHAPTER TWO

Jase led Olivia out of the OCC and into the hallway. Directly across from them loomed the sealed airlock, a constant reminder of their isolation. It was the only threshold between them and the world above, the one door that could lead them back to civilization.

If anything was left.

Above the door, the countdown clock glowed its familiar blue. But now the numbers no longer counted down. They ticked upward, mocking them with each passing day.

When they first entered The Ouroboros, the clock had been a promise—ninety days of the study, ninety days until release. The anticipation had been palpable.

But that changed on Day sixty-six.

An alarm had ripped through the facility, an ear-splitting wail that rattled their bones. Ouro's voice, calm as ever, summoned them to the OCC, where their new fate was delivered.

The communication systems had gone dark. The Ouroboros slipped into emergency protocol. The outside world was sealed away, leaving them blind to whatever the disaster might be or whether they were safe at all.

The countdown ended that day. From then on, the clock only ticked upward, each number a reminder of how long they had been trapped below. Days spent waiting for answers, for escape, for any sign of hope.

None had come.

Jase's eyes flicked to the display, the cold blue glow reflecting in his gaze. He hated the way it reminded him of everything he'd left behind. The guilt pressed harder with every second, but no matter how much time passed, it didn't bring him any closer to finding Eli.

Olivia caught the glance. They all did it when they passed the clock, as if it still held some kind of freedom.

Wanting to break his focus, she said brightly, "You know, Jase, next week makes it officially one year down here. Some of the others were talking about maybe… celebrating." A mischievous edge to her voice.

Jase raised a brow. "Celebrating?" Genuine confusion cut through his tone. "You want to celebrate being stuck down here?"

"Not… celebrate-celebrate," she countered with a grin. "More like… a party. Blow off steam. Mark the occasion. Surviving a whole year down here."

She spun ahead of him, light on her feet, her laughter a stark contrast to the weight that usually clung to the corridors.

Jase sighed, a conflicted frown tugging at his lips. "I don't know… Doesn't that feel a little… disrespectful?"

"Not at all," Olivia shot back, full of conviction. "We've been through hell down here. We can't carry that weight every day. Why can't we have one night to let go? We'll decorate, we'll play music." She caught his hand, lifted it above her head, and twirled beneath his arm, fingers brushing his wrist. "We'll dance. We'll laugh."

Jase's chest tightened at the sight of her spinning, her joy contagious. Despite himself, a smile tugged at the corners of his mouth.

She stopped in front of him, eyes locking with his. "Just one night, Jase. One night where we forget all this bullshit."

Jase met her gaze. "Alright, alright. When you put it that way, it actually sounds kind of nice. But honestly…" His lips curved into a grin. "It was the twirl that sealed the deal. Guess it must mean something to everyone if you're willing to go that far. But—"

He let the word hang, his expression turning serious. "There's one condition."

Olivia narrowed her eyes, suspicion flickering across her smile. "What?"

His seriousness broke into a grin. "No karaoke. Especially from you. Ouro might self-destruct if she has to hear that."

Laughter burst out of them both, echoing down the corridor, filling the hollow air with something alive. Jase couldn't remember the last time it felt this easy, when the weight pressing on them didn't smother every moment. Maybe there really was room for joy, even here.

"Fine," Olivia said with a dramatic pout. "I'll save my talents for the shower, where you can't be graced by them." She bumped his shoulder with hers, grinning wide as they carried on down the hall.

As they stepped into the core, Jase slowed, his eyes drawn to the towering tree that pierced both levels of the facility. The Ficus stretched skyward as if it longed for a sun it would never reach, its deep green leaves rustling in the soft, manufactured breeze.

"I know it's been almost a year," Jase murmured, "but I'll never get used to this view." Wonder still lit his face, the same as on their first day.

Olivia tilted her head, following his gaze. "It's amazing, isn't it? The way the lights shift from day to night, sounds of crickets, birds… even the air." She spread her fingers into the faint current, letting it curl around her hand. "It feels like stepping outside every time." Her amazement was more in the technology of it all, but still, the sentiment was there.

The Ouroboros had been designed to mimic life aboveground, but its beauty was sterile, calculated. Two concentric levels ringed the central core, their symmetry echoing the ancient symbol it was named after—the serpent devouring its own tail. The cyclical nature of existence. The constant intertwining of life and death.

Where endings give rise to new beginnings.

The lower level was where they lived. One wing branched into the male quarters, another into the female—each with three bedrooms along one side of the hall and a communal bathroom across from them. A third wing held the kitchen and dining area, with the living and game room across the hall. The fourth wing contained the fitness center on one side, and a recovery spa with a small pool on the other.

At the center of it all rose the base of the Ficus tree, surrounded by synthetic grass and carefully tended plants. A miniature Eden, manufactured but fragile. It was the closest reminder of the world above, a false freedom to dull the ache of confinement.

The upper level mirrored the design but had only three functional wings, built for function over comfort. One wing housed the Operations Command Center, the Ouroboros's nerve center, while directly across stood the sealed airlock. Another wing contained the greenhouse opposite the workshop and utilities. The last wing held the medical bay, with a laboratory across from it.

Two staircases, perfectly aligned on opposite sides of the core, coiled between the levels, making navigation efficient.

Every element was engineered with precision. Every wing, every room, every door led somewhere—yet nowhere. Despite the lights, the plants, all the amenities, it could never be mistaken for home. It was a machine, cold and exacting, with a single purpose: to keep them alive.

The symbol had once felt inspiring, a promise of survival. Now, after nearly a year underground, it felt more like a curse. Its design reinforced one unshakable truth: the cycle of life would continue indefinitely without escape.

Jase closed his eyes, inhaling deeply. The earthy fragrance that clung to the air filled his lungs—damp soil after rain, a whisper of growth, as if the world above were still there, just beyond the walls. It wasn't overpowering, but it lingered, grounding him, tricking his senses into believing he was somewhere else.

"It's the smell," he said, exhaling slowly. "That's what does it for me. I didn't realize how much I'd miss fresh air. This is as close as we'll ever get."

Olivia smiled faintly, though the wistfulness in her eyes betrayed her.

As they descended to the lower level, the savory aroma of frying potatoes mingled with the rich bite of coffee, drifting through the communal wing. By the time they reached the kitchen, the hydraulic door slid open with a soft hiss, releasing the clatter of pans and the steady sizzle from the stove.

Ryder stood at the counter, spatula in hand, flipping thin slices of potato, their edges already crisping golden brown. She glanced up as they entered, a calm smile spreading across her face.

"Good morning," she said warmly.

Wiping her hands on a towel, she moved toward the coffee machine, where a fresh pot was finishing its cycle, steam curling into the air. "Coffee, anyone?" she offered, lifting a brow.

The kitchen in The Ouroboros always struck Jase as more lab than home. Stainless steel surfaces gleamed under recessed lights, everything too perfect, too polished. Functional, yes—but clinical, as if even eating was just another survival task.

Along the counter, several essential machines were lined up in neat order: a tall food dehydrator and a vacuum sealer beside it, both working to stretch their greenhouse harvests as far as possible.

Next came the most impressive machine of all, the 3D meat printer. Sleek and box-like, with a glass-front interface and three nozzles at its core, it could print anything from synthetic proteins to convincing slabs of meat substitute. Although it looked like something from a sci-fi movie, it was just another part of their world.

But the most important device in the facility stood at the end of the line: the coffee machine. A humble, yet vital lifeline that kept the group going day after day. It gurgled through the last of its cycle as Ryder approached, the rich scent spreading through the air like a comfort.

"Jase will definitely take one, and one for me too, please," Olivia said with a subtle lift of her eyebrows.

Beyond the counter stood the walk-in freezer, its door thick and imposing. When pulled open, cold air rushed out, causing a shiver. Rows of vacuum-sealed meals and rations gleamed behind the frosted glass, shelves labeled and catalogued down to the last packet.

Across the room sat the dry storage pantry. Bins of rice, grains, and powdered milk stacked high, freeze-dried fruits and vegetables arranged in neat rows. Even here, the air carried the sterile scent of regulation and order, reinforced by the soft flicker of the digital panel by the door, always watching, always counting down supplies.

Along the same wall, a double-door refrigerator stood beside open shelves neatly stocked with cookware and dishes. Beyond them stretched the cooking area with a microwave, induction cooktops, and a stove, all streamlined and fully integrated with Ouro. A single voice command, and the cooktops hummed to life at the exact temperature needed. No accidents. No wasted energy.

Every part of the kitchen was built with function in mind. It was more machine than home, with clean lines, metallic surfaces, and a sterile atmosphere.

Despite its clinical nature, the kitchen had become somewhat of a refuge. At the center of the room sat a long metal table, big enough for six. Simple, practical.

Over time it had become more than a table. It was where they gathered, traded stories, shared meals, and bonded as a group. In those small moments, they could pretend that life resembled something they once knew.

"He had the nightmare again, didn't he?" Ryder teased, grabbing two mugs off the shelf. Her shorter, sturdy frame of five-four had her reaching on her toes.

Damian and Ava, already at the table with coffee and plates of food, both glanced at Olivia.

"Yup," Olivia said, striding toward the counter as the mugs began to fill.

"You know I'm right here, right?" Jase muttered, looking around the kitchen.

"Oh, hey Jase!" Ava called, offering a half wave.

"Good morning," Damian added with a nod, his tone calm, steady, as he lifted his mug in greeting.

Ryder handed Jase his coffee, then leaned toward Olivia with conspiratorial intrigue. "So… you didn't ask him, did you?"

Olivia paused mid-sip, her face unreadable. She met Ryder's gaze head-on. "I did."

The room stilled. Everyone looked to each other, waiting for the next move.

"She did," Jase said at last, matching her blank expression. He took a long sip, letting the silence drag as he savored the moment.

Then, with a sudden grin, he raised his mug high. "Hell with it. To one year!"

The tension broke in an instant. Cheers and laughter erupted around the table. For a whole year they had lived the same monotonous routine, but now, finally, they had something to look forward to.

Olivia cut in with a smirk. "But for the record, he said no karaoke. Especially not from me."

"Yeah, sorry, Liv," Ava shot back. "We all agree on that!"

"The people have spoken!" Jase declared, sweeping an arm dramatically to the nodding heads. His gaze drifted to the one empty chair. "Well, almost everyone. Where's Nolan?"

Ava leaned back with a satisfied smirk, her ponytail braid sliding over one shoulder as she stretched.

"Still in the gym, getting extra miles on the treadmill. He's been on a mission ever since I smoked him on the leaderboard last week."

She was the group's engineer, specializing in mechanical systems and keeping the facility running. Hispanic, with dark hair and a wiry, athletic build, she carried herself like someone mid-competition—even at breakfast.

At five-six, she wasn't imposing, but there was a sharpness to the way her dark eyes scanned the table, cautious, assessing, always with a spark of challenge.

"Wait, you beat Nolan?" Damian asked, half-impressed, half-amused.

"Oh yeah." Ava's smirk widened. "You should've seen his face."

Jase had to smile. That was Ava in a nutshell—blunt, sharp-witted, never letting anyone else solve a problem she could tackle herself. Practical, resourceful, and maybe a little too competitive, but it wasn't arrogance. Not really. It was just Ava, always pushing to be better.

"He nearly choked when he saw it," she went on. "Now he's in full-on revenge mode. What he doesn't know..." She leaned forward, lowering her voice. "…is that I was up early this morning, sneaking in extra miles before he even rolled out of bed." She pressed a finger to her lips, feigning secrecy.

Jase grinned, raising his mug toward her. "Brilliant. Secret's safe with me."

"Alpha-Three," Ouro's voice chimed, cutting clean through the chatter. "Report to the lab. Test results are ready."

Damian tilted his head in acknowledgment, leaving the words hanging in the air a little too long. He finished the last bite of his breakfast, carried his plate to the sink, and refilled his mug.

"Well, I'll be in the lab if anyone needs me. Jase, you should stop by later. I can check your vitals. Maybe discuss some things I can prescribe to sleep easier."

Jase waved him off with a forced smile. "If I have time."

The truth sat heavier in his chest than the coffee. It wasn't that he didn't long for a night without terror. It was that he wasn't sure he deserved one.

As Damian left the kitchen, Olivia and Ryder drifted toward the counter, their voices dropping into a whisper.

"What are you two whispering about?" Jase asked, half-joking. Still, a twinge of worry gnawed at him. Were they talking about him?

"Nothing!" Ryder blurted, too quick, her expression giving her away.

"Just about the party," Olivia added, shooting him a reassuring look.

Ava smirked over her mug. "Just tell him. He's going to find out anyway. Might even get him excited."

Olivia's eyes widened at Ava's betrayal. She glanced at Ryder, sighed, and then nodded. No sense keeping it secret now.

"I've been growing extra grapes and potatoes in the greenhouse these past few months," Ryder admitted, her voice soft but steady, carrying that calm authority only she had. "I told Olivia and Ava about the surplus, and we thought it'd be a nice surprise for the party."

Jase wasn't surprised. Ryder was the botanist. She always had dirt under her nails, always found barefoot excuses to linger in the greenhouse or around the Ficus tree. If anyone could coax more life out of this place, it was her.

With her long reddish-brown hair loosely tied back, and that warm, hazel gaze, she looked like she belonged in sunlight instead of steel walls. She was slightly curvy with soft, nurturing features. Her face was kind and open, framed by a heart-shaped structure and freckled cheeks and nose.

She smiled at him now, gentle and reassuring, and Jase felt the weight in his chest ease just a little. Ryder had that effect—nurturing and grounding, like the earth itself.

"A surprise, huh? What would that... wait, are you saying..." Jase trailed off, his mind racing to catch up with what they were saying.

"Ava made a distillery for the vodka, and the wine's been fermenting in a demijohn from the lab," Olivia blurted before he could finish.

Jase blinked, staring at them. "Wine... and vodka?!" He struggled to process it. The formalities of the study felt like another life, but this? Was it reckless? Indulgent? And how the hell had they even pulled it off?

"Don't freak out," Ava cut in quickly, trying to downplay it. "It's not that much. Just enough to make the celebration... enjoyable."

"Commemoration—not celebration," Jase corrected, his voice sharp.

"What?" Ava frowned, caught off guard.

"The party is to commemorate one year," he said, his tone low but firm. "Not to celebrate being trapped down here."

Silence spread across the room. Ava glanced at Olivia and Ryder, guilt flickering on her face. Maybe this had been the wrong time to tell him.

Jase broke the silence, his voice low, almost unsteady at first. "We will remember that we've spent a year underground. We will remember the people we love, people we haven't seen in so damn long." His throat tightened, but he pushed on. "And we will remember every sacrifice, every struggle it has taken to get this far."

Each word landed heavy. He met each of their eyes, making sure they understood—this wasn't just about a party.

It was about sacrifice. Resilience. Endurance.

The women exchanged a look, their faces hard but thoughtful. He was right. This day meant more than laughter and drinks. It meant proving they had made it through.

"And what better way to commemorate all that," Jase added, a grin breaking through, "than with a few drinks among friends?"

The tension cracked, giving way to smiles.

Ryder stepped forward, wrapping him in a tender hug. "Exactly," she murmured.

Jase held her briefly, but over her shoulder his eyes found Olivia's. She gave him a small, knowing smile. They were all in this together, and it was vital to never forget it.

Ryder lingered for a moment, giving Jase's arm a quick squeeze before she pulled away.

"Well, I should actually get to the greenhouse. Since we made it to one year, better make sure we can make it to two. Ava, can you stop by later to check the irrigation system? I think one of the pipes is leaking again."

"Yeah, no problem. I'll change, grab my tools, and be over in a bit," Ava replied.

Ryder walked out of the kitchen, and Ava cleaned up her breakfast and followed behind, leaving Jase and Olivia alone.

Jase shot her a look, brow furrowed. "Forget to mention the wine and vodka part?" Sarcasm edged his voice.

"Nope," Olivia said with a smirk, shaking her head. "It was supposed to be a surprise. One you ruined for yourself. Please don't tell Damian or Nolan. I want to see their faces when they find out."

"Oh, I wouldn't dare." Jase lifted his hands in mock surrender. "But seriously, how the hell do you guys even know how to make that stuff? It's not going to kill us, right?"

"We had a little help from a friend," Olivia said, eyes glittering with mischief. "A little guidance. Made sure we followed the process exactly—even tested samples in the lab to be safe."

Jase blinked, incredulous. "Ouro," he said slowly, letting it sink in. "You had a state-of-the-art AI teach you how to make shelter booze?"

Olivia grinned. "Better than winging it and blowing ourselves up. Or poisoning everyone."

Jase gave a dry chuckle. "You've really thought this through, haven't you?"

He wasn't upset. Just surprised. He hadn't realized until now how much they all needed this—one day to shrug off the weight of the year and just breathe.

"Any other surprises I should know about?" Jase asked, one brow raised, humor threading his voice.

"Well, it wouldn't be a surprise if I told you now, would it?" Olivia shot back with a sly smile.

"Oh God, there's more? What else are you up to?" he pressed.

Before she could answer, Ouro's voice filled the room. "Alpha-One, you are requested in the medical lab."

Jase paused, glancing up toward the ceiling. "Well, that's convenient timing. Ouro helping you out again?"

"I'd be just as surprised as you!" Olivia laughed, clearly enjoying the secrecy.

Jase gave her a long look. "Right. I'm onto you." His gaze flicked upward, half-amused, half-suspicious. "Both of you." He shook his head with a smile and turned toward the door.

Olivia watched him go, sipping her coffee. Warmth lingered on her face for a moment. But only for a moment. The satisfaction of keeping the secret slipped into something heavier, a flicker of concern clouding her eyes. She set the mug in the sink, the levity draining away.

"Thank you," she muttered softly, almost to herself.

"You're welcome," Ouro replied instantly.

Olivia exhaled slowly, rinsed the cup, and headed for the door, already forcing her thoughts toward what came next.

CHAPTER THREE

The greenhouse door hissed open, and a rush of warm, humid air spilled out, wrapping around Ava like a damp blanket. She pushed her tool caddy inside, already regretting the choice of coveralls in the heat.

The air smelled thick and alive—rich soil, wet leaves, and a hint of sweetness. After the sterile tang of steel and recycled air in the rest of The Ouroboros, the shift was almost dizzying. This was Ryder's world.

Rows of green stretched beneath the glow of full-spectrum grow lights, calibrated to mimic sunlight. Tomatoes gleamed red against their vines, lettuces spread in careful layers, and clusters of grapes dangled along their trellises. Potatoes sprouted in rows of dark soil. Every plant seemed to lean into the light, chasing a sun that wasn't really there.

Above the rows, pipes ran the length of the ceiling, their nozzles misting at regular intervals. The spray fell like artificial rain, hissing faintly as it dampened the leaves and disappeared into the soil.

Ava watched the droplets cling to the grape leaves before slipping free, the whole system so precise it looked more like choreography than irrigation.

To the left wall, the spice racks rose in vertical tiers, hydroponic shelves glowing with soft light. Basil, cilantro, rosemary, thyme. Their scents an aromatic promise that Ryder insisted kept their meals from tasting like rations. Ava smirked, remembering Ryder proudly calling them her "soul-saving greens."

Every tool had its place above a small workbench: hand trowels, clippers, even gloves neatly hung. Below, a squat processing machine waited to wash and chop vegetables, while the composting unit beside it gave off a faint musk of decomposing scraps being churned back into fertile soil.

At the far end of the greenhouse, Ryder's hands were buried deep in one of the planters. Beside her stood another hydroponic rig, this one glowing softer, filled with medicinal herbs: aloe vera, echinacea, chamomile, peppermint. Damian called this corner his pharmacy, but Ava knew it was Ryder's way of keeping them alive in more ways than one.

Everywhere Ava looked, there was order and abundance, plants thriving where nothing else could. Stepping from cold steel into this sanctuary always made her pause.

The greenhouse wasn't just a room; it was a promise. Ryder had created a small, thriving world, one that pulsed with a fragile hope for a life beyond the walls of The Ouroboros.

As Ava stepped further inside, warmth clung to her skin, damp with humidity. Ryder, though, looked at ease, like the air was as natural to her as sunlight.

"Hey, Ryder, where's my leak at?" Ava called from the entrance.

Ryder's head shot up, startled, soil still clinging to her hands. She wiped them quickly on her thighs as she crossed the rows.

"Sorry, I didn't hear you come in. Back row, over here."

She led Ava toward a dark puddle spreading across the floor. The leak dripped steadily from above, each drop splashing into the water and rippling out in widening circles.

Ava crouched, studying the puddle before glancing up at the pipe overhead.

"There it is. Same elbow fitting I replaced on the front row a couple months ago." She exhaled through her nose, already irritated.

Ryder folded her arms, watching as Ava hauled a step ladder over from the workbench and set it beneath the pipe.

Ava wiped sweat from her brow with her sleeve and shot Ryder a look. "Damn, I don't know how you spend so much time in here. I'm already sweating, and I haven't even started."

Ryder's smile was soft, almost dreamy as she took in the rows of green. "I love it in here. It's like walking into a hug. After a while, you just stop noticing the heat."

Ava snorted, climbing the ladder. "Yeah, well, I'll be heading straight for the freezer after this. Might have to check the coils while I'm in there."

As Ava worked, her movements were sharp and efficient. Metal fittings clanking, pipes banging into place with quick, forceful adjustments.

Beside her, Ryder moved slower, pruning the tomato plants with patient care, every snip deliberate, coaxing order from the tangle of green.

Two rhythms side by side—one all precision and pressure, the other steady and nurturing.

"What did you think of Jase's reaction this morning?" Ava asked, breaking the silence.

Ryder didn't answer right away, eyes focused on a delicate vine as she trimmed it free.

"We knew he'd struggle with the idea of the party," she said finally. "But I think he gets the bigger picture. He knows how much good it'll do for all of us."

Ava let out a heavy sigh, setting her wrench down on the ladder rung. "Yeah, I get it now. It's not just a celebration. I messed that up, got too caught up in the idea of it."

Ryder paused mid-snip and looked at her, offering a quiet, reassuring smile.

"Olivia and I did the same thing. We just wanted a break. We all do. But Jase is right too, it's not just a party. It's one year of surviving down here, and one year without everyone we love." Her voice softened on the last words, the greenhouse hum filling the silence that followed.

Ava swallowed, climbing down from the ladder slowly, her boots landing with a dull thud against the damp floor. She closed the metal frame with a snap and leaned against it, eyes lowered.

"You know, I'm not sure if I intentionally forgot about Jess, or if it's just this place. The monotony makes it easy to let things slip your mind. Either way, I did."

Her voice cracked slightly, and she forced a short laugh that didn't quite land. "We weren't soulmates, not even really in love. It was still early, but… I wish I could see her again. I wish I hadn't let her fade like that. Jase was right. It's not just about us down here."

For a moment Ryder didn't move. Then she set her pruning shears aside and brushed her dirt-streaked hands against her thighs before stepping closer. Her hazel eyes held that steady warmth Ava had come to depend on.

"I get it. It's easy to forget the world when all you see are the same walls every day. The world feels so far away, sometimes it almost doesn't feel real anymore."

Ava nodded, jaw tight. "Yeah. This place wears you down if you let it."

She drew in a breath, pushing herself upright, as if refusing to sink too deep.

"Still," she added with a faint smirk, "I'm definitely having a couple shots at the party. We deserve it. Who knows when we'll get another chance?"

Ryder's laugh was soft, but it carried through the humid air like a balm. "I'm with you. One night to unwind, to remember we're still human—that's exactly what we need. A little fun's not going to hurt anyone."

Ava glanced around the greenhouse, taking in the familiar yet unusual atmosphere that surrounded her.

"You know, I can see why you spend so much time in here," Ava said, her voice softening.

Ryder's expression shifted, a hint of vulnerability breaking through her usual calm. "It's my escape. Surrounded by these plants, I can pretend I'm somewhere else—anywhere beyond these concrete walls."

Ava leaned back against a row of planters, her gaze distant. "Do you ever think about going back up? Like… if it would even feel like the same world anymore?"

"Sometimes." Ryder sighed, her fingers brushing over a tomato leaf she'd just pruned. "But I wonder if there's even anything left to go back to. And if there isn't… then what? At least we know we're safe here. For now."

"Safe, sure," Ava smirked, crossing her arms. "But living? Not so much. If I could go back a year, before all this, I don't know if I'd sign up again. Even with whatever happened up there… I never thought it would turn out like this."

Ryder let out a soft chuckle, though her voice carried weight. "Yeah. None of us did. But here we are. I guess all we can do is make the best of it."

Ava straightened, wiping her palms on her coveralls. "Alright, this one shouldn't leak anymore. But keep an eye on the middle row, that fitting's probably next."

Ryder smiled, the warmth returning to her tone. "I'll make sure it's nice and humid for you when it does."

Ava rolled her eyes but grinned as she folded the ladder and packed her tools. At the door, she paused, glancing back with a playful smile tugging at her lips. "Don't get too lost in here. We've got a party to enjoy."

Ryder watched her leave, the sound of Ava's footsteps fading into the corridor.

Alone again, she drew in a quiet breath, the thick, earthy air wrapping around her. The weight of the year pressed heavy, but in the steady hum of lights and the rustle of leaves, she found a fragile kind of peace.

***

Damian sat in front of the glowing monitor, the hum of the lab filling the sterile air. His eyes moved over the data with methodical precision, finger tracing down the screen as he read line by line. His face revealed nothing, though every number pressed on him in ways he'd never admit.

The lab was a study in control. Bright lights erased every shadow, metallic counters gleaming under their cold glare. Cabinets and drawers lined the walls, every vial and instrument in its place.

At the center stood a series of workstations, diagnostic machines vibrating softly in the background. A centrifuge ticked nearby, separating samples Damian would check later.

Large monitors on the wall streamed constant data: the group's vitals, greenhouse environmental readouts, and lines of code crawling across the screen like a lifeline.

One side of the lab was dedicated to medical diagnostics: blood analyzers, centrifuges, and microscopes lined the counters, ready to test the group's health. A PCR machine waited with its tray of samples set for amplification. The spectrophotometer's screen glowed faintly, waiting for its turn.

He opened a refrigerated drawer and pulled out a vial of phosphate-buffered saline, checking the label against his notes. With care, he drew a measured amount into a pipette and added it to the sample waiting on the counter, the clear liquid swirling as it mixed.

When he finished, he returned it with the other reagents: formalin, antibiotics, glycerol, enzymes. Everything had its place; one misstep could throw the system into chaos. He shut the drawer, the vibration of the compressor rising again to its low drone.

The other side focused on environmental systems: greenhouse monitoring, air quality, and facility conditions that kept them alive. Shelves held neatly labeled trays: soil cores, leaf clippings, and small root bundles—each marked in Ryder's precise handwriting.

Swabs taken from vents and door seals sat sealed in containers. Even dust samples rested under glass, a reminder that in a closed system, nothing was harmless if left unchecked.

Air quality monitors blinked steadily, their readouts feeding into the large display on the wall. Oxygen, CO_2, humidity: every fluctuation graphed in real time. The screen cast a faint warmth across the sterile lab, a contrast to the sharp tang of disinfectant that lingered in the air.

To Damian, it was the only reminder that life, even here, was still growing.

He dropped a stack of papers at his desk and turned back to the monitor. Forcing his attention to the data, he steadied his breathing. One mistake could mean more than bad results; it could mean the difference between health and collapse. And he couldn't let that weight show. Not yet.

In the hall, Jase approached the door, noting the green light above glowing to signal it was safe to enter. A red light would mean the lab was in lockdown for testing or safety protocols. He stepped inside and found Damian at the monitor, eyes fixed on the data.

"I can't tell by your face if it's good or bad," Jase said, moving up beside him.

Damian glanced up briefly, as if surprised to see him, then turned back to the screen. "That's because I'm still in the data phase."

Jase hesitated, brow furrowing. "Funny. Ouro said I was needed here."

Damian made a distracted sound of acknowledgment, fingers still working the keyboard.

"Hmm. Well… since you're here." He tapped the screen. "So far, all our vitals are clean. No trace of radiation or abnormalities in anyone's system. I'm still waiting on the environmental tests to finish."

Jase smirked faintly. "So that's your good news face? Or too soon to celebrate until the other tests come back?"

"In theory, the environmental side should match," Damian replied, tone steady. "No contaminants in us means nothing should be out there, although it's a possibility. I won't call it good news until I have all the information."

That was Damian—calm, calculating, blunt. He didn't sugarcoat. Facts were facts, and bad news was bad news. Offering false hope would be something that haunted him forever.

"Well, I won't celebrate until we get all the information then," Jase said with a nod. This was far beyond his area of expertise, and he didn't want to assume anything.

"It should be any minute. If you want to wait, we could talk about your sleeping issues, and the options I have to help," Damian said, testing to see if that was the real reason Jase had come by.

Jase shook his head. "No, I'll be fine. Nothing to worry about at this point."

"Okay," Damian replied evenly, "but just so you know, I have some options down here that could really help. Things to ease you into sleep, even medication to take the edge off the stress."

"I'm fine. I don't need any pills," Jase answered, sharper this time.

Damian leaned forward, unflinching. "Jase, you've got to start sleeping. You've been running on fumes for a while now. This isn't about pills—it's about keeping yourself functional. Right now, you're putting yourself at risk for things you don't even realize. Prolonged sleep deprivation can impair your reaction time worse than alcohol. It lowers immunity, spikes cortisol, and wrecks your ability to focus. You can't lead, you can't protect anyone, if you're half-conscious."

"I can't afford to be knocked out, Damian," Jase snapped, frustration tightening his voice. "I need to be sharp. We can barely comprehend what's going on with a clear mind. How am I supposed to manage if I'm groggy?"

"You won't be sharp if you're sleep-deprived," Damian countered softly, but his tone stayed firm.

"And I'm not talking about sedating you. Just enough to let your brain cycle through rest. Even something mild like melatonin, or doxylamine. If it gets worse, zolpidem, eszopiclone. Nothing extreme. Just rest."

Jase shook his head. "You don't get it." He met Damian's glance. "Every time I close my eyes…I see him. Eli." His voice cracked on the name. "He's alone out there, while I'm down here—safe. It's all my fault. So no… I don't deserve to sleep easy."

Damian's expression softened, though his words remained steady. "Guilt doesn't make you stronger, Jase. It strips you down. It clouds your judgment, weakens your body, eats at everything until there's nothing left to fight with. You can't carry the weight of the world if you can't even stand on your own two feet."

Across the room, a machine beeped twice, its screen flashing Test Complete. The quiet sound punctuated the silence, but neither of them looked away.

Finally, Damian stood, stretching his lean frame.

At just over five-ten, he carried himself with a quiet discipline that seemed older than his years. His light brown hair was always neatly combed, a small ritual of order he clung to in a world where control was scarce. The sharp angles of his face, high cheekbones and a strong jaw, gave him a naturally serious look. His deep-set brown eyes rarely softened, always scanning for answers, for solutions.

He wore a lab coat out of habit. Protocol maybe. But Jase suspected it wasn't so much for himself as for the rest of them, a false authority he didn't really need.

At twenty-three, Damian was the oldest of them, a third-year medical student when the world collapsed. He had finished his clinical rotations, just beginning to step into the reality of medicine when everything ended. Now, unfinished as his training was, he was the closest thing they had to a doctor. Their doctor.

And to Jase, that was the strangest part.

Damian was still young, only a few years older than him, but down here the weight he carried made him seem decades older. Forced into a role he never asked for, Damian had become their lifeline.

Jase couldn't help but admire the burden he carried... and pity it too.

Damian and Jase stood shoulder to shoulder before the screen, the hum of the lab suddenly louder, heavier. The vitals had come back clean, but this—this was the test that mattered. If contamination had found its way inside, their survival, everything they'd endured for nearly a year, could already be over.

Jase's pulse drummed in his ears as the data scrolled down the monitor, each line feeling like a verdict. Radiation. Toxins. Decay. The words pressed at the edge of his mind, waiting to appear. He swallowed hard, forcing the question out before silence crushed him.

"Well...?"

Damian didn't answer right away. His eyes tracked the numbers with precision, lips pressed into a thin line. Only when he reached the end did he glance up.

"No radiation in the soil. None in the plants. Nothing in the swabs from the airlock door."

Jase exhaled, the relief rushing out of him in one long breath. "That's definitely good news, right?"

"It means The Ouroboros is working as designed—sustaining life within its walls and keeping out everything beyond." Damian's voice was calm, but not triumphant.

"What it doesn't tell us, and can't, is what the world above looks like. Without the ability to open the airlock doors or pull samples from outside, we still don't know what we're really facing."

Jase nodded slowly, grounding himself. "Fair point. Until we figure out a way to do that, let's keep running these tests every few weeks. Better to stay ahead of anything than get blindsided. Who knows, maybe the data will start giving us hints."

"Once a week," Damian said, his arms folding across his chest, eyes still locked on the screen.

Jase studied him, recognizing the steel beneath the calm. Even in moments of relief, Damian wouldn't let them grow complacent. And maybe that was the only reason they'd made it this far.

At that moment, the lab door whooshed open and Nolan limped through, a grimace flashing across his face.

"There you are, Doc," he groaned, bracing himself against the nearest counter and leaning into it with his full weight.

Damian and Jase turned. Nolan, six-two and broad-shouldered, built from years of relentless training, stood wincing in pain. His physique was all discipline, every muscle shaped by endurance and structure. A square jaw and tightly shaven beard lent him a hardened edge, while his dark undercut gave him a sharp, military precision.

But it was his eyes that stood out. Steel-gray, unyielding, they carried a focus that could intimidate even without words. And Nolan rarely used words—quiet, reserved, always watchful. His discipline was instinct, drilled into him as a Corporal in the Marines.

He'd been selected for the study to provide order, and he treated it like a proving ground: a chance to rise, to show his strength, to test himself in this unorthodox command. For him, survival was more than staying alive. It was a mission.

"What the hell happened to you?" Jase blurted, concern spiking his tone.

"Rolled my ankle on that damn treadmill," Nolan grunted, trying to straighten but wincing again. "I need the doc to take a look."

Damian glanced at Jase, gave a small sigh, and shook his head. "Help me get him across the hall to the med bay."

Jase tightened his grip around Nolan's arm, steadying him as they crossed the hall. The med bay door slid open with a hiss, releasing the sharp scent of disinfectant.

"Up on the table," Damian directed, pointing toward the sleek exam table in the center. The metallic frame adjusted with a quiet hum as Nolan lowered himself down, grimacing.

The room around them gleamed under bright overhead lights. Cabinets lined one wall, meticulously organized and labeled with medical supplies: bandages, gauze, syringes, and medicine vials, each carefully stocked by Damian.

The far side of the room held two patient beds against the wall, each with crisp white sheets and small screens above the headboards displaying heart rates, oxygen levels, and other vitals. Even empty, they gave the place an edge of unease, as if the room itself expected an emergency.

The heavier equipment sat on the other side of the room. A compact MRI unit took up one corner, a miniature model built to do everything that mattered: limb scans, head injuries, neurological checks.

Next to that, a small station held surgical equipment, all sterilized in the autoclave that hummed softly in the corner.

On the counter was a portable ultrasound machine, essential for diagnosing internal injuries, and a sturdy defibrillator ready for emergencies. A medical fridge clicked softly as it cycled, keeping antibiotics, vaccines, and emergency meds chilled.

Despite its small size, the medical bay felt like a miniature hospital, ready for general care to critical situations.

Nolan winced as Damian pressed on his ankle. "Yeah, it hurts when you do that."

"Couldn't handle not being top of the leaderboard for one week, huh?" Jase cut in, grinning.

Nolan's steel-gray eyes shot up, sharp even through the pain. "Ava's cheating, isn't she? How—Olivia hacking the damn board for her?"

Jase just laughed and shook his head.

Damian shifted his grip, fingers probing the inner side of the ankle. "How about when I press here? Or here?"

Relief flickered across Nolan's face. "No. That feels fine."

"Alright," Damian said, his tone steady, clinical. "Now rotate it slowly in a circle. Don't force it."

Nolan grimaced as he turned his foot, the movement stiff. "Little bit of pain, but it's more tightness than anything."

Damian nodded. "That's consistent with a sprain. The ligaments here take the stress. Some ice, compression, and a few days off should do the trick. But let's confirm with a scan before I clear you."

"Be back on your feet just in time for the party," Jase added, watching for Nolan's reaction.

Nolan's eyebrow rose, a smirk tugging at his mouth. "Ah, so they finally pitched it to you, huh?"

"They did," Jase said, his tone light but curious as he leaned in, eyes on the swelling. "What do you think?"

His smirk faded into something more thoughtful. "Seems like a distraction to me," he muttered, flexing his swollen ankle. Then, softer, "But maybe a distraction's exactly what we need."

Jase's lips quirked, but the words landed heavier than Nolan probably meant. Maybe a distraction was exactly what they needed, before the weight of everything crushed them for good.

Nolan gave him a quick, pointed look, his expression slipping back into its usual hard lines. "Just as long as we don't make a habit of it. One night, fine. After that, back to business."

Jase nodded, smiling faintly. He knew that, if anything, Nolan would always have his back in keeping the group focused.

"Well, if you're planning to jump back on that treadmill after the party, let's scan this ankle first and make sure you actually can," Damian said, his grin widening as he prepped the machine.

Nolan gave a half-grin of his own, rolling his eyes as he flexed his ankle again.

"I'll leave you to it, then," Jase said, patting Damian on the shoulder. He headed for the door, calling back without looking, "Oh, and Nolan—Ava's definitely going to torment you for the next few days."

Nolan watched him leave, then dropped his gaze to his ankle. He flexed it once, the joint twinging in protest, before dragging a hand over his face. A sigh escaped him, low and frustrated.

"Shit."

CHAPTER FOUR

Jase stood at the sink, gazing into the mirror, where a soft golden glow highlighted the edges, reflecting his tired expression back at him.

The bathroom, like the rest of The Ouroboros, blended futuristic design with a sleek, sophisticated aesthetic.

Matte black surfaces covered the walls and floors, with subtle gold accents highlighting key fixtures. Recessed golden lighting ran along the trim of the ceiling and floor.

At one end, three shower stalls were separated by frosted glass panels, which lit up with a soft glow when occupied. The showers hummed to life as they powered up, the temperature and water duration precisely regulated by the facility's automated system. Water flowed with perfect efficiency, every drop being recycled and filtered back into the facility's reserves.

At the other end, three toilet stalls were lined up, their touch-sensitive doors opening with a quiet, almost effortless motion, ushering occupants in and out with a soft breath of air.

In the center of the room, three sleek sinks were set into a glossy, dark countertop, their gold-accented faucets dispensing water at a pre-set temperature with a gentle tap. Above each sink sat large, sleek mirrors with gold trim.

Jase ran his hand over his face, feeling the cool water refresh his skin before he reached for a soft, heated towel hanging nearby. Would tonight's sleep be haunted by the unknown, or could his mind finally get the rest it needed?

When he stepped into the hall, he paused. Olivia was there, leaning against the wall with her arms crossed, the ambient striplight softening the edges of her face.

Her expression wasn't sharp or teasing this time, just calm and steady. The kind of look that grounded him when the weight in his chest felt too much to carry alone.

"Hey," she said, pushing off the wall to stand straighter. "I just wanted to check in."

Jase frowned slightly, caught off guard. "What do you mean?"

"Are we good? After this morning… keeping all that from you?" Her eyes dipped to the floor, uncertainty flickering across her face.

Jase hesitated, then let out a small breath. "Yeah, we're good," he said, managing a faint smile. "I know you didn't mean any harm."

Relief softened her shoulders. "I just—I didn't want you thinking we were going behind your back. Or that I'd keep something important from you. We just thought it'd be more fun as a surprise, you know?"

"I get it," he said quietly. "I was just… caught off guard. This day crept up faster than I realized. Guess I've been so wrapped up in my own shit I didn't realize what this meant for everyone else." His voice was heavier now, weighed down by the admission.

Her gaze lifted back to him, warm and steady. "Don't beat yourself up. Down here, it's easy to get stuck in our own heads and forget everyone else is fighting their own battles too. We're all just… figuring it out." A smile tugged at her lips, softening the moment.

She reached into her pocket and pulled out a small, dark blue bottle. "Here," she said, offering it to him.

Jase turned it over in his hand. Melatonin Spray. He arched a brow at her. "Talked to Damian, did you?"

She shrugged, the corner of her mouth twitching. "Maybe. But it couldn't hurt. It's natural, not a pill, so… less intense, right?"

"Yeah," he murmured, his thumb brushing the label.

He glanced back at her, slower this time. "Thanks, Liv. For caring, I mean." His voice caught, softer than he intended. "I'm… not used to people watching out for me."

Her expression warmed, eyes searching his as if she wanted to say more. "Of course, Jase. You're always carrying the weight for everyone else. Just… let me carry some of it too."

The words landed heavier than she meant, hanging between them.

Jase nodded, swallowing against the ache in his chest. "I'll keep that in mind. Really… it means a lot."

"You're welcome." Her smile grew, gentler now, as she rested her hand on his shoulder. Her fingers lingered for a moment longer than necessary before she finally pulled away. "Now get some rest. You deserve it."

She turned, her hair catching in the low light as she walked down the hall toward the female wing. Her footsteps echoed softly, until she disappeared into the dim glow.

Jase lingered, staring after her, that warmth still spreading inside him. Gratitude. Longing. And maybe the dangerous thought that he didn't have to carry everything alone.

Jase turned toward his door. It slid open with its familiar whisper, and he stepped inside.

Like every bedroom in the Ouroboros, his was sleek, minimal, stripped of identity. Dark, muted walls and floors echoed the same modern design as the rest of the facility, trimmed in thin golden lines that glowed faintly at night. The lights shifted with the time of day: warm and golden in the evening, gradually brightening to a crisp white each morning—an artificial sunrise built to keep them on schedule.

In the center sat a full-size bed, its memory foam mattress adjusting to his body temperature through the night. Compartments built into the frame stored his clothes, socks, and shoes, a soft strip of light tracing the base like a low ember.

Along one wall, a closet slid open at a touch, revealing rows of identical black clothing: work, gym, and loungewear, all stamped with the Ouroboros insignia in gold. Functional. Uniform. A quiet reminder of the life they had been assigned.

At the bottom, a cubby held the clothes they'd arrived in, and the set they'd wear when they finally left.

A compact desk stood beside the bed, its black surface doubling as a digital interface for notes and facility data. Above it, a single shelf held the only personal items allowed: a handful of books stacked neatly.

Jase leaned against the desk for a moment, scanning the room. It was perfect in design, efficient in every detail. And yet it could have belonged to anyone. Nothing here was truly his.

He set the bottle of melatonin on the desk, its dark glass catching the dim light. For a moment, all he could see reflected there was Olivia's face, her soft smile and the way she'd pressed the bottle into his hand. The gesture felt almost intimate, like an unspoken promise that he wasn't in this alone.

His hand hovered, then Eli's voice whispered through his memory.

Why'd you leave me?

It had been nearly a year since he'd last seen his brother's face anywhere but in his nightmares. Without them, he wondered if he'd ever see him again.

With a weary sigh, he lay back on the bed and pulled the blanket over him, forcing his eyes shut, begging his mind for silence.

But the darkness offered no peace.

His eyelids twitched, his breath quickened, every nerve braced for what waited in the shadows—terror circling like wolves, patient and hungry.

He opened his eyes again, drawn back to the desk. The bottle sat there like a lifeline. Olivia's smile flickered through his mind once more, urging him on.

Jase grabbed the bottle and sprayed three sharp bursts under his tongue. The mint stung as it settled, bitter and thin. He hesitated, then lifted it again, adding two more spritzes, as if sheer volume could hold back the nightmares.

He stared at the bottle a final time, then set it down and sank into the mattress. His eyelids grew heavy, weighted with exhaustion and fear. Maybe tonight he'd find a sliver of peace. Maybe he'd escape the images that stalked him through the dark.

If not, at least she'd know he tried.

For her.

***

The next morning, Jase stepped into the kitchen, the familiar scent of coffee and rehydrated fruit hanging in the air.

Nolan sat at the table, his wrapped ankle propped on a chair, an ice pack balanced on top. Ryder crossed over from the counter carrying two plates and set one in front of him before sliding into the seat across, powdered eggs and fruit piled on both.

"Hey, how'd the scans come back? Anything serious?" Jase asked, concern edging his voice.

"No, just a sprain. Doc called it," Nolan replied with a shrug.

"Good to hear." Jase grabbed a cup of coffee and a protein bar from the counter.

Ryder shot Nolan a look, frustration flickering in her hazel eyes. "Yeah, as long as he stays off it and actually keeps icing it."

"I'd have been fine making my own breakfast," Nolan muttered, giving Ryder a pointed look.

She rolled her eyes, clearly unimpressed. "Sure."

Jase raised his mug, cutting through the tension. "By the way—either of you seen Olivia this morning?"

Ryder shook her head, already halfway through a bite of eggs. "Not since last night."

Nolan took a sip of coffee. "Neither have I. Maybe she's in the gym."

At that moment, Ava walked in, sweat glistening on her brow as she toweled off. Still in her workout gear, braid tucked neatly over one shoulder, she went straight to the sink for a glass of water. "Who are you looking for—Olivia?"

"Yeah," Jase said quickly. "Have you seen her? Was she in the gym?"

Ava drained half her glass before answering, her voice rough from exertion. "No, just Damian. I did see her in the bathroom early this morning, but not since. Figured she'd be in here by now."

Jase frowned. Olivia was always one of the first up, already moving before the others rubbed the sleep from their eyes. It wasn't like her to be absent in the morning.

Ava's eyes flicked to Nolan's leg propped up on the chair, and a smirk curved her lips. "Looks like I'm leaving you in the dust for good now that you're benched."

Nolan rolled his eyes. "Yeah, yeah. Enjoy it while it lasts. I'll be back on my feet soon enough, and back to looking down at you from the throne."

"Oh, really?" Ava arched a brow. "Didn't you sprain that ankle trying to catch up to me? Face it, the crown was already mine. Now I've got days to pull even further ahead."

"More like tiara, Princess," Nolan shot back with a grin. "When I come back, you'll be begging me to show mercy."

Ava chuckled, tossing the towel over her shoulder. "Sure, Corporal. Keep telling yourself that. I'll just keep racking up the miles in the meantime."

"Ridiculous," Ryder muttered, rolling her eyes but smiling.

Jase laughed with the others, but the sound faded quickly. He'd warned Nolan about Ava's torment, and clearly she was enjoying it. But Olivia still wasn't here. Not in the gym. Not at breakfast.

The thought gnawed at him. The next logical place was the OCC. And if she was already there… then something had to be wrong.

***

The OCC was the nerve center of The Ouroboros, designed with the precision and functionality of a military command room. The walls were lined with sleek, black metal panels, with a bank of computer screens dominating one side, constantly displaying the facility's vital readings.

Next to the screens, a wall of servers stretched floor to ceiling, their faint glow casting an otherworldly sheen across the matte-black concrete. Red and green indicators blinked in rhythm, like the pulse of some massive, unseen organism.

They weren't just machines; they were Ouro itself.

A large console allowed Olivia, and the others, to access Ouro's systems—troubleshoot, or run diagnostics.

At the center of the room, a wide conference table sat beneath two stark overhead lights, whiteboards lining the walls around it. This was where decisions were made, where arguments were had, where their voices bounced against the cold, hard walls.

The OCC was cold, functional, without frills—just as it needed to be. It was a place for decisions, monitoring, and survival. Every flicker of data, every quiet beep, reminded Jase of the truth: the Ouroboros wasn't just keeping them alive. It was also keeping them here.

As Jase entered, he caught Olivia at the console, her fingers darting over the keyboard.

At his entrance, she startled slightly, closing a window with a sharp tap. He caught only a glimpse of text before it vanished—'Project Fallout Kids'.

"Hey," he said, keeping his tone casual, though his brow lifted. His gaze lingered on the now-black screen. "What was that? Everything alright?"

A flicker of surprise crossed her face, gone as quickly as it came. "Oh, nothing. Just a quick diagnostic check. Some of the displays were lagging after yesterday's server maintenance." Her tone was light, almost too quick.

Behind them, the wall of servers hummed louder for a moment, a faint shift in pitch like the room itself was listening.

Jase frowned. He rarely dug into Ouro's systems, but he'd never seen anything with that label before. Still, Olivia's easy tone pressed the doubt back, for now.

He stepped closer. "I've just… never seen that before."

"It was just a reboot, all good," she cut in smoothly, smiling. Then, with a tilt of her head, "What are you doing in here so early?"

The pivot caught him, but he let it go. "Actually, I just wanted to say thanks. For the melatonin." He met her gaze. "For the first time in a while, I actually slept through the night."

Her smile softened, more genuine now. "You did? I'm glad, Jase. You needed it."

"Yeah. More than that, I needed the reminder. Thanks for pushing me to do something I was too stubborn to do on my own."

Olivia rose from her chair and wrapped her arms around him. The hug was tight, grounding. "You're welcome. Sometimes we all just need a little push."

Over her shoulder, the monitors flickered. For the briefest second, lines of code scrolled across the blank console before settling again: 'Reboot complete. System 100%'.

Jase pulled back with a small smile. "Looks like your reboot worked."

"Told you. All good now." She stretched, brushing the moment aside. "Which means I'm done here. And starving. Want to grab breakfast?"

"I'm good. Already had some coffee and a protein bar." Jase said with a smile.

"Suit yourself. I'll see you around later." She flashed him one more smile before slipping out, the door hissing closed behind her.

Jase lingered, staring at the monitors as their steady blink filled the silence. He turned to follow her out, but stopped, the unease coiling tighter in his gut.

Project Fallout Kids.

The words pulsed in his mind. He knew them well enough, it was the name of their study, but never once had he seen them buried in Ouro's coding.

And Olivia, skipping breakfast, heading straight to the OCC, brushing it all off as routine maintenance. It didn't sit right. Was there more to it? Was she keeping something from him again?

He shook his head. After last night, pressing her now would only spark tension. Maybe it really was just the system rebooting, and he was reading too much into it. He wasn't the computer specialist, after all.

His eyes drifted back to the empty console. Maybe it was the melatonin. He'd taken more than the label suggested—five spritzes instead of three. Maybe he was still groggy, his thoughts muddied, nightmares bleeding into waking hours.

His heart wanted to believe that. That it was nothing. That the unease was just a shadow left behind by Eli's voice in his dreams.

With a sharp exhale, he forced the thought away and headed toward the gym. If he couldn't quiet his mind, maybe he could sweat it out.

Behind him, the console flickered once, so faint it could have been a trick of the light. A line of code flashed across the screen before vanishing into black.

Jase never turned to see it.

***

Jase stepped into the gym, the steady beat of a workout mix thumping quietly from hidden speakers. The faint smell of rubber mats and sweat hitting his nose.

The room stretched wide before him, sleek and modern, every detail designed to keep them in peak condition. But for Jase, and for all of them, it was more than that. It was where they burned off the anger, the claustrophobia, the helplessness that came from being trapped underground.

To his left, a line of treadmills and stationary bikes glowed with digital interfaces, the screens looping through virtual trails: beaches, forests, winding city streets.

The machines purred quietly, smooth and efficient, their sensors syncing to each user's vitals, every heartbeat and calorie automatically logged into Ouro's system.

Across the way, the free-weight bench sat waiting, flanked by rows of dumbbells arranged in perfect order, matte black metal glinting under the lights. Nearby, a cable machine stood tall, its gold fittings polished from use, ready to work whatever muscle needed punishing.

The farther he moved into the room, the more the focus shifted from conditioning to combat. Thick mats spread across the floor for grappling drills, while two heavy bags hung from reinforced mounts. One dense for power strikes, the other longer and softer, meant to take the pounding of Muay Thai kicks.

Along the wall, gloves, shin guards, and headgear waited in tidy rows, each piece worn but cared for, ready for the next round of sparring.

Above, the lights shifted easily between warm daylight and cooler tones for high-intensity sessions, casting the whole place in a purposeful glow. Even the shock-absorbent floor seemed alive with energy, designed to take a beating and give nothing back.

Centered on the wall, a large monitor scrolled through workout stats, listing miles run and weights lifted. Ava's name gleamed at the top of the leaderboard, Nolan trailing just below.

Jase let out a faint chuckle, shaking his head at their rivalry, before his eyes caught Damian near one of the bikes with a towel draped over his shoulder.

"Morning, Jase," Damian said, catching his breath. He slung the towel over his shoulder. "Sorry, just finished up. About to head across the hall for a steam."

Jase shook his head with a small smile. "No worries. I slept in a little. Sauna does sound like a good way to wrap things up though. Might have to do the same after my ride."

Damian wiped away sweat with the towel, and raised an eyebrow. "You look more rested than yesterday. Sleep better?"

Jase swung a leg over the bike, grin widening. "Yes, actually. Thanks to you and Olivia, the melatonin worked wonders. Knocked me right out."

Damian paused, his brow creasing. "Wait, you took the melatonin? I thought you were against it."

Jase blinked, his expression tightening. "I was. But Olivia gave it to me. I figured you two talked and she grabbed it for me."

Damian shook his head slowly. "No. We've discussed a few options for her, but nothing about you. I had no idea she was giving it to you."

Jase's hands tightened around the bike handles, wheels in his head spinning faster than his legs ever could. "Huh. I just assumed you'd sent her as a nudge."

"No," Damian said, tone flat and serious. "That stuff stays between me and each of you. Doctor-patient confidentiality. If you want to share your medical information, that's up to you."

Confusion flickered across Jase's face before he covered it with a nod.

He hesitated, then decided to push. "Can I ask you something random?"

"Yeah, sure," Damian said, intrigued.

"Have you ever seen the words Project Fallout Kids in any of the files you work on? Like in your logs, or loading screens, wherever?"

Damian thought for a beat. "Yeah. All our records are under that folder. Medical logs, patient files. Why?"

Jase tried to mask the jolt that ran through him. "Oh. Just thought I saw it on a screen, never noticed it before."

"Well, it makes sense," Damian said simply.

"Yeah, definitely. Think I'm just a little groggy this morning." Jase forced a quick nod, as if shaking it off. "Anyway, enjoy your steam. I've got some mountains to bike through."

Damian gave him a curious look, then nodded before heading out. "Will do."

As the door slid shut behind him, Jase settled back onto the bike, the whir of the machines filling the room as questions buzzed in his head.

Project Fallout Kids.

It made sense that the files would carry the label. Damian's explanation was logical. But Olivia's reaction, the way she snapped the window closed and forced that too-easy smile, stuck with him. And the melatonin… how had she known he'd refused it when Damian offered it?

Maybe it was nothing. Maybe it was just his guilt find a new way to haunt him.

His legs pumped harder, the resistance climbing. He pushed against the pedals like he could grind the unease out of his chest, leave it trailing behind him. But it chased him, clung to him—just as unyielding as the steel walls around them.

For now, he told himself, he'd let it lie. Let it simmer.

But with every pedal stroke, the fire of his curiosity only burned hotter.

CHAPTER FIVE

The flames shrieked as they tore through his childhood home, a living beast of fire gnashing its teeth at the walls. Heat clawed his skin, blistering and relentless, while shadows twisted across the collapsing structure—elongated limbs and warped faces, like phantoms jeering from the corners.

Jase stood frozen, wide-eyed. The fire should have consumed him, but all he felt was the weight of guilt cracking away, replaced with desperate clarity. He could still save Eli. He had to. They could figure everything else out later, after they both made it out.

He surged to his feet, every muscle coiled with purpose, his heart pounding as he lunged toward the next step. But then the wood splintered, the floorboard giving way beneath him. His body fell forward as his leg plunged through, the floor swallowing him whole.

The world around him warped in an instant as the flames vanished. The house now a fading memory of ash, scattered on the wind as it was carried away.

In the stillness, all Jase could hear was the faint whisper of his brother's voice, drifting through the breeze.

"Why did you leave me?"

"Why"

Jase turned, heart clawing at his ribs, as a figure emerged from the smoke—broad-shouldered, familiar. His vision blurred, but for an instant, he swore it was Eli. Relief flooded him, his brother was alive. He was there.

But the figure shifted. The outline blurred.

Eli's face melted into someone else's. The hair shorter. The posture straighter. The eyes—blue, piercing, merciless.

Olivia.

She stood calm amid the ruin, a matchbook in one hand, a single match in the other. Her expression was unreadable, but the cold determination in her eyes sent a chill down his spine.

"Olivia!" Jase's throat tore with the shout, the smoke clawing at his lungs.

She only stared, her expression unreadable.

Too still. Too cold.

This was an Olivia he had never seen before, a stranger wearing a familiar face.

A twisted smile washed over her face. She struck the match along the box. The rasp of it cut through the silence like a scream. The flame erupted from its cage, trembling in her hand, as its rage reflected in her eyes.

Her gaze flicked from Jase to the flame, then back again, until it locked on him.

Hollow.

Cruel.

The match slipped from her fingers.

The world exploded into fire. It rushed him like a starving beast, roaring, tearing the air from his lungs. He felt the heat blast toward him, searing and relentless. Jase didn't move. Couldn't.

As the flames closed in, he accepted his fate, feeling the fire's brutal embrace swallow him whole.

He woke with a violent gasp, drenched in sweat, the echo of her smile seared into his mind. His chest heaved as if the fire still raged inside him. He dragged a trembling hand over his face, but the nightmare clung to him. Olivia's eyes, flickering between love and betrayal, burning deeper than the flames ever could.

Why Olivia?

The question lodged in his mind, sharp and unyielding. In all the countless times he'd been trapped in that nightmare, this was the first time anyone else had stepped into it.

And after the past few days, he couldn't shake the thought that maybe his subconscious was trying to tell him something.

Olivia's face, her cold detached gaze as she watched his life burn, haunted him more than the flames ever could.

He swung his legs over the side of the bed, the chill of the floor against his bare feet pulling him back into reality. Back into the familiar, uncompromising walls of The Ouroboros.

Jase drew in a long breath, though the phantom smoke still clung to his lungs.

Just a dream, he told himself. A cruel trick of guilt, punishing him for letting himself enjoy a rare, peaceful night of sleep. How could he let that vision taint the Olivia he knew—the Olivia who had pushed him to rest, who cared enough to watch his back?

He thought about recording an Echo Loop, to get it out of his head. That's what it was for, after all: tracking their mental state, venting into the system.

But the idea froze him. Ouro heard everything. What if she flagged it? What if Olivia ever found out?

The thought unsettled him more than the dream itself.

But the longer he sat in the dim light of his room, the more the silence pressed in.

Thick. Suffocating.

Doubt curled on the edges of his mind, whispering that the dream hadn't been random at all.

Maybe Olivia was hiding something far more dangerous than just party plans.

***

The next few days drifted by in a dull, repetitive haze. Life in The Ouroboros settled back into its familiar rhythm, each of them falling into their usual routines.

Nolan hobbled through the halls, his ankle wrapped tight, muttering curses under his breath every time he had to slow down. He kept to light duties, inventory checks and minor maintenance that didn't require much movement.

He was restless, but Ryder hovered nearby to make sure he wasn't overdoing it, occasionally throwing him a pointed look that kept him in line.

Ryder herself disappeared into the greenhouse, the only place that seemed to soften her edges.

She bent low over her plants, fingers brushing soil as tenderly as if it were skin. Sometimes she whispered to the tomatoes, or hummed under the drone of the grow lights, her voice muffled by the humid air. The earthy scent clung to her hair and clothes, marking her as if the greenhouse had claimed her for its own.

Ava prowled the corridors like a restless fox, tool caddy rattling at her side. A faulty valve here, a flickering light there—she handled them with ease as she moved from one task to the next. She seemed to relish in the minor inconveniences, as if each problem was a small puzzle waiting to be solved.

For Ava, each day was a reminder that this place depended on her ability to keep it running smoothly.

Damian buried himself in the lab, eyes glassy from hours of scrolling data. Environmental graphs crawled across the screens. Soil reports, air samples, irrigation readouts—all combed with relentless precision. He pinched the bridge of his nose often, fatigue tugging at him, but he never stopped. Even the smallest anomaly made him lean in closer, heart hammering as if the walls themselves were whispering secrets he couldn't afford to miss.

His only reprieve came from occasional checkups with Nolan or a cut on Ava's finger, minor injuries that gave him brief flashes of purpose beyond numbers.

Jase, meanwhile, kept his interactions to a minimum. He kept his distance from Olivia, ducking into another hall when she entered, his excuses flimsy even to himself.

Most of the time it was easy, as Olivia spent her days in the OCC, working with Ouro. But every time he caught a note of her voice, that image burned behind his eyes again—Olivia standing in the flames, the match in her hand. He told himself it was just a dream. Still, suspicion rooted deeper with each passing day.

The days crawled by, each one blending into the next, the monotony of shelter life weighing heavily on all of them. They spoke little about the upcoming anniversary, but it was there, glimmering under the surface. A spark of something human, waiting.

*****

The night before the party the group gathered in the living room, their usual refuge after long days. For once, the air felt different, restless. Like the walls themselves were holding their breath.

The living room in was the simplest room in the facility, yet it held a quiet charm. Unlike the rest of the facility with its sleek surfaces and humming machines, this room was plain, a place meant solely for unwinding.

Two deep couches faced each other across a low coffee table, flanked by a pair of armchairs. The cushions were worn from use, their softness a rare comfort in a world of steel and concrete where the group could sit together.

A modest television hung against the wall, ancient compared to the technology that powered the shelter. It only played Blu-rays, and the limited collection of thirty discs had nearly been cycled through twice.

On the opposite side sat a ping pong table and a foosball table, their surfaces scuffed from heavy use. A chalkboard leaned nearby, scores scrawled and erased so many times the ghost of old victories lingered faintly in the background.

Beside them a large card table sat in the corner, round and sturdy, with enough room for all six of them. Countless late nights had been spent there, shuffling cards, arguing over board games, and chasing away boredom with laughter.

One wall was lined with shelves, their contents eclectic but precious. A scattering of novels, a handful of biographies, and history books that had sparked more than one heated debate. Medical texts with Damian's folded notes stuffed between the pages. Board game boxes stacked neatly beside them, their corners frayed from too many hands, too many nights of escape.

It was the least advanced room in the shelter, yet maybe that was why it mattered most. It's quiet lighting and unadorned walls seemed to absorb the day's tension, leaving behind something softer. Here, amidst the simple furnishings and well-worn games, they found something that resembled home, even if only for a few fleeting hours.

The group was quiet that evening. Conversations stalled, shoulders slumped into cushions, the usual banter replaced by a thoughtful silence.

Jase sank into one of the armchairs, his gaze sweeping across. A place meant for comfort now pressed down on him with the weight of unease. His mind raced with thoughts of his new dream: Olivia in the fire, her cold gaze—it clung to him like smoke.

Nolan was the first to break the silence. "Hard to believe it's been a year," he muttered, shaking his head. "Feels like we just got here… and also like we've been stuck down here forever."

Damian leaned back in his chair, thoughtful. "That's temporal dissonance," he said, glancing at the others.

Nolan frowned. "Temporal what now?"

"It's this weird phenomenon where time feels like it's passing fast and slow at the same time. Probably a side effect of living in a place where every day blends into the next," Damian explained.

Ava raised an eyebrow. "So, I'm not going crazy—it's a real thing."

"Yep." Damian nodded. "When there's no variation in routine, our perception of time gets skewed. Our brains can't decide if we're speeding through the days or dragging our feet. Makes sense, considering we've stared at the same walls for a year."

Ryder sighed, folding her hands in her lap. "Well, whatever you call it, it's definitely messing with my sense of reality. Some days, it feels like we've been down here for a lifetime."

Her words struck Jase with a strange comfort. For once, it wasn't just him wrestling with the weight of time. The cracks were showing in all of them.

Ava leaned forward, smirking. "Is that why you talk to your plants, Ryder? Temporal dissonance?"

Ryder didn't miss a beat. She turned to Damian. "Is there a term for someone who thinks they're funny but isn't?"

Damian smirked, crossing his arms. "Oh, yeah, that's an easy one. It's called being an asshole."

The group burst out laughing, Nolan's booming laugh drowning out the rest. "Doc, even I could've diagnosed that one," he chuckled.

Ava nudged Nolan with her elbow. "Glad to know there's a scientific term for it. Guess it's contagious."

"Nope, it's noncommunicable!" Damian replied, winking at Nolan.

Ava leaned back with a smirk, tapping her chin. "Alright, then. What's it called when someone insists on throwing around big words just to be a smart-ass?"

Damian shot her a mock glare. "Oh, that? That's called being the smartest person in the room. Common side effect of being brilliant."

The group groaned collectively, Ava shaking her head even as her grin widened.

"Actually, you're wrong," Olivia cut in, her tone sharp enough to quiet the room. All eyes turned to her, expecting some well-reasoned correction.

She let the silence hang a moment, then smirked. "It's also called being an asshole."

Laughter erupted again, louder this time, echoing off the walls.

Ava grinned, giving Damian a playful nudge. "Guess it is contagious after all," she teased with a wink of her own.

Jase leaned back in his chair, shaking his head. "Damn. If there's still a world left up there, we better hope these doors open soon, or we might not make it out sane."

The laughter softened, tapering off as Ryder's smile faded, her gaze dropping. "Honestly, that's what's starting to worry me." Her voice grew quieter, more reflective. "It's hard to imagine life outside now. This place is starting to feel like…home. And I'm scared that when those doors do open, we'll find something far worse than what we have here."

A heavy silence settled over the group, the weight of her words hanging in the air. They exchanged glances, each one bearing the marks of the year they'd endured underground.

Tomorrow, they would try to forget, if only for a night. They would gather, enjoy themselves, and cling to whatever piece of normalcy they could grasp.

But for now, they sat together in the quiet. Each one lost in their own mind, barricading off thoughts of the future with thick, unyielding walls—like the ones that surrounded them.

Olivia cleared her throat, cutting through the silence. Her voice was light but deliberate.

"So, about tomorrow… we should probably make a plan for the party. We'll all want to shower and get ready beforehand, so let's say we aim to start around dinnertime?"

"Sounds good to me," Ryder replied, her tone a bit brighter. "I'll take care of the food. I've got a few things in mind that should make it feel special. I could use a hand, though. Nolan?"

Nolan nodded. "Absolutely. Just tell me what to do, and I'll be there."

Ava leaned back, grinning. "Well, I'll bring the wine and vodka. Can't let this party go on without a proper drink, right?"

"Shut up!" Nolan exclaimed, his face a mix of shock and disbelief.

Damian's eyes went wide, a flicker of astonishment crossing his features. "Wait, are you telling me you made wine and vodka down here? When did you become a bootlegger?"

Ava's smile grew wider, her eyes sparkling. "Surprise! Olivia, Ryder, and I thought it would be a fun little addition to the party."

Nolan leaned forward, still shaking his head in disbelief. "Alright, Ava, I've gotta hand it to you. I'm impressed."

"Well, hold off on the applause until you've tasted it," Ava replied with a playful grin. "I still need to filter and bottle everything up. No one's tried it yet."

"I can help with that," Damian offered, but Jase quickly cut in.

"Actually, I'll give Ava a hand with that," Jase said, his gaze flickered to her and she nodded in silent agreement. "We'll make sure the bootlegging operation is handled properly." The excuse was convenient. Helping her meant avoiding pairing with Olivia, but he also had yet to check on the setup.

Olivia smiled, pretending not to notice. "Perfect. I'll handle decorations. It's not much, but I think I can make this place feel at least a little festive."

Damian shrugged, unfazed. "Alright, I'll help you with that. We'll make this place look… well, as good as it can look."

"Thanks, Damian," Olivia said, flashing him a smile. "We'll make it work. How could we not? We are the two smartest people in the room!"

"Asshole!" Ava shouted, prompting a fresh wave of laughter from the group.

The sound lingered, warm and genuine. Ryder glanced around at the faces that had grown so familiar, so vital. For the first time in weeks, gratitude swelled in her chest.

"Then let's make it a night to remember," she said softly, her smile warmer this time.

They all nodded in agreement, anticipation filling the room. For the first time in a while, it felt like they were on the brink of something close to happiness, even if only for a few hours. It wasn't much, but it was enough.

***

After the laughter faded, each of them drifted off to their rooms. Jase lingered behind, drawn toward the Ficus tree rising through the heart of the shelter.

In the dim blue light, its broad leaves gleamed like they were bathed in moonlight. Tiny ceiling lights mimicked stars overhead, and hidden speakers carried the faint chirp of crickets. It was an imitation of the world above, beautiful and hollow.

Jase reached out, letting his fingers brush a leaf, feeling its waxy surface cool against his skin.

Ryder had said this place was starting to feel like home, and as much as he hated to admit it, he felt it too. After a year underground, the familiarity of the walls, the routine, and even the tension had woven into his bones. Home had once meant freedom, but now it meant survival, and this shelter was the closest he had to that.

"Hey."

He turned, startled to see Olivia in the glow of the corridor. She stepped closer, her voice low. "You okay? I saw you slip out here. Thought I'd check in."

"Yeah, I'm fine." He turned back to the tree, avoiding her gaze. "Just needed a moment, I guess."

Her eyes followed his to the tree. "She's got a point, doesn't she? This place is starting to feel different." Her voice faltered. "More home than prison."

"Yeah, I guess so." His tone distant, as he shifted his weight.

He felt her presence beside him, warm and familiar, but his mind kept circling back to the way she'd brushed him off. He knew he should say something, but the words lodged in his throat.

Olivia watched him, the tension between them thickening. "Jase… is something wrong?" Her voice was cautious, and he could hear the concern threaded through it.

"You've been… distant. Did I do something?"

He took a deep breath, considering his answer. He wanted to tell her what was really on his mind, but he couldn't bring himself to do it, not here, not now.

"No, nothing. Just… a lot on my mind lately. This whole year, you know?" he said quietly.

She nodded slowly, but her eyes didn't leave him. "If it's about the party, I already told you—"

"It's not about the party. I just… I need some space. It's nothing you did." He said softly, but in a slightly cold tone.

The lie tasted bitter, but he forced a smile, hoping it would be enough to reassure her, even for just a moment.

She searched his face, her expression a mixture of confusion and something else, something vulnerable.

"I get it, Jase. I just—" She hesitated, her fingers curling around the edge of her sleeve. "I thought… I thought we were good, you know? That we could talk about stuff."

"We are good," he said, his tone warmer than before. But he still couldn't meet her eyes.

For a moment, it looked like she might say something more, but instead, she just nodded and stepped back.

"Alright. Well, I'll see you at the party tomorrow. Goodnight."

Jase watched her walk away, the soft glow of the corridor lights catching in her hair. She cast one last glance over her shoulder, a flicker of disappointment in her eyes, before turning the corner and disappearing into the shadows.

He stood there, alone, with only the faint chirp of crickets to fill the silence she left behind.

The leaves stirred in the artificial breeze, a soft rustle in a room that was otherwise perfectly still. The warmth in the air, the shimmer of stars above, the illusion of an open sky.

It was all manufactured.

And the thought chilled him: maybe his trust in Olivia was nothing but another illusion.

He took a deep breath, feeling the weight of the unknown settle heavy in his chest. There was more to this place, more to this so-called sanctuary, than met the eye. Just as there was more to Olivia's actions than he wanted to admit.

He could sense it.

He felt it lurking beneath the surface, waiting to reveal itself in time.

Until then, all he could do was stand there and question everything. From the walls that surrounded him to the people that he thought he knew.

CHAPTER SIX

The next morning, everyone woke early, a quiet current of energy humming through the corridors of The Ouroboros. It wasn't quite joy, but anticipation, like children on Christmas morning, eager and anxious all at once.

Today marked one year since they stepped into the facility, sealing the doors on the world above. A year underground. A year that had changed everything.

They started in the gym, burning through the nervous energy that clung to them.

Ava and Olivia claimed the treadmills, their strides falling into rhythm, each footfall pounding against the belts in perfect synch. Their pace quickened as if they could outrun their thoughts. Ava's gaze stayed locked ahead, sharp and unwavering, while Olivia glanced sideways now and then, daring her to push harder, faster.

Jase and Damian took the bikes, leaning forward with the same quiet determination. Digital trails flickered across their screens: mountains, deserts, winding roads—landscapes they would never touch again except in simulation. Their breath came heavier with each turn of the pedals, the cadence steady, relentless.

Jase shot Damian a glance, and without a word, they both pushed harder, legs churning as if the right pace might finally carry them out of this place.

Across the hall, the spa offered a stark contrast to the pounding energy of the gym, a sanctuary of quiet water and low light. Nolan and Ryder moved through the compact pool with steady strokes, their reflections rippling across the dark-silver tiles, as the water shimmered under the ambient glow of lights.

Nolan, with his ankle still tender though much stronger, found comfort in the buoyancy—glided smoothly through the water. Ryder swam beside him, her form precise and powerful, testing her breath against the current as if competing with the pool itself. A programmable current allowed for laps or gentle relaxation, the water responding to each swimmer's preferences.

Beyond the water, the spa's recovery stations waited. A recessed cold tub gleamed in one corner, its surface broken now and then by drifting curls of vapor. Across from it, a glass-walled steam room glowed softly, benches of contoured wood just visible through the haze.

Next to it, an automated tanning bed promised a rare boost of vitamin D, its sleek panel glowing faintly in standby. Two massage chairs sat nearby, their controls ready to knead, roll, and pulse away the strain of endless days underground.

Every feature in the spa was designed to not only maintain their physical health, but offer a rare moment of solace underground.

One by one, they drifted from the gym and spa, toweling off the sweat of their workouts before finding their way to the kitchen.

By the time they sat down, the table was crowded with plates of powdered eggs, fresh fruit from the greenhouse, and steaming mugs of coffee and tea.

Their faces were flushed from exertion, but beneath it lingered the lines of a year spent underground: etched in the shadows under their eyes, the stiffness in their movements.

They ate quietly, the clink of silverware against plates and the soft hiss of a sip from a warm cup the only sounds breaking the silence. Every so often someone cleared their throat, or shifted in their chair, but no one spoke. The silence wasn't awkward. It was familiar, heavy, an unspoken acknowledgement of what the day meant.

Jase let his gaze travel around the table. Ryder sat across from him, eyes down on her plate, but her grip on her fork gave her away, knuckles pale against the handle.

Damian, to his right, wore the same distant expression he always did when cataloguing something in his mind, running through numbers only he could see.

Olivia sat beside him, shoulders relaxed, but her eyes flicked from face to face, as though she could read the weight of everyone's thoughts.

Ava and Nolan exchanged the occasional glance, a wordless conversation in smirks and raised brows born of shared endurance.

They didn't need words this morning. The silence carried everything—anticipation, reflection, the fragile pride of having made it this far. Today they would celebrate because they had to. In a world that had abandoned them, this was how they claimed a piece of themselves back.

Tomorrow, the routine would return. But for now, they let themselves sit in this rare moment. Six people sharing breakfast, together, marking a year of survival. A year that had shaped them into something new, something they were still learning to understand.

As Jase looked down at his watch, the weight of the moment pressed heavier. He set his fork aside, drew a breath, and said quietly but firmly, "Alright. It's time."

They made their way out of the kitchen, leaving their empty plates behind. Jase guided them to the upper level and down the wing to the airlock door. The six of them stopped in a half-circle before the door, eyes drawn upward.

The clock glowed in cold blue digits above the door. Each number ticked upward, steady as a heartbeat, the glow painting their faces in faint light. 364 days, 23 hours, 59 minutes. The seconds climbed, one by one, toward 365.

Jase felt a shiver crawl down his spine.

To his right, Ryder's arms were folded tight against her chest, her posture small, guarded. Damian stood tall beside her, arms rigid at his sides, jaw flexing with restraint. Olivia's lips pressed together, a line of resolve hiding whatever storm of thoughts swirled behind her eyes.

On the other end, Ava and Nolan stood shoulder to shoulder, their faces pale in the glow, silent but unflinching.

The seconds ticked closer.

And suddenly, Jase was back there—one year ago: the rush of fear and excitement as they stepped through these doors, leaving everything they knew behind. He remembered the ripple of thrill that had passed through the group, the sense of privilege, of promise. They were strangers, chosen for reasons none of them fully understood. But together, staring into the polished heart of The Ouroboros, the future stretched wide and bright before them.

Jase led the way, his steps steady, his gaze sweeping the gleaming cement walls. This was what he'd always wanted—to be part of something larger than himself, something profound. Even as the echo of Eli's disapproval lingered, he couldn't suppress the smile tugging at his mouth. This was where he belonged.

Olivia entered right behind, her eyes wide with fascination, taking note of the intricate systems, the seamless design. This was her dream: technology beyond anything she'd ever imagined, a chance to learn in ways she never thought possible. She felt a thrill unlike anything before, helping shape a future with tomorrow's technology.

Ava hurried in, her eyes immediately drawn to the overhead piping, dissecting the veins and organs of the facility. Her mind raced with thoughts of the intricacies of each life-support system. She couldn't wipe the smile from her face, this was her playground.

Damian's expression was pure awe, the sterility of the place radiating possibility. To him, it was a sanctuary of science, stripped of distraction, where medicine could flourish. Here, every discovery mattered, and he was part of something groundbreaking.

Ryder stepped in and felt her breath catch. The sterile concrete should have repelled her, but instead she felt a spark of excitement. She'd grown up nurturing life from the soil, and now she would be doing the same in a place that seemed to defy nature itself. She imagined vines curling up sterile walls, the balance of green against gray. For her, it wasn't confinement, it was potential.

Nolan brought up the rear, his presence filling the doorway. Pride straightened his spine, the air of discipline clinging to him like a uniform. He'd been trained to protect, to bring order, and in this new world, he felt a deep sense of purpose. Here, he was part of a mission: a chance to prove himself in uncharted territory.

They gathered in the main hall, eyes filled with a shared awe. They exchanged glances, their excitement nearly tangible as they took in the facility that would become their home.

In that moment, the future felt bright, limitless. They were pioneers, chosen for a study that would push boundaries, shape lives, and test every strength they possessed. And for now, all they saw was possibility.

They hadn't yet learned how quickly awe could turn to unease.

The clock struck 365 days.

No alarm. No fanfare.

Just the quiet truth that they'd made it.

They stood in silence, the weight of it pressing down, each of them carrying it differently. A year underground. A year survived.

After a moment, Damian spoke softly, almost as if to himself. "I don't know why a tiny part of me expected the doors to open." The words felt like a confession.

No one answered.

His thought was theirs too.

That flicker of hope—that the world might still be within grasp—never fully disappeared.

Finally, Ryder broke the spell. She let out a long breath, gave Jase a small nod, and turned for the greenhouse.

Nolan's hand landed on Jase's shoulder, a firm squeeze that said more than words. Then he, too, made his way downstairs.

Ava lingered for only a moment, pride in her eyes edged with something softer, almost sad. She nodded once and left, Damian following close behind, a faint smile tugging at his lips.

That left Olivia. She met Jase's gaze, searching his face for something—understanding, reassurance, maybe both. But after a beat she only nodded and turned away, her footsteps fading down the corridor.

Jase stayed. He stared at the clock, its numbers now ticking up well past the mark. He took a long, slow breath and closed his eyes, letting the silence envelop him. He, too, had harbored a faint hope of that moment being their release.

Jase opened his eyes, and exhaled a deep breath, along with the last bit of his hope.

Then, with a final glance at the airlock door, he turned and walked away.

***

Olivia and Damian stood in the center of the living room, surrounded by an odd assortment of makeshift decorations. Olivia held up a partially inflated medical glove, inspecting it before handing it to Damian.

"Here, tie this one up," she said, moving on to the next glove. "They're not exactly balloons, but they'll do."

Damian chuckled as he knotted the glove, letting it bounce lightly. "Who knew medical supplies would make decent party decor?"

Olivia grinned, nodding at the unrolled elastic bandages hanging over Damian's shoulder. "Well, we work with what we've got. Hang those up like streamers, might add a festive touch."

Damian unfurled the bandages, draping them around the room in loops.

Meanwhile, Olivia carefully placed small bouquets around the room, flowers she'd picked from around the Ficus tree. She adjusted each one thoughtfully, the bright colors adding a touch of warmth to the stark space. She then hung up a few paper signs she'd cut from old printouts, each one bearing simple words like "One Year" and "Together" in blocky letters.

"There," she said, stepping back to admire their work. "Not too shabby for a bunch of medical supplies."

"Not too bad at all," Damian agreed.

In the kitchen, Ryder and Nolan were elbows-deep in flour and potato slices. Ryder slid another batch of thinly sliced potatoes into the hot oil, watching them curl and sizzle.

"These might not be your favorite name brand chips, but they're close enough," she said, stirring them around with a spatula.

Nolan was rolling out pizza dough beside her, his forearms dusted with flour. "I bet they'll be the best chips I've ever had. Wait till they taste this. We'll blow their minds."

Ryder gave him a warm smile, sprinkling a little salt over the finished batch of chips. "I hope so. We might not have the best ingredients, but it's as best as we can do. And, it's not really a party without chips and pizza, right?"

"Exactly," Nolan said, spreading tomato paste over the dough. "Ye of little faith. After this, they'll be begging us to open Ryder and Nolan's Apoc-aly-pizza!"

Ryder snorted, reaching over to wipe flour from his cheek with the back of her hand. She shook her head, smiling despite herself. "You're ridiculous."

Up in the workshop, Ava and Jase were carefully filtering the wine and vodka into clean bottles. The room buzzed with a different kind of energy than the rest of the facility—less sleek, more raw.

The room was her dedicated workspace, filled with tools that hung from mounted pegboards along a wall. Below them, machines stood side by side—a table saw, drill press, band saw, and more. Shelving racks lined a wall, stocked with spare parts, pipes, circuit boards, air filters, and every other component she'd need to repair the facility's complex systems.

It was more industrial than futuristic, humming and clanking in a way that felt almost reassuring. If the OCC was the brain, this was the beating heart.

Toward the back of the workshop lay the vital life-support systems that kept The Ouroboros operational. Towering over the room, the air recycler and blower hummed in steady rhythm, its vents filtering and circulating fresh oxygen throughout the shelter.

Next to it, the water filtration system sat in an organized, flowing design, processing and purifying every drop they used before cycling it back throughout the facility.

The power generator, a sleek black monolith encased in tempered glass, pulsed with a quiet, reassuring hum, its control panel showing digital readouts and status indicators in cool green and blue tones.

A large stainless-steel workbench dominated the center of the room, its surface cluttered with half-finished repairs, blueprints, and scattered schematics.

Amid the organized chaos, Jase and Ava worked side by side, the bottles balanced between tool trays and diagrams. Jase watched as she poured the last of the homemade wine through a filter, the liquid trickling steadily until the second bottle filled.

"So, you're sure this is safe to drink?" He asked, glancing at the bottles with skepticism.

Ava smirked, holding up the vodka bottle proudly. "Absolutely. I used clean equipment, and followed every step exactly as Ouro said. It might not be top-shelf, but it'll do the job."

Jase took a bottle, swirling the liquid thoughtfully. "Alright, if you say so. I trust you… mostly."

Ava rolled her eyes, capping the bottle. "Come on, live a little. We've managed to survive this long—a little homemade booze won't be our undoing. Besides, we tested samples in the lab, and everything came back fine."

"What about the taste? The vodka smells like it should be used to strip paint" Jase said with a wince.

"We're all going to find that out together! We should definitely bring some strong mixers, though." She smiled and handed him a bottle. "But, yeah, it could probably start a car!"

Around the shelter, other preparations were falling into place—flowers and streamers in the living room, the smell of fried potatoes drifting from the kitchen.

With the drinks ready, Ava brushed her hands off and said, "Alright, let's clean up. Party's waiting."

***

The guys arrived first, walking in and admiring the festive look of the living room. They had all cleaned up for the occasion, their usual rugged appearances softened with freshly shaven faces and neatly combed hair.

Jase had swapped his typical Ouroboros-issued work clothes for a white t-shirt with a maroon, long sleeve over-shirt, and white acid wash jeans. It was a subtle, but significant change, one that set the evening apart from their daily grind.

Damian wore a light blue button-down shirt, its sleeves rolled up to reveal his forearms, and dress pants. His typical casual professional look, a reflection of how he always carried himself. Nolan, too, had shed his usual threads, now standing in a dark quarter-zip and grey pants, a contrast to the uniform clothes he typically wore outside of the facility.

Their regular attire, supplied by the facility, was all the same—utilitarian, unchanging, just like the routines they followed every day.

But tonight was different. They wore the few personal items they were allowed to bring with them, creating a clear distinction between the daily monotony of their underground lives and the small slice of individuality they clung to.

As they took in the decorations, Nolan smirked. "This is what the two smartest people came up with?" he said, gesturing at the inflated medical gloves and bandages strung like streamers.

Damian didn't miss a beat. "Sorry, I must've forgotten which wing the party store was in."

Jase smiled. "No, it looks great. Seriously." His eyes lingered on the carefully arranged bouquets, each splash of color brightening the room. He knew this was Olivia's touch, her ability to brighten even the darkest spaces.

"Yeah, yeah, it's fine," Nolan said with a grin. "But I still think a blood bag for a piñata would've taken it to the next level."

The banter was cut short when the women entered, and the room shifted instantly, all eyes turning toward them.

Ryder led the way, her hair loose and softly curled, a rare sight as she almost always kept it tied back. She wore green corduroy overall shorts over a simple white crop top. It echoed her usual work style, but the green drew out the brightness in her hazel eyes, softening her presence.

Nolan's gaze lingered longer than he meant to, his stoic mask faltering with a flicker of quiet admiration.

Olivia followed, her straight blonde hair left loose for once, soft strands brushing her chin and framing her sharp features. A silk top hugged her frame, paired with dark jeans—casual, yet with an ease that made her beauty feel effortless.

Jase's breath caught in his throat as she entered, a sudden warmth blooming in his chest. For a moment, his suspicions dissolved, replaced by the simple way she seemed to light up the room.

Ava rounded out the trio, her dark hair falling freely over her shoulders, a change that softened her usual fiery edge. She wore a dark tank top that bared her toned arms and a pair of well-worn jeans. Confidence radiated from her smile, sharp and sure, as her gaze swept across the room, noticing the awe from the gentlemen.

They offered subtle nods of appreciation—for the effort the women had made, and for their undeniable beauty. More than that, everyone felt different tonight, as if for a moment they had stepped back into the world they'd left behind, closer to the people they once were.

Jase found himself watching Olivia for a second longer than he intended, noticing the soft way her hair framed her face, the quiet confidence in her smile.

Next to him, Nolan's eyes followed Ryder, his typically hardened exterior giving way to a flicker of warmth. Ava smiled knowingly at the small shift in the room's energy.

"I think it looks amazing in here," Ryder said, her eyes sweeping over the room with a smile. She gave Damian and Olivia an approving nod.

Nolan was quick to follow with a smirk. "Not too bad for a bunch of medical supplies and flowers."

Olivia rolled her eyes, grinning. "Oh, we heard you from the hall, mister. We were going to wait to tell you, but... you're the piñata. And Damian gets the first swing."

Laughter rippled through the group, the sound already lightening the room. It only took a few seconds, but the weight of the last year had already begun to lift.

"Well, I don't know what we're waiting for. I say we get things going with a shot!" Ava declared, throwing her arms up dramatically.

"We've been waiting on you to pour them," Nolan teased.

Ava made her way to the table where six glasses sat ready. She popped open the bottle of homemade vodka, the sharp scent hitting the air almost instantly. With careful precision, she filled each glass.

Olivia hurried to help, passing the drinks out with a grin that matched the buzz of anticipation.

The group instinctively lifted their glasses, giving them each a cautious sniff. A chorus of grimaces followed—wrinkled noses, winces, even a small cough.

"Jesus," Nolan muttered, half-laughing, half-choking. "Is this vodka or gasoline?"

"Vodka," Ava shot back with a smirk. "But yes, it's definitely flammable. Suck it up for the first one, then use the mixers if you want to keep your taste buds intact." She gestured to the bottles of juice waiting on the table.

"Supposedly the lab results said it won't kill us." Jase said, raising an eyebrow as he inspected his glass.

With everyone finally holding a glass, Olivia looked to Jase and said, "Would you do the toast?"

Jase glanced around at the group, unsure for a moment, but when he saw each one of them nodding in silent approval, he gave a slight smile. He hadn't prepared anything, and now, with everyone looking to him for the right words, they seemed to escape him. He hesitated, lifting his glass slowly, letting the moment settle.

He glanced at Ryder first. Always so connected to the earth, even down here where the soil and light were artificial. She had nurtured more than just plants this past year. Ryder had been a source of quiet strength for everyone, her kindness and warmth bringing a sense of life to their sterile world.

Next, his eyes moved to Nolan. His ever-steady presence, a man built for leadership, his disciplined mind always on alert, ready to protect them no matter the cost. Nolan's sense of duty was unshakable, even in the face of isolation and uncertainty. Jase had no doubt he would take a bullet for any one of them without hesitation.

Then to Damian, barely the oldest but with wisdom far beyond his years. He carried the weight of their health on his shoulders, constantly tracking vitals, worrying about things the rest of them barely understood. In a year's time, Damian had become their doctor in every way that mattered, saving them more than just physically.

Jase's gaze then turned to Ava, their engineer, whose hands had kept The Ouroboros running day after day. She never backed down from a challenge, never complained about the impossible tasks thrown her way. Her resourcefulness had become their lifeline, her fierce determination driving them forward when things seemed to be falling apart.

And finally, Olivia, sharp and calculated yet warm in the quiet moments when she thought no one was looking. She kept the computer systems running, but more than that, she was always looking out for them. She had been there for him more times than he could count, pushing him forward when his guilt threatened to swallow him whole.

Jase's heart swelled with a deep, unspoken gratitude for each of them. They were no longer the strangers they had been a year ago. They were family now, bound not by blood but by the fire of survival.

He cleared his throat. "This isn't just a party," he began, his voice low but steady. "It's not just noise to drown out the silence. It's proof. Proof that we're still here. That we're still fighting. That we haven't given up."

He let the words hang, his gaze moving from one face to the next.

"I could say a lot about the last year. About what we've been through. What we've lost. What we'll never get back."

His voice dipped for a moment before he drew in a steadying breath. "But, I think the most important thing is…what we've

found. We found each other. And no matter what happens next…
I know we can face it together."

With a simple nod, Jase raised his glass. "To us. The Fallout
Kids"

"Cheers," they echoed, voices soft but full, as their glasses
clinked together.

The vodka burned hot down their throats, and every one of
them winced, but they smiled through it, the fire warming more
than just their chests.

CHAPTER SEVEN

Ryder and Nolan walked in from the kitchen, carefully balancing trays of homemade pizzas and bowls of crispy potato chips. The smell of warm dough and seasoned potatoes filled the air, pulling every pair of eyes toward them.

"Oh my god, pizza? Are you kidding me?" Ava exclaimed, practically bouncing toward the table, her excitement contagious.

"Not only pizza, but some incredible potato chips too!" Nolan added, popping one into his mouth. The satisfying crunch drew a round of attention.

Ryder's smile widened at their reaction. For her, these small moments of joy made all the effort worthwhile. "I wanted to make something special for tonight," she said warmly. "Besides, what's a party without pizza?"

"Ryder, you have absolutely outdone yourself!" Jase said, already reaching for a slice.

Her smile deepened, though she tilted her head modestly. "Well, let's see what you say after you take a bite. I'm not sure how great the freeze-dried mozzarella turned out, but the sauce is fresh from tomatoes I grew. It's the best I could do down here." She sighed with a small shrug.

Jase took a bite, savoring the blend of flavors. Beside him, Ava was already halfway through her slice. They caught each other's eyes mid-chew and nodded in mutual approval.

"No, it's amazing," Ava moaned, eyes closing as if the taste itself was too much to bear. "Absolutely amazing."

"Yeah, it's delicious, Ryder," Jase agreed, genuine gratitude in his tone. He hadn't tasted anything like it in what felt like forever.

Olivia, lounging nearby, popped another chip into her mouth. "Wait until you try these," she teased. "I might finish the whole bowl before anyone else even gets a chance."

Damian reached toward the bowl just as Olivia went for another handful, then pulled his hand back. "Whoa—I'm afraid I'm going to lose a finger."

Ryder laughed, glancing at him. "Don't worry, there's another bowl in the kitchen. I made plenty."

Laughter rippled through the group as they slipped fully into party mode. Music thumped softly in the background, voices mingled, games sparked bursts of competition, and feet tapped along to the beat of their favorite songs.

For the first time in what felt like forever, they touched true joy. Their burdens loosened, if only for a while, as they basked in the rare lightheartedness of simply enjoying one another's company.

***

As the night wore on, the group splintered into smaller pairs.

By the music, Ryder and Nolan danced close, her hand brushing his as she spun with a playful smile. Nolan laughed, his usually serious demeanor softening as he let himself relax for once. His eyes lingered on her every move.

Ryder swayed to the beat, laughter spilling freely as she twirled, her face glowing with contagious joy.

Nolan matched her rhythm, his hand finding hers again. When their eyes locked, a spark passed between them in the dim glow of the room.

Across the way, Damian and Ava had taken over the card table, their game collapsing into a tipsy argument. Ava jabbed a finger at him, her cheeks flushed with mock outrage.

"There's no damn way," she accused, narrowing her eyes. "You're definitely cheating."

Damian raised an eyebrow, a mischievous grin tugging at his lips. "Oh, please. You're just terrible. Face it, Ava—you can't beat me!"

"Bullshit!" she shot back, shoving him playfully. "Let's go again. This time, NO CHEATING." She picked the deck up and started shuffling.

Meanwhile, Olivia drifted to the couch where Jase sat, watching the room with a quiet smile. She eased down beside him, her warmth filling the space between them.

For a moment, they simply sat, comfortable in silence.

"You seem… quieter than usual tonight," she said gently, glancing at him from the corner of her eye.

Jase looked down, swirling his drink. "Just taking it all in. Feels surreal, doesn't it? Laughing like this again."

She nodded, her gaze roaming the room before settling back on him. "Yeah. But maybe that's why it feels important. Nights like this remind us what we have here—something worth holding onto."

Their eyes met, the weight of everything unsaid hanging between them. The music, the laughter, the fragile moments of connection. Pieces of a life Jase hadn't believed possible anymore.

Ryder's laughter broke across the room again as Nolan's hand slipped to her waist, guiding her through a spin.

"That's going to be a problem," Jase murmured, his gaze fixed on the pair, their chemistry impossible to miss.

Olivia followed his eyes, her expression softening. "I don't know," she said with a small smile. "I think it's cute. They fit, in their own way."

She looked back at him, then away, a hint of something unspoken flickering beneath her words.

Jase raised an eyebrow. "Really? That might be the biggest surprise of the week. They're complete opposites, I never saw it coming."

"Oh my god, wait!" Olivia suddenly exclaimed, springing up from the couch. "I almost forgot! I have one last surprise for you all!"

Jase stiffened. A knot of unease twisted in his stomach. His subconscious was right, she was hiding more.

Ryder and Nolan paused mid-dance, curiosity pulling them toward Olivia. Damian and Ava set their cards aside, while Jase leaned forward, pulse quickening.

Olivia crossed to the bookshelf, reached behind a board game, and drew out a thin folder she'd stashed earlier. Turning back, she held it against her chest, her voice calm but threaded with excitement.

"I know how hard this year has been for us. I wasn't sure I could pull this off, so I didn't want to get anyone's hopes up too soon."

Jase's chest tightened.

"A few weeks ago," she went on, "I found a hidden, locked folder on one of the servers while running diagnostics. When I dug deeper, I realized it held something connected to the study—our dossiers. Complete workups on who we are. At first I didn't think I could crack it, but after a few days… and with some help from Ouro… I managed."

Jase shot up from the couch, tension cutting through his voice. "Why would you do that?"

The others exchanged uneasy glances.

Olivia met his stare without flinching. "We all made sacrifices to be here, Jase. We weren't allowed to bring anything with us. But I thought it might matter—to hold onto a piece of what we left behind, even if it's just a memory."

Her hands trembled slightly as she opened the folder and began passing out its contents.

Nolan's brows lifted in awe. Ryder's lips parted as she stared down at her page. Ava gasped, eyes welling with sudden tears. Damian took his in silence, his hand shaking.

At last she stopped in front of Jase. He stood frozen, anticipation pounding in his ears. Olivia drew out the final page and handed it to him, her gaze lingering before letting go.

Jase looked down. His breath caught.

It was a photo of him and Eli from their last camping trip. Sunlight filtered through the trees behind them, their smiles unguarded and easy. Eli's face, carefree and alive, was so far from the haunted expression that stalked Jase's nightmares. It was a sight Jase had nearly forgotten..

His eyes blurred. Tears slid down his cheeks before he could stop them.

"I thought maybe... if you could see him whenever you wanted, it might help," Olivia said softly, watching his face. "Maybe even ease the nightmares."

Jase's grip tightened on the photo as though it might vanish. A different weight pressed on his chest—not dread this time, but remorse. He'd been wrong.

She hadn't been hiding a betrayal. She'd been hiding a gift.

A reminder.

She had given them something precious, something beyond repayment. And he'd let suspicion cloud his trust.

He lifted his gaze to hers, raw and vulnerable. "I can't believe you did this for me...for all of us." His voice thickened with gratitude.

Her smile was gentle, her eyes soft with understanding. "We're in this together, Jase. Some days... we'll need these reminders of what we're still fighting for."

Before she could say more, Ryder swept her into a fierce hug, whispering a broken "Thank you."

Ava rushed in next, laughter spilling through her tears as she wrapped them both. Nolan and Damian exchanged a glance, then joined the tangle of arms.

In that messy embrace, laughter mingled with quiet sobs.

"I don't even know what to say," Damian admitted, blinking fast. "I could never express how much this means."

"Yeah," Nolan added, smiling through the sting in his eyes. "You gave us back a piece of home we thought was gone forever."

Even as they pulled apart, no one let go completely.

Jase wiped his face, drawing a steady breath. He looked at Olivia, voice low but certain. "You reminded us what's still out there. Why we keep going."

Olivia's eyes glistened. "That's all I wanted. To remind us that no matter what we face, we're not alone. Not now, not ever."

They stood in a quiet circle, each clutching their fragment of the past. In that moment, the walls of the Ouroboros felt thinner, their burdens lighter, and the world above just a little closer.

Then the alarm hit.

Shrill, shattering—like glass in their ears, like the walls themselves breaking apart.

Everyone froze. Breath caught. The living room's lights strobed red, every pulse painting their tear-streaked faces in panic. The fragile spell of joy they'd shared only moments ago cracked apart in an instant.

They had lived this before—the alarms, the lockdown, the feeling of the floor dropping out beneath them.

"Ouro, what's going on?" Jase barked, his eyes darting across the group. Fear flickered in every face.

The calm, mechanical voice cut through the alarm with chilling detachment:

"Attention. All personnel report to the Operations Command Center immediately. Emergency protocols activated. This is not a drill."

The words struck like a hammer. Anxiety rippled through them as tears of relief turned swiftly into dread. Ryder clung to Nolan's arm, her knuckles white, while he gave her a grim nod of reassurance he didn't feel.

The one night they'd had, the one taste of normalcy, was ripped away.

"Let's go," Jase commanded, his tone clipped, already pushing them back into motion. Olivia met his eyes, nodded, and fell in step behind him.

Their hurried footsteps thundered down the corridor, alarms pulsing overhead. Each crimson flash chased them through the hall, throwing their shadows against the walls like hunted prey.

By the time they reached the OCC, the monitors were alive with rapid streams of unreadable data. Then the main screen shifted, an enormous alert pulsing at its center:

'RADIATION LEAK DETECTED'

The words seemed to suck the air out of the room.

"A radiation leak?" Damian's voice cracked, disbelief warring with panic. "Impossible. I've swept the facility for weeks, never found a trace."

Jase clenched his fists. "Ouro, where is the leak coming from?"

The AI's voice was steady, cold. "Scanning all systems. Radiation detected in the air circulation system."

The room went silent, then panic erupted in their eyes.

"Our air supply—" Ryder stammered, a hand flying to her mouth.

Nolan's face went pale. "We're breathing it in right now?" His voice pitched higher, like he was pleading for a denial.

Ava froze, chest rising and falling in sharp breaths, before she forced herself into motion.

"Okay, listen. Listen! We need to shut down the air system now. Lock off the greenhouse and kitchen before the food is contaminated. Then isolate the source. If we find it fast enough, maybe we can contain it and repair the breach before the damage is done."

Olivia's voice wavered. "Shut off the air? How much time does that even give us?"

Damian answered before Ava could, his face drained, brows tight with mental calculations. "Not long. An hour, maybe two, before we start feeling it. Less if the leak's severe."

Jase's jaw tightened, but his voice stayed steady. "We don't have a choice. The whole facility could be contaminated if we don't."

Ava snapped into action, fingers flying across the console. "Ouro, Beta-One command: isolate all essential sections. Shut down all ventilation systems. Lockdown every area flagged for possible exposure."

"Executing command," Ouro confirmed, as the faint hum of circulation died. The silence it left behind felt suffocating, as though the very air was slipping away.

Ava's hands trembled over the controls, scanning frantically. "We need to pinpoint the breach. Fast."

Jase stepped in, voice steady despite the storm raging inside him. "Tell us what you need."

"I'll need two here monitoring the readings and calling it out," Ava said, eyes locked on the glowing screens. "The rest of you—search the primary and secondary air ducts. Look for cracks, ruptures, anything abnormal. I'll check the recycler in the workshop."

"I'll stay here with Damian," Olivia said quickly, already moving to the panel. "We'll guide you to the highest readings."

Jase nodded sharply. "Nolan, with me on the lower level. Ryder, take the upper. Ava—get to the recycler. Let's move."

Damian threw them a hard look. "Stay sharp. Radiation levels are low, but don't take chances. If you see anything, report it and get out. Do not linger."

Olivia focused on the screen, working to scan every section of the air system. Her fingers flew over the controls, her brow furrowed in concentration. "Jase, start near the gym. That's where the readings are spiking."

The group grabbed earpieces off the far shelf, fear etched into every movement. Ava sprinted down the railing toward her workshop. Ryder swept along the upper level, eyes scanning. Jase and Nolan vaulted the stairs, taking two at a time. Nolan hit the bottom first, bolting toward the bedroom wings, ignoring the ache in his ankle, fear lending him strength.

Every second mattered now. Every breath could be poison.

Jase slowed as he neared the gym. "Alright, I'm at the start of the wing," he said, voice low but steady. "Everything looks clear at this end. What are the readouts saying?"

His eyes swept the vents overhead, tracing the ducts as he advanced.

Olivia bounced between monitors back in the OCC, then her voice crackled in his ear. "Readings point to inside the gym itself. I can override the door, let you get a peek inside."

"Do it."

Olivia and Damian traded a tense look before her fingers flew over the keyboard. Then the gym door slid open with a mechanical whine.

Damian cut in, firm and clinical. "Jase, without a protective suit, hold your breath as long as you can. Use your shirt to cover your nose and mouth. Anything to minimize exposure to airborne particles."

Olivia's stomach dropped at his words. The implication was clear: every breath in there could kill him.

Damian continued. "I can treat you with iodine pills for minor exposure, but if the levels spike, get out immediately. No hesitation."

With an unsure shake of his head, Jase tugged his shirt over his nose and mouth, drew a sharp inhale, and slipped inside. His gaze flicked across the gym, searching.

In the far corner, a faint light pulsed erratically.

"Light flickering, back corner," he muttered through fabric, voice muffled.

Ava's voice came strained over the comms as she pried at the recycler's panel. "Do you see any cracks? Anything that could cause the leak?"

"Not yet. Getting closer."

"Careful, Jase. Not too close." Damian warned.

Jase crept forward, lungs burning, his diaphragm twitching with the urge to breathe. He bolted back to the doorway, shoved his head into the hall, and dragged in sharp gulps of air. His chest heaved, each breath rasping, before he forced one last inhale and plunged back inside.

The flickering light pulsed faster now, throwing warped shadows across the corner. He inched closer, scanning desperately for damage, the fabric of his shirt damp against his mouth.

Then—darkness. The lights snapped off.

A split-second later, a deafening buzzer shrieked.

Jase whipped around to see the airlock door snap shut, the loud thud rattling off the gym's walls.

Jase leapt to the door in an instance, his free hand grabbing at the seal and pulling with as much force as he could muster.

The door didn't move an inch.

His chest tightened. Air tasted heavier, fouler. Every breath was more precious than the last, his mind racing as fear swelled, threatening to choke him before the radiation ever could.

"Jase, what's happening? The levels have skyrocketed, you have to get out of there. Now!" Olivia shouted into his ear.

"The fucking door slammed shut and I can't open it!" His voice was ragged, panic scraping the edges. "You've got to override it—I'm trapped!" Jase yanked at the seal, fingers white with the effort.

Damian and Olivia exchanged a frantic look. Her hands flew over the keys. "The monitor shows the door is open," she said, voice tight with disbelief. She slammed commands again. "It's not responding. I can't override it, the system thinks it's open!"

"It's definitely not open," Jase snapped, hauling at the door until his arms ached. "It won't move an inch."

Nolan, searching the women's wing, heard the comms and broke into a sprint. "Ryder—grab a pry bar from Ava in the workshop and meet me at the gym door!" he barked. "Ava—get your acetylene torch and wheel it down. We'll try to pry him out first. If that fails, we cut him out."

"On my way!" Ryder's voice echoed as she bolted along the upper level toward the workshop.

Damian went pale at Nolan's plan. "Nolan, if you cut through that door you'll vent the gym. The leak will spread." His voice trembled with the weight of what that meant. "The whole facility could be contaminated."

"Then we pray the pry bar works," Nolan shot back, voice tight but decisive, and kept running.

Olivia paused at the console, a sudden idea forming. "Wait, we can seal the entire wing at the corridor bulkhead," she said, eyes darting over the layout. "We'll sacrifice the gym and spa, but it would stop contamination from spreading."

"No death chamber," Nolan said without hesitation. "We'll do that, then."

Damian's gaze flicked to the readings again. He swallowed hard. "Nolan, whatever you do—do it fast. Radiation is spiking in there."

Nolan reached the door and planted his feet, hands gripping the edge. He and Jase hauled in a raw, synchronized pull.

Metal groaned around the frame, muscles straining, breath ragged on both sides. But the door didn't give. Not an inch.

Ryder's footsteps thundered down the hall before she skidded around the corner, a heavy pry-bar clutched in her hands.

"Here, take it!" she shouted, shoving the metal bar into Nolan's grip.

He jammed the flat tip into the door's seal and heaved back with everything he had. The metal groaned, yielding only a whisper of space—far too little.

He pressed the bar in deeper, searching for more leverage. His forearms began to shake, a primal yell escaping as he pried at the stubborn door. But still, the door refused to move.

Nolan's arms gave out. The bar slipped, the door sealing tight again with a cruel clang. He stumbled back, chest heaving, then growled through clenched teeth.

"Damn it! Ava, where's that torch?" He jammed the bar back in, fighting for the fraction of leverage he'd gained before.

"I'm here!" Ava's voice rang out as she rounded the corner, wheeling the heavy tanks down the hallway. "Hang on, Jase. We'll get you out!"

She stopped next to the door and set the tanks upright. Twisting the knobs on the oxygen and acetylene, her hands moved swiftly to adjust them to the right levels. A sharp scrape of metal on metal sounded as she struck the striker near the torch's tip. A fierce, bright flame burst to life, hissing as it shot out the end of the torch.

"Jase—clear the door!" she called.

Jase backed away, tugging his shirt tight across his mouth. "Clear!"

Ava stepped forward, torch angled for the steel. The flame hissed closer. Then, with a sharp hiss of its own, the door shot open.

Ava recoiled, twisting the valve to snuff the flame. Jase staggered out, eyes wide, skin slick with sweat, one hand still clamped over his mouth and nose.

"Olivia, was that you?" Nolan asked in confusion, as if he missed her comms.

Olivia glanced at Damian, both of them pale with confusion. "Was what me? I didn't do anything. Just get him out of there!"

"I'm out," Jase rasped, coughing into his shirt. "The door just… opened."

Olivia's brow furrowed as she scanned the console. "That wasn't me, it wasn't…" Her voice trailed off as her eyes widened.

"Oh my god. Damian, look at the readings!" Her finger pointed to a sudden shift on the monitor.

Damian's eyes followed Olivia's gesture, his face draining of color. "Guys… the gym's clear. Zero radiation." His hands flew across the keyboard, confirming the impossible. "But now… critical alert in the greenhouse."

"No!" Ryder's scream tore through the comms. She bolted, sprinting down the hall like the floor itself was on fire.

"Ryder!" Nolan roared, taking off after her, Jase pounding at his side. Ava snatched up her tanks, clattering down the corridor in their wake.

Ryder flew up the stairs two at a time, wild with panic. The greenhouse door loomed just around the corner as she reached the landing. She slammed against it with both fists, beating the unyielding metal.

"Open it! Open the door, Olivia!" Her screams cracked as she hammered the door, frantic sobs ripping out of her throat. "You can't take this from us! Not this!"

Nolan and Jase reached her, Nolan grabbing her waist as she threw herself against the locked door again.

"Ryder, stop!" he shouted, yanking her back as she kicked at it like it was holding her child hostage.

"No!" she shrieked, thrashing against him, nails clawing at the steel. "It's all we have! Everything. We'll starve without it!" Her voice broke into a guttural cry, each word tearing out like an animal in pain.

Nolan wrapped both arms around her from behind, restraining her as she writhed. "Ryder—please! We'll find another way!" His voice cracked, raw with desperation. Jase pressed against the door, hands searching uselessly for a seam, his own breath ragged.

"Olivia!" Jase bellowed. "Override the door. Now!"

Back in the OCC, Olivia's fingers slammed the keys, her heart hammering. "I can't! The system's locked out! There's nothing I can do!"

Damian shook his head in disbelief. "This isn't possible, the air's shut down. Radiation doesn't just jump like that. And at these levels…" His voice faltered. "We should already be dead."

Before anyone could respond, a new alarm blared throughout the facility. Not shrill this time—low, resonant, final.

The words 'System Restored' flashed across the monitors. Damian's screen updated as well, 'Air Circulation System Active' appeared, with oxygen levels returning to green.

"Ouro, what's happening?" Olivia asked, her voice shaky. "Where's the radiation leak?"

"No radiation leak detected," Ouro replied, steady and serene. "All systems functioning at 100% capacity."

Damian and Olivia froze, staring at one another, pale with confusion.

At the greenhouse door, Ryder collapsed in Nolan's arms, her body convulsing with sobs as he held her tight against his chest.

Jase stood beside them, fists clenched, eyes darting between the greenhouse and the red emergency lights that slowly faded away.

Ava came racing down the hallway and skidded to a stop, her gaze shifting between them.

"What the fuck is going on?"

No one spoke.

Only Ryder's muffled sobs broke the suffocating silence.

The monitors flickered back to a steady stream of green readouts, their glow watching, unblinking.

One thing was clear—the party was over.

CHAPTER EIGHT

The kitchen was quiet, save for the faint clink of utensils and the low hum of the coffee machine. The group sat gathered around the table, each nursing a mug of coffee or tea. Exhaustion marked their faces. Dark circles shadowed their eyes, movements sluggish, every gesture heavy with the night before.

Jase stared into his mug, watching the swirl of steam fade into nothing. Normally breakfast carried quick conversation or light banter, but today silence pressed down on them. Ryder pushed fruit around her plate without eating, her gaze distant, as though she was staring straight through it into the greenhouse that had nearly been lost.

Ava rubbed her temples and muttered, her voice frayed, "We checked every system, every duct, every sensor—twice. Everything's running smooth. None of it makes sense."

Damian set his mug down with a dull thud. "I don't know about you, but I didn't sleep a wink. My mind kept racing. We've tested the systems over and over, and they're perfect. No malfunctions, no radiation. It's like…we made it all up."

Nolan leaned back, arms crossed, eyes narrowing. "So how do we figure out what actually set the alarms off?"

Jase looked up, eyes sharp as they moved from Nolan to Damian. "We start from scratch. Damian, take swabs and samples from everywhere in the facility." His tone was steady, commanding. "Once you have results, run new ones. Nolan, give him a hand with that."

Damian gave a tired nod. "I'll let you know when I have the results."

Nolan nodded back silently.

"Ava," Jase continued, "check every life support system again. Sensors, chips, wiring. You've already done it, but in the chaos, something might have been overlooked."

Her lips pressed thin, but she nodded.

Jase's gaze shifted to Ryder. Her eyes were still distant. "Ryder," he said firmly, snapping her out of her trance. "Could you work on making a hazmat suit? Maybe use an air filter and some goggles from the workshop. If there had been a radiation leak last night, we weren't prepared for someone to go in and make repairs safely."

Ryder dropped her eyes back to her plate, moving fruit with her fork. "Yeah. I can do that," she said softly.

Nolan glanced sideways at her, catching the truth in her slumped shoulders. She was barely holding on.

Finally, Jase turned to Olivia, who had been watching him with steady focus. "Liv, you and I will head to the OCC. I want a full diagnostic sweep of every system in this place. From life support down to the coffee machine. If there's a bug or a glitch anywhere in the code, I want it found."

Nolan let his arms drop on the table with a flat smack. "Jesus. Even the coffee machine runs on the computer?"

Olivia gave him a half-smile. "No. But I get his point." She turned back to Jase, serious again. "I agree. Whatever happened last night was caused by something, if it's a bug in the computers, I'll find it."

"Good," Jase said quietly, scanning the table one last time.

They were drained, frayed, but beneath the fatigue he saw the determination in their eyes. None of them would rest easy until they had answers anyway.

***

In the lab, Damian moved methodically, swabbing vents, ducts, doorframes, even the gym walls. Each sample was labeled and catalogued with mechanical precision, but the monotony gnawed at him. He leaned back, crossing his arms as another test came up clean. The silence of the lab pressed in, broken only by the hum of equipment and the scratch of his pen. With a sigh, he reached for the next sample, his thoughts chasing dead ends.

Nolan worked at his side, assisting where he could. He'd helped collect samples all morning and now fell into a routine of prepping and passing tools, but the endless string of negatives was wearing him thin. Patience only stretched so far. And with the silence thick around them, his mind drifted. All he could think of was Ryder at the breakfast table—distant, hollow-eyed, barely touching her food.

He swallowed the knot in his throat, pushing it down, and forced himself back into focus. He'd promised to help Damian, and figuring out what caused the alarms might put Ryder at ease.

Across the facility, Ava hunched over her workbench, life support panels spread open before her. She checked each sensor, chip, and wire connection methodically. Her fingers moved carefully, prying apart circuits, scanning components, reseating connectors as she hunted for a faulty part that refused to appear.

She sat back with a huff, rolling her aching shoulders, eyes narrowing at the flawless readouts. For all her effort, nothing failed. Nothing shorted out. And the longer she stared at all the flawless components, the more it gnawed at her. Why couldn't she solve this puzzle?

In the living room, Ryder worked in silence on her makeshift hazmat suit. She'd gathered scraps from the workshop, filters, goggles, thick fabric, and stitched them together with skilled hands. Mending and repurposing had always come easy to her. Long before the Ouroboros, she'd patched and repaired clothes, rarely indulging in something new, not out of necessity, but because it felt wasteful to discard what still had life.

Now, that practical skill moved her hands automatically. But her mind wasn't in it. The stitches were uneven, her needle slipping as her focus faltered. She kept seeing the greenhouse door, the image of it locked tight flashing in her mind. For hours she sat like that, piecing fabric together, her throat thick with the thought that if she lost those plants—the only thing she'd truly built here—then she'd lose herself too.

Back in the OCC, Olivia hunched over her keyboard, eyes burning as lines of code blurred together. She had already run diagnostic sweeps a few times. Every log she combed through, every error report she pulled, all came back the same. Systems at 100%.

Her hands stilled on the keys as she rubbed at her temples, jaw tight. It didn't make sense. And the longer she stared at perfect data, the more her frustration curdled into something sharper. Her gaze slid, just for a moment, to where Jase stood nearby.

He loomed with arms folded, his face set in grim determination. He'd been circling between groups all day, checking progress, offering quiet help, but Olivia could see the weight in his eyes. Like the rest of them, he was exhausted. But there was something else too, a tightness in the way he watched, as if he was waiting for a confirmation of what he already feared.

Her fingers hovered over the keyboard before she finally broke the silence.

"Can I ask you something?" she said quietly. "Why did you react the way you did last night?"

Jase looked at her, brow furrowed. "What do you mean?"

"At the party. When I pulled out the file, before I gave you the picture of Eli." Her voice caught slightly, but she pressed on. "You looked at me like I was a different person. Like you expected me to betray you."

She shook her head, letting out a bitter laugh. "I don't know, maybe I'm being dramatic. But it hurt. After everything we've been through…just never thought you'd look at me like that."

Jase's jaw worked as he looked away, his silence stretching. He thought about his new nightmare, his subconscious telling him something was off. The alarms hadn't been a glitch. He knew that much. But voicing his suspicion now, when everyone was hanging by a thread, would only deepen the cracks.

"I was caught off guard," he said finally, his tone even. "I had a few too many drinks, and it was a surprise I wasn't ready for. I'm sorry I made you feel that way, especially when it was the best surprise I could've asked for."

Olivia searched his face. There was truth layered in there, but also restraint. He wasn't telling her everything, she could feel it. She turned back to the screen, her shoulders stiff as she resumed typing. She didn't answer him, but the silence said enough.

The hours continued to drag on, each of them buried in fruitless work. The silence of the Ouroboros grew heavier, filled only by the scrape of tools, the hum of machinery, the sighs of frustration. By nightfall, the truth settled over them like a weight—whatever triggered last night's alarm had left no trace. They had spent the day chasing ghosts.

***

The group collapsed onto the couch and chairs in the living room, both physically and mentally drained. Remnants of last night's celebration, balloons made from medical gloves, half-filled cups, and wilting flowers, still lingered across tables and walls, but the joy they carried was gone.

Olivia slumped in her chair, her head propped heavily in her hand. "I've gone over every line of code, every program, every server. I even checked that every cable was plugged in. Not a single issue anywhere," she muttered, her voice flat with frustration.

Damian leaned back, head tilted toward the ceiling, a groan rumbling out. "I ran swabs on every inch of this place. Multiple times. Not a trace of radiation."

Ava rubbed her face, then locked her hands behind her head with a long exhale. "I didn't find a damn thing either. But on a brighter note, life support systems are spotless. And I increased water pressure in the showers while I was at it." She forced a half-smile that didn't quite reach her eyes.

Nolan glanced around at their slumped forms, the defeat written plainly across every face. "So… no answers. What do we do now?" The question hung heavy, like he already knew it didn't have an answer.

Silence fell over them. No one moved. They were too drained, too spent, the phantom threat still pressing in around them, unanswered.

Finally, Jase sat forward, a spark of determination cutting through the fatigue. "We get some rest. We wake up. We do it again." His tone was calm but resolved, his eyes wide and stern.

The group exchanged weary glances. Deep down, they knew he was right. Giving up wasn't an option. Not when their lives could depend on it.

After a long pause, Ava stood and crossed over to the card table. A half-full bottle of vodka from last night still waited there. She poured a shot, held it up to the group with a defiant glint in her eye, and said, "See you in the morning."

She downed it, set the glass back with a sharp clink, and strode out, leaving the others in silence.

Jase pressed his lips together, gave the others a nod, and stood. Olivia, Damian, and Nolan slowly followed, shuffling out one by one.

But Ryder remained. She hadn't moved since she sat down, her gaze fixed on the wilted flowers still drooping in their vases. Her hands lay slack in her lap, fingers trembling slightly, as though even lifting them would be too much effort.

Nolan paused in the doorway, watching her. She didn't look back. She just kept staring at the flowers, the last fragile reminder of what she had almost lost.

When she finally spoke, her voice was barely a whisper. "What's the point of any of this?"

The words hung in the air, raw and heavy, as Nolan's chest tightened. He paused for a moment, unsure of the words to say.

Slowly, Nolan approached Ryder, standing quietly at the end of the couch. The words sat heavy in his throat, refusing to release.

Finally, he found the courage, his voice low and earnest.

"I know how much losing the greenhouse scared you. It's… it's everything to you. It's your life. You've poured yourself into it. And for a moment, you thought it was gone. Thankfully, it's not. But you need to know—even if it was gone, you'd still have us. You're more than what you grow down here, Ryder. I don't think I could get through any of this without you."

Ryder's eyes lifted, shimmering with both worry and gratitude. She rose to her feet, her hands trembling slightly as she rested them on his arms. Her voice came soft, but steady.

"It's not just about the greenhouse. I've lost crop fields before," she murmured, glancing down before meeting his eyes again. "What terrified me was losing our food source. Our chance to keep going. Everything was starting to feel good for once, and in the blink of an eye, it was almost ripped away. You…were almost ripped away. That's what broke me."

Nolan's face softened, his hands instinctively rising to cradle her cheeks. His thumbs brushed gently along her skin, grounding her.

"Nothing is going to take me from you," he whispered. "Not while I have anything left to fight with."

He leaned in, and their lips met in a kiss that felt like an anchor—a promise that whatever waited for them, they would face it together. It was the moment they had both been yearning for, stolen from them the night before, now finally theirs.

They lingered in each other's embrace, letting the stress of the last twenty-four hours melt away. In the silence, all the words they couldn't find lived between them.

When they finally pulled apart, Nolan brushed a loose strand of hair from her face, smiling softly at the quiet strength in her gaze. He slipped his hand into hers, their fingers lacing together in a steady warmth.

"Come on," he murmured. "Let's get some rest."

Ryder squeezed his hand, a calm washing over her as she nodded.

Their footsteps echoed softly in the dim corridor. Surrounded by uncertainty and fear, this moment felt like the only true thing she could hold on to.

At her door, Nolan paused, his hand lingering in hers a moment longer.

"Get some sleep," he said, his voice certain. "We'll figure it out tomorrow. Together."

Ryder nodded, their hands finally parting as she watched him head down the hall. For the first time since the alarms, a faint smile touched her lips, the smallest spark of warmth returning to her chest.

***

The days blurred together. Each morning began the same—a quiet breakfast, followed by hours of scouring the facility, inspecting every system, every duct, every shadow of a fault. Each evening ended the same—regrouping in the living room, drained and tense, reporting the same maddening outcome. Nothing. Always nothing.

On one of those mornings, the group gathered around the table, slightly more rested, their resolve hardening despite the grind. Jase poured himself a cup of coffee, slid into his chair, and whistled a low tune as if to cut the silence.

As they ate, he slipped a folded slip of paper to Damian.

Damian's brow furrowed as he read the message, scrawled in blocky letters—'Don't say a word. Meet in men's bathroom tonight before bed. Pass to the next person'.

He gave Jase a sidelong glance, confused yet silent, then passed it to Ava. One by one, the note circled the table, each person pausing with a flicker of uncertainty before handing it on. By the time it returned to Jase, the air around the table had shifted. The silence wasn't just tired anymore, it was curious, wary.

Jase tucked the slip into his pocket without comment, his expression unreadable.

No one spoke. They finished breakfast in silence. But their eyes followed him more closely after that, the secret hanging in the air, sharp and strange.

Olivia pushed her chair back, forcing a small smile. "Well. Back on the hunt we go."

One by one, they dispersed, the weight of routine a little lighter with the promise of what was to come.

***

In the OCC, Olivia combed through flawless diagnostics yet again, her eyes scanning code line by line. Meanwhile, in the greenhouse, Nolan found Ryder bent over a planter bed, gently loosening the soil around a cucumber sprout. She glanced up as he approached, managing a small smile.

"Need a hand with anything?" he asked, grabbing a nearby trowel.

"Actually, could you grab a few samples from the beds along the back? Some of those plants have been struggling, not sure why"

He nodded, filling containers with soil. They worked in easy silence, and when their eyes met, an unspoken understanding passed between them.

In the lab, Damian stared at the steady stream of results crawling across his monitor. Negative. Negative. Negative. The data confirmed what he already knew—no pathogens, no contamination, no radiation. Clean, always clean. He pinched the bridge of his nose, clinging to the slim hope that maybe, just maybe, one line would break the pattern. But the clock on the wall ticked on, mocking him with each passing second.

Out in the corridor, Ava balanced on a ladder, flashlight cutting into the dark shaft of an air duct. She scanned the seams, the metal spotless, then let out a quiet huff as she started to climb down. Jase passed by at the far end of the hall, offering her a quick wink, the faintest grin tugging at his mouth. She returned the gesture with a small smirk of her own before snapping the vent cover back into place.

That evening, they ended the day as they always did—collapsing into the living room couches and chairs, drained from another fruitless search. Reports were given, or rather, lack of them. The absurdity of it all had started to creep in, the tension of those first nights giving way to dry humor.

"I still think it was the coffee machine trying to kill us," Nolan muttered, his head tipped back against the cushion. Damian snorted, giving an exaggerated nod.

"Yeah, lying and brewing decaf instead," Olivia added with a smirk. "Maybe that's why we're so tired."

Their banter bounced around the room, each adding a light-hearted jab as their frustrations started to feel strangely funny.

But every so often, subtle glances flickered across the circle, unspoken reminders of the note that was passed.

Each of them felt the anticipation gnawing beneath the surface, but no one dared bring it up prematurely. They spoke instead about air ducts, monitor readouts, and the most recent lab results, all careful to keep their tones level.

When their nightly chatter wound down, Jase stood, stretching casually. "Well, back at it tomorrow. I'm grabbing a shower, then bed."

Ava caught his eye, then turned to the others with a sly smile. "Oh, bad news, ladies. I was working on something in our bathroom earlier and, uh… forgot to turn the water back on." Her tone was light, teasing. "Guess you'll have to make do with the boys' side tonight."

Olivia groaned, rolling her eyes. "Seriously? It better be clean in there." Her voice carried playful annoyance, but the flicker of anticipation in her glance said otherwise.

One by one, they filed out of the living room. Jase slipped into the men's bathroom first, followed by Damian, then Nolan.

A few moments later, Olivia and Ava entered nonchalant, with Ryder trailing behind, a towel draped over her arm. She spotted Jase, who met her eyes and lifted a finger to his lips.

Jase moved to the shower controls and twisted the knobs. Water roared from all three heads, the steady hiss filling the tiled room. He motioned everyone closer, pulling them into a tight circle just out of view of the door.

In a hushed voice, he began, "Here's the situation. I had Ava shut off the water in the women's bathroom so we'd have a reason to all be in here. Olivia's checked it out, this is the only place where Ouro doesn't hear us. Still, keep your voices low."

The group exchanged wary glances.

Damian whispered, his voice edged with caution. "Why don't we want Ouro to hear us?"

Jase's expression hardened. "We've torn this place apart for days. There's no damage. No malfunctions. Not a trace of the alarms in any logs. But we all saw those readings, something should have been there. If it was real, a faulty sensor, or even a glitch, there'd be evidence."

Nolan leaned forward, eyes narrowing. "So what are you saying?"

Jase let his gaze travel the circle before speaking. "I think Ouro triggered those alarms."

The words landed like a boulder into still water. Silence rippled out.

Ava was the first to find her voice. "So… Ouro's broken?"

Jase shook his head, but Olivia spoke before he could. Her eyes were locked on him, her face pale as the pieces fell into place. "No. Ouro is fine," she whispered. Her breath caught as she turned on him. "That's why you've been so distant. You've suspected this."

Jase didn't answer, but his silence confirmed it.

Olivia's throat tightened as she continued. "You believe Ouro knew what it was doing. The alarms, the 'radiation leak', the fear… it wanted us to experience that. For what?"

He gave a slow nod. "Yeah. I think it saw us falling off track, decided we were too comfortable. So it created an emergency to snap us out of it. To refocus us." He glanced at Damian, "You said it yourself, radiation doesn't jump like that. None of it added up. Because it wasn't real."

Damian tilted his head, his brow furrowing, a grim recognition dawning.

Jase's voice dropped lower, steady and grim. "Ouro's main mission is to keep us alive. When it saw us relaxing, it introduced a threat to remind us what's really at stake. The best way to do that—fear. Without question."

The group shifted uneasily, dread pooling in their eyes. Ryder wrapped her arms around herself, shivering though the room was warm. Nolan clenched his jaw, fists tight at his sides. Damian's usual calm cracked, his eyes darting like the walls themselves might turn on them.

Ava's gaze swept the group. "We're trapped in here," she said, her voice barely more than a whisper. "It can do whatever it wants to us."

The hiss of the showers filled the silence.

"So what do we do?" Ryder muttered at last, her voice fragile, as though she wasn't sure she wanted the answer.

Jase scanned the circle, expression steady. "Nothing. We continue everyday as normal. We keep our routines, we keep up on maintenance. We let Ouro see that we're focused."

Olivia's brow raised, an idea forming. "I think I can lock Ouro out of the living room," she said, voice firm. "We need one place where we can relax and speak privately. Until then, use the bathrooms for these meetings, and keep your Echo Loop neutral."

"Good. Just be careful." Jase said with a nod.

"Listen," He added, low and even, "In a way, this is actually good news. The facility's systems are working perfectly. There's no physical problem we need to worry about. Ouro is just… going to keep us on track."

He started to trace a slow circle in the air with his finger. "We just need to stay aware of that watchful eye. If something unusual happens, we stay quiet, regroup in here, and discuss what to do in private."

The group exchanged tight nods, the pact settling over them like concrete.

"Other than that, we continue on as normal." Jase finished.

A small measure of relief settled over them—their world wasn't collapsing, at least in a mechanical sense. But as they made their way out one by one, a new understanding settled in— Ouro was always watching. It was a reminder to remain vigilant, as they carried this quiet knowledge, close to their chests, through their everyday routines.

And that was exactly what they did.

Life in the Ouroboros fell back into its rhythm, relentless and precise. Days folded into one another, the routines no longer ritual but necessity.

Nolan pushed them through daily exercises, keeping their bodies ready for survival. Damian logged every heartbeat and blood test, each record a reminder of dangers they couldn't see. Ava rotated through the air systems, water filtration, and power supply, patching small faults before they could grow. Ryder tended the greenhouse with quiet devotion, her hands buried in soil, coaxing fragile green sprouts into life that kept them fed.

They laughed where they could, clung to small victories, and bore the weight of confinement with steady silence. At night, they gathered together, speaking lightly, always careful, always aware that Ouro might be listening between the lines. The rule was unspoken but firm—their guarded truths were saved for rare, whispered moments in hidden corners.

Days bled into weeks.

Weeks stretched into months.

And still, hope pulsed stubbornly in their chests—hope that one day, the sealed doors would open.

Until then, they would endure.

Bound to one another.

Surviving in the dark beneath Ouro's eye, clinging to one fragile mission: make it back to the world that left them behind.

PART TWO

MISSION: FALLOUT KIDS

CHAPTER NINE

Jase sat alone, his silhouette slumped against the chair, his gaze locked onto the camera in front of him. His fingers tapped idly on the edge of the console, lost in thought. The faint glow from the monitors illuminated his face, highlighting the strain etched across his features.

For the last 11 months, they'd been playing a dangerous game with Ouro—carefully curated narratives and polished performances designed to keep the AI complacent. It was a delicate dance, this constant tug-of-war between truth and fiction, and he was tired. Tired of the lies, and tired of the secrets that seemed to grow with each passing week.

The screen stared back, unblinking, waiting.

He took a deep breath, his eyes narrowing slightly as he considered his words. How much to say? How much to keep hidden?

After a long pause, Jase leaned forward and pressed the record button, forcing a casual smile as he started his Echo Loop.

"It's been another good week. Everything is running smooth, with only minor maintenance needed every so often. The group is getting along great, and really working well together. Personally, I am feeling really good, and continue to be focused on keeping this group together and pushing forward."

He adjusted slightly in his seat, the faintest tension flickering in his jaw. "It's been another week without my recurring nightmare."

He glanced off to the side, as if seeking strength from somewhere inside him, then he looked into the camera. "Honestly, I think having that picture of Eli helps a lot. I look at it every day, and… I don't know, maybe it just keeps me grounded. I think it makes it easier to focus on what we have to do down here—worry less about where he is, what he's going through. Reminds me that I have to survive down here to get back to him." His voice softened, and he caught himself, feeling the raw edge of his thoughts slipping through.

He cleared his throat, putting the mask back on, the carefully crafted facade he'd worn for so long. "Anyway, that's all for this week. I'll keep you posted if anything changes, but so far, no complaints." He gave a small shrug. "We're just… holding steady."

Jase took a long, slow breath, and forced a soft smile to his face. "This is Alpha-One, day seven hundred and two."

Jase reached out and pressed stop on the Echo Loop, watching the red recording light blink off with a hollow sense of relief. The silence that followed seemed almost too loud, filling the Operations Command Center like an accusation.

He sat back in his chair, the weight of the act settling over him. A year of deflecting and hiding, pretending that everything was fine—that the oppressive isolation had no effect on them, that the walls weren't closing in a little more each day.

 He ran a hand through his hair, his fingers catching in the mess of it, as he closed his eyes for a moment. The weight of his words—every carefully chosen phrase and veiled half-truth—seemed to settle over him, thick and suffocating.

They had managed to keep it together, at least that was what he kept telling himself, and Ouro. And so far, it had been working. They hadn't had another 'emergency' since that night less than a year ago, the one they never talked about. The one that reminded them all how closely Ouro was watching.

The group had adapted, finding a strange rhythm to their underground existence. The routines had become their lifeline, something to cling to when the monotony and isolation threatened to overwhelm them.

The Ouroboros was running perfectly, an artificial oasis beneath the earth. The greenhouse was thriving, lush and green. They had food, shelter, supplies—everything they needed to survive physically.

But mentally, it was a different story.

The toll of their confinement was harder to ignore. The masks they wore, the constant charade of calm, was wearing them down, layer by layer, slowly but steadily. They had learned to act unbreakable in front of Ouro, to keep their fears and doubts hidden behind carefully controlled smiles and empty reassurances. Yet beneath the surface, each of them was fraying, in ways they rarely admitted out loud.

It had taken a few months, a grueling project filled with whispered plans and cautious work, but Olivia had managed to cut Ouro's access to the living room. With Ava's help, she'd isolated that one space from Ouro's all-seeing gaze, creating a haven where they could let their guard down, if only for a little while. It was their one sanctuary, a place where the weight of their secrets lifted, where they could speak freely, let their exhaustion show, even break down if they needed to.

The effect had been immediate. Conversations that had once been guarded, every word chosen with caution, started to flow more freely. They found solace in each other, in the shared understanding that nothing else could provide.

Late-night talks, laughter, moments of vulnerability—they became their therapy, the one thing that kept them from losing themselves entirely to the claustrophobic reality of living underground. In the living room, they were no longer just survivors in a shelter. They were a family. Bound not by blood, but by the shared trauma of their isolation.

Jase gave one final glance around the empty OCC, looking over all the monitors and computer server banks—the brains of Ouro. Pushing himself up from the chair, he squared his shoulders and stood tall, presenting a tough armor. He needed to keep it together, to keep up the facade.

And with his mask back on, he walked towards the door, and back into their carefully constructed lives they'd built.

As the door closed behind him, a new screen opened up on the monitor he had just sat at. 'Analyzing' flashed on the screen, as the Echo Loop he just recorded began to play in the empty room where only Ouro roamed.

***

The med bay was quiet, save for the faint hum of equipment, and a sterile scent hung in the air. Ryder lay on the exam table, muscles tense with anticipation, her fingers nervously wrapped around the edges—knuckles white with the force of her grip.

The table was cold on her back causing a shiver to shoot down her spine. Her eyes, wide and glossed over, held a fierce determination to stay dry and keep the levee from breaking.

For a few moments, Damian said nothing, his brow furrowing in concentration. He glanced at her, catching the barely contained fear in her expression. "It's going to be okay," he said, offering a small, steady nod, trying to project a calm confidence that he hoped would ease her nerves.

Though this was new territory for him—his clinical training covering little of it—Damian was determined to take care of her, to make the experience as reassuring as possible. He could feel her trust hanging in the balance, and he didn't want to let her down.

He adjusted the portable ultrasound machine beside her, a transducer on a long cord connected to a tablet mounted on a stand. His hands moving with confidence despite the unfamiliarity of the procedure. He'd only seen it done a handful of times in his clinical training, but he knew enough to make it work.

Ryder's shirt was rolled up to expose her abdomen, her gaze fixed somewhere past him, as if focusing on anything but the machine and what it might reveal.

"Alright, Ryder," he said softly, his voice a calming anchor in the quiet room. "I'm going to apply the gel now. It'll be a bit cold." Damian offered her a reassuring nod, then squeezed a healthy cold dollop of gel onto her abdomen.

She sucked in a sharp breath at the cold sensation, her body instinctively flinching at the chill. Her grip tightened on the table, but she didn't look at him, her gaze fixed on some distant point in the room. Damian hesitated briefly, letting her adjust to the sensation before he brought the transducer to her skin and gently pressed down.

As he moved the transducer across her abdomen, the screen flickered to life with hazy, shifting images, patterns of light and shadow in grayscale. Adjusting the angle and pressing a bit more firmly against her, he concentrated as he leaned in, maneuvering the transducer slowly to locate the image he was looking for.

The fuzzy shapes on the screen gradually began to sharpen, the haze giving way to something more distinct. "There," he murmured, focus edged with worry. A faint shape floated in the gray static.

Ryder's breath caught, the sound sharp in her chest.

Damian leaned closer, steady hand guiding the probe. His breath caught for a split second, and he felt a sudden, almost overwhelming wave of emotion. He leaned closer, guiding the transducer with precision, angling it to bring the tiny shape into clearer focus.

And there it was—the faint outline of a head, followed by the curve of a tiny spine, arms, and legs folded inwards in the classic fetal position. Then, the faintest flicker—a rhythmic pulse that showed up as a subtle, throbbing glow on the monitor. It was the heartbeat. Steady, resolute, a flickering light of life.

Damian released a breath he hadn't realized he was holding, his relief blending with a deep sense of wonder. "Everything looks good," he murmured, glancing at Ryder. His voice was soft, calm, keeping any trace of his own awe hidden beneath a layer of professionalism.

"The heartbeat is strong, steady. The baby's growing right on track." He pointed to the screen, showing her the outline, tracing the shape with his finger in the air. "See that there? That's the head, and the arms, and those are the legs you've started to feel moving around."

Ryder's gaze finally shifted to the monitor, her eyes widening as she took in the image. She looked almost disbelieving, like she was seeing a miracle she hadn't fully accepted until now.

Slowly, her trembling hand reached up, hovering just over the screen as if she could somehow touch the image, feel the small life that had begun to grow within her. For a brief, unguarded moment, the strength and resilience she always wore melted away, replaced by an expression of pure, vulnerable awe.

Damian gently moved the transducer again, trying to capture different angles, making sure there were no signs of complications or abnormalities. He studied the size, the shape, the position, every inch of the tiny form on the screen, scanning for any signs of trouble. But everything appeared normal and healthy, a quiet reassurance in this world where so little was certain.

"Based on our discussion and what I see here, I'd say you're about 16 weeks," Damian said firmly, his voice calm and steady, betraying none of his own nervousness.

The certainty in his tone masked the unfamiliar terrain he was navigating—he'd never expected to play the role of an OB-GYN, let alone in a place like this. But for Ryder, he needed to exude confidence.

"Would you like to know the gender?" He asked with a raised brow.

Ryder's eyes shot from the screen to his, widening in surprise. She opened her mouth, hesitated, then shook her head. "No…not yet."

Knowing the gender would make it all feel so much more real. She was barely beginning to wrap her mind around the reality of her situation, let alone everything that was about to change. With everything they needed to figure out in the coming months, she wasn't ready to add another thought to consume her mind.

Damian gave a quiet nod of understanding and carefully wiped the gel from her abdomen. Then he met her gaze with a gentle but insistent look.

"You have to tell the others. They're going to find out soon enough, you're going to start showing dramatically. You won't be able to hide this anymore." His voice was firm but compassionate.

He understood how she liked her privacy, how tightly each of them guarded parts of themselves in this isolated life. But he also knew the weight of carrying something like this alone, and he wanted her to have the support she needed.

Ryder's hand instinctively drifted to her stomach, her gaze dropping as she absorbed his words. She nodded slowly, though uncertainty lingered in her eyes. "I know," she murmured, as if convincing herself. "I just… wanted to be sure everything was okay first."

Damian smiled softly, a reassuring warmth in his eyes. "Well, now you know," he said, his voice low and steady. "Everything looks great so far. And, don't worry, they'll understand. They'll be here for you—both of you. Besides, we're family down here, Ryder. That baby is all of ours!"

She gave a small nod, pulling her shirt down as she sat up, her shoulders hunched forward as if the weight of the moment was pressing down on her. Her head lowered, eyes fixed on the floor as she struggled with the reality she'd kept buried until now.

After a beat, she looked up, her gaze locking onto Damian's, her vulnerability stark and raw. "I'm scared, Damian," she admitted, her voice trembling. "How am I going to do this? How are we supposed to bring a child into this small world of ours? Into…whatever's left of the world above? How do I even begin to prepare for that?"

After a long, thoughtful pause, he exhaled slowly, meeting her gaze with a renewed determination. "The same way we've made it through these last two years," he said quietly, a steady resolve anchoring his voice. "As a team. We've faced hard times, and we've come out on the other side. All of us will be here to help you and this baby through whatever comes next."

He allowed a small, reassuring smile to soften his expression. "We may not know what the future holds, but we're not going to let you face it alone. Whatever it takes, Ryder. We're all in this together."

A faint, trembling smile crept across Ryder's face, a glimmer of hope breaking through her fear. The emotions she'd held at bay finally spilled over, a single tear slipping down her cheek, her defenses giving way to the enormity of the moment.

She leaned forward, wrapping her arms around Damian in a gentle but firm embrace, seeking comfort in the warmth of his presence, in the steady strength he offered.

"Thank you," she whispered, her voice muffled against his shoulder, the words carrying a weight that went beyond gratitude.

***

Ryder sat on the cold floor in the far corner of the greenhouse, knees pulled tight to her chest, arms wrapped around them as though they were the only thing keeping her together. Her mind spun with worry, a storm of what-ifs too heavy to silence.

How would she tell Nolan? How would she tell the others? How could she possibly bring a child into this world—a world of concrete walls, artificial light, and recycled air? Life here was already hard enough. Adding a baby felt impossible, like planting a seed in barren soil and expecting it to take root.

It wasn't a question about wanting children or not. She had always pictured herself with kids one day, though never like this. She'd imagined sunlight, open fields, and fresh air. Not concrete ceilings and humming vents.

Even so, she had always been the one who nurtured. The one who cared quietly, who healed, who cultivated life where none should exist. In the greenhouse, she poured herself into her plants, treating every seed, sprout, and bloom like her children. She dedicated herself to them, to their every need—watering, pruning, testing the soil, checking nutrient levels. She even talked to them, her gentle words filling the greenhouse with a warmth that made the synthetic space feel more alive.

But plants were one thing. The Ouroboros was built for that, engineered to sustain harvests. It wasn't built for children. There were no cribs. No soft blankets. No quiet corners to lay a baby down. Nothing about this place suggested a future with children.

The thought hollowed her chest. A child deserved sunlight, grass beneath bare feet, the sky overhead. What could she offer except a concrete cage? Could love alone fill the cracks? Could it counterbalance the absence of a real childhood, the cruel truth that they would be born into captivity?

Ryder's thoughts turned to Nolan, and a fresh wave of anxiety tightened her chest. How would he react? The man she loved was disciplined, a natural leader with a soldier's instinct for survival and structure. His compassion showed in their quiet moments together, but he was also ruthlessly pragmatic. She could already hear his first reaction, practical to the core. Is this really the time? The place?

She knew him well enough to imagine the calculations forming in his mind—how a baby would strain their resources, disrupt routines, and create vulnerabilities they couldn't afford. A baby was unpredictable, demanding, dependent. Nolan hadn't signed up for that. What if he saw this new life as a weakness—or worse, as a burden?

Her heart sank. Telling him felt like handing over a grenade with the pin pulled—knowing it might bind them closer, or shatter everything they'd built.

And yet, she hoped.

She'd seen the warmth in his eyes in rare, unguarded moments. The way his hard edges softened, if only for a heartbeat, when they spoke of what might have been had the world not collapsed. Could that tenderness, that hidden vulnerability, be enough to welcome this unexpected miracle?

The thought sparked a fragile ember inside her. She wasn't alone. Nolan, Damian, Jase, Olivia, Ava, each brought their own strengths. Together, they had survived the impossible. Maybe, if they all believed in this new life, they could find a way. But first, she would have to tell them. She would have to let down her guard, expose her own vulnerability, and hope that they would understand.

Her gaze drifted to a row of seedlings she'd planted days earlier. Tiny, fragile, pushing through soil—yet full of promise. And then she felt that flicker of resolve solidify within her. If those tiny seeds could find a way to grow in this place, then maybe, so could a child.

A surge of warmth spread through her, a fragile but fierce determination taking root. She would find a way to protect this new life, to nurture it, just as she'd nurtured all these plants in this greenhouse. Because this child, her child, deserved a chance to grow and thrive in this artificial world as well.

The greenhouse door hissed open, startling Ryder out of her thoughts. She looked up sharply, arms tightening around her knees.

Nolan stepped in, his tall frame filling the doorway. His expression softened as his eyes swept over the greenhouse, taking in the vibrant rows of life Ryder had carefully cultivated, before landing on her curled in the back corner.

When their gazes met, Ryder's restraint crumbled. Tears spilled down her cheeks, unstoppable.

Nolan's smile vanished. He crossed the room in quick strides, dropping to his knees in front of her. "Ryder?" His voice was sharp with alarm. His hands hovered just above her shoulders, scanning for wounds. "Are you hurt?"

She shook her head, biting her lip, the sob breaking free anyway. She tried to form words, but her throat tightened, refusing to cooperate.

"Okay, okay," he murmured, softer now, steadying himself. "Then what is it? Did something happen?" His hands settled gently on her arms, anchoring her.

Ryder squeezed her eyes shut, trying to hold it in, but the emotions—fear, guilt, hope—were too heavy. She drew a shaky breath, forced herself to meet his gaze, and saw only worry and love there, which made the words harder to speak.

"I..." she started, her voice cracking. She took another breath. "I have to tell you something," she finally said, her voice barely above a whisper.

Nolan nodded slowly, giving her space. "Alright. Whatever it is, you can tell me."

She looked down at her twisted hands, her throat burning. A sob slipped out, and she shook her head with a shaky laugh. "I'm sorry. I don't know how to say it."

"You don't need to apologize," he said gently. "Take your time. Whatever it is, we'll figure it out together, okay."

Nolan waited patiently, his thumb lightly brushing her arm in a calming gesture. That steadiness, that calm, was the only thing keeping her from breaking apart completely.

She leaned forward, pressing her forehead to his chest, and felt his arms close tight around her. Her voice came out as a whisper, almost lost in the hum of the vents.

"I'm pregnant."

Nolan stilled, his breath catching against her hair.

CHAPTER TEN

The next morning in the kitchen, Olivia poured herself a cup of coffee and sat down at the table next to Jase, who was already halfway through his breakfast.

Across from him sat Damian and Ava, both quietly eating while the faint hum of the kitchen filled the silence. It was a rare moment of calm in their otherwise stressful lives, and the group seemed to be enjoying it.

Olivia took a sip of her coffee, glancing at Jase. "You know, if you're going to keep hogging all the peanut butter packets, we're going to have a problem," she teased, pointing to the small pile near his plate.

Jase smirked, pushing one toward her. "Easy now, I can share. Besides, you're the one always taking extra honey packets, so I'm just evening out the playing field."

Olivia rolled her eyes, but her grin betrayed her. "Please, you don't even like honey. That's different."

The door slid open, breaking their back-and-forth. Nolan and Ryder walked in together, relaxed and easy. Nolan's damp hair stuck up from a recent shower, while Ryder, her dark hair pulled into a loose ponytail, carried a faint glow that didn't go unnoticed.

"Well, look who finally rolled out of bed!" Ava said, leaning back in her chair with a smirk. "Missed you at the morning workout!"

Nolan didn't flinch. He poured himself coffee, the rich aroma filling the air, and leaned against the counter. "Yeah, sorry about that. I was beat," he said casually. "I'll make it up this evening."

"Oh, I know you will," Ava shot back, raising an eyebrow.

Ryder slid into the seat across from Damian, her movements too careful to be casual. She offered him a small, private smile, one Damian immediately caught. It wasn't just a smile, it was a thank-you. A silent acknowledgment of the conversation they'd shared the day before.

Damian smiled slightly, and leaned forward, his tone light and warm. "Good morning, Ryder. How are you?"

"Better than I was expecting," she replied, her grin carrying a flicker of mischief.

Ava groaned loudly, dropping her spoon into her bowl with a loud clank. "Oh god, you two are ridiculous. You're going to ruin my breakfast."

Ryder blinked, caught off guard. "What? No—that's not… honestly, we just slept in," she blurted, her voice rising a little too fast.

Ava rolled her eyes, unimpressed. "Okay, if you say so." She let out a short laugh, and turned her smirk on Nolan as he sat down. "So, the rule was an extra mile on the treadmill for being late to workouts. What should the punishment be for missing it completely?"

Nolan pursed his lips like he was giving it real thought. "Fair point. Maybe it should be more." He leaned back, arms crossing. "What do you have in mind?"

"Extra round of sparring," Ava said without missing a beat, her tone smug.

"Two extra rounds," Nolan countered, crossing his arms over his chest.

"Okay, tough guy, but you still have to make up your morning cardio, too." Ava shot back, their playful standoff drawing amused glances around the table.

Jase leaned back in his chair, enjoying the exchange. "Why stop there? Make him do some of your work today."

"Brilliant," Olivia added with a grin, swirling her coffee. "And while he's at it, he can take care of the dishes this morning. We all know how much he loves a clean kitchen."

"Okay, okay," Nolan said, holding up his hands in surrender. "Let's not go overboard. The punishment should fit the crime. I'll clean up, but don't make me spend more time with Ava than I already have to."

The group laughed, throwing more ideas at him. Ryder tried to join in, but the sound caught in her throat. Their late arrival wasn't Nolan's fault, it was hers. Now he was the one paying for it.

Her guilt twisted tighter when she glanced at Damian. His eyes met hers, and she gave him a small, almost desperate look. You were right. Telling Nolan was good.

Damian returned it with a subtle, reassuring smile. Then his brows lifted with a slight head nod—a quiet urging. Now's the time. Tell the rest.

Her stomach dropped. Ryder's pulse thudded in her ears, drowning out the laughter around her. She shook her head quickly, her smile faltering. Not now. Not like this. The thought of saying the words aloud—of seeing their faces shift from joy to shock—was unbearable. What if they weren't ready? What if they thought she'd doomed them all?

Her gaze flicked around the table. Ava and Nolan were still bickering over punishments, Olivia egging them on, Jase leaning back with his easy grin. No one else had noticed. Relief mixed with dread.

Ryder forced herself to take a deep breath, steadying the storm of emotions swirling inside her. There would be a time for this, there had to be, but not now. Not when the group was laughing and teasing, the rare moment of levity filling the room. For now, she would keep this secret close, savoring the small victory of having told Nolan and holding onto the hope that the rest would fall into place when the time was right.

Ryder pushed away from the table and stood up, brushing a stray strand of hair behind her ear. "I should get to the greenhouse," she announced. She turned to Ava, softer. "Please go easy on him, it was my fault."

Leaning down, she pressed a quick kiss to Nolan's cheek. He smiled without hesitation, but Ryder's heart clenched as she turned away, the guilt following her out the door.

Ava watched Ryder leave, her lips twisting into a smirk. The moment the door hissed shut, she leaned across the table toward

Nolan. "Please go easy on him," she said in a mocking tone, exaggerating Ryder's voice. "You're lucky I like her."

Nolan gave her a flat look, though the corner of his mouth betrayed a smile. "You heard her, the blame falls on her."

Ava chuckled as she stood up. "As much as I'd love to keep tormenting you, I've got work to do. Damian has been having power surges in the lab that I have to look into." She dropped her dishes near the sink and shot Nolan a pointed look. "I'll let you handle these. Since you're so eager to avoid me." With a quick wink, she was gone.

Damian stretched, yawning as he rose from his seat. "I should go keep an eye on her, make sure she doesn't break anything in there." He gathered his plate and mug, then set them directly in front of Nolan with a smug grin. "Appreciate the cleanup. Love the accountability."

Nolan groaned. "You're all heart, you know that?"

Olivia pushed herself up from the table. "Well, I don't have much going on today, so I'll give Ava a hand. Make sure those power surges aren't effecting anything else in the facility."

She started toward the door, then glanced back at Nolan with a sly smile. "Don't worry—my plate isn't that dirty. But the pan I used to cook breakfast is going to need some elbow grease!"

Nolan sat back in his chair, sighing heavily as he glanced around the messy kitchen. "Unbelievable," he muttered to himself, shaking his head.

Only Jase remained, arms crossed, leaning back in his chair. "Looks like you're on cleanup duty," he said with a smirk. Then his tone shifted, more deliberate. "But before you dive in, there's something I want to show you in the living room."

Nolan frowned, glancing between the dishes and Jase. "The living room too?"

"I mean, it's just across the hall," Jase said, condescendingly. He motioned toward the door. "Come on, I'll show you."

With a sigh, Nolan stood and followed Jase out of the kitchen, leaving the dishes untouched for the moment.

As they entered the living room, the door closed behind them with a loud thud. The space, like most of the shelter, was nearly pristine. Everything was in its place. The furniture perfectly aligned, the tables cleared, and not a single item left out of order.

Nolan glanced around, confusion creasing his brow. "Well, this should be an easy job. Is this you having mercy on me?" he asked, a small grin playing at his lips.

Jase leaned against the table's edge, arms crossed, expression calm but edged with purpose. "No," he said flatly, giving the room a quick once-over. "Honestly, I thought this place would be messier. But that's not why we're here." His voice dropped lower. "Ouro can hear us in the kitchen, not here."

Nolan's eyes widened. "Oh, shit. I did not pick up on that," he admitted, rubbing the back of his neck. "Thought you just wanted to pile on like the rest of them." He gave a sheepish laugh. "So what's going on?"

Jase straightened, arms falling to his sides, his tone firmer. "Listen, everyone's glad you and Ryder found each other. Seriously, no one's judging that. And so far, Ouro hasn't seemed to have a problem with it either." He paused, his expression darkening. "But you two skipping the workout? That's different. We've gone almost a year without another…incident. All because we've stayed smart—stayed focused. Do you really think sleeping in and missing out on what we've all agreed to follow was the smart move?"

Nolan's grin faded as guilt crept across his face. He looked down at the floor, his hands slipping into his pockets. "I'm sorry," he said quietly. "We didn't oversleep. That's not what happened. I just…I didn't even think about how it might look to Ouro."

Jase's expression hardened, his jaw tightening as he took a step closer. "Wait," he said, his voice sharpening. "You're telling me you missed morning workouts intentionally? To get laid? What were you thinking?"

Nolan raised his hands defensively, shaking his head. "No, no, it's not like that!" he said quickly, his voice tinged with panic. "It wasn't anything like that." He hesitated, glancing at the door to make sure it was still shut. "Ryder and I had some…issues we needed to discuss. Important things."

Jase's brows lifted, suspicion flickering across his face. "Issues?" he echoed slowly, folding his arms. "What kind of issues?"

Nolan's face flushed, and he hurriedly interjected. "Don't worry," he said firmly. "We were careful. We were in the bathroom with the showers running. Ouro couldn't hear a thing."

Jase's eyes narrowed, his stance still tense. "That's not the point," he said. "You're missing the bigger picture. Ouro's always watching, always evaluating. The routines, the workouts, the maintenance—those are what keep it satisfied. Breaking that pattern, even for a good reason, could trigger something we're not ready for. You know that."

Nolan's shoulders sagged, guilt heavy on his face. "I get it, I do. And I'm sorry. I'll make it right, I swear. I just...I didn't think."

Some of the tension drained from Jase's shoulders. He rubbed a hand over his face, clearly frustrated but trying to reign it in. "Look, Nolan," he said more softly, "I get that you and Ryder are dealing with stuff. Everyone's got their battles in here. But we can't afford mistakes. Not now, not ever. You've got to keep your head in the game—for her sake as much as everyone else's."

Nolan finally looked up, meeting Jase's gaze with a determined nod. "You're right. It won't happen again. I'll make sure of it."

Jase studied him for a long beat, then gave a short nod. "Good. Just be smarter about it next time. We have to find the right moments for those things." He smiled, and gave Nolan a pat on the shoulder. "Now, you better get to those dishes. Ava's wrath is probably worse than Ouro's, and I can't save you from that!"

Nolan let out a small, melancholy laugh, feeling the weight of the conversation lift just slightly. "Oh, it's definitely worse," he said, turning to follow Jase back toward the kitchen.

But the weight of Jase's words lingered, a reminder of the delicate balance they all maintained under Ouro's watchful eye.

***

Nolan took a sharp right hand to the face, his headgear shifting slightly from the impact. He stumbled back, fumbling with his gloves to tug it straight. The tang of sweat filled his nose, the sound of Ava's glove still echoing off the gym walls.

Ava bounced on her toes, her ponytail swaying as she gave a cocky laugh. "Oh, that one landed clean!" she sneered, lowering her gloves just enough to smirk. "What's the matter? You still tired? Need another nap?" There was an unmistakable gleam of satisfaction in her dark brown eyes.

Nolan straightened, chuckling as he reset his stance. "That your best shot? My four-year-old niece hits harder!" His tone was light, but the fire in his gaze said otherwise.

He came forward, gloves high, movement smooth and patient compared to Ava's scrappy aggression. A sharp left jab snapped her head back, then another followed in quick succession.

"Come on," Nolan said, his tone teasing but instructive. "Move your head. You're leaving it out there for me." He gave her a small grin.

Ava gritted her teeth, focused now as she tried to close the gap. She wasn't a polished fighter like Nolan, but she had grit.

Nolan kept his stance relaxed, darting in and out of range, peppering her with quick jabs. Ava managed to slip under one, dipping low and throwing a fast left hook to the body that landed.

Nolan let out a light groan, his breath hitching for a split second as the punch connected. "There you go," he said, a hint of pride in his voice. "Way to dip under that. Rotate your hips a bit more when you throw that left hook. You'll get more power in it. Hit the liver hard enough, and even the biggest guy will drop to his knees."

Ava smirked, her chest rising and falling as she panted from exertion. "By the end of this, you're going to be on your knees, begging for mercy," she shot back, her words defiant as she bounced lightly on her toes.

Nolan laughed, shaking his head. He dropped his guard, arms spread wide. "Sure. I'm right here. Make me beg."

Ava narrowed her eyes, shoulders tight as she pressed forward. A quick jab, then another. Both thudded harmlessly against Nolan's gloves. She snapped an overhand right, the impact rattling his guard but not breaking through.

It was the opening she wanted. Nolan's guard was high, his abdomen wide. Perfect for the liver shot he'd just lectured her on. She dipped left, focusing on the movement of her hips, as every muscle drove into the punch. She swung forward, putting everything she had into it, her form tighter this time.

But Nolan was already one step ahead. He slid back, Ava's glove brushing his stomach before her momentum carried her forward. She over-rotated, her hands dropping low, her face wide open.

Nolan saw it instantly. His right hand snapped forward but he held back the power. The glove still caught her flush, knocking her off balance and sending her sprawling to the mat.

Ava hit the mat with a dull thud, her hands and knees catching her fall. Frustration burned across her face as she slammed a fist against the mat. "Damn it!"

Nolan leaned back, his arms outstretched in mock triumph. "Mercy!" he exclaimed, a wide grin plastered across his face.

Ava glared at him, her cheeks flush. "Shut up, asshole!" she shot back, though the faintest smile betrayed her.

Nolan chuckled as he extended a hand toward her. "Come on, get up." His tone softened.

She hesitated for a moment before grudgingly accepting his help. Nolan pulled her to her feet and immediately began unstrapping his headgear and gloves.

"I set you up for that one," he admitted with a grin as he pulled the headgear off and shook out some sweat. "Knew exactly where you were going. But hey," he said, his tone turning encouraging, "you rotated your hips perfectly. Had it landed, it would've been a killer. Might've even dropped me."

Ava smirked, wiping the sweat from her brow with the back of her glove. "Might've?" she said, arching an eyebrow. "Next time, I'll be helping you up."

Nolan laughed, patting her on the shoulder. "We'll see about that." She might not have the skill to beat him, yet, but her grit was undeniable and her progress impossible to ignore.

"Should we hit the cold plunge and sauna?" Ava asked as she unstrapped her gloves, flexing her fingers with a wince.

Nolan wiped sweat from his brow, letting out a breathless laugh. "You go ahead. I've got to hit the treadmill, make up for skipping the morning workout. Can't let myself off that easy."

Ava paused, her hands on her hips as she gave him a pointed look. "No, forget it," she said firmly, shaking her head. "I was just giving you a hard time earlier. You paid your price in here today. No need to overdo it."

Nolan glanced at her, his brow lifting as a smile tugged at the corner of his mouth. "Wow, Ava, look at you. You do have a heart after all." He pressed a hand to his chest in mock shock.

Her lips twitched into a grin, but she quickly masked it with a scowl. "Don't get used to it," she said before giving him a light jab to the stomach with her bare hand.

Nolan chuckled, but the humor faded as his expression turned sincere. "Listen," he started, his tone low and earnest now. "You were right. Missing the morning workout was not cool, and I can't let it slide. I appreciate you calling me out, even if it stung a little." His gaze held hers. "So, you go hit the spa, relax. I'm going to make up for it here. And you have my word, that'll be the last time I skip."

Ava blinked, caught off guard by the sincerity. Then she gave a small nod. "Fair enough, Corporal," she said, voice steady but with just enough amusement to show he wasn't completely off the hook.

She returned her gear to the shelves, the gym suddenly quieter without the sound of their strikes and footwork. At the door, she leaned against the frame with a smirk. "Hey, Nolan," she called out, her tone light but playful. "You'll be begging me for mercy one of these days."

Nolan's crooked smile answered her. "Oh, I'm sure I will. Just not anytime soon."

Ava huffed a laugh, pushing off the frame. "We'll see," she muttered, striding out with her ponytail swaying behind her.

The door hissed shut, leaving Nolan alone in the space. He stood still for a moment, letting the silence settle around him before walking over to the treadmill. As he started it up, the rhythmic sound of his footsteps filled the room, slamming steadily against the moving belt.

With every stride, his mind drifted back to the conversation he'd had with Ryder that morning in the bathroom. Each footfall against the treadmill felt like penance, a rhythmic reminder of why he was here, why he had taken the ribbing from Ava, and why he'd endured the kitchen cleanup without a word of complaint. But even as sweat dripped from his brow, soaking into his shirt, a small, quiet smile tugged at his lips.

He thought about Ryder. Her soft voice, her nervous smile, the way her hand had trembled slightly when she reached for his. He could still hear her words, clear as day, playing on a loop in his mind.

'I'm pregnant.'

The weight of those words had nearly knocked the air out of him, more than any punch Ava had thrown. All the extra work, the teasing, and even Jase's pointed lecture—it all paled in comparison to what was coming. A future that now felt so close and real, despite the chaos of their world.

They could have piled on every punishment they could think of, and none of it would have mattered. Not when he replayed the look in Ryder's eyes, that mixture of fear and excitement as she waited for his reaction. Not when he remembered the way he'd pulled her into his arms, his heart racing with a mix of joy and disbelief.

The treadmill beeped, signaling a new interval, but Nolan hardly noticed. His thoughts were miles away, back in that quiet bathroom, the sound of running water muffling their whispers. His smile deepened as he thought about the life they were creating together, the family they were about to become, who he was about to become.

Father.

The word felt heavy and light at the same time, a responsibility he never expected, but now couldn't imagine turning away from. They could throw every last task at him, every jab and critique, and he'd take it all in stride. Because in the end, it was all worth it.

For Ryder.
For their child.
For their future.
Now he had something real to fight for.

CHAPTER ELEVEN

A few days later, the group gathered in the living room to unwind. Jase and Olivia sat across from each other in the armchairs, Olivia with her legs curled beneath her, a book open on her lap she wasn't really reading.

Ava was sprawled out on one couch next to Damian, who sat upright, sketching idly in a notebook. Nolan sat alone on the other couch, leaning back with his arms crossed, staring off at nothing in particular.

"I'm so bored," Ava groaned, throwing her arms over her head dramatically and letting them flop back down. She stared at the ceiling as if waiting for it to crack open and bring something, anything, different.

"Ping-pong?" Olivia offered, flipping a page without looking up.

Ava sighed loudly. "Too lazy to move."

"Some cards or a board game?" Damian proposed, still focused on his sketch.

"You're all a bunch of cheats," Ava shot back, with a teasing bite.

Damian laughed, finally turning toward her. "Right. That's what it is."

Olivia tapped her book thoughtfully. "It's not movie night, but we could bump it up."

Ava yawned and waved her hand dismissively. "Nah, I'll just fall asleep. Don't want to waste it."

"Well, you've kinda shot down every option," Jase chimed in, leaning forward, elbows on his knees.

"I know. I'm just bored with all that. Same shit, different day," Ava complained, rolling her head to the side to look at Damian. "Got any exciting new ideas, oh wise one?"

"Sorry, fresh out," Damian said with a smirk, closing his notebook.

Just then, Ryder entered from the kitchen, carrying a plate of cookies fresh from the oven. The sweet, buttery scent filled the air, and every head turned. She wore a knowing smile as she set the plate on the coffee table.

"Here," Ryder said lightly. "Try a cookie. Maybe sugar will cure the existential boredom. I call them mini-me's."

Ava shot upright, snatching one without hesitation. "Ryder, you're officially my favorite person." She bit in, her face lighting up. "Oh my god, what's in these?"

Ryder sat beside Nolan, who had already reached for one. Her voice was coy, but her pulse hammered in her ears. "Just something special. You'll figure it out."

Damian grabbed one, chewing thoughtfully. "These are… really good. Pomegranate seeds?"

"Maybe," Ryder replied cryptically, her smile growing wider.

Olivia finally set her book aside and leaned forward, curiosity winning. "Alright, I'm intrigued. You don't bake unless there's a reason. What's the occasion?"

Ryder shrugged nonchalantly, though her heart was pounding in her chest. "No occasion. Just felt like doing something nice for everyone."

Her gaze slid to Nolan. He chewed quietly, the corners of his mouth curved in a private smile. Ryder's heart swelled. The moment was close, but she let the suspense linger just a little longer.

"That's it!" Ava blurted, sitting up so fast her voice cracked through the room.

Everyone's heads turned. Ryder froze mid-breath, her stomach dropping. For one terrifying instant, she thought Ava had pieced it together.

"It's almost the two-year anniversary!" Ava declared, grinning wide. "We should have another party!"

Ryder let out a subtle sigh, her shoulders sinking as her heartbeat slowed.

Jase leaned forward, his brows furrowing. "Whoa, hold on. I know we're all bored, but do you think that's a good idea? Look what happened last time."

Ava waved a dismissive hand, rolling her eyes. "Come on, Jase. That was different. We didn't have this." She gestured around the living room. "Ouro can't hear us in here anymore. As long as we keep it lowkey, she'll never know."

Olivia, who had been quietly enjoying her cookie, glanced at Jase. "I mean, she's not wrong," she said with a small shrug. "We've been smart about everything else. It's doable if we're careful."

"See? Olivia agrees," Ava said with a triumphant grin. "So, come on! Who's in?" She asked, nudging Damian in the ribs.

Damian raised a skeptical brow. "I don't know, Ava. I get wanting a distraction, but a party? That's asking for trouble."

"Exactly," Jase added, his tone firm. "Things have been going good. We're finally in a rhythm—no incidents, no unnecessary attention. Let's not give Ouro a reason to remind us who's in charge."

Ava groaned, slumping back into her seat. "You guys are no fun. Nolan—what about you? Don't tell me you're siding with these stiffs."

Nolan hesitated, shifting his gaze to Ryder. "I don't… that's not…" He faltered, his words trailing off as he struggled to find the right thing to say.

"It's a bad idea," Jase cut in, finishing for him.

Olivia sighed, setting her half eaten cookie down on the table. "Well, let's hear from Ryder." She turned to her, who had been uncharacteristically quiet. "What do you think? Party, or no party?"

Every gaze swung to her. Ryder's throat tightened, her heart racing as she realized the moment was slipping further from her control. She needed to find the courage she had when she walked in.

Her fingers curled against her knees. She dropped her eyes to the floor, drew a shaky breath, and forced the words out, quiet but unshakable. "I'm pregnant."

The room fell utterly silent. Even the hum of the vents seemed louder against the absence of words.

Ava, mid–eye roll, froze in place. Her mouth opened, then shut again before she finally blurted, "Wait… what?" She leaned forward, eyes wide, all trace of her usual bravado gone. "What did you just say?"

"I'm pregnant," Ryder repeated, stronger this time.

Her eyes shimmered as she looked around the room. "I wanted to tell you in a way that felt… special. Because this isn't just my baby. In a way, it's our baby. We've built this life together, and this child is going to need every one of us."

No one moved. Olivia's fingers tightened around the edge of her book, knuckles white. Jase straightened in his chair, eyes wide. Nolan sat frozen beside Ryder, jaw tense, like he'd been holding his breath for her.

It was Ava who finally broke. With a sudden squeal, she launched herself across the couch and nearly tackled Ryder in a hug. "This is insane! You're going to be a mom! We're going to be—oh my god! We're going to be aunts and uncles!"

Her outburst cracked the silence like glass. Olivia rose quickly, her face still stunned but softening into a rush of joy. "Ryder…" she breathed, crossing the room to hug her. "That's… that's incredible. Congratulations."

Damian smiled and leaned back in his seat, nodding his head in approval. "Congratulations."

Nolan slipped his hand into Ryder's, his face breaking into quiet pride. "I told you they'd be happy," he whispered, then raised his voice for the others. "We'll need all the help we can get… but I know we've got this."

Jase was silent, his eyes stayed fixed on Ryder, searching. Responsibility flickered in his features, the weight of what this meant pressing down.

But after a moment, his expression softened. He offered her a rare, genuine smile. "This is big," he said quietly. "But you're right. We're in this together. We'll make it work."

Ryder's breath caught as she scanned the faces of the only family she had left. Relief and joy washed over her in equal measure, tears blurring her vision. "Thank you," she whispered. "All of you. This baby is so lucky already."

Ava finally released Ryder and flopped back down, wiping her cheeks with the heel of her hand. Then she grinned fiercely.

"Okay, forget the two-year anniversary party. We're throwing a party for this. A baby shower! Don't even think about arguing with me, Jase."

Jase groaned, rubbing his face, though the smirk tugging at his lips betrayed him. "Yeah, because arguing with you ever works."

"I'll make the decorations!" Olivia burst out, her excitement spilling over now that the shock had broken. She clasped her hands together, her mind already racing. "Wait… do you know the gender yet?"

Ryder shook her head and glanced toward Damian. "No, not yet. I wasn't ready to know, but Damian does."

All eyes turned to Damian, who suddenly became the center of attention. Ava smacked him lightly on the arm. "Oh my God, how long have you known? You've been keeping this kind of excitement from us?"

Damian smiled, raising his hands defensively. "Ryder came to me a few days ago, and we did an ultrasound. But it was up to her when she was ready to share the news. Although…" He gave Ryder a teasing look. "You all would've started to notice soon enough. She's about sixteen weeks along."

Jase's brow furrowed, his expression turning serious. "Wait, sixteen weeks? You just found out recently? Ryder, why didn't you go to Damian earlier?"

Ryder's smile faltered, her eyes dropping to the floor as she shifted uncomfortably. "At first, I wasn't sure," she admitted softly. "When I missed my first period, I just shrugged it off as stress. But the next one… I started to panic. I didn't know how everyone would react, how we could make this work. I…I just didn't know what to do." She glanced up at Nolan, her voice trembling slightly. "I was scared."

Nolan immediately wrapped an arm around her, pulling her close. "You don't have to be scared anymore," he whispered.

Ryder took a steadying breath, her voice growing stronger. "I finally worked up the courage to see Damian. I needed to make sure everything was okay, that the baby was healthy. But I wasn't ready to know the gender. That would've made it feel too real, and I had yet to tell Nolan."

She looked up at him, her eyes shimmering with emotion. "I wanted to tell him first, and after that, I just needed to find the right way to share it with all of you."

Ava's eyes narrowed playfully as she looked between Ryder and Nolan. "Wait… is that why you two skipped the morning workout the other day?"

Nolan nodded, a sheepish grin tugging at his lips. "Yeah. She told me the night before, in the greenhouse. It hit me like a truck. I couldn't think straight. The next morning, we used the bathroom while the showers were running so we could talk it through."

He turned to Ryder, pressing a gentle kiss to her forehead. "We needed that time to figure out how to handle everything."

Ava looked down, her face flushing with guilt. "Nolan, I'm so sorry." She sighed, her voice softer than usual. "I gave you hell about that, and meanwhile…you were dealing with this." Her voice softened, rare sincerity threading through. "I feel like an ass."

Nolan smiled faintly. "Don't. You couldn't have known. We're all just trying to do our best."

Damian leaned back, a faint smile playing on his lips. "Honestly, I'm glad you told me when you did, Ryder. Everything looks good so far. But going forward, you're going to need regular check-ups—and I mean regular."

"You hear that?" Nolan said, giving her a pointed look. "Doctor's orders."

Ryder let out a soft laugh and nodded. "I hear you. I promise I'll be better. I just needed time…to wrap my head around it all."

"Well, now you're not alone," Olivia said, her voice warm and reassuring. "We're here for you, Ryder. And for this baby."

Jase, quiet until now, finally spoke. His serious expression eased into a small nod. "She's right. We'll shoulder it together. Whatever it takes."

Ava grinned, her excitement bubbling up again. "Oh my god, I'm so excited! A gender reveal and a baby shower! We've got so much to do now."

The room filled with chuckles, the earlier tension finally easing. Ryder looked around at the faces of her makeshift family, warmth flooding her chest. For the first time since she'd whispered the words to Nolan, the fear loosened its grip. Whatever came next, they would face it together.

"Well," Ryder began, her voice soft but steady, "as much as I appreciate all the excitement and enthusiasm… maybe we can save the planning for tomorrow? This announcement took everything out of me, and I think I'm ready for bed." She gave them a tired but genuine smile.

Olivia immediately nodded, her tone gentle. "Of course. We'll brainstorm tomorrow. You just focus on getting some rest, you've earned it."

Ryder's gaze drifted to Nolan. He met her eyes with a quiet nod, and together they rose. Before leaving, Ryder turned back, her hand lingering against the doorframe. "I know this is going to bring extra stress for all of us," she said, her eyes shimmering with emotion. "And I'm sorry for that. But… thank you. Thank you for meeting me with support instead of fear. It means more than I can say."

For a heartbeat, no one spoke. Then Ava broke the tension with her usual fire, waving a hand dismissively. "Stress? Please. I can't wait to be an aunt! Now get some rest before I start shouting out baby names."

The group laughed softly, the heaviness of the moment easing into warmth. Nolan gave Ava a knowing wink before placing a steady hand at the small of Ryder's back. With that quiet, protective gesture, he guided her out of the living room.

The rest of the group sat in silence, the atmosphere thick with a mix of emotions as they each processed the life-altering announcement. Their eyes lingered on the empty doorway, as if the weight of what had been shared still lingered in the room.

It wasn't the silence of shock anymore, it was the silence of reckoning. Of understanding that their world had just shifted, and nothing would be the same.

Olivia was the first to speak, her voice barely above a whisper. "A baby…" She pressed a hand to her cheek, staring at the floor. "It's not just about us anymore. It's about creating a life here for someone who never chose this."

Ava nodded, her usual brash energy tempered by something more thoughtful. "And that's what scares me. We can barely keep ourselves sane half the time. How the hell do we raise a baby in concrete walls and recycled air?" Her eyes drifted to the others. "This changes things. Like, it's not just about survival anymore. It's about building something better. For that kid. For all of us."

Olivia stared off into the distance. "We're going to have to adjust a lot of things. Food rations, space, resources. A baby changes the entire dynamic of how we function here." Her mind jumped tracks, her voice quickening. "We'll need a crib, blankets, baby clothes. " Her eyes widened as she looked at everyone. "Oh my god, what are we going to do about diapers? Bottles? Toys— a baby needs toys!"

Ava leaned back, her expression grim. "Great, Liv. Just throw all the baby panic at us at once. What if something goes wrong? What if—."

"Alright! Let's reel it in for a second." Jase rubbed his face, letting out a long, tired breath. "Yes, there's a lot we need to figure out, and those are all valid points, but…" He gave Olivia a pointed look as she opened her mouth to add more. "But that baby's coming whether we're ready or not. We've faced worse, and we've always found a way. Tomorrow, we'll start making a list of everything we need—supplies, plans, contingencies. But there's no sense in getting worked up about it tonight."

Jase's voice dropped, heavy with unease. "My biggest concern is Ouro. There's no hiding this. And I don't know how she'll see it. A baby could be viewed as a disruption to the mission."

Damian leaned back in his seat, a thoughtful look crossing his face. "Knowing Ouro, she probably already knows. She's been tracking everything in this shelter since day one. Hell, she probably knew Ryder was pregnant before Ryder did. I'd say as long as we stay focused, keep up with our responsibilities, and work together to make this work, she won't see it as a threat."

Ava crossed her arms and raised an eyebrow. "Yeah, but what if she does? You know how she can get when something doesn't fit into her precious algorithm."

Damian shook his head. "She's an AI, not a dictator. Ouro exists to keep this place running—it's mission is to keep us alive. If we show her that we're managing this responsibly, there's no cause for concern."

Olivia frowned, her fingers drumming against the chair arm. "Still… we'd be fools to assume her approval. If she decides this baby destabilizes the mission, it won't matter what we want."

Jase leaned forward. "That's why we need to stay united on this. Whatever happens, we deal with it together. This is bigger than any one of us now."

They all nodded in agreement, the weight of their collective responsibility settling heavily on their shoulders. Each of them understood how much more vigilant they would need to be—not just for the group's survival, but for the fragile new life they were now protecting.

After a moment, Jase's brows furrowed, and he glanced over at Damian with a look of growing concern. "Damian… have you ever delivered a baby before?"

Damian scrunched his nose, inhaling deeply. "About that…" He shifted in his seat, rubbing the back of his neck awkwardly. "I was going to wait until tomorrow to bring this up, but since you asked. No, I haven't. Let's just say I'm very glad I've got six months to prepare."

Ava's jaw dropped. "You're kidding me. Tell me you're kidding."

"Wish I was." Damian gave her a tight, sheepish smile. "But hey, I've got plenty of textbooks, and I'm turning this place into a crash course in obstetrics. My biggest concern right now is breaking the news to Ryder that we don't have an epidural, so she's going to have to tough it out the natural way."

The air was sucked out of the room. Olivia's eyes went wide, Jase turned pale. Ava slapped a hand over her mouth. "Oh my god."

"Oh, it gets better," Damian added. "I'm going to need an assistant. Delivering a baby needs a second pair of hands, so one of you gets to learn the ropes with me."

Ava recoiled instantly, shaking her head so hard her pony-tail whipped. "Oh, hell no. Don't even look at me."

Damian smiled. "Oh come on, Ava. Think of it as a challenge. You love challenges, right?"

"Not ones that involve… uh, blood, and babies coming out of places I don't even want to think about!" Ava shot back, crossing her arms tightly over her chest.

Jase pinched the bridge of his nose, muttering under his breath, "This just keeps getting better."

Olivia tilted her head, her expression thoughtful, calculating. "I'll do it."

The room stilled.

"You will?" Damian blinked.

Olivia nodded, her voice steady. "I've worked under pressure my whole life. I'm not squeamish, and I can follow orders. And it's not like we have a lot of options. So, if it helps Ryder and the baby, I'm in."

Damian clapped his hands together. "Perfect. Welcome to the team, Liv."

Their eyes met—doctor and apprentice bound by necessity.

The others sank back into their chairs, the air heavier than before. Whatever joy they'd felt at Ryder's announcement was now tempered by a sobering truth—survival had just gotten more complicated, and this time it wasn't just their own lives at stake.

***

Ryder lay on her side, staring into the quiet darkness of their room. The weight of the day still pressed on her chest, but there was comfort in Nolan's presence. When he emerged from the bathroom, silhouetted briefly in the dim light, the tension in her shoulders eased.

He slipped under the blanket without a word, curling against her. His arm wrapped protectively around her waist, pulling her close until their bodies fit together like puzzle pieces. For a while, they simply lay there, sharing warmth, letting the silence wrap around them like a cocoon.

Finally, Ryder's voice broke the stillness, barely more than a whisper. "Do you think they were really happy?"

Nolan hesitated, not because he didn't have an answer, but because he wanted to choose the right one. He took a deep breath, his chest rising and falling against her back.

"I do," he said at last. "They're worried. Just like us. But underneath that? Yeah. They were genuinely happy. How could they not be? A baby is…hope. Proof we're still alive. Still fighting. Still human."

A faint smile curved her lips, but it faded as quickly as it came. She turned just enough to glimpse him over her shoulder, her hazel eyes glimmering with fear. "Are they going to resent us?"

Nolan's brow furrowed. His arm tightened around her. "Why would you even think that?" he murmured, low and steady.

Her gaze dropped. The thoughts she had buried finally surfaced. "Because this isn't just about us anymore. It changes everything for them. More mouths to feed, more risks. And what if something happens because of us? What if they think we're selfish for bringing a baby into this world—into this life?"

Nolan's hand moved to her stomach, resting gently over the small swell that had yet to truly show. His touch was grounding, his voice filled with quiet conviction. "Ryder, no one's going to resent us. They might be scared, sure. But they care about you. About us. And this baby…it's not just ours. It's a part of this family. Everyone in that room tonight wasn't just reacting to the news. They were stepping up. For us. For the future."

Ryder closed her eyes, letting his words sink in, but the knot in her chest didn't fully loosen. "But what if we fail?" she whispered. "What if we lose everything?"

Nolan pressed his forehead to the back of her head. His voice was firm, unwavering. "We won't. We'll make it work, one way or another. We've already survived so much. And now... now we've got something worth fighting for."

A tear slipped from the corner of Ryder's eye, disappearing into the pillow. She reached down, intertwining her fingers with Nolan's where they rested on her stomach. "I'm just...scared."

"I know." His voice cracked as he pressed a kiss to her hair. "I am too. But you're not in this alone. We're in it together. Always."

Ryder shifted, turning until her forehead met Nolan's. They stayed like that, breathing together, clinging to each other—sharing fear, sharing hope in the quiet.

"Always," Ryder whispered back.

CHAPTER TWELVE

The next morning, the crew gathered for breakfast. The room felt lighter, a newfound sense of purpose buzzing among them as they ate. Laughter punctuated the meal, and for the first time in months, the weight of everything seemed a little easier to bear.

As the last plates were pushed aside, Olivia tapped her tablet awake. "Alright," she said, cutting through the chatter, "I've started making a list of everything we need to tackle. If I've missed something, speak up." She glanced around the table.

"Let's hear it," Jase said, lifting his coffee and keeping his eyes on her.

"First on the list—food supply. We need to do a full inventory—figure out what we have. We'll also need to boost greenhouse production. This way we'll have a surplus for the later stages of her pregnancy, when she's too tired to keep up with it. Plus, it'll cover the downtime after she gives birth."

Ryder nodded. "Makes sense. I'll get started on maximizing the soil beds and optimizing the crop rotation."

Jase set his mug down, leaning slightly toward her. "I'll be joining you."

Ryder blinked, a slight crease forming between her brows. "What do you mean?"

"Think of it as job shadowing," Jase replied, his tone calm but firm. "If something happens, God forbid, you shouldn't be in there by yourself. And let's face it, someone else needs to know the day-to-day routine for when you need to step back. The greenhouse is all of our lifeline. We can't afford to have its production fall behind. And if it ever stops..." His words trailed off, the silence that followed carrying the weight of what he didn't need to say.

Olivia's stylus stilled against her tablet, her eyes flicking up to meet Jase's. Ava shifted in her seat, arms crossing tight against her chest, as if bracing against the thought. Nolan's jaw tightened, his gaze dropping to the table. Even Damian, usually composed, stopped mid-sip and set his mug down.

Ryder swallowed, her features softening even as the tremor in her smile betrayed how deeply his words struck her. "I'd be happy to have you. Maybe you'll even develop a green thumb."

"We'll see," Jase replied, and though the grin tugging at his lips looked like humor, there was no mistaking the weight behind it.

Olivia cleared her throat, bringing their focus back to her. "Next on the list—baby items. Here's what I have so far: bottles, a crib, clothes, blankets, pacifiers, a baby carrier or bouncer, diapers, and a breast pump. I'm sure there's more, but these feel like the essentials."

Nolan, who had been listening intently, chimed in. "I'll handle the crib. I can repurpose some furniture from Ryder's room, she sleeps in mine anyway. Should be able to craft up something nice in the workshop."

"Perfect," Olivia said, adding a quick note to her list.

Ava leaned back in her chair, arms crossed confidently. "I'll take care of the bottles, pacifiers, and breast pump. The 3D printer should handle most of it, and I've got liquid silicone for the softer parts. Shouldn't be an issue."

"Great," Olivia replied, glancing at Ryder for input.

Ryder hesitated, her hands resting protectively over her stomach. A shadow of concern crossed her face as she looked toward Damian. "What if I can't breastfeed?" she asked quietly. "My mother couldn't, she had lactation insufficiency. What if it's the same for me?"

The shift in the room was immediate. Damian straightened, his expression calm and steady, the kind of reassurance only he could bring. "Ryder, just because your mother struggled doesn't mean you will. Genetics can play a role, but it isn't a guarantee.

We'll monitor closely during your checkups, and I'll be right there every step of the way."

She bit her lip, her worry still etched in the curve of her brows.

Damian continued, more deliberate now. "That said, I've already thought about contingencies. If breastfeeding isn't an option, I'll work on creating a formula. We've got powdered milk, sugar, multivitamins—I can refine a mixture to meet the baby's needs. We'll be ready either way. This is not something you need to lose sleep over."

Ryder exhaled slowly, her shoulders easing. "Thank you," she whispered, gratitude breaking through her anxiety.

The reality pressed in, their fragile world wasn't designed for babies, and even the smallest complications felt enormous.

Olivia broke the silence, her tone purposeful. "Okay. That leaves clothes, blankets, and diapers." She turned to Ryder with a small smile. "I'm no expert with a needle, but I'll help. We're going to need a mountain of cloth diapers, aren't we?"

Ryder's expression softened, warmth lighting her eyes. "Yes, we are. And I'd love your help. Sewing isn't hard once you get the hang of it. I'll teach you the shortcuts." Her face brightened, excitement flickering through the heaviness. "We can make little onesies, matching blankets—oh, it'll be fun."

Olivia laughed, leaning back. "Fun for you, maybe. I'll be proud if I can manage a running stitch."

"That's the beauty of it," Ryder said, her laugh soft and contagious. "It doesn't have to be perfect, it just has to be made with love. And between all of us, this baby is going to have more than enough of that."

Olivia smiled with a hand over her chest. "He or she definitely will. Well, that's all I have on the list for now. Anyone have anything else?"

"Ah, yeah. And it pertains to what you just said." Ava exclaimed with an exaggerated look. "When are we doing the gender reveal? I want to know if I'm going to have a niece, or a nephew!"

Jase looked around the table, contemplating. "How about on the two year anniversary? That'll give us a few weeks to get to work and check some of these things off the list. It'll also be a nice way to welcome in the start of our third year."

Everyone nodded in agreement and the room seemed lighter, as if the task ahead wasn't just another challenge but an opportunity to create something together, a small spark of joy in their meager world.

As chairs scraped back and dishes clinked, Damian's voice cut through the movement. "Hang on a second." He looked to Ryder and smiled, then to Nolan. "Would you like to see your child."

The room froze.

Nolan's eyes went wide, a flush creeping across his face. His hand reached instinctively for Ryder's, their fingers locking together. "More than anything," he said, his voice low but trembling with awe.

Ava practically leapt out of her seat, spinning toward them. "Can I see too? Please...please! After you, obviously, but... please?" Her grin stretched ear to ear, her excitement barely contained.

Ryder turned her head toward Nolan, sharing a quiet smile, then back to Ava. "Yes," she said softly, emotion threading her words. Her eyes lifted to Olivia and Jase as well. "You all can."

***

Ryder lay back on the examination table, her shirt lifted just enough to bare her stomach. The med bay's soft light cast a warm glow across her skin, outlining the calm determination on her face.

Nolan stood at her side, one hand resting on her shoulder while the other clasped hers tightly. His thumb brushed absently over the back of her hand, but the faint tremor in his legs betrayed the storm of anticipation coursing through him.

Sensing his unease, Ryder tilted her head toward him and gave his hand a firm squeeze. "It's okay," she whispered, her hazel eyes steady on his.

Damian wheeled over in his chair, pulling on his medical gloves, the faint snap of latex punctuating the moment. Setting his tablet beside Ryder, Damian plugged in the transducer and adjusted the screen for all to see.

"Just getting prepped," he said, his tone calm but with a flicker of excitement beneath it. He tested the device against his forearm, the screen lighting up with faint static. Satisfied, he glanced at Ryder with a reassuring smile. "Ready for the worst part?"

Ryder grinned, nodding with enthusiasm. Nolan stiffened. "Worst part? What's going to happen?" His voice cracked as his eyes darted between them.

Ryder let out a soft laugh, shaking her head. "Relax, babe. He's talking about the gel—it's just cold and a little weird, that's all."

Nolan exhaled hard, relief flooding his features, though his grip on her hand stayed tight.

Damian offered a small grin as he squeezed a generous swirl of gel onto Ryder's stomach. "No danger here. Just the first introduction."

The gel spread cool and slick across her skin, making Ryder shiver. Damian lowered the transducer, moving it in slow, steady circles.

The screen flickered—shadows, static—and then, almost like magic, the image sharpened. A small, grainy form emerged from the haze.

Ryder's breath caught. "Is that…?" she whispered, her voice breaking on the word.

"That's your baby," Damian confirmed softly. He angled the screen so Nolan could see.

Nolan leaned in, eyes wide, lips parting but no words escaping. Awe hollowed his chest, leaving him breathless.

Ryder squeezed his hand again, tears brimming in her eyes. "That's our baby."

Damian shifted the transducer, pointing to a faint flicker at the center. "There—that flutter. That's the heartbeat. Strong and steady."

The rhythmic thump filled the med bay, steady and sure. The sound seemed impossibly loud, echoing through the sterile walls, reverberating straight into their chests.

Nolan's eyes shimmered, his voice breaking as he looked down at Ryder. "It's real. That's really… ours."

Her nod was small but certain, her tears spilling freely now. "Yeah. It is."

Damian gave them a moment, his expression softening as he watched. Then he nodded at the screen. "Everything looks perfect—size, heartbeat, no complications. Ryder, you're doing great."

Nolan let out a shaky laugh, relief flooding through his voice. "Thank you, Damian. Thank you."

Damian smiled. "It's what I'm here for, but you're welcome. I'll save these images for your records, and I can print a copy for you to keep."

"Yes, please," Ryder said quickly, her excitement breaking through the tears.

As Damian worked at the tablet, Nolan bent down and kissed her forehead, his voice low against her skin. "You're amazing."

Ryder smiled up at him, her eyes glistening. "We're amazing."

For a moment, the weight of the shelter disappeared. The flickering screen, the steady heartbeat, and the fragile spark of new life filled the room with something the walls of the Ouroboros could never contain—hope.

Damian pulled the transducer away, a smirk tugging at the corner of his lips as he glanced at Nolan. "Well… should we?"

Nolan rolled his eyes, grinning. "Honestly? I kind of want to see how long it takes her to barge in." He shot a look at the door, laughing under his breath.

Ryder nudged him with her elbow, equal parts amused and exasperated. "Don't torture her. She's probably been pacing holes in the floor. Go get the others so they can see."

Nolan sighed dramatically and started for the door. Before he reached it, Damian called out, "Careful, her ear's probably pressed right up against it."

Nolan smirked and raised his voice. "Remove your face from the door, Miss Impatient!"

The door slid open with a soft whoosh, and there was Ava, exactly as predicted, her ear inches from the frame. She froze for half a second, then threw her hands up like she'd been wronged.

"Finally!" she exclaimed, brushing past Nolan without hesitation. "Do you know how long I've been out there? Days, probably. Now, let's see that baby!" She made a beeline straight for Ryder and the glowing screen.

Olivia followed close behind, her expression caught between apology and amusement. "What can I say?" she said with a shrug, a sly twinkle in her eye. "You know how she gets."

Jase lingered at the doorway, resting a steady hand on Nolan's shoulder. His tone was dry, but his smirk betrayed him. "You're lucky you opened up when you did," he said. "I was running out of creative threats to stop them from storming in."

Nolan laughed, shaking his head. "Thanks. I wanted to see how long we could go, but apparently, that wasn't very nice." He motioned toward Ryder, now flanked by Ava and Olivia, both leaning in towards the monitor. "Come on. Come meet the baby."

"Gladly," Jase said, stepping inside.

Ava's finger shot toward the screen, her eyes wide. "Look at that! Oh my gosh, Ryder, your baby's heartbeat! That's crazy." She grabbed Ryder's hand with sudden tenderness, giving it a squeeze. "You're growing a tiny little human."

Ryder laughed, her cheeks flushing at Ava's enthusiasm.

"I can't believe we're going to have a baby here," Olivia murmured, her eyes locked on the tiny flickering shape on the screen. Her voice carried a mix of awe and disbelief, as though the idea hadn't fully rooted yet. "It feels… surreal. In the middle of all this chaos, we still get this. A new life."

Her eyes lingered on the screen, wide with wonder, but then slowly drifted to Jase. There was something unspoken in her expression, a flicker of vulnerability that passed too quickly to name. Her gaze narrowed, thoughtful and searching, as if trying to read his reaction.

Jase stepped closer to the monitor, his arms folding tightly across his chest. His jaw clenched for a moment before softening. His eyes stayed fixed on the screen as he spoke, voice low and steady. "You're right. It's surreal." The words held more weight than he let show.

After a beat, he turned to Ryder and Nolan. His expression eased, his tone warming just enough to let something through. "But it's also a reminder. A reminder there's still hope. Still something worth fighting for."

Ryder lifted her head, hazel eyes full of gratitude. She gave him a small, genuine nod. Nolan, though, tightened his grip on her hand, his shoulders squaring as if bracing against the world. "We're going to give this kid the best chance possible," he said firmly, his voice thick with emotion.

Ryder's smile widened, her free hand moving instinctively to rest on her stomach. "I know we will," she said quietly, her confidence lifting the room. "All of us. This baby has an amazing family."

Jase's lips twitched at the corners, almost forming a smile, but he caught himself and nodded instead. He stepped back slightly, giving the couple their moment, though his gaze lingered on the monitor for just a second longer than necessary.

Meanwhile, Olivia's eyes remained on him, her expression unreadable. Her arms folded, fingers tracing the edge of her sleeve as though she had words pressing to be spoken, but she swallowed them back and turned her eyes to the screen instead.

Damian finally spoke from the side, his voice gentle but sure. "This kid's already lucky. They're coming into the world with a team of people who would move mountains for them."

"You're damn right about that," Ava blurted, her grin wide as she leaned closer to the screen. "Now, tell me—does the baby look more like Ryder or Nolan?"

Damian raised an eyebrow, smirking. "It's a little early for that, Ava"

Ryder shook her head, laughing along. "It doesn't matter, as long as it's healthy, that's all I care about."

Ava grinned, nudging Olivia, and whispered. "It totally does. And I'm praying for Ryders genes."

The room filled with a lighthearted laughter, and in that moment, their uncertain future finally had a purpose. They were no longer just survivors, they were a family. Brought together by unimaginable circumstances, but now bound by something far deeper.

***

Olivia stood alone on the upper level, her arms resting lightly on the cold railing. Below her, the Ficus tree stretched toward the artificial light, its glossy leaves catching the glow.

Her gaze was fixed on it, but her eyes stared right through it to something only she could see. She exhaled slowly, her thoughts swirling like the faint breeze of the air circulation system around her. Laughter still drifted faintly down the wing from the med bay behind her, but her gaze didn't break. She needed a moment, just her and the tree.

Her fingers tapped absently against the railing as her shoulders sagged. The weight of the moment, and perhaps more, settling over her. The Ficus tree, a symbol of life, seemed almost mocking in its resilience. She envied it in that moment, its quiet strength, its ability to grow and thrive no matter the circumstances.

"Couldn't have picked a better view," Jase's voice came from behind her, low and easy.

Olivia startled but didn't turn. He stepped up beside her, close enough for his shoulder to brush hers as he leaned on the railing.

"Guess it's the only view," she said with a dry little laugh.

"Still," Jase murmured, eyes on the tree, "not bad for a bunker."

They stood there in silence for a moment, faint artificial chirps filling the gaps. Olivia glanced sideways again, catching the edge of his profile—the set of his jaw, the faint weariness around his eyes—softened now in the quiet moment.

"That was something, huh," she said at last. "The ultrasound."

Jase nodded slowly. "Yeah. Seeing that little thing... in the middle of all this..." His jaw tightened, then eased again. "I never thought I'd see something like that. It's easy to forget what life's supposed to look like when it's not just about enduring."

Olivia let his words settle over her, the truth of them striking deeper than she'd like to admit. She leaned her chin on her hand, fingers brushing her lips. "It's weird, isn't it?" she said softly. "A baby. Here, of all places. It feels like hope. Proof there's more to life than just making it to the next day."

Jase shifted, turning to watch her instead of the tree. His usual guarded look had slipped, replaced with something gentler. "It's more than hope," he said. "It's proof we don't have to give everything up."

Her brow furrowed, her gaze catching his. "What do you mean?"

He hesitated, fingers curling tighter around the railing. "I mean… we've spent so long focused on what we can't do. What we shouldn't do. Like letting ourselves want anything more than survival would somehow ruin everything. But seeing that baby…" His voice faltered, balanced between caution and longing.

Olivia turned toward him, searching his face as he continued.

"Maybe we're wrong," Jase said finally, quieter now. "Maybe we can do both. Stick to the goal…but not lose ourselves in the process."

Her lips parted, but no words came out. The air between them felt heavier now, like the moment had shifted into something neither of them fully knew how to navigate. She looked back at the Ficus tree, her heart beating a little faster.

"I guess it's scary," she said at last. "Letting yourself want more. Hope for more. What if you lose it? What if it all goes wrong?"

Jase let out a short laugh, though there wasn't much humor in it. "Yeah. It is scary." He glanced at her, his voice dropping lower. "But maybe… it's worth the risk."

Silence fell again, but it wasn't empty. It was weighted, their unsaid words crowding the space between them. Olivia felt the pull of his presence, the warmth radiating off him despite the careful distance they always kept. She stole a glance sideways, and found he was already watching her.

For a moment, it felt like everything else disappeared. The hum of the facility, the steady glow of the lights, the weight of the world on their shoulders. It was just them.

Jase's lips twitched into the faintest hint of a smile as they stared into each other's eyes. Their eyes said everything their words couldn't.

And then—

"I cannot wait to hold that baby!" Ava's voice shattered the moment as she barreled into them, throwing her arms around both Jase and Olivia in an exuberant hug.

Olivia let out a soft laugh, lighter than she expected, though something in her chest ached as if she was mourning the moment. She caught Jase's eyes over Ava's shoulder, still heavy with everything left unsaid.

"Yeah," Olivia murmured, her voice steadier now. "I can't wait either."

Ava released them from her hug, stepping back with her usual energy practically vibrating off her. "We've got so much to do, so much to get ready. I'm too excited to stand still, I need to burn this energy off!"

Jase hesitated, glancing at Olivia once more. "Yeah, that's a good idea," he said, straightening and shoving his hands into his pockets. "We should all get to work. I should see if Ryder is ready to show me her sanctum."

Olivia gave a small nod, her lips pressing together in a faint smile. "That sounds like a good idea," she said quietly, watching as Jase turned and walked away. His footsteps echoed faintly down the corridor, growing softer with every step.

As Jase disappeared into the med bay, Ava turned on her heel toward Olivia, her sharp eyes narrowing. "Did I interrupt something?"

Olivia blinked, caught off guard, heat rising in her cheeks. "No, not at all," she said quickly, forcing an easy smile. "We were just… in awe of the baby. That's all."

Ava's grin snapped back into place, her skepticism dissolving into raw excitement. "I know, right? Just a tiny little thing on the screen, and it's already the cutest baby I've ever seen. Just wait until we know the gender! Oh my god, why am I still standing here? I've got so much to do—so much to make. Only three weeks away!"

She practically bounced down the corridor, her voice fading as she disappeared around the corner. "I hope it's a girl!"

As Ava vanished, her smile slowly faded, and she turned back toward the Ficus tree. The branches swayed gently, as if beckoning her to lean on their quiet resilience.

Her gaze settled on the tree, though her focus was somewhere far beyond it again. The charged silence Jase left behind still clung to her skin, an invisible thread pulled taut. Something had shifted, though she couldn't name it.

For the first time in a long time, Olivia let herself wonder what it would mean to want more. To reach for something beyond survival. The image of the baby still glowed in her mind, fragile and full of promise, sparking a reminder she hadn't dared to feel.

Life wasn't just about enduring.

It was about living. About feeling.

She exhaled softly, the corners of her lips twitching into the faintest smile as her fingers gripped the railing a little tighter.

Maybe, just maybe, there was room for more in this world after all.

CHAPTER THIRTEEN

The group gathered three weeks later beneath the Ficus tree on the lower level. Its base had been transformed into a small haven of celebration. Normally, they would have hidden such a gathering away in the living room, safe from Ouro's constant surveillance. But this was Ryder's day, and no place felt more fitting than here—on the grass, surrounded by greenery, where for a moment it almost felt like the outside world. Besides, Ouro already knew. She always knew.

Blankets and pillows formed a wide circle around the base of the tree, inviting them closer together. At its center stood a makeshift table, a plain sheet draped across it, made beautiful by the care woven into its details. Jars of rosemary and lavender filled the air with a calming fragrance, their green sprigs standing like small guardians between bursts of wildflowers Olivia had arranged, vibrant and defiant in their color.

The table held a modest but thoughtful spread of food. A large bowl of salad, bursting with leafy greens, tossed with cherry tomatoes and radishes. Smaller dishes of nuts, dried fruit, chips, and a plate of buttery cookies—rare enough to feel decadent. While a pitcher of citrus and mint-infused water sparkled under the glow of the lights.

But it was Ava's creation that gave the room its wonder. She had spent nights twisting copper wire and soldering LEDs into place, stringing them through the Ficus branches until they glowed like fireflies in the dark. The cascade of warm light bathed the tree and their circle below in a golden shimmer, transforming the cold bunker into something softer, almost magical. Ava had shrugged off their praise, but everyone could see the pride in her work—the way her fingers lingered on the wires gave it away.

The scene was almost otherworldly, as if the Ficus itself had grown into something sacred. Its leaves shimmered under the glow, no longer just a plant in a steel cage but a living beacon, quietly holding their hope. It was a perfect reflection of Ryder herself—natural, nurturing, and brimming with life. For a little while, laughter and soft conversation filled the air, and the bunker felt less like a prison and more like a home.

Earlier that morning, the group had gathered once again in front of the countdown clock, as had become their tradition now. It was a ritual they had come to rely on, even if it carried a bittersweet weight.

The cold, glowing blue numbers flipped over to Day 730—two years in The Ouroboros. No celebrations, no fanfare—just the stark reality of their seclusion. A quiet reminder of what they had endured and what still lay ahead.

The first anniversary had been somber, met with silence that pressed down heavier than the earth above them. Back then, survival had felt fragile, uncertain, as if every day was just borrowed time. Even making it a single year seemed like tempting fate

But now, standing in that same spot, they felt a shift. The silence wasn't suffocating—it was steady, almost reverent. There was warmth in their closeness, a quiet spark of hope in the air. They weren't just clinging to existence anymore. They were beginning to live.

Jase had broken the silence with a simple, steady voice. "Two years," he said, his words carrying more weight than the numbers on the clock. "We've made it this far. We'll make it another."

The quiet reverence that had followed was no longer filled with doubt. His words had been met with quiet nods and murmurs of agreement, a small but powerful acknowledgment of how far they had come and how far they would go.

Now, as they settled beneath the Ficus tree, the memory of that glowing clock felt distant—sterile numbers replaced by the warm light Ava had strung through the branches, the hum of machinery replaced by laughter and the rustle of leaves. Where the clock had marked time survived, the tree marked something greater—the possibility of a future.

This wasn't a party. It was a declaration. Even in the depths of a bunker built to outlast the end of the world, they could still create moments of beauty, love, and joy. Ryder's pregnancy, their bond, the fragile ember of hope they kept alive—it all mattered. They mattered.

Tonight, under the tree's golden glow, it wasn't just a gender reveal. It was a reminder that life, as messy, imperfect, and stubborn as it is, was still worth cherishing.

***

The group sat in a circle on the blankets and pillows, their faces glowing in the soft shimmer of lights. Jase, Olivia, Ava, and Damian leaned close together on one side, laughter and teasing spilling easily between them, while Ryder and Nolan sat opposite, Nolan's arm resting behind her in a gesture that was equal parts protective and relaxed. Just behind them, a pile of gifts had been arranged neatly on a blanket. Each item crafted with care, the result of countless hours of work and thought.

Ava's corner of the workshop had become a storm of clutter—silicone molds, 3D-printed parts, wires, scraps of scavenged plastic scattered across every surface. She grumbled constantly, muttering at stubborn joints and failed molds, but the gleam in her eyes betrayed her excitement. The result was a set of sleek, functional bottles, pacifiers, and even a surprisingly efficient breast pump. But her triumph was the baby bouncer—a cushioned seat, sturdy frame, and dangling toys she'd soldered together herself.

When she revealed it, the group had stared in stunned silence. Ava had shrugged, feigning nonchalance. "It's not rocket science. It's just… baby science." But the flush on her cheeks and the way she lingered when Ryder hugged her told a different story.

Nolan's gift was quieter, but no less powerful. His hands, more used to weapons than tools, had turned Ryder's unused bedroom furniture into a crib. He sanded every edge smooth, built it solid and simple, practical to the core. But he couldn't resist adding a personal touch. Carved on the headboard, a small Ouroboros symbol.

Ryder's breath caught when she saw it. She traced the carving with trembling fingers, tears brimming in her eyes. "It's perfect," she whispered.

Nolan shifted, his usual confidence faltering into something softer. "It'll keep the baby safe," he said, voice low and rough, as if the words themselves were a vow.

Olivia had taken up sewing for the first time in her life, a skill she never imagined she'd need. With Ryder's patient guidance—threading needles, tying knots, stitching fabric—her early attempts were clumsy, her stitches uneven, and her frustration plain. But she kept at it. Over time, her confidence grew, and together they built a small collection of baby clothes, blankets, and cloth diapers.

Olivia added her own flair, stitching tiny patterns into the fabric. Her proudest creation was a miniature version of their black Ouroboros uniforms, complete with the golden circle emblem. When she revealed it, the group erupted into laughter, the sheer absurd cuteness melting their hearts.

Jase, ever practical and resourceful, had turned his attention to making a mobile for the crib. Using lightweight materials from Ava's workshop and 3D printed pieces, he crafted something that was as functional as it was beautiful. Tiny stars, planets, and even a small blue Earth spun gently in balance, each piece painted with careful precision. When he first set it in motion, the planets caught the glow of Ava's string lights, scattering faint reflections across the walls.

"It's not much," he said, scratching the back of his neck, "but I thought the kid could use something to dream about."

Ryder rested a hand on her stomach, her smile soft but certain. "It's perfect," she whispered. And she meant it, because it wasn't just a toy. It was Jase giving her child a universe beyond concrete walls.

Damian's gift was quieter but no less profound. Over the weeks, he had scavenged scraps of leather and paper, carefully binding them into a hand-made baby book. The cover was worn but strong, the pages thick enough to last for years. The opening leaves were personal messages from each of them to the baby. Beyond that, he'd divided it into sections—milestones, drawings, notes, and space for photos—an archive of a childhood unfolding in the most unlikely of places. At the very back, he left a section empty, reserved for the child's own words someday.

When he placed it in Ryder's hands, he did so almost shyly, his voice low. "This is from all of us," he said. "So the baby knows how much they were loved, even before they were born."

Ryder's eyes shimmered as she pulled him into a hug, the simple book heavier with meaning than any gift could carry.

As Ryder gently closed the baby book and set it down on the blanket beside her, her eyes shimmered with emotion. She reached out to Nolan, taking his hand and giving it a squeeze, the gratitude in her expression unmistakable.

Around them the plates were empty, crumbs and stray salad leaves the only evidence of supper. Jase stretched his legs, leaning back on his hands. Olivia sat cross-legged, absently plucking at a loose thread on a pillow. Ava, however, could barely sit still—her knee bounced, eyes flicking between Ryder and Damian. Patience had never been her strong suit.

"Okay, enough waiting!" Ava finally blurted, sitting up straight and clapping her hands together. "We've eaten, we've gifted, we've cried—now it's time to do the big reveal! I'm dying over here!"

Ryder laughed, her hand instinctively moving to her barely visible bump. "I figured you wouldn't last much longer," she teased, then looked to Nolan with a soft smile. "What do you think? You ready?"

"Let's do it," he said, squeezing her hand.

Ava let out a triumphant cheer. "You're up, Doc. Tell us what we're having!"

Damian straightened from leaning against the Ficus base, wiped his palms, and walked to the food table where two small, carefully decorated boxes waited. One box was filled with pink Coneflower petals, the other with blue Cornflower petals, both sets dried and delicately preserved over the past weeks.

He picked up both boxes and gave the group a sly smile. "Alright," he said, voice steady with a hint of showmanship. "Make your guesses while I head upstairs."

The circle erupted in chatter. Ava shouted, "Girl! Definitely a girl!" Olivia countered, smirking, "Nope, I'm calling boy." Jase laughed and hedged, "I'm with Ava, but only because I don't want to hear her gloat later." Nolan and Ryder exchanged a private look and a soft, secret smile. "We'll see," Ryder said warmly, though the anticipation in her voice was unmistakable. Nolan squeezed her hand gently, his expression a mix of excitement and quiet nervousness.

Upstairs, Damian reached the railing and paused, letting the moment stretch. Ava could barely contain herself below; she grabbed Olivia's arm like a child on Christmas Eve. "Come on, come on," she muttered.

Damian set the boxes down carefully, glanced at the eager faces turned up toward him, and called, "Ready?"

The response came in a deafening chorus of cheers, Ava's voice rising above the rest. "Yes! Do it already!"

Damian's grin widened, his usually composed demeanor slipping slightly as he opened one of the boxes. With a smooth motion, he lifted it high over the railing and tipped it.

A shower of yellow petals drifted down, soft as confetti.

"Yellow? What the hell does that mean?" Ava blurted, her face scrunching in confusion as she scanned the others for an explanation.

Soft giggles broke through from Nolan and Ryder, who exchanged knowing glances, both trying to stifle their laughter. Ryder was the first to crack, a laugh escaping as she raised her hands in mock surrender. "I'm sorry, Ava. It was Damian's idea," she admitted.

Damian leaned over the railing, now laughing freely. "That's what you get for being so impatient!" he teased, his voice laced with amusement.

"I swear to god, if you don't throw the real petals down, I'll come up there and throw you down," Ava said, her tone half-joking, but the irritation was clear in her voice.

Olivia bit at her lip to hide a laugh, shaking her head, and gently grabbed Ava's arm as if to hold her back from storming up the stairs.

Damian raised his hands in surrender. "Alright, alright. Are you ready for the real thing?" he called down.

"Damian!" Ava shouted, a mix of pleading and frustration in her voice.

Ryder smiled softly, her eyes gleaming. "We're ready," she called up to him, her hand still resting gently on Nolan's.

Damian lifted the second box high over the railing. "Alright, here we go!" he called, his voice carrying over the circle below. "Three...two...one..."

He tipped it gently, and a cascade of petals spilled out into the air.

The group gasped as a soft rain of pink drifted down, glowing in the string lights like falling rose quartz. They twirled and fluttered, slow as butterflies, before settling on shoulders, in hair, across the blankets—turning the whole circle into a garden blooming underground.

Ryder clapped both hands over her mouth, her hazel eyes brimming with tears. A sob of joy caught in her throat as she looked up into the shower of petals, her face alight with disbelief and wonder. Nolan pulled her into his arms, holding her so tightly it was as if he could shield her and the child at once. He bent to her ear, whispering something meant only for her, his voice trembling against her cheek.

"It's a girl," Damian announced, warmth and pride threading through every word.

Ava shot to her feet, pink petals caught in her hair, and threw her arms skyward. "I knew it! I called it weeks ago!" she shouted, spinning in triumph. "We're having a little girl!"

Jase laughed, shaking his head, knowing he dodged a bullet. Olivia stood quietly, a soft smile playing on her lips as she watched Ryder and Nolan embrace. Her gaze lingered on them for a moment, her usually reserved expression melting into something tender as she brushed at the corner of her eye.

Ryder finally looked up, tears streaming down her cheeks, her face radiant as she locked eyes with Damian. "Thank you," she called up to him, her voice trembling with emotion.

Damian's answering smile was small but certain as he descended the stairs. When he reached the circle, the group collapsed inward, wrapping Ryder and Nolan in a cocoon of arms, kisses, and laughter. For a few minutes, the shelter felt weightless—no walls, no mission, no Ouro. Just joy.

As the noise slowly softened into murmurs and low laughter, Ryder eased back, pulling against Nolan's arm around her shoulders. He felt the shift and gave her hand a tender squeeze, his eyes searching hers.

"I'll be right back," she murmured.

He nodded, his gaze lingering on her as she slipped from his side. His brow furrowed slightly as he watched her with the kind of quiet curiosity only he could offer—steady, patient, always attuned to her movements.

Ryder crossed to the pile of gifts, knelt beside it, and sifted through them until she found what she was looking for. The small onesie made by Olivia—plain black, matching the Ouroboros-issued clothing they all wore—was a quiet reminder of their shared reality.

Ryder held it to her chest for a beat, grounding herself before she reached into her pocket and pulled out a neatly folded scrap of cloth. It was a small rectangle cut from one of her old shirts, faded but familiar. Golden thread embroidered a single word into the material, its uneven stitches glimmering faintly under the string lights as if it was imbued with magic.

The others' voices blurred into a gentle hum behind her as she threaded her needle, the ritual pulling her into focus. Each pass of the thread anchored her heartbeat, the tiny garment in her lap transforming under her hand. When the last knot was tied, she smoothed the patch with her fingers, a faint smile curving her lips.

She stood, holding the onesie carefully against her chest, as though guarding something precious. For a moment, she simply watched the group—their laughter, their teasing, the easy camaraderie that softened the edges of this life they hadn't chosen, but were learning to navigate.

"Already picturing her in it, are we?" Olivia teased, her voice bright as she caught sight of Ryder.

Ryder shook her head, her smile small but full of meaning. "No," she said, her voice calm but heavy with emotion. "I was making it hers."

Those words caught everyone's attention. The hum of conversation faded, and all eyes turned to her. Curiosity, confusion, and something gentler passed between them as they watched Ryder step forward. She exhaled a soft breath and slowly turned the onesie around, holding it up for them to see.

The patch glowed beneath the lights, golden thread spelling out a single word.

Aurora.

The name hung in the air like a revelation. The groups collective gaze shifting from the onesie to Ryder's face, where the shimmer of unshed tears caught in the corners of her eyes.

Jase was the first to find his voice, low and reverent. "Aurora." He let the word linger. "That's...beautiful. What does it mean?"

Ryder lowered her eyes to the stitched letters, brushing her thumb across them as if engraving the meaning into herself. The silence stretched, patient and waiting, until she spoke, her voice quiet but powerful.

"Aurora means dawn," she said, lifting her gaze to meet theirs. Her expression radiated with something gentle, yet powerful. "It's the first light that breaks after the darkest part of the night. It's a promise...that something new is coming. A brighter future. That no matter how bad it gets, there's still a chance for a new beginning."

Her words settled over them like a blessing. No one dared break the silence that followed. For a moment, beneath the glow of Ava's lights, it felt as though dawn itself had reached them underground.

Jase nodded slowly, a thoughtful smile tugging at his lips. Damian, unfolded his arms and let out a quiet breath. Olivia's teasing edge had softened into something gentler—her eyes lingering on the onesie as if she, too, were holding onto the fragile beauty stitched into its fabric.

Ava, uncharacteristically quiet, tilted her head, testing the name under her breath. "Aurora." The word rolled off her tongue like a secret, and her expression softened before a grin finally broke across her face. "It's perfect."

Ryder's chest eased, the tightness loosening. Nolan moved beside her, his hand resting against her back, steady and grounding. He didn't say anything, he didn't have to. The way his gaze lingered on the name, and then on her, said more than words ever could.

"It's beautiful," Olivia said softly. "It suits her already."

The group drew closer, their eyes fixed on the onesie, on the golden thread glimmering beneath the lights. It wasn't just a name. It was a vow—hope stitched into fabric, fragile yet radiant.

For a moment, the shelter felt transformed. The hum of the air systems seemed softer, the walls less suffocating. No one spoke. They only looked—at Ryder, at Nolan, at the name. Even the silence felt reverent, as though they'd been granted a glimpse of something sacred.

Ryder pressed the onesie against her chest, her heart swelling with belief. Warmth and love swirled around them, as the golden light reflected the unspoken promise that it would carry.

Aurora.

The light after darkness. Their new beginning.

The moment shattered.

A piercing alarm ripped through the facility, shrill and merciless. Red light burst across the walls in violent pulses, washing away the golden glow of Ava's lights. The celebration collapsed in an instant, laughter and warmth drowned out by the mechanical scream.

Ryder flinched, clutching the onesie tight to her chest as if she could shield it from the noise. Nolan's arm closed protectively around her, but she barely felt it, her joy cracked open into a cold rush of dread.

Ouro's voice cut through the chaos, calm and unyielding. "Attention. All personnel must report to the Operations Command Center immediately. This is not a drill."

Unease rippled through the circle, laughter and hope collapsing into silence—like dawn eclipsed before it could rise.

CHAPTER FOURTEEN

The doors to the Operations Command Center shot open, hissing sharply as the group stormed inside. Adrenaline surged through their veins, the remnants of their earlier celebration fading like a dream.

Their eyes darted to the wall of monitors, scanning each glowing screen for the telltale signs of another disaster—radiation spikes, structural failures, or breaches.

But unlike the chaos they had braced for, the screens were eerily calm. No flashing warnings. No streams of emergency data. Just the usual, dull glow of system readouts.

"What fresh hell does Ouro have for us this time?" Ava muttered, her voice edged with irritation as her gaze flicked from monitor to monitor.

Unease rippled through them, coiling tighter with each second of silence.

Finally, Jase broke it. "Ouro," he called out, his voice low but steady, "what's going on?"

The alarms abruptly ceased. The red lights blinked out one by one until only the cold fluorescent glow remained. The sudden stillness pressed down on the room like a weight.

Then Ouro spoke. Its voice carried not the usual neutral hum of routine reports, but something flatter, detached. "All personnel, please be seated at the conference table."

Ava spun toward the ceiling, tension crackling in her words. "What the fuck is this?"

Jase's brows knitted. "Ouro," he repeated, sharper this time, "why did the alarms go off? Is there a problem?"

"All personnel, please be seated at the conference table," Ouro replied, identical in tone, stripped of explanation.

The group exchanged uneasy glances, their concern sharpening into dread. Something about the repetition, the refusal to elaborate, felt different. Heavier.

Jase exhaled slowly, his jaw tight. He gestured toward the table in the center of the room. "Alright," he said, his voice steady but wary. "I guess we sit."

Ava muttered under her breath as she moved, her sarcasm laced with unease. "This better be good. Pulling this shit on tonight of all nights…"

One by one, the others followed, their movements slow, reluctant. Each glance at the monitors carrying an unspoken question—what are we walking into?

Jase lowered himself into the chair at the head of the table. His voice was firm, but his eyes betrayed the unease coiled in his chest. "Let's stay calm. We'll hear what Ouro has to say, and then we'll deal with it."

The group settled into their seats, a heavy silence hanging over them as they stared at the monitors and the empty table in front of them.

"Thank you for joining me," Ouro's voice resonated through the OCC, calm and unflinching. It was too calm. "I apologize for interrupting your celebration. Rest assured, there is no immediate emergency."

The group exchanged uneasy glances, confusion etched across every face.

Jase leaned forward. His voice was tight, controlled, but his eyes betrayed the flicker of unease beneath. "Then what was the reason for the alarms? Why call us here?"

"I have received an update to change my parameters," Ouro replied evenly.

The words landed like a shot to their chests. A ripple of shock swept through the group—eyes widening, breath catching, as if they had all lost hope that this day would ever come.

Jase stiffened, pulse quickening as he pressed further. "What kind of update? What does it do?"

Ouro's answer was swift. "The update is called Mission: Fallout Kids. Would you like me to execute the update?"

The room froze. The name itself carried an ominous weight, heavy enough to still the air. For a moment, no one breathed.

Jase turned sharply to Olivia. "Liv—what is this? Do you know anything about this? Is this from up above?" His voice cracked with urgency, almost pleading.

Olivia's lips parted, but no words came at first. She shook her head slowly, her brows knitting as she tried to make sense of it. "I have no idea," she whispered, her voice thin. Then, louder, firmer, as if forcing conviction into herself: "It has to be from them. Who else could send an update to Ouro's system?" Her gaze flicked to Jase, searching for answers she knew he didn't have. Finally, she turned toward the ceiling. "Ouro, what's in the update? What does it include?"

"The update has no notes or specifications. It must be executed to reveal new parameters," Ouro replied, its tone unchanging. "Would you like me to execute the update?"

The weight of the choice pressed down on them. For two long years, they had been cut off from the world above, forced to build their lives in isolation. Now, something, or someone, was reaching through the walls. The promise of answers pressed against the dread of what those answers might cost.

Jase leaned back, scanning the table. Nolan sat rigid beside Ryder, his hand resting protectively against her leg. Ryder had one palm pressed to her stomach, her thumb tracing nervous circles across the fabric of her shirt. Ava's restless energy had bled into stillness, her sharp eyes darting from face to face. Damian's jaw worked silently, his hand hovering over his notebook like he wanted to write something, but couldn't. Olivia sat perfectly still, shoulders tight, fingers tapping against her thigh—calculating, dreading what might come next.

One by one, they met Jase's gaze. Small nods. Silent agreement. Fear was there, but so was the inevitability. They had to know.

Jase inhaled, steadying himself. "Ouro," he said, his voice firm, "Alpha-One command. Execute the update."

"Executing update," Ouro responded. "This may take a moment."

The OCC plunged into silence. The faint hum of servers filled the room like a heartbeat, slow and steady, dragging each second into eternity.

Then the lights flickered. The monitors came alive, lines of code cascading too quickly to follow, streams of commands racing across the screens. Fans whirred louder, the sound swelling until it seemed to press against their ears.

They watched, frozen, as the code halted all at once. Every screen went black.

A beat of silence.

Then Ouro's voice: "Update complete. Please turn your attention to the monitors for briefing."

"Briefing?" Nolan echoed, his brow furrowing. His instincts as a Marine coiled him tight, bracing for impact. "What kind of briefing?"

Before anyone could answer, the main monitor flickered to life: MISSION: FALLOUT KIDS.

"Project Fallout Kids has completed," Ouro declared. "My parameters have changed from study mode to fully operational mode. The armory wing will be unlocked. Tomorrow your training begins."

The words sent a chill down the room, each syllable precise, unfeeling.

Before anyone could respond, the monitors shifted again, this time displaying a sprawling map of the region around the Ouroboros. Red markers pulsed like open wounds across the terrain.

"These are the designated waypoints for Mission: Fallout Kids," Ouro continued. "The mission objective is to search these areas and retrieve priority assets for transport to this facility."

Nolan leaned forward, his voice cutting sharper than usual. "Assets? What kind of assets?"

"Survivors," Ouro replied.

The word detonated inside the room. Chairs scraped. Breaths caught. The air seemed to thin.

Ryder bolted upright. "Survivors? You mean something did happen?"

"Confirmed," Ouro answered, its voice clinical, detached. "Preliminary data indicates multiple survivors within the designated waypoints. Their retrieval is your mission."

Olivia's face blanched, her lips parting as her mind raced. "This can't be real?" she whispered, then louder, more desperate: "Why haven't you told this sooner? What changed?"

"The update was sent as a directive to initiate this facility's primary function—reestablishing human society," Ouro explained. "All prior data regarding external operations was classified and unknown to me until this directive was received."

Jase slammed a hand against the table, the sound echoing in the sterile room. "Ouro—enough." He snapped, his voice raw, breaking the tension. "What happened? Did the world end?"

The silence that followed was suffocating. The monitors went black, reflecting their pale, stricken faces. The only sound was the pounding of their hearts.

"The world as you knew it ceases to exist," Ouro began, the calmness in its tone almost haunting. "It is being referred to as the Genesis Collapse. The event was initiated by the rapid spread of the Serpentis Strain, a highly mutagenic viral pathogen engineered for biological warfare. Its release was an act of global retaliation, escalating beyond containment within a matter of weeks."

The group stared at the monitor, frozen. No one moved. No one breathed.

"Engineered?" Damian's voice was a growl, his fists trembling against the table. "You're saying this wasn't an accident, it was deliberate?"

"Correct," Ouro replied. "The Serpentis Strain was designed to dismantle genetic integrity, resulting in systemic organ failure, neurological degradation, and rapid mortality. Unforeseen mutations rendered all countermeasures ineffective. Global population estimates place survival at less than five percent."

Olivia's lips parted, her mind racing. "Five percent..." she whispered, her voice trembling as if saying it aloud might make it less true. "That means…" She froze, her throat tightening. "That means more than seven billion people are dead."

Ryder's breath hitched, her hands gripping the edge of the table until her knuckles went white. "You're saying billions—billions are gone?" her voice breaking. The number was too large, too monstrous, to comprehend. It wasn't just a statistic. It was every city, every family, every face she'd ever known. Entire lives. Entire worlds. Snuffed out.

Nolan's jaw locked, his fists tightening as he stared at the monitor. Four hundred million, spread across the globe, scattered and desperate, clinging to scraps of existence. His military training had prepared him to process casualties. But this… this was annihilation.

Damian whispered the number under his breath again, as though testing it against reality. "Billions…" His medical mind recoiled at the thought of that much suffering, that much death. "Unforeseen mutations," he muttered, horrified. "God… the scale of it…" His shoulders slumped, and for the first time, he looked utterly defeated.

Olivia leaned back, her eyes glassy, staring through the monitors as if she could see the ashes of the world above. "All this time, we thought maybe… maybe there was still something left," she said, her voice brittle.

Jase didn't speak. His jaw was clenched so tight it hurt, his hands pressed flat to the table as though he could keep them all grounded through sheer will. His eyes flicked to each of them, lingering on Ryder's pale face, then Nolan's rage, then Olivia's hollow stare.

The weight of the number shattered whatever strength they had left.

Ava snapped, her voice cracking with barely contained fear. "So that's it, then? Billions dead while we're locked in here like lab rats waiting for our turn? Why weren't we told about this, why keep us in the dark?"

"My parameters were to ensure the integrity of the study," Ouro replied without hesitation. "The Ouroboros was designed to be a fully functioning shelter for long-term survival, even after the study concluded. Until my directives were updated, I was only allowed to operate under study parameters. I was unaware and unable to gather external data."

"So they chose to keep us in the dark," Olivia said flatly, her voice hollow.

"Affirmative," Ouro replied. "The Genesis Collapse advanced beyond projected containment windows. External conditions have stabilized to a threshold consistent with Phase Two protocol. The directive to commence Mission: Fallout Kids dictates the study phase is no longer the primary objective of this facility. Activation phase is now initiated. Objective: locate, secure, and transport viable survivors and resources necessary for reestablishing societal infrastructure."

Silence fell like a weight over the table, pressing the air from their lungs. The words, Phase Two, activation, and survivors, all blurred together. While one thought cut through Jase like a blade.

He leaned forward, his voice rougher now, stripped of command. "Ouro," he said, his jaw tight. "What about my family?" Jase asked, harsher than he meant. He caught himself, swallowed, then added more quietly, "All of ours. Did they make it?"

"Unknown. The Genesis Collapse destroyed most communication networks. Containment efforts included large-scale bombings of urban areas to eliminate infected populations. Combined with the virus's rapid spread and high fatality rate, statistical analysis indicates it is highly unlikely your families survived."

The words struck like a hammer. Ryder's hands flew to her chest, her breath coming in short, shallow gasps. "They just… bombed them?" she whispered, her voice breaking.

"Yes," Ouro confirmed. Its tone was clinical, merciless. "Major metropolitan areas were prioritized for eradication. Evacuation protocols were attempted. Healthy populations were to be separated from the infected and relocated to secure zones. However, containment measures were rapidly overrun. The Serpentis Strain's spread exceeded all predictive models. Once infection breached evacuation routes and quarantine sites, large-scale bombings of urban centers became the only viable strategy to slow transmission."

The words struck like shrapnel.

Ava shot to her feet, fists trembling. "So they just wiped out everyone?" she spat, her voice shaking with rage." That's the help they got? Bombs?"

"Containment measures were implemented with minimal notice," Ouro replied without hesitation. "The priority was survival of humanity as a species, not individuals. Neutralizing high-density infection clusters was the only option once control was lost."

"That's not survival," Damian muttered, his voice cracking as his head fell into his hands. "That's genocide."

Jase stared at the monitor. His voice, when it came, was low, deliberate. "So what you're saying… is that we're all that's left."

"Negative," Ouro said. Its neutrality made the word colder. "Survivors remain. However, the likelihood of your personal connections among them is near zero. Your mission is to recover and secure these survivors to ensure humanity's continuity."

Nolan's fist slammed against the table, the sound exploding through the silence. "And what if we don't?" he demanded, his voice raw. "What if we refuse to play along with this… this mission?"

"The success of Mission: Fallout Kids is imperative for the human race," Ouro replied. "Failure to comply will result in automated protocols designed to preserve the mission at all costs. This facility exists for the sole purpose of executing this directive. Noncompliance is not an option."

The hum of the servers filled the stillness as their breaths came ragged, the enormity of what they'd just heard hollowing them out. For a moment, no one spoke. No one moved. They weren't just trapped underground anymore. They were the last fragile thread of humanity, and Ouro was tightening the noose.

The monitors shifted, flickering through a grim sequence of images—grainy satellite views of gutted cities, broken highways choked with abandoned cars, and sprawling camps of gaunt, hollow-eyed survivors huddled around dying fires.

"Survivors have been identified in rural areas where environmental conditions allowed for temporary stability," Ouro explained, its tone flat against the devastation on-screen. "These individuals exhibit genetic immunity to the Serpentis Strain and are critical to humanity's restoration. Their retrieval is of the utmost priority."

Damian's head snapped up, his voice sharp with concern. "Wait, what about us? How are we supposed to go out there? Are we immune?"

"Yes," Ouro replied. "Analysis of your blood panels over the past two years confirms complete resistance to the Serpentis Strain. This resistance is not random. You were selected for the Ouroboros initiative because of specific genetic markers identified during pre-screening."

Damian straightened slowly, his eyes narrowing in thought as the pieces clicked together. "That explains it," he murmured, his tone steady. "All the endless testing we went through before coming down here... they weren't just routine clearances. They weren't just looking at our health, they were looking for resilience. People whose systems could stand up to... almost anything."

The realization rippled through the group, silent but sharp.

Olivia swallowed, her voice barely steady. "So... we're safe?" she asked, her tone fragile, teetering on the edge of hope.

"Resistant to airborne and person-to-person transmission." Ouro clarified. "However, resistance does not make you invulnerable. Direct blood exposure can still result in infection. Hostile survivors—those driven to desperation—pose a significant threat. Additionally, there are those who were infected with the Serpentis Strain but did not succumb to it."

Ryder straightened in her seat, her stomach twisting. "What does that mean?" she asked, her voice barely above a whisper.

"The virus has produced unpredictable mutations in some individuals," Ouro said evenly. "The nature and scope of these mutations remain uncertain. You are advised to exercise extreme caution during encounters with such individuals."

The coldness of that warning shook them to their core. The images on the screen seemed to shift from tragic to menacing, every shadow in the ruined world carrying unseen threats.

Nolan leaned forward, his jaw tight. "So we're not just rescuing survivors. We're stepping into hostile territory, with desperate people and God-knows-what roaming around. What's the protocol for engagement?"

"Engage with non-lethal methods when possible," Ouro instructed. Then, after a chilling pause: "However, mission parameters prioritize the safety of your team and the retrieval of immune survivors above all else. Lethal measures are authorized and should be considered the first option."

The group fell silent as the full scope of their mission became painfully clear. Not only would they be venturing out into a world they hadn't seen in years, but they would also be facing dangers worse than in their nightmares. This wasn't just a rescue mission, it was a battle for survival. For themselves and the future of humanity.

"To assist your efforts," Ouro continued. "BioPulse Scanners can be constructed in the workshop. These devices will identify carriers of the Serpentis Strain and confirm immunity among survivors. All necessary materials are available within the facility. Fabrication instructions will be uploaded to the system archives immediately following this briefing."

Nolan's arms crossed tightly. "They'll work in the field?"

"Yes," Ouro replied. "Accuracy rate is 99.8%."

Jase gave a short nod. "Is there anything else?"

"That is all for now. The countdown clock has been updated. You have 150 days to prepare before the doors open." Ouro stated.

The group's eyes widened. The moment they had waited for—hoped and dreaded for in equal measure—was finally real. But as the shock settled, Jase's brow furrowed. "Why so long, Ouro? Why 150 days?"

Ouro's voice remained calm and direct. "You will need this time to train as a cohesive unit. The mission requires more than individual strength. You must function as a team capable of operating in hostile environments and combat scenarios. Additionally, this timeline aligns with the estimated conclusion of Ryder's gestational period, ensuring her safety and the safe delivery of the child before initiating operations."

The group exchanged glances, a mix of relief and unease—they could deal with one issue at a time, but they were still on their own.

Nolan reached for Ryder's hand, squeezing it gently before turning back to the ceiling. His voice was steady, but his eyes were sharp. "Where do we train? How do we prepare for something like this in here?"

"When this briefing concludes," Ouro replied, "I will unlock the armory wing. Within, you will find everything necessary for your training. The training program will include physical conditioning, tactical drills, and strategic planning. Alpha-Two, you will oversee daily progress and objectives."

Nolan straightened in his seat, shoulders squaring with a renewed sense of purpose. "Understood," he said, his voice firm.

The room felt unbearably heavy, the weight of Ouro's revelations pressing down on them like an unrelenting tide. Silence stretched, thick and suffocating, as the group tried to absorb the enormity of what they'd just heard.

Olivia sat motionless, her wide eyes glassy, as though her mind had shut down under the weight of it all. Ava's leg bounced furiously, the restless energy of fear barely contained. Damian gripped his pen so tightly it left an imprint on his fingers. Nolan's hand was firm around Ryder's, his thumb moving over her knuckles in steady, protective strokes, while she clutched the onesie in her lap.

For two long years, they had lived in limbo, clinging to fragile hope while the walls of the Ouroboros shielded them from the horrors above. Deep down, they had always suspected the truth, a gnawing certainty that the world they once knew was gone. But to finally hear it, every agonizing detail, was a fresh wound and a loss too immense to understand.

The reality of what lay beyond the shelter doors was far more horrifying than any of them had dared to imagine. Death. Desolation. A world reshaped by chaos. And now, the knowledge that they would soon face it, armed with uncertain tools and a daunting mission, was more than they felt prepared to bear.

Jase sat at the head of the table, his jaw clenched as he scanned the room. He could see it in their faces: the fear, the grief, the overwhelming sense of despair. He wanted to say something, anything, to pull them back from the brink. But even he wasn't sure where to start.

He tilted his head back, drawing in a deep, steadying breath before exhaling slowly. His gaze swept over the group, locking eyes with each of them as if willing his resolve to pass to them. When he spoke, his voice was firm, unwavering.

"This isn't what we expected," Jase said. "But let's be honest—we always knew. We felt it. We just didn't want to face it." His throat tightened, but he forced the words through. "Now we know. And we can't change any of it. We can't bring anyone back."

He leaned forward, his hands gripping the edge of the table, his eyes hard with determination. "But we can choose what we do next. Now we step up. Not just for ourselves, but for everyone who's still left out there. They're counting on us now."

"Affirmative," Ouro replied. "This concludes today's briefing. Good luck, team Fallout Kids."

As they pushed away from the table and stood, a heavy mechanical groan echoed through the Ouroboros, reverberating in the floor beneath their feet.

Nolan glanced at Jase, eyebrows lifting. "Guess our armory's open."

Jase's expression stayed steady, cautious. He gave a small nod. "Guess so."

The group hesitated only a beat before following his lead out of the OCC.

In the hallway, instinct pulled their gazes upward. The countdown clock glared down at them, its blue glow spilling over their faces—somber, uncertain, and pale with fear.

But this time the light seemed sharper. Alive.

150 days, 10 hours, 7 minutes.

The numbers burned into their vision. For two years the clock had mocked them, ticking upward in cruel defiance of hope. Now, at last, it was counting down.

But the moment felt nothing like triumph. It was hollow, like the first gasp of air after nearly drowning. Not freedom, but the reminder of how close they had come to suffocating.

Jase exhaled slowly, tearing his gaze from the glow. "Let's keep moving," he said, his voice quiet but firm.

The others followed without a word, the glow of the countdown behind them now. But its presence lingered, etched into their minds—a witness, a warning. The countdown had begun, but it felt less like a promise of release than the start of another kind of clock. One measuring their survival.

At the end of the wing, their steps faltered as their gazes shifted right. For two years, that section of the upper level had been nothing more than a seamless wall.

Now, it wasn't.

A corridor stretched open into a newly revealed wing, its dim overhead lights flickering awake as though roused from decades of slumber. The air spilling out was cooler, metallic, carrying the sharp tang of a space untouched until this moment.

For a long moment, no one spoke. The group stood frozen, their eyes scanning the unfamiliar hallway, trying to reconcile its existence with the two years they had spent believing this section of the Ouroboros was solid, impenetrable.

"Son of a bitch," Ava muttered, breaking the silence. Arms crossed tight, her dark eyes narrowed at the hallway, as if glaring hard enough might force an explanation. "There was another wing there this whole time."

Damian's head shook slowly, his lips curving into something caught between disbelief and a bitter smirk. "And not one of us questioned why the lower level had four wings and this one only had three." His voice was low, almost to himself. "Makes you wonder what else Ouro's been hiding."

Silence thickened as the words hung between them.

One by one, their eyes shifted to Damian.

CHAPTER FIFTEEN

The group gathered at the entrance to the newly revealed wing, their anxious eyes fixed on the dimly lit corridor before them. For all the mystery surrounding it, the layout mirrored the other seven wings of the Ouroboros—an identical stretch of hallway leading to a distant dead end. The walls were smooth and sterile, interrupted only by the usual sliding doors on either side.

But one feature stood out. On the right side of the hall, a bay of glass windows lined the hall, each pane spotless and gleaming under the fluorescent glow. Below the windows, a polished metal ledge ran the length of the bays, with stools evenly spaced beneath it. It felt less like part of their shelter and more like an observation deck, designed for someone to watch.

Their footsteps echoed in the untouched space as they drew closer. Peering through the glass, their reflections blurred against what lay beyond.

On the left, a four-lane, 50-yard gun range stretched into the distance, lit bright as day. Each lane was equipped with a highly advanced target retrieval system, with a touch screen control panel. Customizable training courses included flashing lights, moving and turning targets, and randomized patterns. A live video feed displayed an image of the target with detailed data—shot placement, trajectory, reaction time, and overall score. All fully integrated into Ouro's system compiling detailed performance metrics.

But it was the right-side windows that stole their breath.

Behind the glass sprawled something far larger—a tactical training course carved into the underground world like a mock battlefield. Half was forest—artificial trees, shrubs, and uneven terrain designed to mimic the outdoors. A programmable lighting system simulated different times of day, while a shallow stream of running water wound through the course, adding an extra layer of realism and forcing them to adapt to varied terrain.

The forest blended seamlessly into an urban zone. This resembled a city street corner with cement barricades, shattered storefronts, and a few alleys leading into a single-level building. The building was set up with narrow hallways, cornered rooms, and a stairwell. Everything could be rearranged with a command to Ouro, creating endless configurations to ensure no two sessions were ever the same. It was the most advanced CQB training room in existence.

The entire course was equipped with motion sensors and sound emitters that simulated combat—gunfire, shouting, and chaos. Sensor-equipped targets were programmed to move unpredictably, along with tactical objectives, dummy hostages to rescue, and supplies to retrieve. It was designed to teach them how to move as a unit, communicate effectively, and strategize under pressure.

The group stood frozen, drinking it all in. It wasn't just a gym or a shooting range. It was a proving ground. A place to break them down, rebuild them, and prepare them for the war waiting beyond the shelter doors.

Jase's eyes swept across the room, his jaw tightening. "This is… a lot."

"Yeah," Ava muttered, her gaze darting from the mock forest to the urban maze. "They didn't just want us to survive. They wanted us to fight."

Nolan folded his arms, nodding toward the training course. "Yeah. And if it's half as bad out there as it sounds, we're going to need this. If we can't move as one, we're done before we even begin."

The group fell quiet, their attention settling on him. One by one, they nodded. If anyone understood the importance of unity, it was Nolan. His military training had drilled into him that no mission could succeed without coordination and trust.

Nolan unfolded his arms, his sharp gaze sweeping over the tactical course one last time. His demeanor was calm, but there was a spark of determination behind his eyes.

"This," he said, gesturing toward the space, "is where we build our shooting and team skills." He paused, a faint grin tugging at the corner of his lips. "Let's go see the tools."

They turned toward the opposite wall, where a sliding steel door waited like a sealed vault. Nolan led the way, his boots striking the floor in steady rhythm. With a sharp hiss, the door parted.

Blinding white light poured into the hall as overhead fixtures snapped on in perfect sequence. The air inside carried the sharp tang of oil and gunmetal, with a faint whisper of burnt powder buried deep in the stillness.

The sight beyond stopped them cold.

The armory felt like a secret showroom, clinical and immaculate, but with the hush of something dangerous. Dark matte-gray walls framed the space, while thin bands of golden LED traced the ceiling and floor, giving the polished black concrete floors a subtle sheen. At the center of the room a large Ouroboros 'O' inlaid into the floor seemed to glow, a quiet emblem of authority that made the place feel almost ceremonial.

The room was divided into two distinct halves. On the left, rows of shotguns, rifles, and pistols gleamed under the lights, each mounted with clinical precision along the walls. A holographic display under each section identified the models, specifications, and use. Every category was represented, every gap accounted for—BENELLI M4 shotguns, SIG MCX SPEAR rifles, HK MP5K submachine guns for close quarters, CHRISTENSEN ARMS MPR rifles for long range, and even SIG XM250 machine guns.

Nolan's eyes widened as he moved along the displays, the faint scent of oiled steel thick in the air. Stopping at the vast selection of rifles, he let his fingers brush over the cold metal of the MCX-SPEAR, its lines familiar, its weight promising. Taking it down, he worked the charging handle, checked the ejection port, then shouldered the weapon and squeezed the trigger.

Click.

The soft sound echoed in the pristine room. Jase stepped up beside him, watching. "What do you think?" he asked, his voice quiet but curious.

Resting the rifle upright against his shoulder, Nolan's smile was small but genuine. "Just like the rest of this place," he said, his voice tinged with awe. "Top of the line. It's everything we could need, and more. We'll be ready for anything."

With that, he set the rifle down on the central workbench, a broad slab of black steel flanked by heavy gun vises. The table dominated the center of the weapons side, built for cleaning, repairing, and customizing the arsenal. Wide drawers beneath held brushes, oils, spare parts, and precision tools, while a suspended LED bar above cast a bright, clinical light that left no detail hidden.

The opposite half of the armory was equally formidable. Storage racks lined the walls and the center of the room, filled with meticulously arranged ammunition boxes, each labeled by caliber and type. Shelves held an array of suppressors, optics, flashlights, lasers, and other accessories—all neatly organized and easily accessible. Other racks held tactical and survival gear—compact backpacks, gas masks, trauma kits, durable rations—everything they would need to live and fight beyond the shelter's walls.

At the center of the armory, a golden 'O' glowed faintly from the floor. Along the walls on either side, three large open lockers faced three identical ones across the room. Each locker had a digital nameplate above that displayed their project codenames. Inside hung military-grade clothing, plate carriers, ballistic helmets, reinforced boots, gloves, and climate-adaptive outerwear. Every piece was perfectly fitted for its intended wearer, as if Ouro had been preparing them for this moment all along.

Ava approached her locker, looking up at the display reading 'Beta-One'. Her brow furrowed as she traced the glowing letters with her eyes. She then dropped her gaze down into the open-faced locker, slowly taking in the sets of military-grade clothing, boots, and other gear. Her fingers brushed over the fabric, noticing the fit and precision.

Her voice cut through the silence. "Why is this stuff custom-fit to us? If the armory was hidden this whole time, how do they have our sizes set in our lockers?"

Ryder moved closer, drawn by the unease in Ava's tone. She glanced at Ava's gear, then turned her attention to her own locker, labeled 'Beta-Two'. Inside, she found the same setup, each item unmistakably made for her.

"She's right," Ryder said, her voice measured but laced with unease. "This doesn't make sense. We didn't even know about this place. How is it stocked for us?" She gestured to the tailored clothing. "Like it was waiting for us all along."

With that, Jase, Damian, Nolan, and Olivia made their way to their respective lockers—each finding gear cut to their measurements, down to the smallest detail.

Ava leaned back against the steel frame, crossing her arms. "So why keep it hidden if it was made for us?"

Olivia's eyes narrowed, her mind working through the implications. She took a step forward, tilting her head toward the ceiling. "Ouro," she called, her voice sharp. "If we weren't given access to the armory until now, how is it stocked with gear for us? How were you ready with all of this?"

The AI's voice responded almost immediately, smooth and detached, as though anticipating the question. "During the project phase, it was determined that the armory and associated equipment would remain inaccessible until a final feasibility test was conducted. Pending analysis of your mental stability and group cohesion, the last week of the project schedule would have included opening the armory and initiating a series of tests to evaluate its effectiveness in operational scenarios."

Ava frowned, shaking her head. "So this was always the plan. We just didn't know about it."

"Correct," Ouro replied. "The armory and its contents were prepared in advance based on your biometric and physical data—–collected during your onboarding and regular health evaluations. This ensured the equipment would meet the required standards for each individual, had the test phase proceeded as planned."

Olivia crossed her arms, glancing at Ava. "So the world ended before we reached it."

"Affirmative. The armory's readiness was always part of this facility's design."

Ava exhaled sharply, rubbing the back of her neck. "Convenient," she muttered, glancing at Ryder next to her. "Still feels like they were planning for us to fight a war instead of testing out their facility."

Ryder's gaze lingered on the gear, her voice dropping to a whisper. "Maybe that's exactly what they were planning."

Jase turned from his locker, his gaze sweeping over the group, each of them caught in their own storm of emotions. He took a slow, measured breath before speaking, his voice steady but carrying an edge of authority.

"Listen," he began, "I get that this is overwhelming, because it is. Whatever hope we had left for the world was just ripped away. Ouro dumped a mountain of information on us and we haven't even had a chance to take a breath, let alone process any of it."

He paused, his eyes meeting each of theirs in turn, grounding them with his presence. "Before we all lose our shit, let's sit down and take a few deep breaths."

His words carried a quiet strength, the kind of steady reassurance they all needed in the moment. Jase's demeanor wasn't commanding so much as anchoring, giving them a moment to pause and collect themselves amidst the chaos that had been thrust upon them.

One by one, they sank into their benches and the cold floor, the tension easing just enough to keep them upright. Damian sat on the bench in front of his locker, hunched forward, elbows braced on his knees. His mind churned with questions, while his usually steady hands clenched into fists, betraying the unease he tried to suppress.

Ryder lowered herself carefully to the floor at her locker, her arms circling her stomach. She kept glancing toward the gear, her thoughts drifting to the child growing inside her and the uncertainty of bringing a life into a world she'd never seen. The thought was both terrifying and oddly grounding.

Nolan sat rigid, his posture taut as a wire. His training demanded composure, demanded he hold fast, but nothing in his life had prepared him for this truth. He was going to be a father, yet he might be raising that child in a wasteland. The pressure pressed down on him like a tidal wave.

Olivia perched on her bench with her head in her hands, her mind running wild with calculations and strategies, desperate to make sense of everything they had learned. She felt the familiar pang of guilt, a sharp reminder of the secrets she carried. Even now, surrounded by the group, she felt alone in her thoughts.

Ava sat cross-legged against her locker, her sharp eyes scanning the room, catching the subtle cracks forming in everyone's armor. She wanted to spit, to scream, to rage at the ceiling—but instead, she rubbed at her temples, forcing her thoughts into motion. Anger could be useful if she aimed it right.

Jase lowered himself to the floor with a heavy sigh. He leaned back against the bench, tilting his head up, his breath steady but weighted. The silence of the armory pressed on him, heavier than steel. His words had steadied them for now, but inside, another fire burned.

For months, the thought of Eli had haunted his dreams. The uncertainty of his fate had burned deep scars in his mind, with every outcome spiraling into horror. Night after night, his subconscious fed the flames of fear and guilt, until they consumed him. With time, and Olivia's support, the nightmares ebbed, and he made an uneasy peace with the unknown.

Now, with the truth of the Genesis Collapse laid bare, that fragile hope splintered. The fire reignited, scorching through his mind once more, stoked by the haunting question—was Eli out there somewhere—or had he been swallowed whole like the billions Ouro had condemned to ash?

The room stayed silent for what felt like an eternity, only broken by their heavy breaths. Each of them lost in their own storm of thoughts, their own fears.

Finally, Jase broke the silence, his voice quiet but resolute. "It's not fair," he said, the words dragging the air down with them. "We didn't ask for this. We just wanted to be part of something bigger, something special. We didn't know we were saying goodbye to our families forever."

He hesitated, his shoulders sagging as the realization settled in. "It doesn't feel real. I can see it on all your faces—you're all wondering what the hell we're supposed to do now."

His eyes swept across the group, meeting each of theirs in turn. Exhaustion. Fear. A desperate need for direction he wasn't sure he could give.

"As I see it, we've got two choices," Jase continued, leaning forward slightly. "We can stick to Ouro's plan. Train, prepare, and go out there as a team when the doors open. Or…" He was reluctant to finish, his gaze dropping to the floor. "We can go our own way. Look for our families, our friends. Try to piece together some kind of life—even if it's not the one Ouro has in mind for us."

The room felt like it was holding its breath. Ryder's eyes flicked toward Nolan, and in that brief glance, they exchanged a thousand unspoken fears and hopes. Damian looked down at his hands, his brow furrowed in thought, while Ava crossed her arms, her expression unreadable but her mind clearly racing.

Olivia finally lifted her head, her lips pressed into a thin line. Her voice was quiet, but it landed like a hammer. "It's him, isn't it? You think Eli's still out there." Her eyes shimmered, grief rising like water behind a dam.

Jase's gaze snapped to her. He exhaled slowly, his voice a rasp. "No," he admitted. "I don't." The truth cut sharper than he expected. He forced himself to look at the rest of them. "But I can't say the same for your families. For your loved ones. And I won't ask you to make the choice I've already made for myself."

His voice caught, then steadied. "Each of us have to decide what's worth fighting for. Who's worth risking everything for."

The silence that followed was deafening.

Jase leaned back, running a hand through his hair, and swallowing hard. "It's not an easy choice," he said at last, firmer now. "And I don't know what the right answer is—hell, I don't think there is one. But each of us needs to decide for ourselves. And whatever we choose, we'll have to live with it. All of us."

His words lingered in the stillness, settling deep in their bones. No one moved, but every one of them felt the weight of the choice pressing on their chest, suffocating and inescapable.

Minutes dragged on, heavy and silent, as everyone wrestled with the weight of the decision. Each one sat locked in their thoughts, searching for answers that didn't exist.

Finally, Damian broke the stillness. I have a responsibility," he said, the words carrying a quiet weight. All eyes turned to him. "I didn't finish medical school to do nothing. I became a doctor to help people. I don't know how much good I can do in a world like this, but here in this facility, with Ouro's resources, maybe I can make a difference. I need to try. I need to help whoever's left out there."

His gaze shifted to Jase, and he gave a small, resolute nod. Jase returned it, his expression unreadable, though a glimmer of pride shone in his eyes.

Across the room, Ryder exhaled shakily and rose to her feet, brushing a stray tear from her cheek. Her voice trembled, but her words did not.

"This is my family now," she said, hazel eyes bright with emotion. "We wouldn't have made it this far without each other, and we won't make it out there without each other."

She looked to Nolan, who had already pushed up from his locker, moving beside her. His gaze swept the room, hard but unwavering.

"I've spent my life training to fight, to protect, to survive. That's what I know, what I'm good at. And I'll do it for all of you, for this family. Out there, it's going to be chaos. But if there's even a chance we can bring some order to it, we owe it to ourselves and to whoever's still alive, to try."

Ava shifted against her locker, arms crossed, her brow drawn tight as though she were measuring every risk. With a sigh, she pushed upright, shaking her head.

"Let's be real, if I'm not here keeping everything from falling apart, you won't last a week." The sharpness faded, and for a moment her walls cracked. "But the world Ouro described... it doesn't sound like a place you should go alone."

Olivia had remained silent, head bowed, hands knotted in her lap. Her silence was heavy, her thoughts distant, until finally she lifted her gaze. Blonde strands of hair framed her face, clinging to damp cheeks. Her eyes searched Jase's, hesitant but unflinching.

"You're sure, Jase?" she asked softly. Her voice trembled. "You can really let him go… and stay with us?"

Jase exhaled sharply, the weight of the question hitting him harder than he expected. He looked down for a moment, his jaw tightening as he grappled with the storm of emotions threatening to break through. When he finally raised his head, his voice came low, almost a whisper.

"No," he admitted, his breath hitching. "He'll always be with me, in my thoughts, in my dreams, in everything I do. That's something I can't let go of." His voice faltered, then steadied. "But I'm doing this for him. For Eli. The guilt of leaving him haunted me for so long, but I've learned to live with it. What I can't live with is making that same mistake again. With all of you."

Olivia's lips trembled. A tear slid down her cheek before she could stop it. Her voice wavered, then hardened.

"If he's out there, if there's even the smallest chance…" She drew a steadying breath, steadying herself. "I promise you, Jase. We'll find him one day. Together."

Her words hung in the air like a vow. She stood, deliberate and grounded, the color returning to her face.

"I don't know what's waiting for us out there." Her gaze swept the room, lingering on each of them. "But I know what we'll always have in here. Each other. That's how we move forward."

Jase nodded, his throat tight. A quiet strength rippled through the group as her words sank in. This wasn't just a choice, it was a commitment. A promise to face whatever waited beyond the shelter doors together.

Jase scanned the room, his eyes lingering on each of them. Ryder, standing tall though her eyes shimmered with tears. Nolan, his arm firm around her shoulders, steady as ever. Damian, steady and resolute. Ava, her sharp wit masking a deep loyalty. Olivia, her quiet courage steadying them all.

He nodded, the weight in his chest a little lighter. "All right," he said, his voice steady. "Nolan—you start training us tomorrow. Whatever's waiting when those doors open, we face it as a team."

Back in the Operations Command Center, a monitor flickered to life. Their six names glowed across the black screen, each marked with a fresh green check. Ouro did not speak, but the silence was louder than words.

Noncompliance was never an option.

CHAPTER SIXTEEN

The group gathered around the workbench in the armory, a mix of nerves and purpose hanging in the air. Despite little sleep after yesterday's emotional gauntlet, they were on time and ready. The morning workout and a quick breakfast had steadied them. But now, surrounded by weapons, the gravity of what lay ahead began to sink in.

Nolan stood at the head of the steel table, his posture rigid, every movement disciplined. Behind him, the walls glimmered with racks of rifles, pistols, and shotguns, each aligned with clinical precision. Across from him, the others waited, curiosity and apprehension written across their faces.

Reaching up, Nolan selected two weapons from the racks: a tan Sig MCX-Spear LT chambered in 5.56, built for precision and reliability, and a Staccato HD P4.5 pistol, its heavy frame promising accuracy and control. He set them on the table with deliberate care, the soft clink of metal punctuating the silence.

He looked at the group, his gaze settling on each of them before he spoke.

"All right," he began. "Today we're starting with the basics. Target practice. This is just about getting comfortable—handling the weapons, aiming, firing." His voice was calm but carried the authority of a man shaped by training. "Familiarity before anything else."

He paused, scanning the group. "Anyone have experience shooting?"

Jase and Ava raised their hands. Jase shrugged, casual but steady. "A few times. Mostly pistols, an AR once or twice."

Ava's tone was brisk, matter-of-fact. "Pistols and a hunting rifle. My dad hunted."

Nolan nodded approvingly. "Good. That'll make this a little easier for me. I'll start with you two on the range since you've got some experience. Once I'm confident you're squared away, I'll come back and walk the rest of you through the basics. Until then…" He pointed to the monitor mounted on the wall beside them. "Ouro will play some instructional videos. These will break down how each weapon works, so pay attention. It's important you understand how they function before you even think about pulling a trigger."

Damian, Ryder, and Olivia exchanged uncertain glances before nodding, their collective sighs of relief almost audible. None of them had any real experience with firearms, and the thought of holding, let alone firing, a weapon felt overwhelming.

"Jase, Ava," Nolan continued, gesturing toward the weapons rack, "grab a Spear and a Staccato each. I've got mags, ammo, and ear and eye pro already set up at the range. Let's move."

Jase and Ava stepped forward, each taking their time selecting them from the racks. Jase tested the weight of the rifle in his hands, his fingers brushing over the rail system as he adjusted his grip. Ava handled her weapons with confidence, inspecting them briefly before nodding to herself.

As they moved towards the door, Nolan picked up the weapons he'd set on the table, his gaze shifting back to the others. "I'll be back in a bit. In the meantime, watch the videos and take notes if you need to. Understanding these weapons could make the difference between surviving and not out there."

The steel door slid shut behind them, leaving Damian, Ryder, and Olivia in the quiet hum of the armory. The monitor flickered to life, Ouro's voice filling the room with a smooth narration of the arsenal. The three exchanged uneasy looks before turning to the screen, ready to absorb whatever they could.

Jase and Ava followed Nolan across the hall to the range. Jase shot her a sideways glance, his tone teasing. "You ready for this?"

Ava smirked, her hand tightening on the rifle. "Ready to show you how it's done? Always."

Nolan glanced at them, his expression stern but not unkind. "Let's see if either of you can impress me first."

***

The air in the shooting range shifted to a cold, smoky scent that sharply filled their lungs. The space was lined with 4 lanes, each one marked with glowing indicators above. Behind them, running along the windows that faced the hallway, stood a table stocked with ammo, magazines, and protective gear.

"Jase, you're on lane 1. Ava, lane 4," Nolan said in a commanding tone, his voice sharp and precise. "Drop your weapons on the shooting benches, then come grab your gear." The shift in his demeanor was palpable, and Jase and Ava straightened instinctively, sensing the gravity of the moment.

They approached their lanes, placing the pistols and rifles carefully on the benches. The metal was heavier than they'd expected. Not just the weight you could feel in your hands, but the weight that settled in the chest. Jase felt a faint buzz of nerves at the base of his neck, while Ava's fingers twitched slightly, betraying her outwardly calm demeanor.

"Gear up," Nolan ordered, nodding toward the table.

The pair moved swiftly, joining him at the table stocked with magazines, ammo, and protective equipment. Jase grabbed a pair of Walker's Razor electronic ear muffs and slipped them over his head. The world around him muffled into silence until he flicked the dial, turning on the internal speakers. Ava adjusted her glasses, the clear lenses slightly fogging as she first exhaled.

"Start with pistols," Nolan said. "Seven yards. Slow, deliberate shots. Work on grip, sight alignment, and a smooth trigger pull. I'll move between lanes and check your mechanics. Questions?"

Both shook their heads silently, determination settling in their features.

"Good. Grab your mags and head to your lanes."

Jase returned to his lane and the overhead light and control panel flicked on. The pristine black walls of the bay seemed at odds with the raw violence they were about to unleash. He tapped the screen, selecting a seven-yard distance. The target retriever whirred to life, a crisp silhouette gliding down the lane, stopping with a metallic clink. A few lanes over, Ava did the same, her focused movements mirroring his.

Jase picked up the Staccato HD. The textured grip bit into his palm, unfamiliar yet instinctive. He slammed a magazine into place, racked the slide, and the metallic snap echoed through the bay.

He took his stance, planting his feet shoulder-width apart and slightly bending his knees. His left hand came up to brace the grip, palms pressed tightly together as he extended his arms forward. Slowly, he raised the pistol, aligning the sights with his eye-line and the center of the target. His breath slowed, his chest rising and falling rhythmically as he exhaled.

When the moment felt right, he squeezed the trigger.

Boom.

The report of the pistol cracked through the air, reverberating through his body. The recoil kicked back into his palms, but he held firm.

Boom.

Boom. Boom.

Boom.

A steady rhythm of shots echoed across the range as Ava joined in, her shots tight and deliberate. At first her first shots were precise, then the pistol's kick surprised her and a round pinged wide. She recovered, forced her shoulders down, and the next strings tightened back to center.

The smell of burned powder grew, and the ventilation's low whine filled the spaces between shots. Nolan moved steadily between lanes, hands behind his back, voice cutting through the racket.

"Wider stance. Give yourself a base."

"Lean into it. Don't let the recoil push you back."

"Smooth trigger. Don't flinch."

Magazines emptied quickly. Slides locked back, signaling their progress. They grabbed fresh magazines, slapped them home, released the slides, and went again. Rhythm built into a machine—load, aim, fire, reset.

This continued on for a bit until Nolan had them pause, stepping between the lanes to inspect their results. He nodded approvingly.

"All right," Nolan said, motioning toward the control panels. "Let's step it up. Set the targets to 15 yards. This time we're working on speed and precision. Start from the combat compressed position. Weapon tucked at your sternum. On my command, bring it up, acquire the sights, and fire a controlled double tap. Both shots center mass."

Jase and Ava nodded, determination etched into their expressions. They tapped the touchscreen again, and the targets slid farther down the lanes, their silhouettes shrinking into the distance.

They reloaded, mags slamming home with crisp clicks. Pistols close to their chests, elbows tucked, they waited. Coiled springs.

Nolan stood behind them, his voice sharp. "Ready. Go!"

Boom. Boom.

Jase's shots rang out in succession, his arms snapping up with controlled precision as he fired.

Boom. Boom.

Ava followed suit, her shots echoing simultaneously as his.

"Faster," Nolan barked. "You're overthinking. Trust the mechanics. Trust yourself."

They reset, bodies tight, and at his next command the shots came quicker, more fluid. The echo of gunfire filled the lane in rapid beats, smoke curling into the cold air.

Jase felt the tension in his forearms, the kick in his palms, but deeper still was the weight of it—each shot a promise of survival or failure.

Ava gritted her teeth, her competitive edge lighting her up. She tightened her grouping, her rounds stitching closer together. A smirk flickered at the edge of her mouth.

Nolan paced behind them, his voice steady and relentless. "This isn't just about shooting, it's about control. Out there, hesitation gets you killed. Sloppiness gets your friend killed. Keep it tight. Keep it clean. Again. Go!"

Boom-boom.

Boom-boom.

The rhythm carried on, steady and merciless, until their targets were riddled with tight groupings. With each shot, Jase and Ava's movements became smoother, faster, sharper—until the motions began to settle into muscle memory. The hesitation was gone. They moved as though the pistols were extensions of themselves, each trigger pull an act of focus rather than fear.

He crossed his arms, eyes scanning their stances and the control in their movements. Then a sharp nod.

"Guns down."

In unison, Jase and Ava lowered their pistols, fingers off the triggers, setting them on the benches. They stepped back, chests heaving, adrenaline humming in their veins.

***

Back in the armory, Ouro continued playing instructional videos on the various weapons. Damian's eyes lingered uneasily on the pistol on the screen, tracing its cold lines. He flexed his hands, frustrated by their slight tremor. He had spent years learning to stitch wounds, to save lives. Now he was expected to take one.

"I don't know if I can handle this," he murmured under his breath.

Ryder sat on her stool, her arms wrapped protectively around her stomach. Her gaze stayed fixed on the monitor, but her thoughts drifted. She had never wanted to touch a gun. Never thought she'd have to. But for her child? For Nolan? She swallowed hard and whispered under her breath. "This is for your future, baby girl."

Olivia leaned forward on the bench, eyes sharp as she scribbled notes. Mechanics, terminology, safety procedures. She repeated them under her breath, memorizing them as if sheer precision could drown out her nerves. Her pen tapped against the page in a steady rhythm.

***

"Good," Nolan said. "Let's move on to the rifles. Keep the targets at fifteen yards. Start slow. One shot at a time. Focus on the feel of the rifle—the weight, the recoil, the control of it. Precision comes first."

Jase and Ava exchanged a brief look and stepped toward the equipment table. They grabbed Magpul PMAGs, lightweight polymer thirty-round magazines with clear windows for quick round counts, and returned to their lanes. The overhead lights snapped on as the targets reset, sliding out and locking into place with fresh sheets.

Jase lifted the rifle, its weight heavier than the pistol, but just as balanced. He braced the stock against his forearm, and slid a magazine in smoothly. Pulling back the charging handle and letting it spring forward, he chambered a round. The action felt smooth, precise, and powerful. Ava mirrored his movements, her own rifle coming to life with a faint metallic snap.

"Take your time," Nolan said as he paced behind them. "Rifles are a different game. They're more stable, but they demand more discipline. Control your breathing. Align your sights. Don't rush it."

Jase shifted into position, planting the rifle's buttstock firmly into his shoulder. His cheek pressed against the stock as he peered through the SIG TANGO6T scope, aligning the crosshair with the center of the target. He adjusted his grip on the handguard, steadying the rifle as he took a deep breath and squeezed the trigger.

BOOM.

The rifle thundered. A concussive blast jolted through him, far stronger than anything the pistol produced. The sound still rattled his ears despite the ear protection.

BOOM.

A few lanes down, Ava fired her first round. The sharp crack echoed through the range as the rifle kicked against her shoulder. Her shot was slightly off-center. She frowned and adjusted her stance.

Nolan moved between them, his calm but authoritative voice cutting through their heavy focus.

"Jase, lean your right shoulder into it more," Nolan said. "Offset your feet. Let your stance absorb the recoil."

Jase nodded, shifting his weight forward slightly and firing again. The next shot was smoother, the recoil feeling less jarring.

"Ava," Nolan said, stepping behind her. "Tighten your C-grip on the handguard and drive the rifle with that hand. You're letting it drift up at the last second. Your right hand can be looser. It's just there to pull the trigger."

Ava adjusted her grip, her brows furrowed in concentration. She fired again, the shot landing closer to the bullseye.

The range came alive once more as the two fired in steady succession. The sharp crack of the rifles echoed against the walls, punctuated by Nolan's instructions. After several magazines and repeated adjustments, Nolan called out, "Stop."

Jase and Ava lowered their rifles. Their arms ached and sweat dampened their foreheads, but they stood taller now. Confidence grew with each shot.

"All right, let's take it up a notch. Targets to 25 yards. This time I want controlled bursts: three rounds at a time—two to center mass and one to the head. Keep those shots tight and on target. No spray-and-pray bullshit. Precision and control."

Jase and Ava nodded, their faces set with determination. They reloaded fresh magazines and settled into position once more.

"Ready. Go!"

BOOM-BOOM. BOOM.

BOOM-BOOM. BOOM.

The sound of controlled bursts filled the room as the two fired in unison. The rhythm was different now—quicker, more deliberate, yet no less focused.

"Good. Get that third shot off faster. Ready. Go!"

BOOM-BOOM. BOOM.

As they continued, their movements became fluid and instinctive, the rifles an extension of themselves. Nolan's voice, firm and guiding, pushed them harder, instilling the discipline that would mean the difference between life and death outside the shelter.

By the time the last magazines ran dry, they were drenched in sweat, arms aching, their targets marked with tight clusters. Nolan nodded in approval, his gaze softening slightly.

"Guns down," he said with a hint of satisfaction. "That's enough for now. You both did well, better than I expected. But don't let it go to your heads. This is just the start. We'll drill this again and again until it's second nature."

Jase and Ava carefully set their rifles down on the benches in front of their lanes, their movements deliberate as if each gesture was a mark of respect for the weapons in their hands. They exchanged a quick glance, a mixture of pride and exhaustion. Ava let out a slow breath, shaking out the tension in her shoulders, while Jase wiped a bead of sweat from his temple.

Nolan stepped toward them, his tone shifting from instructor to something more relaxed. "Now it's time to bring the others in," he said, motioning toward the door. "We'll walk them through everything: safe handling, basic mechanics, and firing positions. Then we'll get them on the range. I'll lead the drills, but I want you two helping me in here. You guys have enough under your belt to help them catch up."

Jase raised a brow, "You think we're good enough to help?"

"Yeah," Nolan replied without hesitation. "They'll need more one-on-one attention than you did, and I can't be everywhere. If you see the same mistakes I corrected with you, fix them. Go slow. Help them get comfortable. Think you can handle that?"

Ava straightened, a confident smile forming. "We've got this."

"Good," Nolan said, nodding. "Let's get moving."

The three exited the range, leaving behind the lingering scent of gunpowder and the steady hum of the ventilation. As they made their way back toward the armory, the muffled cadence of Ouro's training videos drifted down the hall, accompanied by the low murmur of Damian, Ryder, and Olivia. Waiting. Watching. Bracing themselves for what came next.

***

The group rotated through the range over the rest of the day, each stepping into their lanes with hesitant strides and wide eyes. Nolan, Jase, and Ava worked seamlessly as a unit, guiding the others through the basics.

Jase kept his voice calm and steady as Olivia gripped the pistol, her hands trembling slightly. Ava broke the mechanics down for Ryder in sharp, simple steps, her focus cutting through Ryder's obvious unease. Nolan, ever the commanding presence, circled constantly, adjusting grips, correcting stances, and repeating safety checks until they became muscle memory.

"Widen your stance. Balance first," Nolan said as Damian handled the Staccato with visible nerves. "This isn't just about aiming. It's about control."

Hours passed in a blur of muffled shots and the rhythmic cadence of Nolan's instructions. Each member of the group cycled through magazines, their confidence slowly building as they became accustomed to the feel of the weapons in their hands.

The transition to rifles followed the same rhythm. Nolan drilled them on posture and recoil management, while Jase and Ava offered steady encouragement. Ryder flinched at the rifle's first booming shot but steadied under Ava's guidance. Olivia focused with quiet intensity, each magazine smoother than the last. Damian, analytical as ever, made small adjustments until Nolan gave a curt nod. "Good. Keep that up."

When the final rounds punched through paper, Nolan called them off the line. "That's enough for today," he said, fatigue in his voice but no compromise. "You've made progress. But this is only the start. Out there, you'll only get one chance to do it right. We'll drill until it's instinct. Which means we'll be back at it tomorrow. Pack it up."

They began gathering their gear, movements slower now, weighted with fatigue. Jase drifted toward Olivia, giving her shoulder a quick pat that lingered just a second longer than casual. A tired grin pulled at his lips. "You did really well. How'd it feel?"

Olivia pulled off her ear protection, cheeks flushed, her breath shaky. "Loud. And... a little terrifying. But I think I'm starting to get it." She managed a faint smile, though her hands slightly trembled as she set the rifle down.

Jase leaned closer, his voice dropping into a teasing warmth. "You'll get used to it. First time's always the hardest." His eyes caught hers, steady. "Honestly? You were better than I was my first time. I'm impressed."

A flicker of a smile tugged at her lips. "Oh, so you're admitting you weren't perfect at something?"

Jase laughed, rubbing the back of his neck. "Not at first. We can't all be you."

Olivia rolled her eyes, though her shoulders eased as a small laugh escaped her. "Oh, too bad."

Their eyes met again, an unspoken connection passing between them before Olivia broke it, glancing down to double-check the safety on her rifle. The moment lingered in the air, subtle and unspoken, before Jase straightened and gave her one last encouraging nod.

"Good work today, Liv. Really." His voice softened as he turned away, the faintest hint of a smile still on his face as he walked toward the others.

Olivia watched him go for a moment, her fingers brushing the strap of her rifle, before she shook her head, exhaling quietly as the weight of the day settled into her bones.

Nearby, Ryder was carefully setting her pistol back on the table, her movements slow and deliberate, as if she were still processing everything. Ava stepped up beside her, her sharp, calculating gaze softening just enough to show she'd noticed.

"I'll take your guns back for you," Ava offered, her voice gentler than usual. She reached for Ryder's pistol and rifle. "You've had a long day. Go rest. Get something to eat—or, I don't know, go hug a plant or whatever it is you do. Just keep my niece happy in there."

Ryder let out a small laugh, the tension in her shoulders loosening. "Thanks, Ava. I probably should lie down for a bit." She brushed her palms over her thighs, voice quieter. "This was… more intense than I thought. But I'll get there. I have to."

"You will," Ava said firmly, giving her a short nod. "Couple more reps and it won't rattle you so much. But for now? Take a break. You earned it."

Ryder smiled softly and headed for the door. Ava watched her go for a moment, then turned back, methodically organizing the gear.

Nolan glanced over. "Thank you."

Ava shrugged, her edge creeping back. "She's no good to us if she burns out on day one. And besides, it was for my niece. She's not even born yet, and she's already out on the gun range."

Nolan smirked and shook his head.

When the last weapons were stowed, the reinforced door hissed shut behind them. As they started walking down the hall, Nolan stopped and nodded for Jase and Ava to hang back.

"Good work in there," he said, his tone warm then turning firm. "Tomorrow, we go harder. Everyone needs to get comfortable with these weapons. That's the foundation. Then—the hard part begins."

Jase and Ava traded uneasy glances, brows furrowed.

Nolan didn't answer their confusion right away. Instead, he turned toward the wide observation window.

Beyond the glass sprawled the tactical training course, an underground battlefield of shadows and obstacles. Broken walls, doorways, and overturned furniture created a twisting urban maze. Sandbags, trees, and dirt mounds shaped an outdoor kill zone. Mannequins with motion sensors stood scattered everywhere. Some obvious, others hidden.

This," Nolan said, nodding toward the course, "is where it gets real."

Jase and Ava stepped closer to the glass. Ava's posture stiffened, her eyes scanning the tight corridors and blind corners.

"You think static targets are tough?" Nolan continued. "Try clearing a room when the enemy could be anywhere. Or everywhere. And you won't be alone. You'll move as a team—communicate under pressure, cover each other's backs, know when to push and when to hold. One mistake in the real world. Game over."

Jase and Ava looked at each other, then back at the sprawling course. The weight of his words settled deep. This wasn't just about learning to fire a weapon. It was about instinct. Trust. Teamwork.

And they only had a short time to get it right.

CHAPTER SEVENTEEN

Over the next month, the group trained relentlessly. The rhythm of their lives no longer felt measured in days or weeks but in progress—the tightening of their aim, the quickening of their reflexes, the way their movements became second nature. Shots grew truer, teamwork tighter, and their roles within the Ouroboros began to crystallize.

Nolan kept the weapons training structured and relentless, breaking them into rotating groups of three while the rest focused on daily duties. Every session pushed them harder—timed drills, moving targets, firing on the move. Each day blurred into the next, marked by the constant grind of survival and preparation—and the looming shadow of the world above.

They grew familiar with the entire arsenal, though not all at the same pace.

Olivia proved the most precise, her analytical mind thriving with long-range rifles. The Barrett MK22 became her weapon of choice. She relished the quiet challenge of calculating distance, windage, and corrections, her steady hands delivering round after round with clinical precision.

Jase and Ava proved the most versatile, adapting quickly to nearly every weapon they touched. They excelled with AR rifles, often side by side, their competitive streaks pushing each other harder. Ava, though, developed a particular fondness for the SIG XM250—a belt-fed light machine gun whose brutal power thrilled her.

Nolan often shook his head at her enthusiasm. "I'm glad we've got it," he said one day as she tore through a target downrange. "But I hope to hell we never need it."

Ava smirked, resting the weapon across her shoulder. "If we do, they'll regret that I'm the one behind it."

Damian and Ryder lagged behind the others, struggling with recoil control and precision of heavier weapons. Damian's hands were built for sutures, not triggers. Ryder's nurturing instincts clashed with the violence of every shot. Yet neither quit. They found steady success with pistols and submachine guns—smaller calibers that matched their control. They weren't the most accurate shooters, but each session built confidence, resilience replacing hesitation.

Life outside the range carried its own rhythm. Jase spent his off-hours in the greenhouse, learning from Ryder how to coax life from the soil. At first he was clumsy, knocking over pots, over-packing soil, but Ryder's patience soon turned him into a capable helper. It became a familiar sight—Jase crouched beside a row of lettuce, dirt streaking his arms, while Ryder knelt nearby, her growing belly brushing the planters as she loosened the soil with delicate hands.

Ava poured her downtime into the facility's mechanical systems, fixing minor issues before they became serious. On quieter days, she prowled through storerooms, tallying supplies and muttering about shortages and surpluses.

In the med-bay, Damian trained Olivia. Together they pored over medical texts and practiced with the equipment, Olivia's hands shaky at first but steadier each time. Ryder's pregnancy weighed heavily on them all, but especially here—it was a constant reminder that their knowledge might mean the difference between life and death. Damian's calm demeanor steadied Olivia's nerves, and her resolve sharpened under his guidance.

By the month's end, the group was transformed. Their bodies stronger. Their aim steadier. Their confidence tempered. Not by arrogance, but by the sobering knowledge of what lay ahead. The range no longer echoed with hesitant shots but with the sharp, disciplined rhythm of survivors preparing to fight.

They were far from perfect. But they were ready for the next step.

***

Nolan gathered the group in the armory to brief them on their next steps in training. He stood behind the steel workbench, palms braced on the surface, while the others stood around the far side. The atmosphere was heavier than in earlier meetings. Weeks of training had reshaped them—straighter stances, sharper focus, eyes fixed on him.

"We've spent the last month honing your shooting," Nolan began, his voice calm but edged with command. He gestured over his shoulder at the wall of weapons, each one gleaming under soft backlighting. "You've learned how every one of these fires and handles. You've come a long way."

The group exchanged brief glances. Jase's jaw set hard. Olivia's small nod showed her mind was already racing ahead. Ava folded her arms, a smirk tugging at her lips. Ryder shifted uneasily, fingers twitching at her sides, while Damian tried to hide his nerves with a subtle adjustment of his stance.

Nolan leaned forward, his eyes sweeping across them. "Now it's time for the real training."

No one spoke, but their posture said enough. Ready or not, they understood what he meant.

"From here on out, we shift to combat training," Nolan said. "You'll learn to move—individually and as a team. Clearing rooms. Running formations. Maneuvering through different environments. This isn't about shooting anymore. It's about surviving real-world scenarios." He paused, locking eyes with each of them.

"I won't lie to you," he continued. "This will be the toughest training we've done yet. We've only got a few months left to prepare. I'll need every ounce of effort you've got. But if you commit, if you give it everything—I'll make sure you're ready for anything out there."

Ava unfolded her arms, her voice slicing through the tension. "We're ready."

"Good," Nolan said, a faint smile breaking his severity. "First order of business. Starting tomorrow, everyone wears their battle belts around the facility. Set them up however you want— your pistol of choice, extra mags, IFAK—whatever setup works for you. You need to get used to carrying that gear all the time. Find the layout that's most comfortable for you."

He gave them a moment to absorb that before continuing. "After a few weeks, we'll start running plate carriers too. Twice a week, we'll hit the treadmills fully kitted. You need the strength and endurance to move in full gear as easily as you move without it."

Ryder's eyes widened slightly, and she exchanged a nervous glance with Damian, whose lips pressed into a thin line. Olivia raised a skeptical brow but kept her composure, her mind likely racing through the logistics. Jase let out a small, low whistle, while Ava's smirk grew, her excitement barely hidden.

Nolan caught their reactions and crossed his arms, his tone unwavering. "Yeah, it's going to suck. But when the time comes, you won't even notice the weight. You'll be faster, stronger, and more efficient because of it. And most importantly, there won't be any distractions. Everything has to be second nature."

The room fell quiet. None of them looked thrilled, but they all understood. The time for comfort was over. They were about to step into a world they barely understood, one that was unforgiving. Being prepared was their only option.

"Tomorrow, I'll start with Jase, Ava, and Olivia on the training course," Nolan continued, his voice steady and commanding. "Ryder and Damian, you'll stay on the range to refine your shooting. We'll rotate after each session so everyone gets equal time. We'll start slow. Focus on fundamentals, but things will ramp up quickly. It's going to get tough, so get some rest. You're going to need it."

He let the weight of his words settle, then gestured to the racks along the wall. "Before you head out, grab your battle belts. Set them up how you like. If you need help, ask."

Boots scuffed against the floor as the group moved toward the gear. Jase held a belt up, already imagining its weight in motion. Beside him, Ava buckled hers on immediately, cinching it tight around her waist with a sharp tug.

Ryder hesitated before reaching for one. "What's an IFAK again?" she asked softly.

"Individual First Aid Kit," Damian answered, sliding a belt into place around his hips. "Tourniquet, bandages, stuff to stop bleeding. You'll want it on you in case something happens."

Ryder nodded, brow furrowing as she studied the pouches. "Right. Got it."

Olivia, always the pragmatist, laid out her gear on the workbench, methodically arranging each item with precision. She secured a drop leg holster to her right thigh, adjusting the straps until it fit snugly but didn't restrict her movement. On her left side, she set up a drop leg magazine holder, carefully tightening it and testing the accessibility. She crouched, shifted, tested draws and reloads, then adjusted until her movements flowed clean.

Nolan watched them with a critical eye, stepping in occasionally to offer advice. "Jase, position your holster closer to your hip—too far forward, it'll slow you down. Ava, make sure your tourniquet is somewhere reachable with either hand. Ryder, don't overload the belt—you want it functional, not cumbersome."

The group followed his instructions, tweaking and adjusting their belts until they felt as comfortable as possible. By the time they were done, the armory carried a different energy—less apprehension, more focus. The belts around their waists were a physical reminder of the path they were on now, but somehow made it less terrifying.

"Good," Nolan said, stepping back to survey them. "Square everything away tonight. Tomorrow morning, these belts go on first thing, and they don't come off. Training, chores, meals—it doesn't matter. The more you wear them, the more natural they'll feel. This gear isn't just equipment. It's part of you."

The group nodded, their faces set with determination. Ava gave her belt one last tug and smirked. "Damn, I look like a total badass, right?"

"Something like that," Nolan replied with a faint grin, though his tone remained serious. "Dismissed. Get some sleep."

As the group filed out of the armory, Nolan gently placed a hand on Ryder's shoulder. His touch lingered a moment before he said, "Hey, you two. Hang back." His voice had lost its usual edge, softened as his gaze shifted between her and Damian

When the others were gone, he turned fully to Ryder, his expression warm but serious. "Ryder," he began, lowering his hand, "With all this new training, you won't be doing anything too intense. I know you want to contribute, but your health, and the baby's, come first." His voice wavered slightly on the last words, a flicker of vulnerability breaking through.

Ryder let out a soft sigh of relief, her hand instinctively brushing over her stomach. "Thank you. I've been trying to figure out how far I can push myself without risking anything, and it's been weighing on me. I don't want to hold anyone back."

Nolan stepped closer, his tone gentle but firm. "You don't have to worry about that. We'll find a balance. I still want you to learn the basics. Enough to feel confident and prepared for after the baby comes. The more you know, the safer you'll feel. And the better I'll feel. You don't need to run drills with the rest of us, but I'll make sure you're ready to handle yourself if the worst happens." He reached for her hand, giving it a light squeeze.

Damian cleared his throat, his professional demeanor breaking through the moment. "I was hoping we wouldn't put her through all that intense training. She can stay active, exercise and shoot, but anything too physical? It's just not smart right now."

Nolan nodded, meeting Damian's eyes with quiet appreciation. "That's why I'm pairing you together. You'll keep an eye on her, Doc. If something doesn't feel right, you pull her back. No questions. I know you've got her best interests at heart, same as me."

Ryder smiled softly, her fingers tightening around Nolan's. "Thank you. Both of you. It means a lot to know I've got you watching out for me."

Nolan shifted his gaze to Damian, his tone becoming more pragmatic. "Now, as for you. I know this isn't exactly your area of expertise, but we're going to focus on turning you into an effective combat medic. It's one thing to keep your cool in the med bay, but when things get chaotic out there—bullets flying, people shouting—it's a whole different game. You'll need to move, think, and keep sharp under pressure. It won't be easy, but I'll get you ready."

Damian exhaled, resolve settling in his expression. "I'll do whatever it takes. I won't let anyone down."

Nolan's lips curved into a small smile before he looked back at Ryder, his voice softening once more. "And you, you're not slowing us down. You're doing exactly what you need to do. Don't ever think otherwise."

Ryder's eyes glistened as she nodded. "I won't. And I promise I'll stay strong. For all of us."

Nolan leaned in, pressing a gentle kiss to her temple. "That's all I could ever ask."

He stepped back, his tone lifting slightly. "Alright, let's get some rest. Tomorrow's a new day, and we've got plenty of work ahead."

***

Nolan pulled back the charging handle on his SIG MCX-SPEAR LT. The metallic clack echoed across the range. He crouched low, rifle tight to his chest, breath steady, muscles coiled.

The sharp blast of a horn split the silence.

Nolan sprang into action, sprinting toward the wooded area that marked the starting zone. Boots hammered gravel, then dulled to the soft thud of dirt as he hit the tree line. His eyes cut left, right, every nerve alive, every motion wired into discipline.

A CRACK rang out, the sound of simulated gunfire ricocheting off the trees.

Nolan dove behind a tree, pressing his back against the bark as he aimed his rifle toward the source of the sound. Finger poised outside the guard. Waiting.

Ahead, 40 yards out, a silhouette zipped between trees, half-hidden by foliage. The pop-up target swept left to right, its black figure blurring against the green. Sweat slid down Nolan's temple as he leaned out, finding his line.

Another gunshot rang out, closer this time, spurring him into action. Nolan dropped to one knee, adjusted his aim, and squeezed the trigger in a fluid motion. The suppressed rifle whispered its fury. The target jerked—its red LED flashing center mass—then dropped into its slot.

Nolan didn't linger to celebrate. He sprinted, low and fast, diving behind a fallen log. The course was alive now. Gunfire cracking, voices shouting through speakers, targets shifting in the brush. Another silhouette popped up to his left, this one stationary but partially shielded by a wooden barricade.

Nolan flattened, crawling forward, barrel sweeping ahead. He moved with the precision of a predator stalking its prey, inching forward until he had a clear angle. His finger squeezed the trigger again—two shots this time. Pop-pop. Both hits, the target flashing red before slumping back into its base.

He sprang to his feet and pushed forward, moving between trees and obstacles. His breathing was measured, even as his heart hammered in his chest.

Then, a target on a pulley system screamed across a clearing. Nolan hit the dirt, body snapping into prone. He tracked it, scope slicing across its erratic sprint. Another burst of simulated gunfire cracked overhead, but he tuned it out.

Breath in. Exhale. Squeeze. The round caught center chest. LED flashed—target dropped.

Nolan pushed himself up in one fluid motion, slinging the rifle to low ready as he broke into a sprint. His boots pounded against the dirt path, the sound swallowed by the simulated chaos of war—distant gunfire, shouting, and the whirring of the course's automated systems.

Ahead, the terrain shifted abruptly, the wooded area giving way to the urban environment. A broken-down vehicle, cement barricades, and shattered storefronts lined a small makeshift street corner designed to mimic the chaos of a city under siege. The course's second act.

Nolan immediately dropped into a crouch, moving swiftly toward a cement barricade partially surrounded by rubble. He pressed his back against it, scanning the area ahead with quick, practiced movements.

A target popped up to his left, partially obscured by a rusted-out sedan. Without hesitation, Nolan snapped in that direction, bringing his rifle up and firing a double-tap. The target's LED blinked red as it jerked back and disappeared.

Another burst from a doorway across the street, its movement erratic with loud gun shots. Nolan shifted, peeking out from the edge of the barricade. He steadied his aim and squeezed the trigger. The target dropped with a sharp crack of the bullet.

Before he could adjust, a third target swung into view from behind a crumbled wall spitting simulated fire. Nolan rolled, came up on a knee, and cracked a single precise shot. The LED flared red as the target collapsed, vanishing back into its hiding place.

Nolan remained low, his breathing measured despite the exertion. He scanned the area for any additional threats before shifting his focus forward. The street ahead narrowed into a dead end, culminating in the final stage—a two-story building designed for CQB training.

Its facade was riddled with simulated damage—cracked walls, boarded-up windows, scorch marks—forming a realistic training ground. The structure loomed ahead like a challenge waiting to be conquered. Tight hallways, blind corners, and the kind of intensity only close-quarters combat could deliver.

Nolan glanced back, checking his six. Clear. He moved forward, every step deliberate, ready to breach.

The horn blared twice, signaling the end of the run. Lights flooded the arena. The exercise was over.

Nolan hit the mag release. The half-full magazine thunked into his palm. He tucked it into a pouch, racked the charging handle to strip the last round, and flipped the safety on.

"Clear!" he barked, automatic, the sound a compact snap that cut through the adrenaline haze.

He moved back to the staging area where Ava, Jase, and Olivia waited in full kit—boots, battle belts, plate carriers—their faces lit with awe and a hint of intimidation. They'd watched every stride, every decision—smooth, fast, surgical.

"Damn," Ava said, hooking her thumbs under her plate carrier straps, voice edged with genuine admiration. "That was pretty badass."

Olivia tilted her head, pragmatism masking the flutter under her ribs. "If that's the standard, we have work to do."

"By the time the doors open, you'll all be moving like that," he said, his voice calm but firm, a promise more than a boast. "But it's not going to happen overnight. Training like this takes time, discipline, and repetition."

Nolan set his weapon down on the table behind them, his gaze sweeping over the group. "Here's how we're going to start. First, we're going to walk the course together with empty weapons, no ammo. I'm going to show you how to position yourselves behind cover. What works and what gets you killed. You'll learn how to move between cover points, keep your weapon ready, and stay situationally aware. These basics are critical."

The group nodded, their expressions serious as the weight of what he was saying settled over them.

"For the next few days, that's all we'll focus on," Nolan continued, pacing slowly in front of them. "You'll practice moving, crouching, and using cover until it becomes second nature. I'll walk you through it step by step, and we'll repeat it until you're comfortable."

"What happens after that?" Olivia asked, her arms crossed as she studied him intently.

"Once you've got the basics down, we'll move on to something more realistic," Nolan said, his tone shifting, a hint of challenge creeping in. "We'll start using simunition—marking rounds. They're non-lethal but still give you a clear sense of where you're hitting. It'll feel like real shooting, but it won't kill anyone if you screw up. And to make it more… motivating," he added with a small smirk, "you'll be wearing FTVs—Feedback Tactical Vests."

"Feedback vests?" Jase asked, raising an eyebrow.

Nolan nodded. "They're specially designed vests that'll give you a slight jolt if the targets hit you. The idea is to simulate the consequences of bad positioning or poor movement. If you leave yourself exposed, you'll feel it. Trust me, it's not fun—but it's effective. You'll learn real fast to stay low, stay quick, and stay covered."

Ava's lips curled into a small, amused smile. "So, basically, we get zapped for screwing up?"

"Exactly," Nolan said, his tone matter-of-fact. "Better a small shock in training than a bullet in the field. The goal is to get you comfortable making split-second decisions under stress."

The group exchanged glances, a mix of apprehension and determination in their eyes.

"You've all improved your accuracy," Nolan went on, his voice dropping into something heavier. "But accuracy is the least important thing now. This is about thinking. Problem-solving under fire. Knowing when to move, when to hold, when to fight. Out there, you won't face paper silhouettes. You'll face people, desperate people—who know how to move, think, and fight. This training isn't just for your survival. It's for the survival of everyone in this group. So we do it right."

Jase cracked his neck, rolling his shoulders like he was gearing up for a fight. "On your lead."

"Good," Nolan said. "Grab your rifles. Follow me." He gave them one last look, his expression resolute. "We've got a long road ahead."

Nolan lead them toward the first section of the course, a mock woodland environment with scattered trees, low bushes and dirt mounds. One by one, the group followed Nolan's lead, practicing their movements and adjusting their stances under his watchful eye. He barked corrections as they moved.

"Olivia—lower your center of gravity. Don't overextend your stride."

"Ava—pivot smoother. Don't let your barrel drift."

"Jase—cleaner transitions. Get your eyes on the next cover point before you move."

Despite his commands, their movements stayed clumsy, uneven. They hesitated at cover, tripped over footing, and left themselves exposed more often than not.

Nolan watched them stumble through the last barricade, sweat and frustration heavy on their faces. It was a start, but nowhere near enough.

At the far end, the CQB house loomed in silence, a jagged shadow against the lights of the arena. Nolan's gaze lingered on it. With only five months until the doors opened, he knew this team had a long way to go.

CHAPTER EIGHTEEN

Three months later, the med-bay door slid open with a soft hiss, and Ryder stepped inside. Her silhouette had changed dramatically, her belly now fully showing at 35 weeks. She moved carefully, one hand resting instinctively on her stomach as she crossed the threshold, mindful of her body's limits.

Damian was already waiting, standing beside the examination table with his medical tablet in hand. His gaze softened as he saw her. "Hey, there," he greeted, setting the tablet down. He stepped forward to offer his hand, helping her up onto the exam table. "How are you feeling today?"

"Big," Ryder said with a small laugh, brushing a strand of her dark hair behind her ear. "And a little sore. But nothing out of the ordinary."

Damian nodded, his expression a mix of affection and professionalism. "That's expected. You've been doing a good job taking it easy, though." He grabbed a blood pressure cuff from the nearby tray. "Let's see how you and our little one are doing."

He slid the cuff around her arm, gently tightening it as he positioned the stethoscope against her skin. The familiar hiss of the cuff inflating filled the room, and Ryder watched him with a calm, trusting gaze. After a moment, Damian nodded in approval.

"Blood pressure's good," he said with a small smile, jotting down the numbers on his tablet. "That's one less thing to worry about."

Ryder exhaled a breath she hadn't realized she was holding. "Good to hear. It's hard not to think about all the things that could go wrong."

"That's my job," Damian reassured. "You just focus on staying comfortable and let me handle the worrying." He set the cuff aside and rolled his stool closer. "Alright, let's check on the baby."

Ryder leaned back as Damian powered on the portable ultrasound. The screen flickered to life. He squirted gel across her stomach, and she winced at the coldness before smiling at his apologetic glance.

"Here we go." He pressed the transducer gently against her skin, moving until the picture resolved. The room fell quiet. Then the rapid, rhythmic whoosh of a heartbeat filled the air.

"There it is," Damian said softly, eyes fixed on the screen. The baby's heart beat strong and steady. He angled the monitor toward her. "Looking good. Head down, plenty of fluid, measurements right on track."

Ryder's eyes shone as she gazed at the grainy image. "Hi, Aurora," she whispered, reaching to brush her fingers against the screen. "I can't wait to meet you."

"It won't be long now," Damian said, his voice gentle. He wiped her belly clean with a warm towel, then took her hand. "You're doing everything right. You and the baby are in great shape."

"Thanks, Damian," Ryder said, squeezing his hand. "For everything. I don't know what I'd do without you."

"You'll never have to find out," he said firmly, then allowed a small smile. "Now, tell me how you're feeling overall. Any swelling? Cravings? Anything else I should know?"

Ryder leaned back against the table, laughing softly. "Cravings are fine. The swelling, though… my feet don't even look like my feet anymore."

Damian chuckled as he glanced down. "They're still your feet, but swelling can happen. Let's up your water intake and make elevate your legs when resting. That should help, but if you experience any rapid swelling or pain—especially headaches, vision changes, or abdominal pain—tell me immediately. It could be a sign of preeclampsia."

He got up and moved across the room, stripping off his medical gloves.

Ryder nodded, then tilted her head, her curiosity edged with unease. "What about breastfeeding? Are there signs now that could tell if I'll have trouble?"

Damian leaned back against the counter, arms folded thoughtfully. "I know you're worried about that. Most of the time we can't predict challenges this early. But there are a few things I can monitor—breast tissue changes and whether you start producing colostrum in the final weeks. Colostrum's that thick, nutrient-packed milk your body makes before your actual supply comes in."

Ryder's brows knit. "And if I don't? My mom struggled with it. She couldn't feed me the way she wanted, and I remember how much it haunted her." Her voice thinned, betraying the weight of that memory. "What if I end up the same?"

Damian shook his head, his tone firm but kind. "Not producing colostrum before delivery isn't unusual. Some women don't see it until after.birth, and it's perfectly normal. But I hear you. If you want to be proactive, we can try hand expression in the final weeks—gentle stimulation to help encourage milk production. We can collect and store some colostrum, that way, even if your milk is delayed, you'll have a supply ready."

Ryder's hands curled over her belly, her eyes fixed on them. "I can't fail her."

"You won't," Damian said with quiet certainty. He picked up his tablet and pulled up a set of diagrams. "It's simple, manual expression into sterile containers. I can walk you through it and give you bottles for storage. It's not about perfection. It's about giving yourself options."

Ryder studied the diagrams, then looked back at him, her voice low. "Maybe we can start in a couple weeks. I want to do everything I can."

"Absolutely," Damian said, a reassuring smile softening his face. "One step at a time. For now, focus on eating well, staying hydrated, and getting rest. That's the best foundation for both of you."

Damian paused, his expression softening as he chose his words carefully. "There's one thing I need to tell you, but I don't want to upset you. Given the circumstances here and the fact that the med-bay wasn't prepared for a birth, an epidural won't be possible. You'll have to go through labor and birth the natural way." His voice was gentle, bracing for any reaction.

Ryder didn't flinch. Instead, she nodded, a warm, calm smile spreading across her face. "It's okay," she said, her voice steady. "I kind of figured that already."

She took a deep breath, grounding herself. "Honestly, I'd probably choose the natural route anyway. It's something I've always wanted to experience at its purest—at least the first time. I know it's going to be painful, but... she'll be worth it."

Damian's tension seemed to melt away as he exhaled, his shoulders relaxing. "I should've known you'd handle it like this. You're stronger than you realize, Ryder"

Ryder gave a quiet laugh, her eyes meeting his with gratitude. "Thanks, Damian. I really appreciate you taking the time to explain everything. It makes me feel... a little less overwhelmed." Her smile genuine, a quiet reassurance that she was ready for what was to come.

"That's what I'm here for," he said, giving her a supportive nod. "You're doing great, Ryder. Just keep taking it one day at a time, and before you know it, you'll be holding Aurora in your arms."

At the mention of her baby's name, warmth spread across Ryder's face, her eyes softening. Aurora wasn't just a dream or a hope. She was her future, and she couldn't wait to meet her.

***

In the armory, the harsh overhead light illuminated the workbench, where tools and weapon parts were scattered. Olivia, Nolan, Jase, and Ava worked in focused silence, the rhythmic clink of metal and quiet conversation filling the space.

Jase leaned over his rifle, hands deftly working to replace the pistol grip with one featuring a more vertical angle. He tested the feel of the new grip, rolling the rifle in his hands as if already moving through the course in his mind. He turned his attention to the gas block, fine-tuning it for optimal performance when suppressed.

Across from him, Ava's rifle was laid out with the precision of her workshop bench. She tightened the mount on a Trijicon RMR Type 2 red dot, fixing it offset beside her scope. Nolan had convinced Jase to run the setup last week, and after seeing how quickly he transitioned between long-range and close-quarters targets, Ava wasn't about to be left behind.

Olivia and Nolan worked across from one another, their focus on other weapons and a small pile of accessories. They were attaching red dots and weapon lights to each Flux Defense Raider X they had.

Nolan was adamant that every weapon in the armory be fully outfitted and combat-ready before the doors opened. With the armory overstocked with various accessories, every weapon would be in their purpose-built configurations for quick deployment in an emergency.

"That should do it," Jase said, breaking the quiet as he shouldered his rifle. He gave it a final inspection, then grinned. ""Let's see if this tuning is any better. I'll be on the range if anyone needs me."

Ava smirked, setting down her wrench and reaching for her rifle. "Not without me. I just finished installing this offset dot, and I need you to help me zero it. I always forget the correct way to turn the screws."

Nolan chuckled without looking up. "Point of impact, Ava. For the millionth time—point of impact."

Ava rolled her eyes dramatically but grinned as she slung her rifle. "Yeah, yeah, easy as that."

Jase stood at the door, motioning for Ava to follow. "Come on, I'll show the engineer."

"Oh, shut up. You know it's confusing," she shot back, falling into step beside him as they exited.

Nolan watched them go, shaking his head with a small smile. "I really enjoy how much that confuses her."

Olivia smirked. "Same. But Jase is definitely catching hell for that comment."

Nolan laughed under his breath before returning to his work. The armory settled back into the cadence of metal on metal, the quiet focus of preparation.

After a few minutes, Olivia glanced up from her weapon, her voice soft but deliberate. "So," she said, "how are you holding up? With… everything?"

Nolan froze, his hands stilling on the optic he'd been tightening. He looked up and met her eyes. He didn't need to ask what she meant.

He exhaled, running a hand over his cropped hair. "I'm… managing. Trying to stay focused. Ryder's a rock, but it's a lot." His voice dipped lower. "The baby's almost here, and I keep thinking about all the ways I have to keep them safe. But there's only so much I can prepare for, you know? The rest is just… faith that I won't screw it up."

Olivia set her pistol down, leaning forward slightly. "You won't. That fear just means you care." She tilted her head, her expression thoughtful. "You've been training us all like our lives depend on it, because they do. That same dedication? That's what's going to make you a good father. Ryder knows it. We all know it. She's lucky to have you to lean on during all this."

Something in Nolan's posture eased, the steel in his shoulders softening. For a moment, the weight didn't feel so crushing.

"Thanks," he said quietly. "That… means a lot."

Olivia picked up the rifle she'd been working on, turning it over in her hands. "And for what it's worth, if you need someone to step up, carry more of the load, anything at all… I'm here. Just say the word."

Nolan paused, his screwdriver hovering mid-turn. There was something steady in her voice, that dependable edge he'd always admired. He shook his head, voice sincere. "Thanks, Liv. But you've already stepped up plenty. Helping Damian with the delivery. That's more than anyone should be asked to do. But I'm glad it'll be you in there, helping her through this. Ryder needs someone who can keep their cool, and you've got that in spades."

Olivia pressed her lips into a faint smile, gaze dropping back to the rifle. "Me too," she said softly.

For a moment, only the soft clink of tools filled the room as they fitted parts to the weapons. It was a quiet, shared understanding. One that didn't need words.

Nolan broke the silence, his tone light but probing. "What about you, Liv? How are you holding up?"

Olivia blinked, caught off guard. "Me?" She glanced at him, then quickly back at her weapon. "I'm fine. Same as always."

"Come on," Nolan said, leaning forward, his forearms resting on the edge of the table. His voice was casual, but his eyes were sharp. "You're always fine. But really—how are you doing? With the baby coming, the training… everything."

Olivia hesitated, her hands stilling mid-assembly as his question sank in. She didn't meet his gaze right away, focusing instead on tightening a screw on the rifle. Her fingers moved methodically, as if the task could shield her from the weight of the question.

"It's… overwhelming," she admitted finally, her voice quieter than before. "But we don't really have the luxury of falling apart, do we? I just focus on what needs to be done. That's enough for now."

Nolan tilted his head, studying her. "Fair enough," he said, though he didn't sound convinced. Then he added, almost casually, "And what about Jase?"

Her hands froze. She glanced up sharply, surprise flashing across her face. "What about him?"

Nolan shrugged, a knowing smirk tugging at the corner of his mouth. "You two are close. Always have been. Anyone can see it. Just saying—lean on him if you need to."

Olivia's cheeks flushed faintly, but she masked it with a dismissive laugh. "We're a team, Nolan, and we're focused on that. Anything else you're thinking is of your own imagination."

"Sure," Nolan replied, drawing the word out just enough to make her narrow her eyes at him. "Maybe that's what you both tell yourselves."

Olivia rolled her eyes, though the gesture lacked conviction. "Drop it," she warned, her voice more flustered than firm.

Nolan laughed, lifting his hands in surrender. "Hey, I'm just saying. We all see it."

He returned to the weapon he was working on, his tone shifting, softer now, more sincere. "It's okay, you know. To let someone in. To want that. Especially now. It's a dark world out there, Liv. Hell, it was bad enough before it went to complete shit. No one would think less of you for not wanting to go through it alone."

Olivia didn't respond, her gaze dropping to the weapon light in her hands. She tightened another screw, her expression carefully neutral, though tension flickered in her jaw. "We've all got enough to worry about," she said at last, her voice quieter. "That's all it is. Making sure we're ready for what's coming."

Nolan studied her another moment, then gave a small nod. "Okay, Liv."

The armory fell quiet again, broken only by the click of tools and the things left unsaid. As Nolan focused on his weapon, Olivia turned his words over in her mind like a stone in her palm, rough-edged and impossible to ignore. She tightened her grip on the gun, her thoughts drifting to Jase before she could stop them. It wasn't something she could afford to dwell on. Not now, not ever.

***

Later that evening, the group gathered around the dinner table, their plates pushed aside and the air filled with the lingering warmth of a meal shared among family. The black trays stamped with the Ouroboros insignia sat empty now, crumbs and smears of sauce all that remained.

Ava leaned back in her chair, arms crossed, a sly grin tugging at her lips. "Remember when Damian tried to make pancakes that first week?" she said, eyes sparkling. "We had to scrape them off the griddle like cement."

The table erupted with laughter. Damian groaned, rubbing the back of his neck, though a reluctant smile slipped through. "Hey, I never claimed to be a chef. You all still ate them. Half a bottle of syrup gone in one morning."

"Because it was the only way to choke them down!" Ryder laughed, one hand resting protectively on her bump. "We didn't want to hurt your feelings."

"Alright, true," Damian conceded with a laugh. "That's why I stick to the lab and med-bay. The kitchen is all yours."

"At least you can brew coffee," Jase said with a grin. "Unlike Nolan."

That set the table off again. Nolan threw up his hands. "Okay, hold on! You know that damn thing has a mind of its own. Don't know why we need such an elaborate machine to brew coffee. I still think Ouro was doing it to mess with me."

Olivia smirked. "Yeah, the highly sophisticated AI that manages our entire survival just wanted to mess with you by screwing with the coffee machine."

The laughter rolled on, filling the room in a way that felt like oxygen, a reminder of how far they'd come.

"I gotta say," Ryder began once the laughter died down, her voice more reflective, "we've come a long way since those first few months. Back then, we were just… here. You know? Not really sure what the point of any of this was. Now, I feel like we're completely different people. Even with everything looming over us."

The table fell quiet. Their eyes distant, each of them remembering who they'd been when this all began.

"Yeah." Olivia nodded slowly. "It's strange, isn't it? Thinking about who we were back then. Scared. Lost. Unsure of everything."

Her voice caught briefly, but she steadied it.

"And now… we've grown so much. All of us. And as terrifying as it is to think about what's up there… I think we're ready. Or at least as ready as anyone can be."

Jase leaned forward, resting his forearms on the table, his gaze moving from one face to the next. "To see who we were when we first walked in here, and who we are now…" He let the thought hang before continuing, his voice low and steady. "I'm proud of us. We've all been through dark days—even before we knew what had happened to the world. And somehow, we stayed strong. We forged ahead. We did it together."

The words lingered, each of them remembering their worst days, and how they had pushed through.

"Thirty-five days from now," Jase finally said, "those doors are going to open. And one thing I know is that whatever's waiting out there, we'll be ready to face it. Because together, we can get through anything."

Ryder reached across the table, her hand finding Jase's. Her eyes shone with gratitude as the others murmured their agreement. It reminded them why they had survived, why they had fought so hard.

Across the table, Olivia's gaze lingered on Jase. Her expression calm, though her eyes betrayed the turmoil beneath. She tried to keep her face neutral—proud, even—but something else lingered beneath. Something deeper. Something raw. She couldn't stop seeing him differently now, her heart pulling in ways she had spent months trying to ignore—even if she'd never admit it.

Nolan cleared his throat, his expression shifting. The warmth in his eyes gave way to something heavier. Something serious. "There's something I need to say," he began. Instantly, all eyes turned to him.

"For the last few months, I've been leading you through the training," Nolan said, his gaze moving from one face to the next. "And I've been proud to do it. Proud of all of you—how hard you've worked, how much you've grown. I don't think any other group could have done what we've done down here."

He paused, drawing in a breath. "But with the baby coming… it's time for a change. A change I believe is best for all of us."

His eyes flicked to Ryder, vulnerability breaking through for just a moment. Ryder's hand instinctively tightened over her stomach, her expression unreadable.

Nolan's voice steadied. "The truth is, I can't be the one to lead us anymore. Not in the way we'll need once we're out there. My focus has to be on my family. On keeping Ryder and the baby safe. I can't risk that getting in the way of the decisions that will keep the rest of you alive." His eyes softened on Ryder, then turned back to the group.

"And that's why," Nolan said, his gaze locking on Jase, "it's time for Jase to take back his role as leader of this group."

The room went still, a collective inhale. Jase's brow furrowed, his mouth parting in protest.

"Nolan, no," Jase said, his voice low and resolute. "You've been the one holding us together. You built this—the training, the discipline. You've carried us farther than I ever could. I'm not—"

"Yes, you are," Nolan cut in firmly.

"I'm not ready!" Jase snapped, louder now, his hand pressing flat against the table. His eyes burned as he looked around the table. "You all think I've got this figured out? I don't. Half the time, I don't even know what the hell I'm doing. I've made mistakes—big ones. If I screw up out there, it won't just be on me. It'll be on all of you."

His words hung heavy in the silence.

Nolan leaned forward, his voice steel. "Every one of us has made mistakes. But you were the one who pulled us through the worst of it. Day after day, when this place felt like it was going to break us. You made sure we didn't fall apart. That's leadership, Jase. You carried us when none of us knew how."

Jase shook his head, his chest tight. "That wasn't leading. That was me…stumbling forward…because there wasn't another option."

"Exactly," Nolan said, his tone unyielding. "And you still got us here. That's why it has to be you. I trained you all to fight, but I can't lead you into what's coming. My priorities are divided now. Yours aren't. And like it or not, we already look to you. We always have."

Jase's gaze dropped to the table, his jaw working. The fight bled slowly from his posture. When he finally looked back up, his eyes met Nolan's. The doubt hadn't vanished, but beneath it flickered something else—acceptance, heavy and unavoidable.

"You're sure?" He said at last, voice rough. "You're all sure?" His eyes swept the table, desperate to see the conviction he couldn't yet find in himself.

Nolan's lips tugged into a faint smile. "It's what's best. For all of us."

Olivia reached out, her hand brushing Jase's arm. "We've always followed your lead," she said softly, conviction in her voice.

"And we always will." Her hand lingered before retreating, but her gaze didn't, holding his until she finally forced herself to look away.

The others echoed their agreement in quiet voices, each voice sincere. They all bore scars, carried their own fears—but in that moment, gathered around the table, they drew strength from one another. The path ahead was uncertain, but with Jase at the helm, they felt ready to face it. Together.

Jase exhaled, the weight in his chest settling into place. He gave a small, reluctant nod.

"Alright," he said softly.

CHAPTER NINETEEN

Almost a month later, Ryder found herself once again sitting in the hallway of the armory wing, her favorite perch overlooking the training course. Through the bay windows, she could watch the team as they moved below, their silhouettes weaving through obstacles with purpose and precision.

Every detail held her attention—the clipped hand signals, the clean transitions between cover, the silent communication that made them look less like individuals and more like a single, cohesive unit.

At the center of it all was Jase. His voice carried through the comms with calm authority, his movements steady and assured. The hesitation she remembered from months ago was gone. Now he moved with the weight of command, each order sharpened by confidence earned the hard way. Nolan, Damian, Olivia, and Ava followed seamlessly, covering each other's blind spots, their rhythm forged by months of relentless repetition.

Ryder watched quietly, pride rising in her chest. Pride in them, in how far they'd come. Pride in herself, too, because even if her training had been slower, Nolan's patience had never wavered. Room clearing. Moving efficiently. Confidence with her weapon. No, she couldn't run the course with them. Not now, not with the baby growing inside her. But she didn't feel left behind. She knew her time would come. And when it did, she'd be ready.

The comm system crackled, snapping her out of thought. Jase's voice cut through, steady and commanding.

"Alright, form up at the shoot house. We're running this one live. No stumbles this time. Olivia, you're on point. Nolan, you're trailing. Ava and Damian, you're with me."

Ryder's gaze shifted to the far end of the course, where the shoot house loomed. Her pulse quickened. Jase's orders were firm, confident, carrying the weight of someone who no longer doubted himself. Someone the others followed without question.

Below, the team assembled at the entrance to the shoot house.

Jase stood in the center, his rifle resting against his shoulder, scanning their faces. He raised two fingers in the air, signaling to stack up on the wall.

Olivia slid to the door first, back to the wall, weapon low but ready. The others fell in behind her, precise, disciplined.

"Breach," Jase ordered through their headsets.

Olivia shoved the door open and flowed in. The rest followed like water through a crack.

"Clear left!" Olivia's voice cut sharp as she swept her sector.

"Clear right!" Ava echoed, moving in sync with Damian, eyes darting to every corner.

""Move!" Jase barked, stepping in behind them. "Damian, left door. Nolan, on me. Olivia, hold center."

The split was seamless. Damian pressed to the left, Ava covering. He gave her a glance, then yanked the handle and went in.

"Contact!" Damian snapped, weapon rising. Two sharp cracks. Target dropped.

"Clear," he called, Ava already covering his six.

Meanwhile, Jase and Nolan moved down a narrow hallway toward a larger open space. Jase's hand came up in a fist—stop. He tilted his head, listening for movement beyond the corner.

"Two targets, left. Nolan, on point. I'll cover."

Nolan rounded the corner without pause. Two silhouettes. Two clean shots. Both down.

"Clear," he reported, voice steady.

"Olivia, move up! Ava, take rear. Damian, regroup on me," Jase commanded, his tone firm but composed.

The team moved as one, their footsteps almost silent against the floor. They entered the final room, a large open space with multiple obstacles. Jase pointed to Olivia, then to a high vantage point on the left. "Overwatch."

She scrambled up, taking position. "Eyes on," Olivia reported, her voice steady. "Two targets, back right corner."

"Ava, Damian, peel right," Jase ordered. "Nolan, cover fire, on my call."

Ava and Damian darted to the right, their steps quick and low.

"Engage!" Jase's voice cut through.

The room erupted in a controlled storm of gunfire and movement. Nolan laid precise bursts, pinning the targets. Ava and Damian cut up the right side, flanking hard. Both opened fire. Two silhouettes dropped, and silence fell over the shoot house.

"Clear," Olivia confirmed from her perch.

Jase swept the room one last time, rifle raised. Then he lowered it, nodding once. "Good work."

The team exhaled, shoulders easing, the adrenaline bleeding off. Jase's gaze lingered a beat longer on Nolan, giving him a silent nod of respect before turning back to the group.

"Alright, let's regroup outside. We go again. Ouro, reset the shoot house—change it up!" Jase ordered.

"Copy that, Alpha-One." Ouro's voice echoed back.

The group gathered outside the shoot house, restocking magazines and grabbing a drink of water. Meanwhile, the low rumble of machinery echoed faintly from inside the shoot house. The mechanical sounds of shifting panels and sliding barriers filtered out, interspersed with the clattering of moving targets resetting into new positions. The metallic grind was a reminder of the facility's ability to challenge them in ways no ordinary training could. Every run was different, and every scenario unpredictable.

They checked gear in silence, the air thick with focus. This course demanded more than stamina. It demanded total awareness.

Then the mechanical noise cut off, leaving an eerie stillness.

"Shoot house reset. Scenario randomized. Proceed when ready," Ouro announced.

Jase slid his last magazine into place and turned to his team, resolve sharpening his features. "Same approach. Watch your corners, call your shots, stay tight."

They nodded, eyes hard, breathing steady. Jase raised two fingers. Stack. Olivia slid into position at the door, hand on the handle. The others aligned behind her, rifles ready.

A silent nod passed between them.

"Bre—"

A horn blasted.

"Simulation paused," Ouro's voice sliced through the stillness, cold and clinical. "Alpha-Three, Beta-Two requires your immediate medical attention."

The words froze them in place. For a beat, no one moved, the air vibrating with shock.

Then, as one, their heads snapped toward Damian.

The silence shattered.

"RYDER!" Nolan's roar cut like thunder, raw and panicked.

He bolted before anyone could react, boots hammering the floor as he sprinted for the exit.

***

They found Ryder slumped against the wall outside the armory wing, legs stretched out, her breaths short and ragged. Sweat glistened on her forehead, her hands clutched tight against her stomach.

"Nolan," she gasped, her voice trembling but steady. "It's happening. The baby's coming."

Nolan dropped beside her in an instant, his face etched with panic and resolve all at once. "Ryder, I'm here. We're all here."

Damian was already kneeling, snapping on gloves, his med kit open. "Ryder, I need you to focus on me," he said firmly, his voice calm against the storm. "How long have you felt contractions?"

Ryder winced, her body seizing as another wave hit. "I—I don't know. Maybe an hour. They weren't this bad until now."

"Damn it, Ryder," Nolan muttered, gripping her hand like a lifeline. "You should've said something."

"I didn't want to slow anyone down," she panted, her breath hitching.

"We can talk about that later," Damian snapped, pulling Nolan's eyes back to him. "We need her in the med-bay, now."

Nolan moved to lift her, but Ryder shook her head, stubborn even through the pain. "I can walk." She tried to rise, only to grimace and collapse back down.

"No way," Nolan said fiercely. "We're carrying you."

Together, he and Jase lifted her, one supporting her shoulders, the other her legs. Ryder groaned, clutching Nolan's arm like it anchored her to the earth. "You're okay," he murmured, his voice cracking before he forced it steady. "Breathe, Ry. Just breathe. We've got you."

Damian kept pace beside them, his eyes sharp. "Ryder, your breathing's too shallow. I need you to take slower, deeper breaths, okay? In through your nose, out through your mouth."

She nodded weakly, trying to match his rhythm, but another contraction tore through her, pulling a whimper from her lips. "It's too soon," she whispered, fear breaking through. "We're not ready for this."

"Yes we are," Nolan reassured her as they turned the final corner toward the med bay. "You're so ready to be a mom, Ryder. We've got this."

The med-bay doors hissed open, lights already bright and sterile. Jase and Nolan eased Ryder onto the exam table while Damian rolled up his sleeves, all business.

"Jase, thank you, but I need you to wait outside with Ava. Olivia, you're with me. Ready to deliver a baby?" He asked with a slight smile.

Olivia's face was pale, but her eyes burned with focus. "I'm ready."

"Good." Damian's tone left no room for doubt. He gestured to Nolan. "Stay by Ryder's side. Keep her calm. Help her focus on her breathing."

Ryder let out a strangled cry as another contraction seized her, tears springing to her eyes. Nolan held her hand in both of his. His voice trembled but didn't break. "Just breathe, babe," he said softly, his forehead pressed against hers. "You can do this."

The med-bay doors slid shut behind Jase and Ava, leaving the world outside suspended in silence, while inside, everything came down to Ryder's ragged breaths, Damian's calm instructions, and Nolan's whispered words of love.

"That was more intense than I was expecting. She's in good hands though," Ava said, arms crossed as she leaned beside Jase. Her tone was calm, but worry flickered in her eyes.

Jase nodded, exhaling slowly, though his jaw clenched. "Yeah. I know. Still feels wrong, just standing out here doing nothing." As his eyes drifted to the door.

Inside, the med-bay pulsed with quiet urgency. Damian scrubbed his hands at the sink, snapping on fresh gloves, every motion deliberate. Olivia mirrored him, tying her hair back in a tight knot before slipping on her own gloves and sterile gown. The sharp scent of antiseptic filled the air.

"Olivia, focus on me," Damian said, arranging instruments on a tray with practiced precision. "This is going to get intense, but we'll handle it."

Olivia swallowed hard, then nodded. "I'm good." Her voice was steady, but her breath caught as she glanced at Ryder—her hand clutched Nolan's, her face twisted with pain, sweat beading at her temple. "What do you need me to do?"

Damian gestured to the monitors. "Vitals. Blood pressure, heart rate. Call it out if anything spikes or drops. If I need more, I'll guide you step by step."

Ryder let out a strangled cry as another contraction ripped through her, her back arching against the table. Her nails dug into Nolan's hand, leaving red crescents on his skin.

Nolan's voice was soft and steady as he tried to keep her calm. "You're doing amazing, Ryder. Just keep breathing. We're so close."

Ryder turned her face slightly, tears spilling despite her grit. "It hurts, Nolan," she whispered. "God, it hurts."

"I know, baby," he murmured, brushing damp strands of hair from her face with his free hand. His own eyes glistened. "But you can do this. You're stronger than the pain."

Olivia's eyes flicked between the monitor's steady beeps and Ryder's trembling form. For the first time since stepping inside, she felt her nerves fall away. Her hands steadied. Her focus narrowed. She wasn't just the coder anymore, they needed her to be something more.

"Vitals holding steady," she said clearly, her voice cutting through the rising tension. "She's doing good."

Damian glanced at her and gave the faintest nod of approval before turning his full attention to Ryder. "Alright. Let's bring this baby into the world."

***

Damian positioned himself at the foot of the table, his eyes scanning Ryder's progress. His brow furrowed, though his voice stayed steady. "Okay, Ryder, you're fully dilated. But the baby hasn't moved down as much as we'd like. With the next contraction, I need you to push hard. Understand?"

Ryder nodded weakly, gasping, sweat dripping from her temple. "I'll… I'll try."

Nolan wiped her forehead with a cloth, his voice low, anchoring. "We're almost there, Ryder. Just hang on."

A few minutes passed, and Ryder bore down with everything she had, screaming through gritted teeth as her fingers crushed Nolan's hand.

Damian's frown deepened. The baby wasn't moving.

Olivia moved to Damian's side. "Is something wrong?" she whispered.

"Too soon to say," He replied, calm but clipped. "Let's give her another chance."

Moments later another contraction built, Damian's voice cut through the tension like a lifeline. "Alright, push Ryder! Push!"

Ryder's scream echoed against the sterile walls, her body trembling with the effort. Olivia's eyes darted to the monitors, her heart rate climbing with the strain, but Damian's focus never wavered.

Outside, Jase paced like a caged animal, Ava tapping her arms against her chest. Ryder's cries leaked faintly through the doors.

"She's strong," Ava muttered.

Jase stopped, his forehead pressing against the wall. "Stronger than me."

Inside, the air thickened with every groan.

Damian leaned back, murmuring low to Olivia so Nolan couldn't hear. "Shoulder dystocia—the baby's stuck." His eyes narrowed on Olivia. "We'll try repositioning first. Be ready."

"What do you need?" Olivia asked, her voice level, though her eyes betrayed a flicker of worry.

"Suprapubic pressure." He pointed above Ryder's pelvis. "When I tell her to push, apply hard pressure here. I'll guide the baby's shoulders." He turned to Ryder, his voice calm. "Ryder, I'm going to need you to give me one more big push, okay? Just one more."

Ryder nodded, tears streaking down her face as she braced herself.

The next contraction hit like a wave. Damian guided Ryder's legs into position. "Now! Push, Ryder! Push!"

Ryder cried out, Olivia pressing firmly above her pelvis as Damian maneuvered. Nolan pressed his forehead to Ryder's, whispering through clenched teeth, "Push, baby. Push!"

But the baby didn't move.

"It's not working," Damian said tightly, stripping his gloves, his eyes on the monitor. "The baby's shoulder is lodged too firmly, and Ryder's blood pressure is dropping."

Nolan's head whipped up, panic breaking through. "What does that mean?!"

Damian met his gaze, calm but urgent. "It means we can't deliver naturally. Her blood pressure is dropping fast, it's too dangerous—for both of them. We have to do an emergency C-section. Now."

Ryder's eyes widened in fear, her voice trembling. "A C-section? But—"

"There's no other choice," Damian said firmly but gently. "I know this is scary, but we need to act quickly to save both you and Aurora"

Olivia was already moving, pulling out surgical instruments with trembling efficiency. "Damian, what about anesthesia?" She asked, her eyes wide.

Damian hesitated for a second. His face masking the hard decision he was making in his head. "There's no time, her vitals are too unstable. We'll have to use ketamine to sedate her enough to perform the procedure."

Ryder's breathing hitched, her voice a whimper. "Wi... will it hurt?"

Damian knelt beside her, his eyes soft but resolute. "Ryder, I won't lie to you. It'll dull the pain and put you in a dissociative state, but you'll feel everything. It's not perfect, but it's the only option we have right now."

Tears streamed down Ryder's face as she nodded, her voice barely a whisper. "Do what you have to...just save her."

Nolan pressed her hand to his chest, his face pale but resolute. "I'm right here. Just look at me, Ryder. Don't look anywhere else. Just me."

Damian moved fast to the med cart, drawing ketamine into a syringe with practiced hands. "Low dose intramuscular," he said to Olivia, his voice clipped. "It'll dull the pain and keep her calm enough for me to work."

He injected the ketamine, and within moments, Ryder's eyes glazed, her breath slowing as the drug took hold. Her words slurred, fragmented. She didn't resist as Damian and Olivia prepped, but her body twitched under the haze.

"Scalpel," Damian ordered.

Olivia passed the instrument, her hands steady even as her chest tightened. She caught Nolan's eye, giving the faintest nod.

The first incision cut the sterile air. Ryder's scream ripped through the room, primal, shaking the walls. Her body arched violently against the table.

"It burns!" she gasped, thrashing. "Fire—everything's on fire!" Her cries broke into sharp, incoherent fragments as the ketamine warped her senses.

Nolan's expression twisted with helplessness, his jaw clenched as tears streamed down his face. He moved to hold her down with one arm, his other hand trembling, as it brushed her damp hair away from her forehead. "You're okay, Ryder," he whispered, though his voice cracked with emotion. "You're so strong. Focus on me."

Ryder's body trembled violently, a haze of pain and confusion. Her eyes glazed over, a flicker of something distant in her gaze. "Please... hurting... everything..." Her words were barely coherent, but her desperation was unmistakable.

Damian's hands moved with a calm intensity, cutting through the layers of tissue with precision. Blood pooled, and Olivia suctioned furiously, clearing the area as Damian worked. But the blood didn't stop, it seemed to flow faster than they could manage. Her heart pounded in her chest as she glanced at the monitor.

"Her vitals are dropping," she called, voice tight.

"I know," Damian muttered, jaw set. "Almost there."

Ryder's screams grew weaker, her body almost limp beneath their touch. She was slipping, drifting further away with each labored breath.

"I see it..." she murmured, her voice barely a whisper now, distant and unfocused. "A door... it's ahead of me..." Her eyes fluttered, staring at the ceiling as if seeing something beyond the sterile lights above.

Nolan's voice cracked as he leaned closer to her face, his words more of a plea than comfort. "Stay with me baby, I'm right here. You're so strong, Ryder. Just hold on. Please."

Damian worked as quickly as he could, his brow was furrowed with concentration. Ryder's breathing was shallow now, each breath more labored than the last. As his hands reached the uterus, he worked with extreme care, knowing every second mattered.

Ryder's voice barely broke through. It was there, fragile, but still fighting. "Save...her..."

Damian cut through the final layer, sweat beading at his brow. His hands reached in, careful but quick, maneuvering the tiny shoulders free.

Seconds stretched, Ryder fading, the room collapsing into a tunnel of beeps and breath.

Then Damian pulled the baby free, lifting her into the harsh light. His chest heaved, his voice raw with relief. "I've got her."

A moment of silence filled the room, thick and heavy.

Then, like sunlight breaking through storm clouds, a piercing cry filled the med-bay.

Damian's shoulders sagged. "She's okay," he said softly, voice thick with relief as he handed the slick, squirming newborn to Olivia.

She wrapped her up quickly, clearing the baby's airways with delicate hands, her heart swelling as she heard the tiny, but powerful wail of life.

At Ryder's side, Nolan still gripped her hand as if willing her to stay tethered. His voice cracked with awe and relief. "You did it. She's here. Aurora's here."

Ryder's eyes fluttered open, her lips trembling. "She's...okay?"

"She's perfect," Nolan whispered, a broken smile twitching at his mouth.

But Ryder's hand went limp. She was still conscious, but her mind was no longer in the room—it was somewhere else completely.

"Ryder," Nolan murmured, tears streaking down his face. "You did it. She's here." But she didn't respond.

Damian's head snapped up at the monitor, voice sharp. "I need to close her up—now. Olivia, keep monitoring the baby. Let me know if anything changes."

The next few minutes blurred. Damian's hands moved with desperation, trying to stop the bleeding. Olivia hovered nearby, eyes flicking between the baby and the crashing vitals.

Ryder winced, her voice faint and far away. "Nolan… the door. I see the door." Her eyes stared past the ceiling, unfocused. "If I walk through it… I'm dead."

"Damian, she's crashing!" Olivia shouted, her voice tight.

Nolan pressed his forehead to hers, brushing sweat-soaked hair back with trembling fingers. His voice broke into a plea. "Don't go through that door. Please. Stay here, with me. With our baby. She's perfect, Ryder. Just like you. Stay with us."

Her eyes flickered, barely a spark. "I wo...won't..."

"Good," Nolan whispered, leaning closer. "Stay here. She needs you. I need you."

Her eyes drifted shut again, exhaustion overtaking her, but her lips shaped one last whisper. "I love…"

Nolan leaned down, pressing a kiss to her forehead. "I love you."

***

Jase paced in the hall outside, his boots striking the floor in restless rhythm. Each turn was sharper than the last, like he was trying to carve his anxiety into the concrete beneath his feet.

Ava sat against the wall, knees hugged to her chest, arms wrapped tight around them as if she could hold herself together by sheer force. Her face was still, unreadable, but her eyes never left the sealed door.

"This doesn't feel right," Jase muttered, raking a hand through his hair for what felt like the hundredth time. He stopped, swallowed, then spun on his heel. "I've never been around someone giving birth before, but that—" His voice cracked. "That didn't sound normal."

Ava's chin rested on her knees. Her voice was quiet, thin. "Damian said there was no epidural. But…" Her brow furrowed, her eyes flicking to the door. "Yeah. That sounded worse than I thought it would. Way worse."

Jase's pacing quickened, his heart pounding in his throat. Just as he passed Ava again, the med-bay door slid open with a soft hiss.

They both froze.

Olivia stepped out. Her face was streaked with tears, her eyes red and raw, her composure unraveling the instant she saw Jase. Without a word, she collapsed against him, arms wrapping tight around his torso.

Jase stiffened, startled, before his arms came up, pulling her in just as fiercely. Over her shoulder, he met Ava's gaze. She was already on her feet, pale, her hands curled into fists at her sides.

"Olivia," Jase whispered, afraid to ask the question. "What happened?"

Olivia didn't answer. Her body shook against him, muffled sobs soaking into his shirt. Jase tightened his hold, dread clawing through him.

"No... no, no! Is she—" Ava's voice faltered. She couldn't finish.

Olivia pulled back just enough to grip Jase's arms, her eyes burning with emotion. "Ryder and the baby... they're okay," she breathed. Relief and heartbreak twisted her features all at once. "But it was close. Too close."

Jase exhaled a breath he hadn't realized he'd been holding, his shoulders sagging. Ava leaned against the wall, her head tipping back, her eyes fluttering shut as the weight bled out of her posture.

"Damian's still with her," Olivia continued, her voice hoarse. "She lost a lot of blood. But she's stable now. She's going to need some time to recover."

Ava's hands twisted in her sleeves, knuckles white. "And the baby?"

Olivia's lips trembled, and then—at last—a small, tearful smile broke through. "Ask him," she said, her voice cracking with exhaustion and wonder.

Ava turned to see Nolan standing at the doorway, cradling the tiny bundle in his arms. The golden 'O' crest on the blanket caught the faint hallway light as he stepped forward, each movement careful.

"Ava, Jase," he said quietly, his voice thick with emotion. "Meet Aurora."

Ava's breath hitched, her usual composure cracking. "Aurora," she whispered, edging closer. Her guarded gaze softened into something almost luminous as she looked down at the baby.

Jase froze, heart pounding. He slowly stepped closer, his voice rough with awe. "She's... she's so small."

"She's perfect," Nolan said, a weary, proud smile tugging at his mouth. Aurora stirred in her sleep, tiny fingers twitching against the blanket.

"She looks like Ryder," Ava said, her voice unsteady with wonder.

"She does," Nolan murmured. But his smile faltered, and his eyes flicked back toward the med-bay.

"How is she?" Jase asked quietly.

Nolan exhaled, shoulders sagging. "She's sleeping right now. Damian's keeping a close eye on her. She lost a lot of blood during the birth." He paused, his grip on the baby tightening just slightly. "Damian had to transfuse a unit of blood to stabilize her. Thank God he started storing our blood a few months ago. If he hadn't…" He trailed off, shaking his head as if banishing the thought. "We're lucky to have him, is all I know."

Jase exhaled slowly, running a hand over his face. "We owe him. And Ryder." He looked at the baby again, his voice dropping to a whisper. "And her."

Nolan nodded, his gaze lingering on Aurora for a moment longer before he let out a quiet sigh. "She needs to rest too," he said softly. "I should get her back inside."

Nolan turned toward the door, but then hesitated, and looked back over his shoulder to Olivia. "Thank you," he said simply, his voice raw with gratitude. Then stepped into the med-bay as the door slid shut behind him.

Olivia leaned against the wall, wiping her eyes, her hands trembling.

Jase laid a steadying hand on her shoulder. "You did amazing. You and Damian both."

Olivia let out a shaky laugh that broke into a sob. "It wasn't just us. Ryder… she's stronger than we ever gave her credit for."

Ava's voice was quiet, certain. "She always has been."

For a moment, the three of them stood in silence, the weight of it settling over them like a heavy fog.

Jase finally broke it. "Let's give them some space," he said. "They've been through enough for one day."

They turned from the med-bay, walking into the dim corridor. Behind them, the faint echoes of Ryder's screams still clung to the walls—a reminder of how close they'd come to losing everything. Or more importantly, what they could lose when the doors open.

PART THREE

THE SERPENT'S TAIL

CHAPTER TWENTY

Early morning had settled over the Ouroboros. The facility lay in a rare, peaceful silence, so different from hours before when Aurora's cries had echoed through it. Nine days had passed since she was brought into the world, cut from Ryder's abdomen in a desperate act to save her. In that short time, the infant had become the heartbeat of their world. She was proof that hope could still exist in a place carved out of despair.

Jase sat alone in the Observation Command Center, his face illuminated by the pale glow of the monitors. The others were still asleep, still too early for their routines to begin. He stared at the small camera mounted above, its lens staring back at him like an unblinking eye. He wasn't sure why he had come here.

Echo Loops ended the moment Ouro received the mission update. What had once been a mandatory part of their routine, now belonged to a distant past, a relic of who they used to be. And yet, Jase felt the pull. Some part of him needed to leave one final entry.

He sat motionless, his thoughts circling, pulling him back through everything they'd endured over the past two and a half years. He thought of the fear that had gripped them when that first alarm sounded. The panic, the disbelief, as the world above was locked away. He thought of the endless trials that followed—grueling, heartbreaking, relentless—and how each had tested them to the core.

But most of all, he thought of what they had become.

Against all odds, they had survived. They had adapted, endured, and risen. Together, they had been reshaped by fire and loss—hammered into something harder, sharper. They weren't the naïve kids who had walked into the Ouroboros. They were scarred, but unbroken. They were something greater.

And then he understood why he was here.

Tomorrow, the doors of the Ouroboros would open. They would step into a world forever changed, one they didn't truly know. It could be the day they died. But it wasn't fear of death that had brought him here, it was the need to leave something behind.

Jase realized he needed to leave one final entry. Not for himself, and certainly not for the others, but for anyone who might still be watching. Anyone who might someday stumble upon these recordings and wonder who they were, what they had endured.

He wanted to tell the whole truth. Not just the pain, the loss, the fear. But the resilience they had found along the way. Who they had become. Not broken survivors, but warriors shaped by the unforgiving world around them. They had evolved, become stronger, more determined. Now they were ready to step into the unknown, to face whatever lay ahead. Ready to fight for whatever was left of the world and the chance to rebuild it.

Jase leaned forward, his finger hovering over the button to start the recording. He took a deep breath, letting the weight of his thoughts settle into something solid, something real. For the first time in a long time, he knew exactly what to say.

With a firm press, the red light blinked to life. Steady. Waiting.

And Jase didn't hold back.

He let it all out. Every struggle, every triumph, every hard-fought moment of the past two and a half years. He spoke of the dark days, when survival felt impossible, when the fear of the unknown pressed down heavier than the walls that surrounded them. He spoke of the nights filled with doubt, when despair whispered louder than hope.

But he also spoke of the light. The laughter found in stolen moments. The rituals that gave them some sense of normalcy. The fragile joys they had clung to in the midst of a broken world.

And then, he spoke of them.

"Damian," he began, his voice softening. "The reluctant med student who became our lifeline. He didn't ask for this responsibility, but he shouldered it anyway. Every stitch, every diagnosis, every tough call—he faced them with courage forged under fire. He saved us time and time again."

Jase's lips curved into a faint smile. "Ava—the engineer who refused to let anything fall apart. Not our machines, not this shelter, and not even our hope. No matter how many setbacks came her way, she never let them break her. She's been our backbone, keeping everything running when it should have fallen apart."

His voice grew steadier as he continued. "Nolan—the soldier who became more than our shield. He took all our fear and uncertainty and forged them into strength. With every drill, every hard truth, he pushed us to become something strong enough to survive out there. And through it all, he's carried more than just our safety—he's carried the responsibility of preparing to be a father in this world. And still, he never wavered."

Jase's expression softened as he thought of Ryder. "And Ryder—she found a way to nurture life, even in the darkest circumstances. In a world that feels so dead, she's been our reminder that there's still beauty to fight for. And now, with Aurora, she's given us the most precious thing we thought was gone forever. Hope."

His breath caught slightly as he spoke the last name.

"Olivia—the sharp mind that guided us through every crisis. She saw angles the rest of us missed, made calls we didn't want to make, and kept us going when we couldn't see a way forward. She's been our guide, whether she wanted to be or not."

He hesitated, his voice softening as his gaze flickered to the empty space beside him, as if she were there. "She's… more than that, though," he murmured, the words heavy with something unspoken.

"She makes you believe you can rise even when you're broken. She shows you strength you didn't know you had." His gaze moved back to the lens. "Olivia has been my compass through all of this, in more ways than she knows."

He let the silence stretch, gathering his thoughts before his voice softened, almost imperceptibly. "I don't think any of us would've made it this far without her. I know I wouldn't have."

His throat tightened as he fought to keep control, the weight of what he'd said settling over him.

"These people aren't just participants in an experiment," Jase said, his voice raw. "They're my family. We came here as strangers, each with our own fears and scars. But together—through heartbreak and loss, through victory and laughter—we've become something unbreakable."

His gaze hardened, a quiet storm brewing in his eyes. "Together, we've forged a bond that nothing, not even the end of the world, can shatter. And now…" He paused, letting the weight linger. "Now we're ready. Ready for whatever awaits us beyond those doors."

He leaned forward, eyes locking on the camera, his presence commanding the space. "And what comes next, you ask?"

His voice softened, edged with steel. "This place is called the Ouroboros, the serpent devouring its own tail. We've reached the tail, where endings give rise to new beginnings."

A faint smirk touched his mouth before he continued.

"We are the Fallout Kids. And now…" His eyes narrowed, voice steady with conviction.

"…now it's time for the Genesis Rising."

***

In the kitchen, Jase sat alone at the table, his hands curled around a steaming mug of coffee. The quiet hum of the shelter enveloped him, a stark contrast to the storm of emotions that had raged inside him just a bit ago.

Steam curled lazily from the cup as Jase stared into it, his mind replaying the words he'd spoken in the Echo Loop. He wasn't sure if anyone would ever hear them, and honestly, it didn't matter. For the first time in what felt like an eternity, a sense of relief washed over him, as though the heavy burden he'd carried had finally been lifted. It was cathartic, a confession he hadn't known he needed to make. Raw, unfiltered, and real.

He took a slow sip, the warmth grounding him. The silence stretched, unbroken, until the soft hiss of the sliding door broke through. Glancing up, he saw Ava, Damian, and Olivia step inside. Their presence pulled him from his thoughts, warming him more than the coffee ever could.

"Morning, Jase," Ava said, stretching as she shook off the last of her sleep. "First one up, huh? Aurora wake you again?"

Jase chuckled and leaned back in his chair. "Nah, just thought I'd enjoy a quiet cup for once." He gave her a wink.

Ava peered into his mug and grinned. "Yeah, looks like you had plenty of peace." She gave him a playful pat on the back as she passed.

He lifted the mug toward her, grin widening. "More than I was expecting."

Olivia smirked from across the room, her sharp eyes sweeping over the group. "Who's hungry? I'll cook."

Ava perked up immediately with an exaggerated groan. "Me. I'm starving!"

"Same here," Damian said, raising a hand like a kid in class.

Olivia turned to Jase, her smirk softening into a playful smile. "What about you? Some food to go with that peace?"

"Sure," he said, smiling back. "That sounds wonderful."

"Alright then," she declared, rolling up her sleeves with dramatic flair. "Eggs and 3D-printed sausage for everyone. You're welcome in advance."

She selected the settings on the printer, then moved to the dry pantry. As she mixed powdered eggs in a bowl and the sausages hummed to life nearby, the kitchen filled with the smell of breakfast and soft chatter.

Before long, the sliding door hissed open. Nolan walked in behind Ryder, who cradled Aurora in her arms. Aurora let out a soft coo, her tiny head nestled against Ryder's shoulder.

"Morning," Nolan said, his voice low but warm as he glanced around the room. His protective gaze lingered on Ryder as she moved gingerly to a chair.

Ryder offered a tired smile as she eased into the seat, wincing slightly but brushing it off. "Good morning, everyone," she said softly, her voice still laced with exhaustion but full of love as she looked down at Aurora.

Nolan grabbed a coffee, then rested a hand on Ryder's shoulder before sitting beside her. She adjusted her shirt and positioned Aurora to nurse. The baby latched easily, and Ryder exhaled as her hand brushed tenderly over Aurora's dark hair.

Jase watched them with a faint smile, his coffee forgotten for a moment. It was a rare sight, something pure in their manufactured world.

Olivia glanced over her shoulder from the stove, her expression softening as she noticed Jase. "Breakfast is almost ready," she said, her voice gentler now as she tried not to disturb the peaceful scene between Ryder and Aurora. Moments like this, quiet, ordinary, were rare, and she wanted to stretch them as long as they would last.

The sausages sizzled as she rolled them in the pan, the smell of spice and oil mingling with the faint hum of the shelter. In another pan, the eggs waited, fluffy, golden, perfectly cooked. Olivia plated everything with surprising care, setting a meal in front of each person before sliding into her chair with a content sigh.

"Alright, everyone, dig in," she said. Then, with a mischievous glint, she added, "And don't worry—" She set a bottle down in front of Ava. "I didn't forget your hot sauce."

Ava's grin was instant. "You're a saint," she said, already reaching for it.

Across the table Ryder smiled faintly, her voice apologetic. "I'm sorry about last night. This little one was in a mood. We tried everything, but she wouldn't settle. I'm sure you all heard." She rubbed Aurora's back gently as the baby snuggled against her chest, breathing softly, the picture of innocence.

"Yeah, I tried everything," Nolan added, shaking his head with a weary smile. "Rocking her, singing—none of it worked. She was determined to make sure we all knew she was unhappy."

"Oh, don't worry about it. Slept like a log," Ava said, waving a hand, though her smirk betrayed her.

Damian swallowed a mouthful of eggs. "Same. Didn't hear a thing."

Ryder blinked, incredulous. "Really? She was screaming. I thought for sure one of you would come banging on the door."

Olivia leaned back, the corner of her mouth lifting. "Not a peep," she said lightly. "Ava made us some silicone earplugs the other day. Worked like a charm."

Ryder's jaw dropped. "You're kidding."

Ava shrugged, unapologetic, as she dunked a piece of sausage into hot sauce. "Sorry, babe. I love my niece, but she's got some serious lungs on her. Figured you'd want us rested enough to help during the day."

Nolan chuckled and shook his head. "You know, I should've guessed. I thought it was suspicious that none of you so much as stirred when she was wailing at full volume."

"You're serious?" Ryder said, narrowing her eyes at Olivia. "You slept with earplugs?"

Olivia raised her hands in mock surrender, grinning unapologetically. "Hey, don't look at me like that! I don't want to rub salt in the wound, but Ava's a genius for thinking of it."

Ryder groaned, letting her head fall back against the chair. "You're all traitors."

Laughter filled the kitchen, light and easy, echoing off the walls like something almost forgotten. For a moment, the worries beyond the shelter didn't exist. For a moment, they were just people sharing breakfast, breathing in the peace while they still could.

As the laughter faded, Olivia got up to refill her coffee and glanced over her shoulder at Ryder and Nolan. "You're doing great, you know," she said softly. "We all know it's not easy, but she's lucky to have you two."

Ryder smiled down at Aurora, who was now sleeping peacefully against her chest. "Thanks," she murmured, her voice warm and tired, but full of quiet pride.

Jase set his mug down deliberately and leaned forward as the easy air around the table shifted. "Alright, let's get serious," he began, his eyes sweeping the room. "Tomorrow, the doors open."

The words hung in the air for a moment, heavy with anticipation and trepidation.

"It's not exactly the celebration we'd imagined," Jase said, his gaze sweeping the table, "but it's what we've been waiting for. Today, we make sure we're ready. No loose ends, no mistakes. Here's what needs to happen."

He turned first to Ava. "Ava, I need a full systems check. Doors, ventilation, water—everything. If something fails while we're out there, it could compromise the shelter. We can't afford that."

"On it," Ava said with a nod, already mentally mapping out her checklist.

"Damian," Jase continued, "go over the med-bay. Restock everything you can and run diagnostics on your equipment. If any of us get hurt, you're our lifeline."

Damian's posture straightened. "I'll run full inventory and sterilization cycles. It'll be ready."

Jase nodded, then looked toward Ryder. "Make sure Aurora's supplies are squared away—formula, diapers, blankets. Everything she might need. Want to make sure you're covered."

Ryder nodded to Jase. "Thank you."

"Olivia," Jase said, his gaze shifting toward her. "I want a full diagnostic on Ouro. If there's even a flicker of instability in the system, I need to know before those doors open."

Olivia gave a short nod. "I'll comb through everything—system logs, power flow, security functions. I'll make sure there are no surprises."

"And finally," Jase said, glancing at Nolan, "you and I will handle weapons and load-outs. We check every mag. Every strap. Every kit. No room for error."

Nolan gave a short, approving nod. "Understood."

Jase exhaled, leaning back slightly, letting some of the tension ease from his shoulders. "Look, I know this is a big deal. We've been waiting for this moment for a long time, and I trust every single one of you to do what needs to be done. But once today's checks are finished..." He hesitated, his tone softening. "Take tonight for yourselves. Enjoy this place while it's still home. Be with each other. Because once those doors open..." He paused, meeting each of their eyes. "Everything changes. And I don't know when we'll get another chance to just breathe."

A hush settled over the group. Ryder glanced down at Aurora, her thumb brushing the baby's tiny hand. Nolan's palm rested gently on her shoulder. Ava leaned back, folding her arms, her usual edge tempered by something almost tender. Damian sipped his coffee in silence, nodding to himself. Olivia stirred her cup, her sharp eyes flicking toward Jase—steady, thoughtful, and a little sad.

For the first time in a long time, they weren't thinking about survival. They were thinking about each other.

***

The rest of the day unfolded in a steady, methodical blur of preparation. Each of them moved through their final checks with the focus of people who understood what was at stake.

In Ava's workshop, the clang of tools echoed off the metal walls as she muttered under her breath, the hum of machinery swallowing her frustration. Across the facility, Olivia sat at her console, the faint beeping of diagnostics breaking the stillness as lines of code scrolled across her screen. Her sharp eyes traced every flicker, hunting for the smallest anomaly.

In the med-bay, Damian worked with surgical precision, restocking and reorganizing, his movements deliberate and calm. Meanwhile, Jase and Nolan occupied the armory, their actions practiced and in sync—loading magazines, checking safeties, testing straps.

They had done this a hundred times before. Drills, maintenance, rehearsals. But today carried a different weight. Every sound felt amplified, every movement purposeful. This wasn't another drill. This was the last one.

The Ouroboros had been their home for so long, its walls shielding them from the chaos of the world above. Now, as they prepared to step into the unknown, it was more than just a shelter, it was their sanctuary. Whatever waited outside, they would always have this place to return to.

As evening fell, the group naturally gravitated toward the living room. Nothing was planned, but the pull to be together was instinctive, like moths drawn to a flame. The small, dimly lit space had an almost sacred coziness, its worn furniture arranged in a circle that felt more like an embrace than simple seating.

They talked for hours. Not about the mission or the dangers waiting above, but about the moments that had made this place theirs. The inside jokes. The strange routines. The nights of laughter that had kept them sane. For a few hours, the looming future didn't exist.

When Aurora stirred, Ryder instinctively rocked her back to sleep, her voice a soft hum barely audible over the quiet. The sight of the tiny infant curled against her chest silenced whatever conversation was left. She was proof of everything they'd fought to preserve—fragile, innocent, alive.

The conversation faded into a companionable silence, one born of deep trust and connection. For a while, no one moved, each person content to sit in the stillness and soak in the presence of the others.

Eventually, one by one, they peeled off and retreated to their quarters for what little rest the night would offer.

***

Olivia stepped out of the bathroom and into her room, the faint light from around her bed casting a warm glow across the floor. She pulled on a pair of soft shorts and an oversized T-shirt, the fabric brushing lightly against her skin. As she sat on the edge of the bed, her hands gripping the blanket, a familiar tightness pressed against her chest.

Two and a half years.

They'd lost so much—friends, family, a world they once knew. Now, with tomorrow looming, they stood on the brink of losing everything that remained.

Her heart twisted at the thought. Regret was a quiet but relentless companion, whispering of all the things she wished she had done differently. Words she'd held back. Decisions she hadn't made. Emotions she'd buried. She felt the sting of every unsaid word and every moment she'd been too afraid to seize.

What if tomorrow brought her a lifetime of regret?

The thought sent a jolt of panic through her, sharp and un-compromising. She exhaled shakily, pushing it down as she fell back onto the pillow and pulled the covers over her. Her hand hovered over the switch, ready to plunge the room into darkness. Sleep wouldn't come, only thoughts that spiraled, but exhaustion was winning.

Then, a soft knock broke the silence.

Her hand froze midair. For a moment, she simply stared at the door, her pulse quickening. She rose slowly, her bare feet silent against the cold floor as she crossed the room.

When she opened the door, her breath caught.

Jase stood there, his frame outlined by the dim hallway light. His features were tired, shadowed—but his eyes held something raw, something she'd never seen so clearly before.

"Jase?" she whispered. "What's wrong?"

He didn't answer right away. The silence stretched, charged, their gazes locked in a thousand unsaid things. Olivia's heart thundered in her chest, the sound so loud she wondered if he could hear it.

And then, without warning, Jase moved.

He stepped forward, closing the distance in a heartbeat. One hand cupped her cheek, the other found her waist. Before she could speak, his lips were on hers.

The kiss was urgent. Almost desperate. As though every un-spoken word, every stolen glance, and every suppressed feeling had rushed to the surface at once. Olivia melted into him, her hands gripping the fabric of his shirt as her racing heart drowned out every thought except him.

In that instant, there was nothing else. The shelter, the Ser-pentis Strain, the weight of survival, it all vanished. There was only Jase, his touch grounding her and setting her aflame all at once.

She pulled him inside as the door slid shut behind them. Their movements were uncoordinated but instinctive, a mixture of urgency and raw emotion. Jase's hands framed her face, his touch both protective and desperate, while Olivia clung to him as though letting go would shatter the fragile moment.

For once, there were no doubts.

No fear.

No walls between them.

Only the fire that had waited too long to ignite, and the fragile promise that whatever tomorrow brought, they would have each other tonight.

CHAPTER TWENTY-ONE

The next morning, Jase lay beside Olivia, his eyes tracing the soft rise and fall of her breathing. Her blonde hair spilled across the pillow, a few strands brushing her lips as she slept. The faint glow from the overhead light outlined her in gold, and for a long moment Jase simply watched her, memorizing the quiet details he'd denied himself for so long.

Last night had felt inevitable.

For months, they'd resisted it—clinging to discipline, to duty, to the fragile boundaries they thought would keep them safe. But now, lying beside her, he couldn't remember why they'd fought it. Maybe it was fear—of losing focus, of complicating the fragile dynamic of the group, of the undeniable uncertainty of their future. But none of that mattered now.

He reached out, his touch gentle as he ran a finger through her hair, brushing it from her face. Olivia stirred, a quiet murmur escaping her lips as she shifted closer to him, her hand resting against his chest. Her eyes fluttered open, hazy with sleep but sharpening as she looked up at him.

"Morning," she murmured, her voice rough with sleep but soft, almost disbelieving.

"Morning," Jase said, his voice low and warm. He didn't need to say anything more.

Olivia blinked lazily, a teasing glint in her eyes. "Is it already time to get up?" she asked playfully as she stretched, the blanket slipping off her shoulder.

Jase smirked. "No, not yet." He leaned down and kissed her. First her forehead, then her lips. Slow and tender, lingering as if to imprint the moment before it faded.

When they finally pulled apart, Olivia smiled, her breath warm against his cheek. "You're quiet this morning," she said, studying him. "Not regretting it, are you?"

He shook his head. "No. Not for a second." His hand brushed down the side of her face, his thumb resting along her jaw. "I didn't want to leave this morning without this—without you. Not after everything."

Olivia tilted her head, curiosity softening her expression. "Why now?" she asked. "What changed?"

Jase hesitated, then exhaled. "Because I realized something. Every time we walk through those doors, we don't know what's waiting for us, or if we'll come back. And the thought of never telling you how I feel, never having this, it was too much. I didn't want to waste another second pretending I don't care about you the way I do."

Her breath caught as her fingers gently found his where they rested against her cheek. "You've always cared, Jase," she said. "Even when you didn't say it, I could feel it. And the truth is, I've always felt the same. Even when I tried not to."

Her confession hung between them, fragile but freeing. "We've been holding back for so long," she said, her voice trembling slightly. "I almost forgot why we started."

"Hope," Jase murmured, the word leaving him like a sigh. "We thought it would make things easier. That if we stayed focused, kept pretending things were normal, maybe the doors would open, and the world would still be waiting for us. Like it was before."

Olivia's thumb traced lazy circles across his skin. "Instead, we built walls," she said. "Around ourselves. Around each other. Thinking it would keep us safe." She paused, her eyes glistening faintly. "But all it did was keep us from what we really needed."

"Each other," he said.

She nodded, a bittersweet smile tugging at her lips. "Each other," she echoed.

Jase leaned in again, resting his forehead against hers. For a moment, neither of them spoke. The world outside those steel walls could have been gone for centuries, and still, in that sliver of peace, they would have found meaning.

Jase shifted slightly, breaking the soft stillness between them. His voice came low, thoughtful. "I dreamt of Eli again the other night."

Olivia turned toward him, curiosity flickering in her eyes. "The nightmare?"

He shook his head, his gaze fixed on the ceiling. "No… not the nightmare. It was different this time. It didn't feel like a dream at all. It felt real, like I was actually there with him."

She rolled to her side, her expression softening. "What do you mean?"

Jase hesitated, his hands gesturing faintly as he tried to find the words. "I don't know how to explain it. I could see him, hear him. It wasn't like before. No guilt, no fear. Just… peaceful."

Olivia's brow furrowed, empathy stirring in her calm eyes. "What happened?"

Jase exhaled slowly, his voice quiet but steady. "We were standing outside, in this field. The sky was clear, blue like I haven't seen since before all of this. Eli was there, smiling at me. Not just smiling, he looked happy. He looked just like he did when we were together."

He paused, his voice growing steadier as he continued. "He told me he was proud of me. Proud of how I kept going, of who I've become. He said what we're about to do—it matters. That people need us. And then…" His voice faltered briefly. "He told me to stop carrying the guilt. He said it wasn't my fault. That it's time to let it go."

Olivia's eyes glistened as she watched him, her hand reaching out to rest gently on his arm. "Jase…"

He met her gaze, a faint smile pulling at his lips. "The strange thing is… I believed him. For the first time in years, I didn't feel that weight. It was like he took it with him, wherever he is. He said we'd see each other again one day, but not to worry about that now. That I have my own path."

Her hand tightened on his arm, her voice soft but resolute. "He's right. You've carried enough for one lifetime. Maybe it's time to let yourself live, too."

Jase breathed out, his chest rising with something that felt almost like release. "I think I'm finally starting to."

He leaned in, his lips meeting hers again in a slow, deliberate kiss, gentle but full of meaning. When they parted, their foreheads rested together, breaths mingling in the still air. For the first time in what felt like forever, the space between them felt light—no walls, no guilt, no pretending. Just them.

Olivia's lips curved into a small, knowing smile. "So… it's not time to get up yet?" she whispered, brushing a teasing kiss against his neck.

Jase smiled, eyes glinting with warmth. "No," he murmured, "not quite yet."

Olivia's finger traced lightly down his chest, her gaze soft. She leaned closer, her voice just above a whisper. "Maybe we should get some more rest then. Got a big day ahead of us." she added with a mischievous smile, her finger drifting lower along his stomach.

"I'm feeling quite rested, actually," Jase said, a smirk pulling at his lips.

"Good, me too," she said as her hand moved below the sheet. She leaned in and kissed him as she slowly slid on top of him, pulling the covers up around them and using every last minute they had to themselves.

***

Two hours later, Jase, Olivia, Nolan, Ava, and Damian gathered in the armory. The usual casual conversation was absent, replaced by a thick silence that settled over the room like a weighted vest.

Each person sat at their locker, the weight of the moment pressing heavily on their shoulders. Damian stood apart from the others, leaning against the workbench with his arms crossed, his jaw set in quiet contemplation. This was it. The day they had been preparing for. The day they would finally step out of the Ouroboros.

At the far end, Jase sat with his foot propped up on the bench, methodically lacing his boots. The black leather creaked under the strain, each pull grounding him in the present. His mind raced, running through contingencies, mapping out every scenario he could anticipate. But no matter how much he prepared, the weight of responsibility pressed against his chest. They were about to step into an unknown world, and they were looking to him to lead them through it.

He exhaled sharply, shaking off the doubt. Not now.

Jase stood and reached for his battle belt, locking it around his waist with a firm click. The sidearm settled against his hip, cold and familiar. He secured the thigh straps, tugging them once to check the fit. The weight was comforting in its own way. He looked around the room. No one spoke, but an understanding passed between them.

They were ready. They had to be.

Across from him, Olivia adjusted her plate carrier, her fingers working quickly as she secured each pouch's Velcro or zipper, the soft snick of fabric echoing through the quiet room. Every motion was deliberate. Yet tension coiled beneath the surface, a tight knot in her chest that refused to loosen.

She strapped her tablet to the back of her plate carrier—out of the way, but in close reach. The tablet was her lifeline in The Ouroboros, and it would be the same above ground—giving her quick access to maps, and control of a small drone for live overhead visuals.

As she slipped on her helmet, the matte black surface caught the overhead light. Its weight pressed down on her, grounding her, steadying her. Don't overthink. Don't let them down. The mantra looped quietly in her mind as she exhaled through her nose, her jaw set hard.

Beside her, Ava sat in front of her own locker, her focus intense as she tightened the straps of her knee pads to a snug fit. Hanging from a hook beside her, an Eberlestock Switchblade backpack, heavy with tools and gear—everything she might need to salvage, fix, and survive.

She paused briefly, her fingertips brushing over the reinforced seams of her plate carrier. The stitching steadied her more than words could.

"Focus on the details. Fix the problem," she muttered under her breath, something she recited before every repair or challenge that seemed impossible.

She tightened the straps with a firm tug, securing her armor as if they were now one and the same. Her dark eyes flicked toward the others, reading their faces, their body language, the subtle way their tension was written in every movement. She drew strength from it. Even with the uncertainty pressing in from every side, they were here. Together. And that, more than anything else, was enough to steady her hands.

Across the room, Nolan stood at attention, his back straight as he fastened his battle belt. The click of his holster settling into place was sharp, a sound that seemed to linger in the room long after it faded. His hands moved with unthinking precision, the routine as ingrained as breathing, as his fingers brushed over the cold metal of his rifle.

Just another mission, he told himself. But even as the thought crossed his mind, his breath hitched at the lie. This wasn't just another mission. This was their life now. The world was different. There was no going back.

His gaze drifted to Ryder's locker, her untouched gear in stark contrast to everyone else's. His chest tightened, guilt settling like a stone. She was waiting in the hall, safe with Aurora. Though that should have brought him comfort, it didn't. Gratitude warred with dread. He was leaving them behind.

Focus, Nolan. One foot in front of the other.

At the end of the row, Jase sat in still for a moment before standing, sliding his rifle sling over his shoulder and letting the weapon hang in front of him. He cleared his throat, his voice firm but steady as he pressed the button on his mic.

"Alright," he said, the words slicing through the quiet. "Comms check. Sound off."

Responses came quickly, crisp and confident, a reassuring rhythm.

"Ava, loud and clear," Ava said, her voice cool and controlled as she tightened the last strap on her helmet.

"Olivia, good to go," Olivia said, calm and focused despite the weight in her tone.

"Nolan, solid copy," Nolan said, his voice calm and professional even as the tightness in his jaw betrayed what he felt beneath the surface.

"Damian, good check," Damian said, his calm tone steady as he adjusted his stance at the workbench.

Olivia looked to Damian, her gaze sharp. "Comms are synced," she confirmed. "Once we're topside, signal range to the Ouroboros will drop. We'll only be able to reach you at short range. It's going to be patchy."

Her eyes swept the room, making sure everyone was in sync. "But," she said, her voice firmer now, "we should be able to communicate with each other over several miles above ground. If we get separated, we've got some range."

She glanced at Jase one last time, locking eyes with him as a silent exchange passed between them—a mix of trust, concern, and something deeper.

"Good," Jase said, his voice low, cutting through the still air. "But we stick to the plan. Stay together. Watch each other's backs. We make it through."

He turned toward Damian, his tone sharpening just a fraction. "Since we won't have constant comms, you'll have to stay ready for our return. If anything goes wrong, we'll keep radioing in until we're within range. Don't hesitate to act if needed."

"We'll be here—ready and standing by," Damian gave a firm nod, his voice unwavering.

"Good." Jase's tone softened slightly, but his focus didn't waver. "If everyone's set, let's head to the airlock. It's almost time."

The words felt final. There was no more room for doubt.

Nolan slung his rifle, his voice low but commanding. "Stay sharp. No unnecessary risks. We all make it back."

The others nodded, their movements silent and sure. Then, without another word, they turned as one and headed out of the armory, their footsteps echoing down the corridor like the slow, steady beat of a countdown.

***

The blue glow of the clock seemed brighter than ever, its cold light sharp against their eyes, searing through their vision as they watched each second tick. Each moment passed with the heavy thud of their heartbeats, slow and deliberate.

Three minutes remained.

The group gathered in front of it, their faces taut with the shared weight of this familiar but no less daunting moment. They had stood here before, clinging to the faint hope that the doors would one day open. But now, with that hope finally realized, it felt less like salvation and more like dread.

Once again, the world as they knew it was ending.

Something entirely new was about to begin.

Ryder stood beside Nolan, cradling Aurora against her chest. The baby's bright eyes followed Nolan's finger as he made soft, playful faces, his voice low and soothing. Ryder's free hand curled around his waist, grounding herself in the quiet strength of his presence. Nolan's arm came around her shoulders, steady and protective, a silent vow he didn't have to speak.

A few steps away, Damian stood beside Ava. Neither spoke. The silence between them wasn't awkward, it was weighted and purposeful. Ava glanced his way, her lips quirking into a small, knowing grin. She winked, the playful glint in her eyes an unspoken reassurance, we've got this. Damian pressed his lips together and answered with a single nod.

Across from them, Jase and Olivia stood close, their fingers intertwined. The simple touch steadied them both, an anchor in the storm of anticipation closing in around them. Jase's eyes flicked to Olivia, a moment of quiet connection stretching longer than it should have, as if time itself had slowed. He studied her face—her determination, her quiet strength—and for a moment it was just the two of them in the room.

Without hesitation, he leaned in, his lips brushing hers in a kiss that was measured and full of meaning.

Across the room, Ava noticed. Her eyebrows rose, a teasing grin breaking the tension. She nudged Damian with her elbow and said, just loud enough for everyone to hear, "Well, it only took you 860 days to finally do that."

Laughter rippled through the group, the moment easing the tension that hung in the air.

But the levity was fleeting.

Jase turned back toward the clock, the glow reflecting off him. He drew a slow breath and spoke. "Ouro, what's the procedure for entering and exiting? Will the facility remain sealed while we're out?"

"When the countdown completes, the airlock doors will be unsealed," Ouro replied, its voice calm and clinical. "The doors will remain locked at all times. Authorized team members may enter or exit through facial and voice recognition. Entry will not be permitted under duress."

The group exchanged uneasy glances. Ryder furrowed her brows. "What does that mean?"

Nolan answered before anyone else could. "It means the doors won't open if we're being forced—at gunpoint or otherwise."

"Affirmative," Ouro confirmed. "The security of this facility is of the highest priority. Any survivors encountered must be vetted and tested before entry. All personnel are reminded to use BioPulse Scanners on any human contacts to ensure your safety and their integrity."

Jase nodded, his voice firm. "Copy that, Ouro."

He glanced over at Damian first, then his eyes shifted to Ryder, holding Aurora. His voice softening. "At least we know you three will be safe in here while we're out."

Ryder nodded, clutching Aurora closer. The infant's tiny hand grasped the edge of her mother's sleeve as if sensing the tension in the room. Ryder's eyes glistened, not with fear, but fierce resolve. "We'll be here when you get back," she said quietly.

The clock continued its merciless descent. Thirty seconds.

Nolan stood close beside Ryder, his hand resting gently on her shoulder before sliding down to cradle Aurora. His eyes softened as he looked at his daughter, her tiny face calm, her fingers curling in her sleep. He leaned down, pressing a kiss to her forehead and whispering, "Be good for your mom."

Ryder's heart clenched at the tenderness in his voice. Nolan's presence was her anchor, his steady composure the thing that kept her from unraveling. But beneath it, she could feel the same fear that gnawed in her own chest, the dread of what might happen out there.

He met her eyes, and for a fleeting second, the mask of discipline slipped. She saw the worry there, the fragility he tried so hard to hide. Then, without a word, he leaned in and kissed her, slow and sure. It wasn't rushed or desperate, but deliberate. A promise. A vow. His lips lingered just long enough to leave her breathless before he pulled back.

"I love you," he said softly, his voice steady but weighted with meaning.

Ryder nodded, her fingers brushing against his as if to hold onto him for just one more heartbeat. "I love you too," she whispered.

As they all turned their attention back to the clock, the final moments ticked away. The tension in the room seemed to stretch out, each second hanging heavier than the last.

3...

The group held their breath, hearts pounding in unison.

2...

Fingers tightened around grips and straps, each one silently preparing for whatever waited beyond the steel.

1...

Silence.

Then the room shuddered as the facility's low mechanical whir came to life. A deep, resonating hum filled the silence like the earth itself groaning beneath the weight of the moment. The massive steel doors groaned in protest as they slowly slid apart, reluctant and hesitant, as if the very walls of the Ouroboros were unwilling to release them.

Red warning lights pulsed along the edges of the blast door, casting the group in waves of crimson and shadow. The first barrier slid open with a deafening clunk, revealing a second set of thick glass doors.

The overhead lights flickered, flaring brighter with each pulse as the airlock came online. Beyond the glass, the narrow stairway loomed in the dim light, a dark tunnel rising toward the unknown.

Jase exhaled slowly, centering himself. The tension in the air pressed down like gravity, every eye turning to him. This was the moment they had trained for, the one they'd dreamed about and dreaded all at once.

He faced the door, his voice calm and full of finality.

"Ouro," he said. "Open the doors."

With a soft, decisive whoosh, the glass doors slid open. The sound was strangely final, like the world itself exhaling after holding its breath too long. A rush of air seeped through the widening gap. It was dry, stale, and lifeless—heavy with the scent of dust and the passage of forgotten time.

No one moved. The group stood motionless, their weapons gripped tight, the act more reflex than readiness. Their hearts pounded as they stared into the dark tunnel, its faint light stretching ahead like a promise, and a warning.

Jase looked over his team one last time. Olivia's calm focus. Ava's determined stare. Damian's steady composure. Nolan's protective strength, and Ryder's quiet courage as she held their future in her arms.

His jaw tightened. His chest lifted with one last controlled breath.

Without a word, Jase stepped forward. His boots struck the cold concrete with slow, calculated force, the echo of each step rolling through the chamber like a heartbeat in the void.

He didn't look back.

The Ouroboros had protected them. Forged them.

And now, it was letting them go.

The Fallout Kids were finally returning to the world.

CHAPTER TWENTY-TWO

The team made their way up the tunnel, each step echoing softly in the confined space. At the top, the heavy steel door hissed open, revealing a dimly lit basement. The air shifted, less sterile, more alive. It carried something faintly foreign: dust, age, the faint whisper of wind filtering through unseen cracks. It was the first breath of the outside world.

They climbed the narrow staircase, their boots creaking on old wood. With every step, the air grew fresher, the scent of pine faint but unmistakable. When they reached the top, a small rustic log cabin stood before them, worn by time but still standing firm. The wooden beams above groaned softly as they stepped inside, the structure exuding a quiet solitude, untouched and waiting.

The cabin was simple, almost cozy. A couch and a pair of mismatched chairs faced a small wood stove, their fabric faded but intact. Stacks of firewood were piled beside the stove, ready for the colder months. Papers and yellowed maps cluttered the desk in the corner—remnants of another life: a ranger station, a forgotten outpost. A single lamp sat at its center, its shade tilting slightly, casting faint shadows across the clutter.

A narrow kitchenette occupied one wall, its modest appliances coated in a fine layer of dust. Through a small window above the sink, light filtered through thick trees, scattering faint beams across the counter. Specks of dust drifted lazily in the sunlight, tiny ghosts of stillness suspended in air that hadn't been disturbed in years.

Toward the back, a short hallway opened into a small room—a bed, a cracked mirror, and a half-open bathroom door. The sheets were folded neatly, waiting as though the person who last lived here might return any moment. The whole place felt caught between past and present, frozen in quiet stasis.

For a long moment, no one spoke. The cabin felt both familiar and strange. Earthly, yet foreign after years underground.

"I know we were blindfolded when they brought us here," Ava said finally, her voice low with wonder, "but I never would've guessed this was the entrance."

Nolan gave a small huff of amusement, the corner of his mouth lifting. "Kind of the point," he said, his tone light but edged with thought. It was a simple truth, a reminder of just how carefully they'd been hidden away.

Jase's eyes swept the room once more before he turned toward the front window, where sunlight strained faintly through the glass. "Doesn't look like anyone's been through here in a long time," he murmured. "Must be pretty isolated."

Then, as his gaze lingered on the narrow band of light, his grin spread—soft, disbelieving, almost boyish.

"Hey," he said quietly, but the word carried. "Who wants to feel the sun on their skin?"

The words hit them like a spark in dry tinder. For a heartbeat, no one moved. Then smiles began to form—small, hesitant, but real. The air shifted, lighter now, charged with something fragile and pure.

Without another word, they followed him toward the door. Their steps quickened, hearts thudding in unison, pulled forward by the promise of the light beyond.

As they stepped outside, the world they had been denied for so long opened before them. For a moment, none of them could breathe.

The light hit first.

Not the sterile white glow of the facility, but real sunlight— brilliant, golden, blinding. It poured over them like fire and warmth all at once, searing their eyes and forcing tears that weren't just from the brightness. Jase froze, blinking rapidly as his vision blurred, his heart pounding with disbelief.

Above them stretched an endless sky. Impossibly wide, impossibly blue. Wisps of clouds drifted lazily across it like soft brushstrokes. The trees ringing the clearing blazed with autumn's final colors—amber, gold, and crimson leaves shifting gently in the wind. Every movement of the branches sent a cascade of color drifting down like burning embers, settling on their shoulders, hair, and boots.

The air hit next—a rush of pine, damp earth, and something sharp, wild, and clean. It filled their lungs like lightning. Each breath hurt in the best way, almost too much after years of recycled air and sterile filters. Damian inhaled deeply, coughing once before laughing through it, as though the air itself was overwhelming his body.

For a long moment, no one moved. They stood there, small beneath the vastness of the open sky, listening to the faint hum of wind through the trees and the soft creak of the cabin behind them. The silence was alive.

Then Olivia moved first.

Her hands trembled as she reached for her helmet buckle, the metal clasp popping open with a faint click. She ripped it off and tossed it aside, her blonde hair catching the light as it spilled free. Her eyes shone with tears as she tilted her head back, closing them against the sun. The warmth touched her skin and a sound, half laugh, half sob, escaped her lips. She spread her arms wide, the sunlight washing over her face as she spun slowly, laughing harder now, freer than she had ever been.

Ava watched her frozen for a second. Then she laughed softly, a breathless disbelieving sound, as she pulled off her own helmet. The wind tangled through her hair as she turned her face to the light.

"God…" she whispered, her voice breaking. "It's perfect."

Then she spun once, arms out, letting the sun pour over her, the breeze catching in her clothes. She felt weightless.

The emotion rippled through the group like a wave. Damian let out a shaky breath, eyes glistening, before lifting his face to the sky and spreading his arms wide as his laughter joined theirs.

Ryder smiled, tears slipping down her cheeks as she turned to Nolan. She slipped her hand into his, clutching Aurora close with the other. Together, they stepped into the sunlight, turning in slow, careful circles as Aurora's tiny giggle broke through the air, a sound so pure it nearly brought Jase to his knees.

He stood back for a moment, watching them—his family—spinning, laughing, alive. His chest felt too tight to contain his heart.

Then slowly, he reached up and removed his helmet. The cool air brushed his face, sunlight striking his skin. It was almost too much—the warmth, the scent, the open sky. He closed his eyes, tilted his head back, and breathed in. The wind brushed across his cheeks, through his hair, and over his armor. He felt the ache in his throat before he realized he was smiling.

For that single, fleeting moment, their first beneath the open sky in years, the world didn't feel like a cage.

It felt infinite.

Minutes later, the weight of their emotions began to settle, and the rush of freedom gave way to something quieter—clarity, fragile and profound. One by one, they stopped spinning, their boots finding the ground again. The laughter faded into breathless smiles, replaced by a reverent stillness as they finally took in the world around them.

The forest stretched out in all directions. Dense trees, their leaves alive with the colors of fall, forming a natural barrier from the rest of the world. The ranger outpost stood at the heart of it all—small, unassuming, half-consumed by nature. Its isolation felt like both a blessing and a challenge, offering safety and separation, but also a reminder of how far removed from everything they were.

The small cabin was nestled against the backdrop, its weathered wooden walls blending seamlessly with the rugged environment. The stone foundation and slanted roof gave it a solid, grounded feel, as though it had always belonged here, hidden from the world for years.

In the corner of the property a radio tower stood. Its metal frame rusted and worn, but sturdy. The tower had once been the outpost's lifeline to the world, but now it stood surrendered to time. Its antennas were bent and broken, the metal frame streaked with rust like veins of decay. Beside it, a small barn loomed in silence, its wood darkened by years of rain and sun.

The heavy doors hung slightly crooked, rattling gently in the wind.

An 8-foot fence surrounded the property, tall and sturdy, offering a false sense of security.

The world was quiet. Not peaceful, quiet in the way a forest goes silent when something is watching. The occasional rustle of leaves or snap of a twig underfoot.

As Jase surveyed their surroundings, the reality of their situation settled into his bones. They had a long way to go, and the work had just begun.

He took a deep breath and steadied himself. "Alright, let's get to work." His voice cut through the silence, sharp and grounding. "Ava, check that radio tower. See if it's got any juice left. Anything we can use to boost comms. We need long-range contact with the Ouroboros. I'd rather find out now if that's possible."

"On it," Ava said, already jogging toward the tower.

"Damian, check the fencing," Jase continued, his gaze sweeping the perimeter. "Make sure the gate's secure, see if anything looks compromised."

"Will do," Damian said with a brief nod, his jaw set as he began walking towards the fence line.

"Liv," Jase turned toward her, his voice softening but no less firm. "Get eyes in the sky. Launch the drone and scout the area, see if there's anything we should be concerned about. See if we can figure out where we're at or a direction we should head toward."

"On it," Olivia said, unfolding her drone. The whir of its rotors broke the quiet breeze as it lifted off, disappearing quickly into the treetops.

"Nolan, you're with me." Jase's tone shifted, a hint of caution creeping into his voice. "Let's clear that barn. Area looks secure but let's make sure."

"Copy that," Nolan responded with a nod, his expression focused as he fell into step beside Jase. The weight of the moment was heavy on him, but it felt familiar. The focus, the quiet readiness. They had a job to do.

Behind them, Ryder adjusted Aurora in her arms, her eyes following the group with quiet focus. "Need me to do anything?" she asked softly, her voice steady despite the fatigue in her tone.

Jase paused, his expression softening. "Yeah," he said, nodding toward the open land around them. "You've got all this land now, start planning out the farm. Think long-term."

Ryder's eyes lit up slightly at the mention of the farm, a spark of purpose igniting within her. "I'll get on it," she said with a soft smile.

Jase and Nolan moved toward the barn, their eyes sharp, alert, and focused. They stacked up side by side next to the large sliding door, their backs pressing against the weathered wood. They paused, listening intently for any sound from within. No movement, no rustling. Nothing.

Jase glanced at Nolan, his gaze steady, signaling him to proceed. He pushed the door open just enough to give Nolan space to slip through. The faint sound of the door's metal tracks sliding open was barely perceptible, but to them, it felt deafening.

Nolan moved like a shadow through the narrow gap, his weapon up, the safety already off. His bright tactical light sliced through the darkness of the barn's interior.

Jase followed close behind, his movements fluid and silent, scanning the darkened room with equal vigilance. His eyes darted to Nolan's right, checking their perimeter as they advanced slowly, covering each angle as they moved along side one another.

The barn was heavy with the smell of oil, dust, and stale air, the remnants of years of disuse. Along the walls, shelves sagged under the weight of various tools—spanners, lubricants, oils, and other forgotten necessities. A couple of chainsaws hung from the wall in front of Nolan, their blades caked with grime and dirt. Further down the wall, a pair of gas cans sat on the floor, their red and yellow hues faded.

On Jase's side, a sledgehammer rested against the wall beside a post hole digger, both tools well-worn from past use. A coiled-up section of chain link fence lay nearby, tangled and waiting to be used, while a large metal tank, marked with the word gasoline, loomed ominously, its surface coated in a thin layer of grime.

Their steps slowed as they reached the center of the barn, where two large, heavy objects sat under black tarps. After one last sweep, Jase gave a silent nod. Clear.

"Give me a hand with these tarps," Nolan said, his voice steady but laced with anticipation.

Together they gripped the edges of the tarps and pulled. The thick fabric fell away with a heavy rustle. Both men froze.

"Oh, shit," Nolan said, eyes wide.

Jase stood motionless, taking in the sight before them. Two Polaris Ranger XD 1500s sat beneath a thin layer of dust, their forest-green paint still intact. Faded Forest Ranger decals marked their doors, while trailers waited behind them, hitched and ready for whatever haul they demanded.

Jase let out a low whistle, awe threading through his voice. "Well, I'll be damned."

Nolan's expression broke into a faint grin. "Guess we won't be walking everywhere after all. How much gas is in that refueling tank?"

Jase stepped toward the tank, wiping grime off the gauge with his thumb. "Eighty-five percent full," he muttered. "Two hundred-gallon tank."

Nolan let out a low huff, his expression shifting from surprise to quiet satisfaction. "This is already off to a better start than I expected," he said, shaking his head in disbelief.

"Yeah, you could say that," Jase responded, but his voice was quieter now, more thoughtful. He crossed his arms, looking around the barn and the wilderness beyond. "But we can't use these right away. We need to check out our surroundings first, see how isolated we truly are. These engines will be like sending up signal flares."

Nolan nodded, understanding the caution. "Absolutely," Nolan said, his gaze turning toward the barn doors. "Just glad we have them for the future. When the time's right."

Jase glanced over to Nolan, meeting his gaze with a nod. What lay ahead was clear in his expression. "Let's regroup with everyone. Time to move out and survey the area." His voice was firm, the subtle urgency beneath it unmistakable.

Jase and Nolan made their way back to the front of the cabin, their boots crunching through a carpet of fallen leaves. Ahead, Ava stood beside Olivia near the porch, her expression set in its familiar mix of irritation and focus.

Jase raised an eyebrow, glancing between them. "What's the word on the tower?"

Ava crossed her arms and exhaled through her nose. "Control panel's fried," she said. "Looks like it took a lightning strike—burned out half the wiring, the fuses, the relays… the works."

"Can you fix it?" Jase asked.

"Yeah," Ava replied, her tone clipped but confident. "It's repairable. Give me a couple days and some time in the workshop." She hesitated, her eyes cutting toward Olivia. "But… Liv's drone might've found something better."

Jase turned to Olivia, intrigued. "What'd you find?"

Olivia's voice was steady, but there was a faint undercurrent of excitement. "Mostly forest. Dense cover, ridge-lines, hills in every direction. But about three or four miles east, on top of a rise…" She paused, tapping at her tablet. "There's another tower."

Jase frowned, surprise flickering across his features. "Another radio tower? That close?"

Olivia shook her head. "Not radio. Cellular. Which is what makes it interesting." Her fingers danced over the screen, pulling up the image. "If we get our tower operational and rewire that one as a signal relay, we could boost comms to maybe a hundred-mile radius."

Ava gave a small nod beside her, eyes bright. "It's a hell of a stretch, but doable. We'd just need access to the base of the tower and a few good parts."

Jase's jaw tightened, the possibilities spinning through his mind. "Three to four miles east," he repeated under his breath. He looked at Olivia, then back toward the trees. "Alright. Plot the course. If we move fast, we can make it there and back before dark."

Olivia nodded and immediately pulled up her map, fingers flicking across the tablet as the drone's coordinates overlaid the terrain.

Damian and Ryder appeared from around the cabin, Aurora bundled in Ryder's arms, the baby's quiet coos barely audible over the whisper of the wind.

"How's the fence?" Jase asked, his tone all business.

Damian gave a quick nod, his gaze tracking the fence line. "It's all intact. A couple spots could use some reinforcement, but it's sturdy all around. There's just one gate." He pointed straight ahead. "That big one right there. It's big enough to drive a vehicle through."

Jase's mouth curved slightly, a hint of a grin breaking his focus. "Yeah, about that," he said. "Nolan and I found two side-by-sides in the barn, and a large fueling tank full of gas."

Ava blinked, disbelief flashing in her eyes. "Wait, you're joking? We've got wheels?"

"Two of them," Jase confirmed, amusement flickering in his voice. "But they stay put for now. Until we get a better idea of our surroundings, we need to stay low and avoid drawing attention."

Ava's shoulders deflated just slightly at the news, but she nodded in agreement, understanding the need for caution.

"Okay," Olivia said, her voice steady as she looked up from her tablet. "I've got the course plotted. It'll take us a couple of hours to reach the tower—manageable terrain, nothing too steep."

Ryder, who had been listening quietly, turned to Nolan. "Where are you headed?" she asked, her tone edged with concern.

"There's a cellular tower about four miles east," Nolan explained. "We're hoping to salvage parts to fix our radio tower. Maybe rework that one to boost our signal. If it works, we could reach nearly a hundred miles out."

Jase stepped forward, his voice cutting through like steel. "Everyone, load up. Damian, head back inside with Ryder and Aurora. We'll be back before dark, but if that doesn't happen, stick to the plan."

Damian gave a quick nod. "Stay ready, but stay inside the facility. If we don't hear from you by nightfall, wait until morning. Then come above ground and try the comms."

"Exactly," Jase said, his tone firm, and then turned to the rest of the group. "If we get separated and lose contact, don't go looking for us in the dark. Get back here and wait until morning. No heroics. Running around in the dark will only cause more harm than good."

The group nodded as the weight of the plan sank in.

No simulations. No drills.

Just the world.

Waiting.

"Alright," Jase said quietly. "Let's move."

Nolan stepped forward, his expression softening as he bent down, his hand brushing gently against Aurora's blanket. He pressed a kiss to the baby's forehead, whispering, "I'll be back soon, little one." Then he rose and met Ryder's eyes.

"I'll be back soon," he said again, the promise catching in his throat before he kissed her slow and certain, as if trying to memorize the feel of her before turning away.

Ryder's chest grew tighter as she watched Nolan join the others. Damian stepped beside her, resting a steadying hand on her shoulder.

Her grip tightened on the small bundle in her arms, her gaze never leaving Nolan's retreating form. Her heart felt heavy, but there was an undeniable strength in the way they moved, united and determined, even in the face of the unknown. The promise of connection, the hope of reaching out to others—made this mission all the more urgent.

As the group disappeared into the distance, Ryder and Damian turned and made their way back to the cabin, retreating to the safety of their underground sanctuary.

Ryder turned one last time, looking off into the horizon, as she whispered to herself, "Be safe."

The world outside was beautiful, but beauty could be deceiving. The quiet that followed their departure wasn't peace—it was the hush before something unseen stirred.

They didn't know what they would find. Only that they were no longer trapped below. And for the first time in two and a half years, every step carried them deeper into freedom, and closer to danger.

CHAPTER TWENTY-THREE

The group moved through the dense forest cautiously, their footsteps light and calculated, muffled by the thick carpet of fallen leaves. The trees towered above them, casting long shadows across the ground. The air was damp with an earthy scent of fall, but there was an edge to it, a sharpness.

Jase led the way, his senses on high alert, every rustle in the underbrush or shift of a branch making him pause, analyzing the sound. His rifle was held low, but ready. His movements deliberate and controlled. Nolan stayed close, his eyes constantly scanning their surroundings, his posture rigid as he shifted between trees and foliage, rifle at the ready.

Behind them, Ava and Olivia moved like shadows, their eyes flicking to the sides, alert for any threat from the flanks. Ouro's words still rang in the back of Ava's mind—"Lethal measures are authorized and should be considered the first option." The phrasing lingered, clinical yet ominous, and she found herself wondering what exactly lurked in the shadows.

They advanced in a seamless formation born of months of training. But this wasn't a simulation. This was the real world. And the forest didn't feel right.

They were halfway to the tower when Jase's instincts flared. His hand shot up. A tight, silent fist. Halt.

The group froze. In an instant, the mood shifted from alert to electric. They slipped behind trees and rocks, lowering their profiles. Every movement controlled and silent.

The forest seemed to hold its breath.

Somewhere in the distance, a crow called.

Then nothing.

Jase's eyes narrowed, his focus laser-sharp as he scanned the distance for any sign of movement. The hairs on the back of his neck prickled. The tension in the air felt suffocating. Something wasn't right. His grip tightened on his weapon, his mind racing through possible scenarios, none of them good.

Moments felt like hours as they waited, poised on the edge of action, their bodies coiled with nervous energy. Jase's gaze flicked between the trees. Olivia's breathing quickened. Ava's thumb brushed over the safety. Even Nolan's stance shifted, more defensive now. His gaze cold and calculating.

Then the movement came.

Between the trees—slow, deliberate.

Jase raised his hand, signaling Nolan to hold position. The shape emerged from the brush.

Two deer cautiously stepped into view. Their coats shimmered with a soft, dull brown that blended with the autumn leaves. Their heads lifted in perfect unison, ears twitching as they scanned the clearing, oblivious to the humans watching from the trees.

The forest exhaled.

Jase gave a subtle shake of his head, signaling to the others. Slowly, the group relaxed, but they stayed low, watching the deer for a moment longer.

"Looks like we've got fresh game," Nolan said, his voice low, but with a hint of satisfaction. "We can hunt these woods for meat when we need it."

Jase nodded, his eyes still on the deer. "Yeah, better than printed meat. Also, makes me feel like we are pretty isolated out here."

"Yeah, good sign that there's not an immediate threat around." Nolan agreed.

After a moment, Jase gestured for them to move. "Stay sharp," he said quietly. "Let's keep moving."

The deer turned, bolting deeper into the trees, vanishing as quickly as they had appeared. The group rose from their cover, every sense still raw, their caution sharper than before.

As they resumed their path toward the tower, the forest closed in again. And though the light broke through the canopy in fractured beams, it no longer felt warm.

It felt like a spotlight.

***

An hour later the cellular tower came into view, its silhouette rising above the trees like a jagged spear of metal piercing the sky. As the trees thinned, a small clearing emerged. At its far edge, the tower loomed—tall, imposing, standing like a sentinel above the land. It seemed to stretch toward the sky like a beacon of hope.

Jase held up a hand, his fingers tight in a fist. The group stopped immediately, dropping to a crouch. Every instinct told them to be cautious. They were close, but not yet in the clear.

Nolan crept forward a few feet, his rifle raised, scanning the perimeter. Every step was deliberate, boots sinking into damp earth. The air felt heavy here.

He paused, glancing toward the tree line. "It's clear," he called softly over the comms, but his voice carried an edge.

Jase gave a single nod. "Alright," he murmured. "Secure the area first. Then we'll get to work." His eyes swept over the landscape.

The team fanned out, slipping into formation. Ava and Olivia flanked the rear, eyes sweeping for movement between the trees, while Jase and Nolan advanced on the front. The forest around them whispered with the faint rattle of branches and the chirr of insects, a sound that somehow made the silence feel louder.

As they approached the base of the tower, the chain-link fence came into view, its rusted mesh glinting weakly in the sunlight. A small building sat beside it, a squat maintenance shed with boarded windows and peeling paint, its door sealed shut. It looked harmless, but Jase's gut twisted. In this world, harmless never meant safe.

The gate's padlock was covered in layers of grime. Ava knelt beside it, pulling a portable torch from her pack. The soft hiss of ignition cut through the air, followed by the molten smell of burning metal. The torch's flame carved through the lock until it snapped free and fell to the ground with a dull clink.

Ava looked up, her voice low. "We're in."

The gate creaked open, protesting against years of neglect. One by one, they slipped inside, crouched low, moving with silent precision. Olivia and Ava split off, each circling in opposite directions along the fence line. Their eyes darted between the tower, the shed, and the forest beyond, scanning every corner for movement.

Meanwhile, Jase and Nolan approached the small building, a faint crunch of gravel underfoot as they moved. Jase drew a pry bar from his pack, fitting it into the seam of the door. He pulled back as the old hinges groaned, the door snapping open with a screech that set his teeth on edge.

Inside, the air was thick with dust and decay. Faded papers clung to the walls, their corners curled from dampness. Shelves sagged under the weight of rusted tools and cracked containers. A single fluorescent light tube hung from the ceiling, long dead, its casing covered with dust and cobwebs.

Jase swept the beam of his flashlight across the room. Nothing but forgotten equipment and silence.

Nolan took a step back, scanning the area again before giving the quiet signal.

Jase nodded, signaling to Ava and Olivia. "All clear. Bring it into the tower."

Olivia and Ava crossed the clearing, joining Jase and Nolan at the base of the tower. The structure loomed above them. An iron skeleton of rust and cable, its frame groaning faintly in the wind. The sound was eerie, hollow, like the tower itself whispering to the sky.

Ava's sharp eyes swept over the control box bolted to the tower's base. Even at a glance, she was already assessing the damage, her fingers flexing unconsciously, itching to start.

Jase unclipped his helmet and pulled it off, his hair falling slightly messier than usual. He ran a hand through it, shaking off the weight of the gear.

"Alright, you two have at it," he said, his voice steady but carrying that edge of command that made everyone listen. He nodded toward the maintenance shed. "There's gear in that building. Looks like spare parts and tools. You should check it out."

He met Nolan's eyes, the silent understanding between them instant.

"Nolan and I will cover the perimeter. Call if anything feels off."

Ava set her rifle down beside Olivia's and nodded toward the building. "I'll start with the control panel. You salvage what we can use from that shed."

"On it," Olivia replied, as she turned toward the building.

Ava popped the panel door open with a metallic creak that made her wince. The faint smell of rust filled the air. She exhaled slowly, inspecting each connection, the metal casing of the panel covered in a thin layer of dust but still intact.

"Let's see what we're dealing with," she murmured, prying at a fuse box with her multitool.

The wires had definitely seen better days, a few years of missed maintenance was apparent. She began checking each circuit, her mind calculating the best approach. "This might just work," she said, as the wind caught the tower again. Its groan vibrated down the long steel frame. She froze for half a heartbeat, glancing up, then exhaled and went back to work.

Meanwhile, Olivia pushed open the shed door with her boot. The hinges squealed in protest. Light filtered weakly through the cracked window, illuminating rows of shelves crammed with tools and equipment. It looked abandoned for years, but not destroyed—just forgotten, a sign of its remote location and accessibility.

She began to take stock, mentally checking off the things they might need—wire cutters, spare fuses, relays. There were some spools of copper wire and a few solar panels stored in one corner. Nothing brand new, but it was a treasure trove of usable parts. Olivia made her way through the shelves, inspecting boxes and miscellaneous supplies.

She crouched and picked up a bundle of relays, inspecting the worn labels, the slight corroding on the contacts. "Perfect," she muttered to herself, setting them aside along with a few spools of wire and an old voltmeter.

When she straightened, the silence pressed in again. No birds. No wind. Only the faint moan of the tower. For the first time, she realized how exposed they were, how loud even the smallest sound could be out here.

She shook the thought away, gathering the parts as she headed for the door. With what she had found, and Ava's ability to piece things back together, the tower might just come back to life. It wasn't much, but having been left in the dark for so long, even a flicker of connection would mean everything.

Meanwhile, Jase and Nolan were stationed near the fence line, where the land sloped gently down into a broad valley below. From here, they had a clear vantage over the forest canopy, a sea of autumn gold and rust stretching as far as the eye could see. The view was beautiful, but there was an eeriness to it too.

Nolan unscrewed his canteen and took a long drink, his eyes continuing their slow sweep across the tree line, the distant hills, and the empty clearing leading back toward the tower.

"Nice and quiet," Nolan muttered, glancing over at Jase.

"Too quiet," Jase replied, his voice low and thoughtful. He scanned the horizon, his expression unreadable. "Doesn't really feel like the end of the world."

Nolan gave a short, dry laugh, his mouth curving into something that wasn't quite a smile. "Yeah," he said, glancing toward the tree line again. "Feels like it's waiting to jump out and surprise us."

Jase's eyes lingered on the horizon as the faint breeze tugged at the collar of his jacket. "Waiting for us to get comfortable," he murmured.

Nolan grunted in agreement as he took another sip of his water.

A few hours later, Jase, Nolan, and Olivia stood at the base of the cellular tower, watching as Ava finished climbing down. She descended carefully, adjusting her harness as she made each deliberate step.

When her boots finally touched the ground, she unhooked herself from the safety line and exhaled, brushing the dirt from her gloves. "We're done," she said, her voice carrying a tired satisfaction. "Rewired the circuits, swapped out the bad fuses, rerouted power through the solar backup. Once we get the Ouroboros tower back online, this one'll boost the signal for miles."

Olivia stepped forward, giving an approving nod. "We also found extra relays and wiring inside the shed. They're old, but usable. Once we get back, we'll replace the fried ones in our tower. It should all be up and running tonight."

Jase smiled. A rare, genuine expression that softened the usual edge in his features. "Good work," he said, his tone sincere. "Being able to talk to the Ouroboros from out here changes everything. We'll be able to split up without losing contact."

His eyes moved between Olivia and Ava, lingering a moment before he straightened. "If that's everything, let's pack up and move out. We can take it slow on the way back and still make it before nightfall."

The group quickly gathered their gear, each of them taking a moment to ensure they hadn't left anything behind, and then Jase led the group toward the gate. The sky above them was cloudless, a fading orange glow signaling late afternoon had arrived.

The walk back felt lighter with their goal accomplished, but Jase's mind was already racing ahead—to tomorrow's repairs, the next mission, and what might be waiting when they ventured farther out. He adjusted his gear, his steps quickening, not out of urgency, but momentum. For the first time in a long while, he felt forward motion.

As they passed through the gate, the forest stretched before them again. Dense and shadowed, whispering with the soft rustle of wind through the trees. The path home waited like an open door.

Ava slowed suddenly, one hand brushing the strap of her pack. "Wait," she muttered, her brow furrowing. Then her eyes widened. "Damn it. My screwdriver—left it at the control panel."

Nolan glanced over his shoulder, the faintest smirk ghosting across his face. "Seriously?"

Olivia turned toward her, her voice calm. "Go ahead. We'll wait here." She glanced toward the tree line, her instincts prickling despite her casual tone. The forest felt different now, like eyes were watching them from direction.

Jase, several paces ahead, didn't hear them. His focus was forward, already mapping tomorrow's plan. The soft crunch of his boots on the forest floor was rhythmic—steady, almost hypnotic—as he drifted ahead of the others.

"Be right back," Ava said quickly, jogging toward the tower, her ponytail bouncing with each stride.

Nolan gave a small nod. "Don't worry. We won't leave you," he called after her. Olivia stood beside him, her eyes darting between Ava and Jase's fading silhouette way up ahead.

Jase reached the edge of the trees and slowed, his hand unconsciously tightening around his rifle grip. The evening light filtered through the canopy, fractured into shards of gold and shadow. For a moment, he let himself breathe it in. The quiet. The illusion of peace.

Then something shifted.

A sound—barely audible, but there. A soft crunch of leaves that didn't belong to him.

He froze. His head tilted slightly, listening. Nothing but the wind. Still, the fine hairs on his arms lifted, that familiar low hum of instinct crawling up his spine. He turned back to the group, suddenly realizing they weren't behind him.

"Hey," he called, his voice steady but sharp enough to carry. "What's going on? Why'd you stop?"

Ava appeared at the gate, jogging toward Nolan and Olivia, holding something above her head. Her voice came through his earpiece, faintly breathless but playful.

"Forgot my screw—"

Her words broke mid-sentence, replaced by a shrill, panicked scream that cut through the static.

"JASE! BEHIND YOU!"

Out of the corner of his eye, Jase caught movement. Quick, erratic, and unnatural. Before he could react, the figure burst from the underbrush, revealing itself right in front of him.

The creature's eyes were wild and bloodshot, bulging with unnatural intensity. Its mouth hung open in a snarled grin, revealing jagged, broken teeth—sharp and ready to strike. The thin, long tongue flicked in and out, slithering with precision as if tasting the air for any sign of prey.

Jase froze. The thing was moving too fast, too fluid. Its limbs bent at grotesque angles, its fingers long and sharp. The skin stretched tight across its frame, a sickly yellow-green that seemed to shimmer with unnatural smoothness, broken only by the texture of its scales. Despite the horrifying appearance, it retained a twisted, familiar form, both recognizable and alien at the same time.

It was a mutated human. One of the unfortunate souls cursed by the Serpentis Strain, the virus that had ravaged the world and left these horrors in its wake.

A Serpent.

Jase's training kicked in. His rifle snapped up, the sights aligning—

But the creature lunged, shrieking through broken teeth, its tongue snapping toward him like a whip.

Before he could fire—

Thwack.

The Serpent dropped instantly, crumpling mid-charge. A spray of dark, viscous blood hit the ground near Jase's boots as the creature struck the dirt with a wet, sickening thud. The echo of the shot hung in the air for a moment before silence returned.

Jase's breath came sharp and uneven, his heart hammering as he spun toward the source of the shot. Nolan stood fifty yards away, rifle raised, smoke whispering from the suppressor.

"You good?" Nolan's voice was calm, but his eyes betrayed the adrenaline beneath.

Jase gave a short nod, his gaze snapping back to the corpse. The creature lay twisted at his feet, the faint twitch of a leg stilling as the last remnants of life bled into the dirt. He stepped closer, his eyes scanning every inch of it.

The thing's body was thin, malnourished, but powerful and built for speed. Scales glistened across its arms and ribs. Its fingers ended in blackened claws, cracked but sharp. The human remnants—its torn clothes, its proportions—made Jase's stomach churn.

Then the world fell silent.

No wind.

No birds.

No sound but the faint crackle of his own breathing in his headset.

And in that stillness—

The Serpent shot back to life.

Its back arched violently, bones popping as a guttural, inhuman noise bubbled from its throat. Its hand clawed at the dirt, reaching and convulsing.

"Shit!" Jase shouted, instinct taking over. He fired again—one sharp, precise shot.

The suppressed crack echoed through the trees. The Serpent's head snapped back, and then it went still for good, the second bullet buried deep through its skull.

Jase's chest heaved as he stared down at the corpse. His hands trembled against the rifle's grip, though he forced them still. His mind struggled to catch up, to understand. This wasn't a nightmare.

It was real.

By the time Nolan, Olivia, and Ava sprinted up behind him, the air still smelled of gunpowder and blood. Their boots crunched to a stop beside him, and all three froze when they saw it.

Ava's hand went to her mouth, her eyes wide with disbelief. "What. The. Fuck…" she whispered.

Jase slowly turned to them, his eyes hard and steely. "This… this is what the Serpentis Strain did to the world," he said quietly, each word weighted with emotion. It wasn't disbelief anymore, it was a quiet, simmering rage settling in.

Nolan shook his head, anger flashing behind his eyes. "Ouro left this shit out of the briefing." His grip on his rifle tightened, knuckles white. "They fucking knew what was out here."

Olivia's eyes flooded with tears before she could stop them. "Oh my God…" she breathed, stumbling a step forward. "This is it. This is what happened to everyone. The Genesis Collapse—it was real." Her voice trembled as a soft sob escaped her lips. "It's all true."

Jase crouched down beside the corpse, his jaw locked. He reached out, forcing himself to look at it up close. The texture of the scales, the stench, the faint heat still radiating from its flesh. "We don't have time to freak out right now," he said. "We can do that later."

He rose slowly, eyes steeling with a grim focus. "Right now, we need to focus. We need photos and samples of this… thing. Anything Damian can analyze. He needs to figure out what we're dealing with."

He looked up, meeting each of their eyes in turn. Olivia's grief, Ava's shock, Nolan's fury. And beneath it all, the creeping realization that whatever waited beyond these woods… was worse than they imagined.

Olivia wiped her eyes and nodded quickly, though her hands trembled as she began snapping pictures with her tablet. The coldness of the task slowly numbed her to the horror before them.

"Before we touch anything," Jase said, his voice cutting through the quiet like a blade, "let's test the BioPulse scanners. Make sure they actually work."

Ava gave a quick nod, pulling the handheld scanner from her pack. The small device came to life with a muted hum, its screen casting a faint blue glow across her gloves. She aimed it at the corpse. The light pulsed steadily as the device processed.

"99.9% Serpentis Strain detected," Ava said, her voice steady though a trace of unease crept in.

Jase frowned, his jaw tightening. "Try it on me."

Ava angled the scanner toward him. The pulse shifted, re-calibrating as the hum deepened for a second before blinking green.

"0.0% Serpentis Strain detected," she read aloud, then quickly turned the scanner back toward the Serpent. The numbers on the display shifted again. "99.9% Serpentis Strain detected."

The confirmation hit like a weight.

Jase exhaled through his nose, slow and deliberate. "Guess they work," he muttered, his voice tight. "Alright, go ahead. Carefully, gloves on. Collect whatever you can. We need Damian to see this."

Ava moved closer, snapping on gloves from her kit, and began collecting samples—tissue, blood, and anything else she could gather. Despite her professional demeanor, her eyes betrayed her. Fear flickered beneath the surface as she worked quickly, her movements fluid but hesitant.

By the time they finished, the forest had gone still again. Too still. A soft wind shifted through the trees, carrying with it a whispering rustle of leaves.

Then—silence.

Jase's head snapped up, every instinct flaring. His grip on the rifle tightened as his eyes scanned the tree line. "We need to move," he said, his voice low but firm. "Now."

They didn't question it. Training overrode fear. In seconds they were moving, weapons ready.

"Back to the tower," Jase ordered. "Behind the fence. Stay low, eyes open."

The wind picked up again, brushing through the branches like something alive. The rustling grew louder, closer. The sensation of being watched pressed on them, thick and tangible.

The group fell into defensive positions. Nolan crouched near Jase, rifle aimed toward the trees, while Ava and Olivia flanked them, eyes darting between the shifting shadows.

The noise stopped.

For a breathless moment, no one moved. Then—

CRACK.

A heavy branch snapped in the distance. Another rustle followed, deeper this time, heavier. Something large was moving through the woods.

Jase's finger hovered on the trigger. "Get ready," he whispered.

The noise grew, crashing through the underbrush.

Closer and closer.

Then it burst into the clearing.

A massive wild boar charged out of the tree line, its bristled hide catching the light, tusks glinting as it snorted and barreled past them, oblivious to their presence.

Everyone froze, weapons raised, breaths held—until it disappeared into the opposite side of the woods, leaving only silence and the echo of their pounding hearts behind.

Jase exhaled hard, lowering his rifle.

Nolan let out a short, shaky laugh, wiping sweat from his brow. "Should've shot it just for scaring the shit out of us."

The tension broke, but only slightly. Beneath the fleeting laughter was something heavier, an understanding that this world no longer belonged to them.

Jase's stance straightened again, his expression hardening. "Liv," he said, "Get the drone up. Scan the area. We need to know if there are any more Serpents around." His eyes flicked over the fence line. "I'm not leaving the safety of this fence until we know it's clear."

Olivia didn't hesitate. She slung her tablet from her pack, fingers flying over the controls as she powered up the drone. The soft whir of its rotors filled the air, a mechanical heartbeat that steadied her nerves.

The drone lifted, rising above the tree line. Its camera fed a live image to her tablet—panoramic sweeps of forest, valleys, and the broken world beyond.

"Nothing nearby," she murmured as she guided it higher and further out, expanding her search area.

Then her breath caught.

Far beyond the trees, at the edge of the horizon, a faint gray thread coiled upward—thin, wavering, but steady.

Her pulse quickened. "Jase..." she said softly, her voice tightening.

He turned toward her, catching the look in her eyes.

She pointed toward the horizon.

"Smoke," she whispered.

CHAPTER TWENTY-FOUR

Olivia's brow furrowed as she focused on the drone feed, her fingers flying over the controls as she tried to get a better angle on the distant smoke. It remained far off, too faint to discern any real details.

"It's too far to see what it's coming from," Olivia said, her voice tight with unease. "It's to the Southwest… maybe 10-12 miles out."

Jase's jaw clenched, his eyes narrowing as he stared into the woods. "Is there anything around us? Anything else that is an immediate threat?"

Olivia shook her head, her focus never leaving the feed. "No. Nothing. The area's clear." Her voice steadied, but the knot in her stomach didn't ease. She hesitated, watching the thin trail of smoke coil upward. "Jase, what if that's a campfire? It could be survivors." She turned to him, her tone edged with both hope and urgency. "We can't just leave them out there. Not with those things in the woods."

Jase's gaze flickered back toward the horizon, his mind already working quickly to prioritize their immediate mission. "It's possible," he muttered, but his tone remained firm, dismissive. "But right now, we need to focus on getting back. We get the tower powered up, then we can worry about survivors. Tomorrow." He paused, looking at each of them. "We can't afford to stay out here any longer than we have to."

Olivia's hands tightened on the controls. She understood his logic, he was right, but the unease wouldn't leave her. Smoke meant fire. And fire meant people… people who might need help.

Before she could respond, Ava leaned over her shoulder, squinting at the tablet. "Hold up," she said quietly. "See that ridge? Southwest, a few miles back." She pointed at the topography lines on the map overlay. "If we loop around to higher ground, we can get a clean visual with the drone from there. It won't take long, and we'll still make it back before dark."

Jase's head turned toward her, weighing the proposal. The sun was already dipping behind the treetops, spilling the forest in long, amber shadows. The air had that quiet, expectant stillness that came just before nightfall—the kind that made your instincts sharpen.

"It won't hurt to check," Nolan said, breaking the silence. His tone was calm but firm, every bit the pragmatist. "We're already out here. Better to know what we're heading into tomorrow than walk in blind." He looked at Jase with a shrug.

Jase met Nolan's eyes, then turned back to Olivia, his thoughts clearly conflicted. The group had made it this far, a little longer wouldn't hurt, especially if doing some recon meant they would be better prepared. Still, the risk of another encounter with a Serpent weighed heavily on him.

He exhaled slowly, the decision sitting heavy in his stomach.

"Alright," he said finally. "We'll take the detour. Quick look, then straight back. No more detours after that."

Olivia's expression softened, a flicker of relief in her eyes as she redirected the drone's course. The path on her screen shifted, marking the route toward the ridge.

As they set off, their steps found a renewed rhythm. The air cooled as dusk deepened. The forest came alive with the chirp of crickets and the whisper of wind through the trees. Jase led the way, his rifle steady in front of him, his mind split between command and the gnawing intuition that whatever waited beyond that ridge could change everything.

* * *

An hour later, they reached the high ground just as twilight settled across the land. The world had turned to muted gold and shadow, the horizon burning faintly with the last light of day.

When they crested the ridge, the smoke was there, clearer now, twisting like a ghost against the dying sky.

A faint, acrid scent drifted on the breeze, barely perceptible but enough to quicken their pulse. It wasn't just campfire smoke. It was older, harsher.

Jase narrowed his eyes, his voice low. "That's not just wood burning."

The group stood in silence, watching the thin column rise against the horizon—their awe slowly giving way to unease. Whatever burned out there had a story, and it was waiting for them.

"Alright," Jase said, his voice steady but sharp. "Get the drone up."

Olivia nodded immediately, pulling it from her pack. She powered it on, the rotors cutting through the air above the ridge. Meanwhile, Jase, Nolan, and Ava fanned out, their boots shifting over dry soil and fallen pine needles. The light was fading fast, the forest below them bathed in deep gold and shadow.

Jase crouched low, rifle angled downward, his eyes scanning the tree line. Every rustle, every flicker of movement felt amplified.

Olivia guided the drone, her hands steady but her breath shallow as she tilted the camera toward the horizon. On her screen, the faint column of smoke still wound its way into the darkening sky.

Then—

Crack.

The shot tore through the silence like lightning splitting the air. The echo rolled across the ridge, sharp and violent.

Everyone froze.

Another shot rang out, closer this time. Then another. Short bursts. Frantic.

"Direction of the smoke," Olivia said, her voice barely above a whisper, eyes darting between the drone feed and the horizon.

Jase's blood went cold. His hand tightened on his rifle as instinct took over.

Then, faint but unmistakable, they heard a voice—a raw, panicked scream carrying across the valley. The words were unintelligible, but the desperation was clear. Someone was begging for help.

"Shit," Nolan muttered.

More gunfire erupted, louder now, followed by a scream that curdled into silence.

Jase's mind snapped from thought to action. "Someone's in trouble," he said, his voice clipped, commanding. "We move. Now!"

He didn't wait for agreement. Nolan was already shifting his rifle, boots digging into the dirt as he started down the slope. Ava fell in behind him without hesitation, her expression set and hard.

"Olivia, pull it in!" Jase called.

"I'm on it!" she replied, her fingers flying across the controls. The drone dropped fast, the rotors whining as she caught it mid-air and shoved it into her pouch.

Jase's eyes met hers for a heartbeat. A flash of understanding, urgency, and fear. Then they moved.

"Stay sharp," he warned, his tone low but firm. "We don't know what's down there."

They broke into a run, weaving through the trees as the forest closed in around them. The sunlight bled away with every step, the underbrush growing darker, more hostile. Branches clawed at their sleeves as the crunch of boots and gear cut through the stillness.

Minutes passed. It felt like hours. The gunfire had stopped, but the yelling continued—distant, fractured, and full of terror.

"Keep moving!" Jase barked, pushing through a thick wall of brush. His voice carried a hard edge now, born of urgency and the unshakable sense that they were running toward something they weren't ready for.

And the closer they got, the less certain Jase became that anyone would be left to save.

***

Finally, they reached the crest of a steep hillside. Below, the valley stretched out in a wash of shadow and fading light. Dense trees gave way to a small clearing tucked deep inside. Through gaps in the canopy, flashes of movement flickered—shapes, voices, rising tension.

Jase dropped to one knee, scanning the valley. His voice was low. "Olivia, set up overwatch on this ridge. We'll move down and try to get a visual."

Olivia nodded, already assessing her surroundings. "Copy that," she replied, her voice tight with focus. "They'll hear the drone from this close, so I'll only have eyes on through the scope."

Jase gave a quick nod, understanding the decision. "Call out anything that moves." He turned to Nolan and Ava, signaling them to move quietly down the hill.

As she settled in behind the ridge, Olivia's movements were quiet and practiced. She dropped to her stomach, braced her rifle against her shoulder, and adjusted the scope. She was the eye in the sky now, the silent guardian.

Jase, Nolan, and Ava began the slow descent. They moved like phantoms. Each step deliberate. Every breath measured.

Olivia's eyes narrowed, following them closely through the scope. She watched their every movement, her focus sharp as she scanned the ground ahead while they made their way down the slope.

They moved cautiously through the underbrush, each step deliberate as they closed the distance to the group of strangers below. The forest provided natural cover—fading light filtering through the trees, shadows stretching long as the breeze rustled and twisted the branches. Every step hidden by the very woods they moved through.

Through the magnified glass, Olivia shifted her focus farther into the valley below. Eight people, armed and tense, formed a semicircle around a man on his knees. His hands were bound behind his back, his head bowed, his face streaked with dirt and blood.

"You knew!" a woman's voice rang out, sharp with fury. "You knew your brother was infected and didn't tell us!"

Another voice followed—male, angry, brittle. "You put us all at risk!"

Jase's hand went up, signaling a halt. He crouched lower, straining to see through the brush. The scene below came into focus.

The group stood in a rough semicircle, rifles trained on the kneeling man. They were ragged, their clothes dirty and faces gaunt but fierce. The desperation in their eyes was unmistakable—the look of survivors who'd seen too much.

The man on his knees tried to speak through swollen lips. "I didn't know," he rasped. "He never told me—he wasn't—"

The words were cut short by the crack of a fist connecting with his face. He fell sideways, spitting blood. One of the armed men stepped forward, shouting, "Don't you fucking lie to us! Your brother turned, and now he's out there hunting us!"

A realization hit Jase like a cold blade to the gut. He glanced at Nolan.

"They're talking about the Serpent," Nolan whispered, barely audible. "The one from earlier."

Jase's jaw tightened. "Yeah." His voice was grim. "And they think he's still out here."

His stomach twisted, but he kept his focus. They needed to get closer, needed to see if they could stop this. "Ava," Jase said quietly, his voice low but urgent. "Cover us from here." Ava nodded, her rifle at the ready.

Jase and Nolan moved silently, steps light, bodies low, as they crept through the shadows. They were careful and deliberate, focused on the group ahead, whose attention was fixed on the man kneeling before them. Their voices rose and fell in angry whispers, but the man's silence spoke volumes.

They found perfect cover, two large boulders partially obscured by thick undergrowth. Jase and Nolan tucked in tight, crouching low with their rifles ready—waiting, watching. Jase's mind raced, trying to figure out their next move, but his gaze never left the scene unfolding before them.

The woman, her face hard with anger, stepped forward. She reached out, gripping the man's hair and yanking his head up.

"You're no better than him," she spat. "You brought this down on all of us."

The man's breath came in ragged sobs. "Please! I swear I didn't." His body swayed on his knees, his face pale, his eyes hollow.

"Jonah is dead because of the two of you." Her voice was cold. Final.

For a moment, it seemed like time slowed, the entire world holding its breath.

BANG!

The shot rang out like thunder, a crack that echoed across the forest.

The man's body slumped forward, his face crashing into the dirt—the wet smack of skin against earth punctuating the silence.

Olivia froze behind her scope, the sound echoing up the hillside. "Jase," she whispered into her comm, her voice trembling. "They just executed him."

Jase's stomach dropped, realizing Serpents weren't the only monsters waiting in the world. But his training overrode the shock—his hand shot up, signaling Nolan and Ava to stay low.

This was over. The man was dead. There was nothing more they could do.

Then the forest shifted—

Snap.

A sharp noise split the silence, echoing down the hillside. He spun toward the sound.

Ava.

As she repositioned, she stepped on a fallen branch. The snap was small but lethal in the quiet woods.

Below, the armed group froze. Then, as one, their heads turned toward the sound.

In that moment, they knew they weren't alone in the woods.

And then all hell broke loose.

"Contact!" someone shouted. Muzzles flashed in the twilight, the first shots cutting through the air with violent precision. Bullets tore into bark and dirt, snapping branches, hissing past like hornets.

Jase and Nolan dropped behind a fallen log, taking cover.

"Ava!" Jase shouted, his voice drowned out by the chaos.

The forest, once calm, now roared with violence—every echo ricocheting off the trees.

"We need to move!" Jase yelled, fumbling for his comm. "Now!"

Without waiting, he rose halfway, firing controlled bursts toward the attackers. The rifle's recoil vibrated through his arms as he laid down cover fire for Nolan, who broke from the log and sprinted through the trees.

"Moving!" Nolan's voice crackled over the comm, breath ragged. He dove behind another log and returned fire, muzzle flashes strobing across his face. "Go, Jase, move!"

Jase surged forward, but gunfire ripped into the ground near his boots, forcing him flat again. Dirt exploded around him. He couldn't move, his position had been compromised.

"Jase, stay down!" Olivia's voice cut through the chaos, sharp and commanding in his earpiece. "I've got you covered. Wait for my call!"

Her words were a lifeline, steadying his breath as she squeezed off a shot. The crack of her shot echoed through the trees. The trunk in front of one of the shooters splintered as the round tore through the bark, forcing them to duck behind it.

Meanwhile, Ava was already in motion, her rifle joining the symphony of chaos. She repositioned with swift precision, laying down cover fire for Nolan as he sprinted toward her, his movements sharp and fast.

The forest burned with sound—gunfire, shouting, the metallic tang of adrenaline thick in their throats.

Olivia's scope flicked to Nolan and Ava. "Jase is pinned!" Olivia barked through the comms, clipped but calm. "Ava, Nolan, flank left and suppress! On my mark, Jase—you run like hell."

"Copy that." The response echoed through their comms as they fell into sync.

Their combined fire tore through the underbrush, forcing the attackers to dive for cover. The air shimmered with heat and gunfire. Olivia tracked every movement through her scope, searching for an opening.

"Get ready." Olivia's voice was calm, but heavy with what was coming.

Jase inhaled sharply, coiling like a spring. He shifted to a crouch, one leg forward, ready to sprint. The chaos around him faded into muffled silence as instinct took over.

Then—she saw it.

"Clear. Move! Now!"

Just as he was about to move, something flickered behind him—

A shadow.

"JASE!" Olivia's voice cracked over the comms, shrill with panic. "Behind you!"

He half-turned, but it was too late.

Something heavy slammed into the back of his skull. The impact exploded into blinding, white-hot pain behind his eyes. He crumpled to the ground, the rifle slipping from his grip. His vision tunneled—shadows and light swirling—before everything went black.

"Jase!" Olivia screamed, fear and rage tightening her throat as she zoomed in on his motionless form. No response.

A figure stepped out from behind the tree.

The woman.

The executioner.

Her face was cold, her eyes hollow. She loomed over Jase's limp body, the butt of her rifle still raised over his skull.

"Jase!" Olivia screamed into the comm, her voice breaking. "Jase, get up!"

No response.

The woman prodded his body with her boot, then raised her rifle, aiming straight for his head.

Time froze.

Olivia's finger tightened on the trigger. The bullet flew, cracking through the air.

The woman's body jerked violently as the shot hit its mark, her figure twisting before she disappeared behind the tree she'd emerged from.

Silence fell again, thick and suffocating.

Olivia's scope stayed locked on the spot where she'd fallen.

No movement. No breath.

Her chest rose and fell in ragged gasps as her hands trembled against the rifle. "Jase…" she whispered, her voice barely holding together. "Please be alive."

Jase lay still. His body was unmoving, but Olivia could see the faintest rise and fall of his chest. He was still breathing.

Her voice trembled as she called out in desperation, "Jase! Can you hear me?"

Nolan and Ava were still trading fire with the attackers, gunshots snapping through the trees. The attackers' focus shifted toward them—too many muzzle flashes in the dark.

Then Ava cried out, her voice slicing through the chaos. "I'm hit!"

She clutched her arm as blood bloomed through her sleeve, soaking the fabric.

"Shit!" Nolan ducked beside her, dragging her behind a tree. "We need overwatch—now!"

Olivia snapped back into action, forcing her panic down. Her rifle cracked once, twice. Precise, controlled shots forced the attackers back behind cover. Smoke curled from her barrel, the recoil jarring her shoulder.

For a fleeting moment, the woods went still.

She swept the tree line through her scope again, searching for Jase.

"Where's Jase?" she whispered, her heart racing. She was aimed at his last position, but he was gone. Panic tightened in her chest. "Jase?" she called again, but there was no response.

"We need to move," Nolan said over the comms, his voice steady but strained. "We're outnumbered and Ava is wounded. We have to fall back."

"Where's Jase? Do you have him?" Olivia's voice came out in a frantic rush as she turned, scanning the woods again, desperate for any sign of him.

"Ava, move!" Nolan's voice was urgent but determined as he helped her to her feet, his hand steady despite the chaos.

Olivia's stomach dropped. "Jase, come in." Static filled her comm. "Jase?"

No response.

"Overwatch, cover fire. Now!" Nolan commanded as he and Ava started running up the hill.

Olivia fired a few fast rounds, but the darkness was closing in, and her targets were hard to find. Nightfall was descending, bringing with it the weight of the unknown.

The gunfire began to taper off. After a long, drawn-out pause, it stopped. The attackers had retreated, leaving behind nothing but the eerie calm of the woods.

Olivia's chest heaved as her gaze raked through the shadows of the woods. Nothing moved. Smoke from spent rounds hung low, the acrid tang of gunpowder heavy in her throat.

Nolan and Ava reached her position, stumbling the last few feet—their footsteps heavy with fatigue and the weight of what they'd just been through. Ava's arm was wrapped tight in cloth, the fabric dark with blood.

Nolan's face was pale, jaw clenched. "We need to go," he said, his voice low but commanding. "Now."

Olivia lowered her rifle. "Where's Jase?" she asked, panic creeping into her voice as she turned to him, her breath hitching.

Nolan hesitated just long enough for the silence to cut deep. "He never made it to us." The pain in his eyes spoke volumes.

Olivia's chest tightened, a cold, nauseating feeling settling in her stomach. "We can't leave. He's still down there." Her voice cracked as her eyes darted back to her scope, searching the place she'd last seen him. Her hands trembled as she scanned the area, desperate for a glimpse of him, any flicker of movement.

"Jase, come in. Can you hear me?" she whispered into the comms, her voice barely audible, as if calling out into the void, hoping for a response that wouldn't come.

The air felt colder now, unmoving, like the woods themselves were holding vigil.

"Liv—listen to me." Nolan's voice softened, but urgency burned beneath it. "He's probably gone silent under cover. If we stay, we risk all of us getting pinned again. We'll come back at first light."

Olivia shook her head, eyes darting through the scope one last time. The clearing was empty now, just shadows and trees and the faint glimmer of shell casings in the dirt.

"Please answer me, Jase…" she whispered into the comms, her voice cracking. "Please…"

Nothing.

Nolan placed a firm hand on her shoulder, his voice quiet but resolute. "We stick to the plan. We go home. If he's alive, he'll find us. And if not…" He trailed off, his expression unreadable.

Her hand trembled as she lowered the rifle, the hopeless silence louder than any gunfire.

She swallowed hard, tears stinging her eyes. She wanted to scream, to tear back through the trees and find him, but the weight of Nolan's words held her in place.

Olivia nodded, her breath catching. *"Stick to the plan,"* she repeated softly, as if saying it would make it true.

The three of them turned toward the woods, the forest eerily quiet now except for the crunch of their boots. Olivia paused once, glancing back over her shoulder.

The ridge below lay dark and still. No movement. No sign of Jase. Only the wind whispering through the leaves, carrying away the echoes of the fight.

"Jase…" she murmured, one last plea to the night.

Then she turned, swallowing the ache in her throat as they disappeared into the trees.

The forest gave no answer.

CHAPTER TWENTY-FIVE

The next morning, a bright beam of sunlight shone down, warming Jase's face. He felt its heat spread across his skin, a strange comfort against the ache in his head. For a moment, the warmth felt familiar. Safe. He thought he was back in his bunk in the Ouroboros, the steady hum of the facility's air circulation somewhere just out of earshot, the smell of sterilized air clinging to everything.

But the air didn't hum. It breathed.

Slowly, his eyes flickered open. The world around him blurry, edges soft and undefined, as if he were seeing through a fog. His hand rose instinctively to shield his eyes, his fingers catching the light and feeling its warmth—real sunlight.

He was still in the forest.

Pain throbbed where the rifle had struck him, a deep, pulsing ache that made his thoughts sluggish. He closed his eyes again, the brightness too harsh, his body heavy and unresponsive. Every muscle ached. When he finally pushed himself upright, his hand pressed to the ground—and froze.

It wasn't dirt.

His heart kicked in his chest as his eyes snapped open. The forest was gone. The cold soil, the trees, the scent of moss. All gone.

He was inside.

A cluttered room surrounded him, sunlight pouring in through a wide window that overlooked nothing he recognized. The light filled every corner, dust drifting lazily in its path. The air smelled of wood, old paper, and something faintly metallic. He sat on a narrow cot, his armor and weapons stripped away, but his wrists were free. For a second, that absence of restraint was more unsettling than if he'd been tied up.

His brow furrowed as his feet slid off the edge of the cot, boots waiting neatly below. It was disorienting—too familiar, like how his gear was always laid out for morning drills back in the Ouroboros. He hesitated before slipping them on, the laces left untied, his mind too foggy to bother with details.

He stood, unsteady at first, the room tilting slightly before settling. His hand went instinctively to the back of his head, brushing against the lump that throbbed beneath his fingers. The pain was sharp, but it grounded him—it reminded him that this was real.

His gaze shifted to the far wall. A large office desk stood there, its surface a chaotic sprawl of papers, maps, and photographs. The wall above was pinned with more of the same—lines connecting locations, scribbled notes, old printouts yellowed with time.

He took a few slow steps forward, the boards creaking under his boots, his body sluggish but propelled by the need to take in his surroundings. His fingers brushed across the papers, the edges rough beneath his calloused skin. The writing was hurried, cramped, unfamiliar. None of it made sense.

His eyes landed on a map pinned above the desk—mountainous terrain, a cluster of red marks surrounding a spot labeled "Sector 12." He frowned, tracing the contour lines, trying to make sense of it. For a moment, the fog in his mind threatened to drag him under again, his thoughts looping through half-formed fragments of memory.

The ambush. The gunfire. The woman's face.

Then came a sound.

A floorboard creaked behind him.

A voice—low, calm, edged with something he couldn't name.

"So, they finally let you out of your cage, did they?"

Jase's heart seemed to stop. The words hit him like a jolt, snapping him out of the fog. His breath caught, the world tightening around him.

He turned slowly, every movement drawn tight with tension.

The figure stood framed in the doorway, bathed in sunlight, familiar yet impossible.

For a heartbeat, Jase couldn't breathe. The room blurred, reality bending under the weight of disbelief. His mind scrambled for an explanation. Maybe he was dreaming, maybe the concussion was worse than he thought.

But the man in front of him didn't fade.

The world narrowed to his face, the years collapsing between them in a rush of shock and grief.

Jase's throat went dry. The word came out as a whisper, almost broken.

"Eli?"

***

Miles away, the usual stillness of the Ouroboros was pierced by the occasional cry of Aurora, awake and hungry. The sound cut through the quiet morning, a small reminder that life kept moving.

It should've been another unremarkable morning in the shelter. But for Nolan, Ava, and Olivia, the weight of the world had pressed down on them all night long.

They had returned late the night before, their faces pale and drawn, exhaustion etched deep into every line. They had walked the last stretch home in silence, the echoes of gunfire and screams still ringing in their minds. None of them had spoken much since.

Ava leaned against the wall near the kitchen door, her head bowed, her left arm hanging at her side. Damian's work had been quick. Precise, even. The skin-like hydrogel he'd applied had sealed the bullet graze, closing the wound by nearly ninety percent in just a few hours. It should have been a relief, a small victory. But every time she flexed her fingers, the sting in her arm burned sharper. It wasn't the wound that hurt anymore, it was the gnawing uncertainty about Jase.

"We need to talk about it," Nolan said finally, his voice low but sharp in the quiet. He paced the floor, boots scraping softly against the concrete, the furrow in his brow deepening. "He's still out there, and we need a plan."

Damian sat at the table, his fingers wrapped around a mug of coffee, the exhaustion of a sleepless night written across his face. He'd spent most of the night in the lab, running tests on the Serpent samples they'd brought back, staring at the impossible results until the numbers blurred. But even now, sitting there, his thoughts kept circling back to the images they brought back—that grotesque, inhuman thing. It wasn't exhaustion that haunted him, it was the realization that the world outside was far worse than they'd ever imagined.

Ava finally pushed herself away from the wall, her movements tight and purposeful despite the exhaustion weighing on her. "We have to go back," she said, her tone flat but unyielding. "That was the plan. If they're not back by morning, we go after them."

Across the room, Ryder looked up from where she sat, gently rocking Aurora. The baby stirred, letting out a soft sigh, but Ryder's gaze was fixed on Ava and Nolan. The thought of Jase—of him being out there alone—twisted in her stomach. "He still hasn't radioed in?" she asked quietly, her voice taut. "Are you sure the tower's working?"

Ava shot her a sharp look. "It's working. Olivia and I fixed it while you were sleeping." Her voice carried more frustration than anger.

Nolan raised a hand in a calming gesture. "Relax. She's just asking questions, trying to help." He turned back to Ryder. "No, he hasn't radioed back. Just silence."

Ava sank heavily into a chair, collapsing into it like something inside her had finally given out. She rubbed at her eyes, her voice raw. "I'm sorry, Ryder. I haven't slept, and this is my fault," she muttered, bitterness creeping into her voice. "Stupid fucking branch..." Her voice cracked. "I should've known better. Might as well have used a megaphone to announce we were there."

Nolan's words were firm, cutting through her self-blame like a blade. "Stop that. It's not your fault. This is what it's like out there now. We let our guard down last night, got too close to a situation we shouldn't have been in. We learn from it, and we move forward."

His eyes locked on hers, steady and unflinching. A quiet assurance in a world that no longer offered much of it.

Ava's gaze softened, her shoulders slumping as she gave him a small, weary nod.

"Now," Nolan continued, his tone shifting from compassion to command, "we focus on today. Get food in us, gear up, and move out. We don't have time to waste."

He glanced around the room, scanning for any sign of Olivia. "By the way, where is she? Don't tell me she went out alone…"

Ava hesitated, the pause long enough to give him his answer before she spoke.

"No," she said finally, her voice low, almost hesitant. "She's in the OCC. Been there all night. Calling for Jase. Over and over."

The silence that followed was suffocating. No one spoke. The air itself seemed to grow heavier, pressing down on them.

***

Olivia sat alone in the Observation Command Center, the hum of the equipment filling the room like white noise against the chaos in her head. Screens glowed dimly before her, lines of data and static radio signals flickering in an endless loop. Her voice was hoarse from calling Jase's name through the comms, each unanswered transmission chipping away at her hope.

Eight hours had passed since they'd made it back. Eight hours of silence. It might as well have been forever.

But Jase was still out there. He'd been left behind.

She left him behind.

And the weight of that failure sat heavy on her soul, dragging her deeper into a pit of despair she didn't know how to escape.

Her eyes drifted to the screen in front of her, where a digital map displayed the area where everything had gone wrong. Olivia traced the route again, the lines and waypoints she'd plotted overnight intersecting into a web of desperation.

Where would he have gone if he was hurt? Which route led downhill? Where could he have taken cover?

None of it helped. None of it made sense.

Her gaze shifted to the ridge marked on the map—the very spot where she'd been perched the night before, watching through her scope. The memory hit her like a physical blow—Jase falling, the chaos below, her finger frozen on the trigger a heartbeat too late.

The image replayed in her mind until her vision blurred with tears she couldn't stop. Her fist slammed into the desk, the crack of it sharp against the quiet room.

"Jase, if you can hear me…" she whispered, her voice breaking. "I'm coming to get you."

She pushed back from the desk, the chair screeching across the floor as she stood.

She was done waiting.

Without another word, Olivia turned and walked toward the door, her steps echoing down the hallway.

She couldn't sit there another second, clinging to static and hope.

She was going to find him.

***

Jase stood frozen.

The world around him seemed to blur, sound draining from the air until all he could hear was the pounding of his own heartbeat. His chest tightened, his breath catching as if his body had forgotten how to move, how to breathe.

The figure in the doorway didn't move either.

He was both familiar and foreign at once—like a ghost wearing the skin of someone Jase used to know. The face was the same, and yet not. Life itself seemed to have carved its story into his skin, chiseling away the boy Jase remembered and leaving something harder. Rougher. The jaw was more defined, the frame broader, the posture unyielding.

But it was the eyes—those unmistakable blue eyes, his own reflected back at him—that stopped Jase cold.

They were older now, edged with something sharp and hollow. The faint warmth that once lived there—the flicker of mischief and light—was buried beneath exhaustion and scars time couldn't heal.

Eli's hair was darker, longer than Jase had ever seen it, brushing against his brow. There was a quiet authority in the way he stood. He didn't look lost.

He looked like someone who had survived the fire and learned to command it.

His presence carried a new intensity. A hardened strength. Though the man standing before Jase had been forged from the stone of his past, the world had carved something new out of him.

"Welcome back, big brother."

The voice broke the silence like a crack in glass.

Jase's breath hitched.

It was Eli's voice, familiar in tone, but changed in texture. Once full of energy and life, it now carried an edge, a rasp of something endured. The warmth was gone, replaced by something steadier. Guarded.

Jase felt his pulse quicken as he opened his mouth, but the words wouldn't come. He forced himself to take a step forward, his legs unsteady as he stopped a few feet away. He wanted to reach out—wanted to confirm this was real.

His voice, when it finally came, was hoarse, thick with emotion.

"You're alive..."

The words came out in a whisper, the weight of everything they had lost—everything that had brought them here—packed into them.

Eli's lips twitched into a faint, lopsided smile that didn't quite reach his eyes.

"Well, some might argue with that," he said dryly. "But yeah... alive."

For a moment, they simply stood there. Two brothers, staring at each other across a gulf of years and loss.

Then Eli lifted his arms slightly, the motion casual but tentative, as if he wasn't sure Jase would close the distance.

Jase didn't hesitate. He stepped forward and pulled Eli into a hug so fierce it nearly knocked them both off balance. His arms locked around him like a man clinging to a lifeline, his breath catching against his brother's shoulder.

"I can't believe it," he murmured, his voice breaking. "I thought I'd never see you again. Thought I lost you."

Eli held him just as tightly, though something about it felt restrained, as if part of him had forgotten how to be held.

"Not yet," he said quietly.

The words were simple, but the weight behind them was immense.

"Came close a few times. But those stories… they'll have to wait."

He pulled back, his hands settling on Jase's shoulders, the grip firm and grounding. For a moment, neither of them spoke.

Jase swallowed hard, the question forming before he could stop it.

"What about Mom?"

Eli's eyes shifted away, the light in them dimming. His jaw tightened. He gave the smallest shake of his head.

"Hmm."

It wasn't even a word—just a sound. A sound full of loss.

That was enough.

Jase's gaze dropped, his chest hollowing as the truth settled like a stone. Deep down, he had hoped that maybe… but no. Hope had always been dangerous in this world.

He nodded once, forcing the emotion down, steadying his breath. When he looked up again, his eyes met Eli's—brimming not just with grief, but with something steadier.

Something almost like peace.

There was warmth there now—faint, but real. "It's good to see you," Jase said quietly.

Eli's expression softened just slightly. "You too, Jase."

"How are you here? I mean… how am I here?" Jase's voice cracked as his mind struggled to catch up. His eyes darted around the room again, scanning every corner like it might somehow explain how he'd gone from the forest floor to this.

He shook his head, overwhelmed. "Actually… where the hell are we?"

Eli started to laugh, a deep, gravelly sound. One hand slipped from Jase's shoulder while the other gently guided him forward.

"Come have a look."

His tone was low and steady, carrying that quiet weight Jase had come to recognize as something dangerous, something earned.

Still dizzy, Jase followed, each step unsteady. His boots scuffed lightly against the floor as he approached the light.

When he reached the window, the world opened up before him—

His breath caught.

A compound sprawled across the land below. What had once been a quiet, forgotten corner of the world had been transformed into a fortress. The old state park administration building now stood fortified and repurposed, its weathered structure hardened with barricades and reinforced walls.

The main building rose at the center, overlooking the entire compound like a watchful sentinel.

High, rusted fencing wound its way around the perimeter, layered with scrap metal and barbed wire. Guard towers rose at intervals along the line, their silhouettes cutting into the gray sky as sentries scanned the surrounding forest for movement.

Fields of farmland stretched beyond the inner walls, rows of crops carefully tended to feed the growing community within. Solar panels dotted the roofs of several buildings, angled toward the weak light filtering through the clouds—a fragile lifeline of power in an otherwise dying world.

Closer to the center of the compound, bunkhouses, workshops, and medical tents had been arranged with careful purpose. Outside one of the workshops, two men worked over the stripped frame of a vehicle while sparks jumped from a welding torch. Fires burned in steel barrels across the grounds, their orange glow casting flickering shadows beneath the darkening sky.

People moved between buildings with quiet determination. A pair of children darted between the paths near the bunkhouses before a woman shooed them back toward the inner yard. Guards paced along the fences, rifles slung and eyes sharp, watching the tree line beyond the walls.

But it was the symbol on the gate that caught Jase's attention.

Painted across the slab of salvaged metal was a slender serpent coiled into the shape of an S, its body split by a vertical blade driven straight through its center. The sword formed a rigid T, its cross-guard cutting across the serpent's upper curve, pinning it in place. At the top, the creature's head hung severed from the line of its body, jaws frozen open in a silent snarl.

Eli stood beside him, his reflection faint in the glass.

"Welcome to The Severance, Jase," he said, his voice carrying a quiet flicker of pride.

Amidst it all, there was a sense of community—people moving between buildings, speaking in low voices, tending the land, keeping the place alive and functional. It was a sanctuary built on the bones of what had once been a quiet government-run park. Now it stood as something else entirely: a beacon of survival in a world that had long since forgotten what it meant to live without fear.

Jase stood there for a moment, taking it all in. His breathing slowed as the full weight of the place settled over him.

This wasn't just a refuge.

It was a statement.

A symbol of defiance, of resilience, of survivors who had fought and clawed their way back from the edge of extinction.

"This..." His voice barely carried above a whisper. "You built this?"

Eli nodded once, his gaze fixed on the compound below. The faintest trace of weariness crossed his face.

"Yeah," he said quietly. "Me—and the people you see down there."

Jase's eyes moved across the settlement, drifting from person to person as they worked, talked, and carried on with the quiet rhythm of survival. Then his gaze settled again on the painted emblem near the gate—the sword through the body of a serpent.

"The Severance," he said slowly, testing the word. "Why that?"

Eli followed his gaze to the symbol below. His expression shifted, hardening slightly, as if the question carried a weight Jase couldn't yet see.

He turned back to him, the faintest curve touching his mouth. "Someone has to sever the head of the serpent."

The words settled heavily between them.

It wasn't just a mark.

It was a message.

Jase frowned slightly, still trying to piece it together.

Eli clapped him once on the back, the gesture both grounding and dismissive.

"Come on," he said quietly. "You've missed a lot."

Jase didn't move. His eyes searched Eli's face.

"Missed what?"

For a moment, Eli just looked at him.

Then a faint, humorless smile tugged at his lips.

"Everything."

He turned and started toward the door.

"We've got a lot to talk about."

***

Back in the Ouroboros, Olivia was alone in the armory.

She moved through the shelves with sharp, focused motions. Her hands didn't tremble, but her breath came fast and uneven as she crammed supplies into her rucksack—MREs, med kits, fire starters, anything she could carry.

She wasn't coming back until she found Jase.

Or until she found what was left of him.

As she zipped the bag shut, the door slid open. She didn't flinch. She was too focused to stop.

Nolan and Ava stepped inside, their faces unreadable as they exchanged a quick glance.

Olivia kept moving.

Nolan spoke first. "There you are," he said carefully, concern threading through his voice. His eyes dropped to the packed bag. "What are you doing, Liv? You're not going out there on your own."

That broke something in her.

Her head snapped toward him, eyes blazing. "I'm not waiting anymore!"

Her voice echoed off the concrete walls, sharp and raw. The words came out cracked with emotion, every syllable carrying the weight of sleepless hours and hollow silence.

"He's out there, Nolan! He could be hurt—dying! And we're just supposed to sit here and do nothing?"

Ava shifted beside Nolan, her jaw tightening as Olivia's words echoed through the room.

Olivia took a step closer, her chest heaving. "You don't get it. Every minute we waste down here, I see him fall. I hear it."

Her hand trembled as she gripped the strap of her bag. "So either help me, or get the hell out of my way. Because I'm done sitting here pretending he's just going to walk in."

The room went still.

Ava stepped forward, her demeanor calm. "We're not here to stop you."

Her voice was steady, as though she understood exactly what Olivia was feeling. She exchanged a brief glance with Nolan before turning back to Olivia.

"We're here to go with you."

Olivia blinked, the words landing harder than she expected. Suddenly the weight of everything—her heart, her mind, her body—threatened to overwhelm her.

Her lower lip trembled, the response caught in her throat.

For a moment, she couldn't speak.

Nolan tilted his head slightly, one brow lifting in quiet challenge, his eyes softer now.

"You ready to go find our boy?"

That simple question shattered the last of Olivia's resolve. The dam cracked. Her lower lip quivered as the tears she'd been holding back finally broke free.

She lunged forward, wrapping her arms around both of them in a fierce embrace. "Thank you," she breathed, her voice shaking.

Nolan let out a rough chuckle, patting her back. "Alright, alright. Let's gear up and go get our guy." He pulled back, meeting her eyes with quiet determination. "Pack your night vision. We're not coming back until we find him."

He glanced at Ava, steel flashing briefly in his voice. "And if we run into that group again… we'll have the upper hand this time."

Olivia wiped her eyes, steadying herself as the fire returned to her chest. She slung the rucksack over her shoulder.

"Oh, I'm hoping we do."

CHAPTER TWENTY-SIX

Eli and Jase sat in his office, the weight of their conversation hanging between them.

The room reminded Jase of the OCC back in the Ouroboros, though this place lacked the technological perfection of the bunker. It was rougher. Pieced together.

One side of the room was dominated by a large rectangular table, its surface scattered with papers, empty mugs, and documents that looked like they'd been hastily reviewed. Behind it, a massive map covered the wall, crisscrossed with markings and notes—locations, patrol routes, danger zones.

On the opposite side stood a large wooden desk positioned in front of a wide window that overlooked the compound below. Two chairs sat on either side of it.

And in those chairs, the brothers faced each other—close enough to reach across the desk, yet separated by years neither of them could explain away.

"So, yeah…" Jase said, his voice low, rough with exhaustion. "My first Serpent encounter was probably with the guy your people were after last night. I can show you where we left him, if you want."

The words carried a mix of resolve and lingering shock, the memory of the creature still echoing in his mind.

Eli didn't answer right away, his expression hardened.

His eyes drifted to the map on the wall behind Jase, scanning the marked routes and patrol zones like he was running the numbers in his head. Small colored pins dotted the terrain—red, yellow, and black—marking patrol paths, serpent sightings, and places the Severance no longer traveled after dark.

His jaw flexed, a muscle twitching in his cheek as he shook his head.

"No."

His voice was flat.

"All that matters is that it's dead."

Jase blinked, caught off guard by the finality in his tone. It was the way Eli said it, like the answer should have been obvious.

"What do you mean that's all that matters?" he asked, frowning. "That was someone once. Doesn't he have family? Someone who'd want to bury him?"

Eli leaned back in his chair, the old wood creaking beneath him.

"You got lucky, you know," he said finally, his voice quieter now but heavy with memory. "In the beginning, people just got sick. They died slow. Painful. Nothing you could do but watch… or end their suffering."

His gaze dropped to the desk before lifting again, his eyes colder now.

"But then the mutations started. We thought we had it under control—small cases. Nothing like what you saw."

He paused, the corner of his mouth tightening.

"Now? The fully mutated ones can tear through a squad in seconds. Hesitate, and you're dead. Get bit, and you end up one—immune or not."

The words settled like lead in the room.

"So yes, he was once human. He had loved ones. But all they care about now is that it's dead."

Jase's stomach twisted. The thought of how close they'd all come—how close he had come—gnawed at him.

Then the door creaked open.

A woman stepped inside, her arm in a sling, followed by two others. The air in the room shifted immediately, charged with presence.

Eli stood, his posture straightening into something colder—command.

He turned toward Jase, the edge softening slightly in his voice. "Let me introduce you."

The woman stepped forward. Even injured, her presence filled the room. Jase's stomach tightened as the recognition set in. It was the woman who had calmly executed the man on his knees the night before.

"This is Isabella," Eli said. "My girlfriend."

She gave Jase a curt nod, sharp eyes appraising him.

Isabella looked every bit the warrior. Standing at 5'9", her lean, sinewy build reflected the strength of someone who had spent years surviving in a harsh world. Her sun-kissed skin bore the marks of time and battle—faint scars, rough hands shaped by years of hard labor.

Her long black hair was pulled back tightly, with braids running along the sides of her head. Her piercing brown eyes stayed alert, constantly sizing up people and situations with quiet, practiced intelligence. Her face was angular, framed by high cheekbones and a no-nonsense expression that made it clear she wasn't someone to underestimate.

"Nice to officially meet you," Jase said, his voice steady but edged with curiosity. "What happened to your arm?"

Isabella's eyes flicked down, then back up, unimpressed.

"One of your friends shot me last night," she said flatly, as if it were just another inconvenience in a long list of them. "Plate stopped it—cracked a rib, maybe two. Dislocated my shoulder when I hit the ground."

She gave a small shrug with her good arm, the motion stiff and deliberate.

Jase's stomach dropped. The realization hit hard and fast—Olivia.

His girlfriend had nearly killed his brother's girlfriend.

"Must've happened after I was knocked out," he muttered, sharper than he meant to.

Eli didn't dwell on it. He pivoted with the practiced ease of someone who'd learned when to redirect a volatile moment.

"This is Wyatt," he said, gesturing to the man standing beside Isabella. "My right hand. Been with me since the beginning."

Wyatt stepped forward, offering a firm handshake. There was a calmness in his presence that immediately set him apart.

He stood an inch or two taller than Jase, built lean but solid. The sun had tanned his skin into a weathered bronze, and faint scars traced along his forearms like thin topography lines. His sandy-blonde hair was unruly, complementing the scruffy beard that gave him a rugged, almost untamed look.

But it was his eyes that caught Jase's attention.

Sharp blue eyes, the kind that belonged to a man who always seemed to be thinking two steps ahead. Cautious. Observant. Ready.

He carried the quiet gravity of someone who'd survived too much to waste words.

"And this," Eli continued, "is Riley. Wyatt's sister. Our scout, and probably the only reason half of us are still breathing."

Jase could feel her assessing him, weighing him, deciding whether he was worth the oxygen he breathed. She gave a brief nod, her gaze already drifting back toward the window, as if part of her attention was always somewhere else.

Riley was small and compact, her frame wiry and efficient. Her dark hair was cropped into a sharp pixie cut—practical, just like her. Her blue eyes were intense and alert, constantly scanning her surroundings.

A pale scar cut down her cheekbone beneath one eye, a single brutal accent on an otherwise striking face.

Like her brother, Riley didn't waste words. She preferred action.

When she finally looked away, the air in the room seemed to ease, though not by much.

"Nice to meet all of you," Jase said after a beat, sincerity threading through his words. "Thank you for protecting my brother during all this. You have my endless gratitude."

Isabella met his eyes. "Don't thank us," she said coolly. "We wouldn't be here without him."

The comment hung in the air—part respect, part warning.

Eli cut through it with a sharp inhale. "Enough of that," he said, gesturing toward the large table. "Let's sit. Time to talk about what really matters."

They took their seats around the table. The wood was scarred, its surface a map of burns, cuts, and stains from years of hard use.

Eli leaned forward, his elbows braced on the edge, his green eyes settling on Jase. The weight of the past, and the present, pressed heavily on his expression. He looked almost haunted.

"Jase," he began, his tone low and deliberate, "it's time you learned the truth. The truth about everything."

The words landed like a tremor.

Jase didn't respond right away. His gaze flicked from Eli to Isabella, to Wyatt and Riley. Each of them wore the same expression—somber, resolute.

The air seemed to grow heavier, the sounds of the compound fading until there was only the steady thud of his own heartbeat. He swallowed hard, bracing himself for whatever came next.

"The Genesis Collapse—it wasn't some natural disaster or accident that got out of control. It wasn't a terrorist group or some foreign enemy."

He paused, his gaze locking on Jase. "It was caused by a man named General David Yuros."

The name hung in the air.

"He was in charge of a secret government program developing advanced warfare projects."

Eli's voice hardened. "Our government, Jase."

Jase's eyes narrowed, his pulse beginning to climb.

Eli's jaw flexed. "The foundation of the program was an advanced artificial intelligence," he said. "Highly sophisticated. Designed to change warfare forever. Its goal wasn't just to fight wars, it was to win them before they even began." He paused, watching Jase absorb it.

"And it worked. It created concepts, strategies… even new technologies that were immediately pushed into development."

His voice darkened.

"One of those was the Serpentis Strain. A weapon of mass destruction engineered to wipe out the enemy without dropping a single bomb."

The words hit Jase like a blow. "They created the virus?"

Eli nodded. "But here's the kicker, Jase." His voice softened slightly, though the tension in it remained. "The AI didn't just create the virus—it created the cure alongside it."

"The plan was to release the virus, then sell the cure to their allies—at a price that would make them kings of the new world. Their enemies would be left begging for salvation."

He leaned back slightly. "What better way to win than to hold all the cards? Control the world through salvation."

Jase's blood ran cold. He couldn't look away. "You're saying they made it on purpose… and planned to profit off it?"

"The real kicker?" Isabella cut in, her voice razor sharp. "The cure didn't actually fucking work."

Eli met her gaze, his expression grim. "No. The cure didn't work."

He paused, letting the weight of that sink in. "The world went to hell after that. The virus spread across the globe, unstoppable. Panic turned to violence. Governments collapsed. Cities burned."

His eyes hardened. "The collapse wasn't just from some virus. It was greed. Lies. Corruption."

He leaned back slightly. "The AI's plan failed… and humanity paid the price for it."

The room felt suffocating. Jase's fists clenched against the table, his knuckles turning white. "All this… because of them."

Eli exhaled through his nose, the sound heavy.

"That's not all."

He looked up, meeting Jase's eyes. "There was another project developed alongside the virus."

Eli hesitated for the first time.

"Project Fallout Kids."

The words froze Jase in place. "What are you saying?" he asked, his voice barely above a whisper.

"It was a contingency plan," Eli said. "If the virus failed… if the world went nuclear… they needed a way to rebuild."

He gestured toward the map pinned to the wall. "So they designed high-tech shelters. Housing hand-picked immune individuals—people they could use to 'take back the world' after the chaos ended."

Eli turned back to Jase, his voice quieter now, "Self-sustaining environments, all run entirely by the same AI that created the Serpentis Strain."

Jase's mind reeled. His pulse pounded in his ears. "Ouro..."

Eli didn't answer. He didn't have to.

Jase sat frozen, his mind numb, his heart a storm of confusion and rage.

"So everything..." His voice faltered for a moment. "Everything that's happened—the suffering, the death, the end of the world—it was all planned. All aimed at controlling the world."

He swallowed hard. "And I've been living in one of their fucking experiments. Training. Preparing. Becoming exactly what they wanted me to be..."

His jaw tightened. "A soldier for their future wasteland."

Eli's stare never wavered. "Yeah."

He leaned forward, his voice low but steady. "That's exactly what I'm telling you."

The air between them crackled, the truth thrumming like a live wire.

Eli spoke again, slower this time. "Earlier you asked why it's called the Severance. We're not just severing the world from serpents."

He paused, glancing around the table at Isabella, Wyatt, and Riley before returning his gaze to Jase.

"We're severing the world from you."

***

Damian stood near the airlock doors, his stance casual but his expression reflecting the weight of the moment. His arms were crossed over his chest, eyes scanning the group.

Olivia and Ava stood in front of him, both women radiating a quiet intensity. Nolan and Ryder flanked them, Aurora safe in Ryder's arms.

It was the final moment before they left.

"Since the tower is up and running, we'll be able to stay in contact the whole time," Damian said, his voice steady, though an undertone of urgency lingered beneath it. "I'll be in the lab running tests on the samples you brought back. I'll try to learn more about the Serpents and the virus—fill in some of the gaps Ouro had. But until then, don't take any chances if you come across one."

Ava glanced down at the bandage on her arm, a quiet reminder of the close call she'd had. Her expression hardened slightly as she looked back at Damian.

"Honestly," she said, "I'm more worried about running into people. They shoot first and talk never."

Damian gave a small nod, his jaw tightening. "Yeah… watch out for them too, I guess."

His gaze shifted to Olivia, a flicker of concern crossing his face. "If you find Jase—"

"When," Olivia cut in, her voice low and sharp, her certainty leaving no room for argument.

Damian hesitated, caught off guard by the edge in her tone. Then he nodded. "When you find him… if he's hurt, radio back with your location. I'll take one of the side-by-sides out. Don't risk moving him if he's not stable."

Silence settled like dust, heavy and still. Olivia didn't break his gaze. Unyielding. Unreadable.

Nolan stepped toward Ryder and kissed her goodbye, his lips lingering as if he could hold the moment in place. When he finally pulled back, his hand cupped her cheek for a brief second before he stepped away.

His attention shifted to Damian. "I don't know when we'll be back," Nolan said. "But we'll stay in contact. Be safe." He gave Damian a firm pat on the shoulder.

Damian nodded, the faintest flicker of emotion passing through his usually guarded expression. "You too."

The words were sincere, but part of Damian's mind had already drifted back to the lab, to the samples waiting for answers they desperately needed.

The airlock doors hissed open. A rush of cold air swept through, smelling of rain, soil, and the living world above.

Nolan took point, rifle in hand, and glanced back at Olivia and Ava. "Let's move."

They stepped into the tunnel, boots striking the concrete in unison. Every sound seemed sharper, every echo louder, as if the Ouroboros itself were watching them go.

For Olivia, there was no turning back now. She had crossed this threshold before—once as the architect of chaos, and now as one forced to face its consequences.

When they emerged from the cabin, the world felt different. A low growl of thunder rolled across the sky. The sun was gone, devoured by the coming storm, as rain began to fall in slow, heavy drops. Wind swept through the trees, heavy with the scent of rain and damp soil.

Olivia tilted her head back, watching the storm begin to gather its strength. It felt like a reflection of what churned inside her, a fury that had been building since the moment Jase disappeared.

Lightning split the sky, and for an instant the light caught in her eyes—burning gold, not with fear, but purpose. Energy surged through her, every muscle in her body coiled and ready.

But this wasn't just another storm.

It was a warning, a reckoning coming to this broken land.

Her gaze dropped from the sky to the path ahead. Jase—her partner, her anchor—was the only thing driving her now.

Thunder cracked again, closer this time.

She exhaled slowly, tightening her grip on the rifle as she stepped forward into a world she was only beginning to understand.

But this time she wouldn't be a passenger in it.

This time she would make it bend to her will.

***

Jase pushed his chair back, the scrape of wood against the floor breaking the suffocating silence. His hands trembled as he rose, his breath shallow, the air itself suddenly too heavy to pull in.

"No," he said, shaking his head slowly. "No, this is—this is crazy. It can't be true." His voice was low, like he was trying to convince himself just as much as everyone else. "How could you even know this?"

"It's the truth!" Isabella shot to her feet. Her voice sharp as a blade, frustration barely contained. "Every last damn word is the truth."

Her eyes burned with conviction, with the kind of certainty that made Jase's stomach twist.

Riley didn't flinch. Her posture remained tense but controlled. Her sharp blue eyes locked onto Jase, ready to strike at a moment's notice. There was no hesitation in her gaze. Only cold, hard resolve.

Eli stood slowly, steadying a hand on the table as if grounding himself. His other hand lifted toward Isabella, a quiet motion that stopped her mid-breath. The air between them felt thick, like a storm on the verge of breaking.

When he spoke, his voice was low and controlled, but every word carried the weight of something lived, not told.

"It's hard to hear, I know," he said. "It's worse to accept. But it's all true. Every word."

The silence that followed was unbearable.

Jase stared at him—his brother, the last piece of family he thought he'd lost—and searched his face for even the smallest flicker of doubt.

But there was none.

Only the cold, unflinching truth.

When Eli spoke again, his tone shifted—rougher now, stripped bare, as if he had been holding this in for far too long. "I never wanted you to do the study, Jase."

The words came slowly, heavy with regret. "You knew that before you went in. You knew I felt there was something off about it. And still…"

He exhaled sharply. "You went."

The words opened a floodgate. Memories rushed back—the arguments, the tension before the collapse, the last night they spoke.

Eli rubbed a hand across his face before he continued. "After the world went to shit, after cities fell, I thought we were all dead. Hell, I thought you were dead."

He gestured toward the others, his voice softening. "But then I found these people. We clawed our way through the ashes. We kept going. Kept fighting. Because we knew there had to be a way to survive. A way to make things right."

His gaze drifted briefly across the room before settling again. "And slowly, we started taking back a piece of the world. A small piece of what we all lost."

Eli turned back to Jase, his expression hardening. "We started searching for answers. Answers about the Genesis Collapse—what caused it, who pulled the trigger, and how we could stop it."

He paused, and for the briefest moment his eyes softened.

"And then… we searched for you."

The words struck Jase like a bullet through the chest. This place, these people, this moment—everything—existed because Eli had never stopped.

Even when the world had burned. Even when hope had turned to ash. Eli had kept fighting. Because somewhere out there, his brother might still be alive.

Standing here now, Jase could feel the weight of that devotion in every word.

It was heavier than gratitude.

It was guilt.

"And in all that," Eli continued, quieter now, every word final and absolute, "this is what we found. This is what I found."

He gestured toward the map-covered wall, littered with papers, photos, and scribbled notes—years of obsession pinned together in chaotic order. "It's all there," Eli said. "Everything we just told you."

Jase turned, his pulse pounding in his ears.

Each piece of paper, each photograph, felt like another wound carved into the surface of the truth. Red lines stretched across the map, crisscrossing the world like scars. The faces staring back at him—scientists, generals, test subjects—were all part of the machine that had destroyed everything.

"Have a look for yourself," Eli said, his tone flattening into something cold and resigned.

He pointed to one of the photos. "That one on the left, that's General Yuros. The prick himself. Get a good look at the man who ended the world."

Jase's eyes locked onto the image.

The man in the photograph stared back with controlled, almost regal stillness—a face carved from steel and ambition. The architect of this nightmare. The man whose vision had unraveled the world.

Jase stepped closer, narrowing his eyes as he studied the photo.

But then—

something else.

His gaze drifted, catching another figure beside Yuros. A woman. Younger. Standing just behind his shoulder.

Jase's breath hitched. He leaned closer, disbelief creeping in like slow poison.

The hair.

The curve of her jaw.

The eyes.

Those eyes.

He slowly reached up, his fingers brushing the edge of the photograph.

"That's..." Jase's voice faltered, the words catching in his throat. "That's... she's part of my team."

Lightning flashed outside, washing the room in stark white light.

Isabella froze mid-breath. Wyatt straightened, confusion flickering across his features. Riley's hand moved instinctively to her sidearm, though she didn't draw it.

All eyes turned to Eli.

Now they were the ones stunned. The truth they'd been unraveling began to twist, becoming something none of them had expected.

Eli stepped forward, the color draining from his face. He looked from the photograph to Jase, realization dawning in real time. "Jase," he said slowly, each word heavy as a confession, "that's General Yuros's daughter."

The room went still.

"She developed and coded the AI."

His gaze flicked back to the photograph—the two figures standing side by side.

"He named it after her."

The world seemed to tilt beneath Jase's feet as the pieces slammed into place.

The logic.

The empathy.

The control.

The way Ouro always seemed to respond to one person above all others.

His voice was barely a whisper, trembling with disbelief. "Olivia…" he breathed, the name catching on his tongue.

"Olivia Yuros."

Outside, the storm finally broke.

And somewhere, miles away, Olivia Yuros walked through the rain straight toward him.

The End

From the ashes of Genesis… they will rise.

Book Two

The Fallout Kids: Genesis Rising

Coming Soon

Join the Fallout Kids

For updates on future releases, bonus content, and announcements:

Website
TheFalloutKids.com

TikTok
tiktok.com/@thefalloutkids

Facebook
facebook.com/TheFalloutKids

X
x.com/@The_FalloutKids

Instagram
instagram.com/The_FalloutKids

Threads
Threads.com/@the_falloutkids

Bluesky
bsky.app/profile/thefalloutkids.bsky.social

About the Author

A graduate of Ithaca College with a degree in Creative Writing, Jordan also works in the film industry as an Assistant Director—an experience that shapes the cinematic scope and pacing of The Fallout Kids.

Jordan Weir is currently at work on the next installment in the series.